I NEED YOU

TO LOVE ME

By GENICIOUS

Sins for Cigarettes

I Need You Series

I Need You To Hate Me

I Need You To Love Me

I Need You To Save Me

I NEED YOU

to love me

I NEED YOU BOOK TWO

GENICIOUS

Special Edition

ISBN: 978-0-6454792-8-7

https://genicious.com

To my amazing readers,
may the stars align.

1

Monster

Ace

Monsters exist in the form of souls. They rest in the deepest fragments, and it isn't until they awake that they become alive. I often question when I stopped looking for monsters under my bed. When did I stop being alarmed about walking down an alleyway at night in the most dangerous city?

It's relatively straightforward, though. The day I stopped being fearful of monsters is the day I became one.

It's confronting to catch your reflection daily and meet everything you were afraid of becoming glaring back at you. The shadows in my eyes flame with wickedness, fight for dynamism. I thrust it all to the back, unwilling to come to terms with the vile creature lurking within me.

The receptionist stands behind the grand desk in front of me. Her scarlet hair tumbles around her face like an ardent blaze. She lifts her head, her eyes widen in recognition, and she slides her black-rimmed glasses down her nose to gain a better look. Speckled-amber eyes stare at me in astonishment. "You're Ace Blackwell."

"I don't know what you're talking about," I reply with a lofty grin. It's my go-to response when I'm recognized in public.

"Do-do you have an appointment?" she stumbles over her words, and color surges to her face. She busies herself by glancing at the computer screen in front of her, searching for my name in the schedule.

Women react one of two ways when they see me—intimidated or starstruck. Occasionally, a bit of both.

"No."

She glances up from her computer. "Ah, I see. I'm afraid he's not to be interrupted," she apologizes like she doesn't want to displease me. Looking down, she adds, "He also doesn't take on new clients—"

"That's too bad." I turn toward the office before she has time to finish her sentence.

I shove my hands deeper into my pockets as I stride like a man on a mission through the halls of the most influential law firm in the state. I glimpse in the rooms that have their doors wide open but don't find who I'm looking for.

The receptionist's heels click behind me on the porcelain floors in an attempt to catch up. My strides are too extended for her short legs, four steps of hers for one of mine. I scan the frosted glass doors for the name I'm after and notice it once I reach the very end of the hallway. The largest office on the floor.

I step in without bothering to knock, fortunate it isn't locked. It's impressively large with the bare minimum—a desk with chairs, industrial filing cabinets, and an antique wooden bookshelf that I assume is for decorative purposes only. Unhurriedly, I pull out the chair across from him, scraping the legs against the floor, and occupy it. His office is everything I've supposed it would be. The exemplification of privilege and ego. The apple mustn't have fallen too far from the tree.

A phone is pressed to the man's ear, and a lazy, crooked smile is embedded on his face. It fades into a eerily familiar line when he realizes someone has marched into his office without his permission.

I did my research vigilantly. Twenty-eight. Not married. Doesn't have children. His mother died when he was ten. A reputable lawyer from the outside, but we all have demons. Some more than others.

"I'll talk to you later, sweetheart." He ends the call and leans forward in his seat, acting surprisingly mild. Like I'm an invited client instead of an unsolicited intruder.

Recognition flickers in him. He knows who I am, or at least a part of my identity. Splendid. We don't need to waste time on introductions. Frankly, I'm not a fan of them.

The receptionist appears behind me, out of breath. "My apologies. I did inform Mr. Blackwell you requested not to be disturbed and aren't taking on new clients. But he was..." she searches for the appropriate word, "adamant."

I turn to face her, and her eyes narrow into slits as she glares at me, undoubtedly afraid my insolence will land her in the bad books with her boss. I shoot her a dazzling smile. The lines between her brows fade, but she purses her lips.

The man in front of me waves his arm. "That's fine, Lucy."

She scampers out, the apologetic expression lingering.

I pluck a pen from the desk and twirl it in between my fingers while I continue to examine the office. There's inadequate décor for me to be this entertained, but I manage to give my attention to every corner, ignoring the glower from the man in front of me.

When I don't bother speaking, he caves. "To what do I owe your company?" His voice appears solid and sonorous.

I've never spoken to the man. I've never even heard of him until a few days ago. But my distaste for him flares in my veins—the resentment buried just mere inches below my skin.

I preserve a grin on my face. The condescending one that frequently pisses people off. "I need a lawyer. I heard you're the best."

2

We Meet Again

CALLA

I used to think if I ignored my pain, it would eventually fade. But I've come to discover pain is alive. It pleads for compassion. It desires to be heard—whether it be in the form of your wails or your thoughts. It's not something you can put in a bottle, screw the lid on, and throw away in hopes it won't find a way back.

It took me four years to realize that. And yet there are still times when I choose to turn my back on it, to push it to the side when I can't endure it anymore. A short-term solution to an inexorable feeling.

There's a rough knock on my door that drags me out of my thoughts. I rush toward it, hoping it's not someone canvassing for a politician or a church organization looking for volunteers or donations.

Living in the cheapest apartment in New York City has some perks, but security measures aren't one of them. Anyone can stroll inside the building without a keycard, and there are often people loitering at the entry. I've become accustomed to not answering my door after the sun sets.

It may seem like I'm complaining, but I'm not. I'm grateful I'm able to afford my own place on my low wage as a junior journalist.

Opening the door, I encounter a guy who appears to be in his mid-teens. I notice the package in his hands before glancing back at his tanned, freckled face.

"Are you Calla?" His voice is smooth, still in between the stages of breaking.

I give a slight nod. "I am."

"Here." He thrusts the box at me and turns on his heel to leave, stuffing his hands deep into the pocket of his washed-out jeans.

"What's this?" I ask, puzzled.

He glances back and shrugs. "From Mr. Stryker."

I examine the box in my hands. It's matte black with a white velvet ribbon. I quickly shout, "Thank you," before he disappears down the stairs.

I met Niklaus Stryker two months ago. He's a handsome lawyer who holds history with my boss, Jennifer. We instantaneously connected at a work event.

Nik is famous for never losing a case. They don't just call him "Stryker" because it's his last name. He strikes his opponent down in court, like a bolt of lightning, no one stands a chance against him. He's a partner in New York's most prestigious firm—Stryker & Portman.

Oreo meows near my feet, and I close my apartment door, ensuring to lock it behind me. My therapist recommended I get a cat. Apparently, they help with self-healing, stress, and mental health. "Their purrs help heal us," she said. At times, I wonder which one of us actually needs the therapy.

Oreo leaps on the bench and nudges me with his head. I comply with his requests and rub him under the chin before staring blankly at the box, afraid to open it. Oreo prods me again, and I sigh. "You want to see what's inside?"

He meows, and I raise an eyebrow. I've lost the plot if I believe a cat can talk to me. I reach for the box and tug at the ribbon that's holding the lid closed. My mouth falls open. Inside lies a stunning, silky red dress with a card on top.

Looking forward to this evening with you.

-Nik

Nik and I have only been on two dates. He flew to London on a business trip shortly after we met. However, we kept in contact and Facetimed while he was gone, more times than I expected we would. He's quite the charmer and appears to be very put together, unlike the other men I've dated in the last couple of years. Not one's lasted more than a month. At this point, I'd argue I haven't really dated them at all. They have all been…arrangements, merely something to fulfill my needs. I'm setting a record with Nik, but I expect him to reveal his skeletons soon enough.

I glimpse at the tag and then do a double take. I grab my phone and dial Nik's number to tell him I can't accept the dress.

"Sweetheart," he answers, his voice low and warm, implying he's not in a meeting yet.

"Nik, I can't wear this."

"You don't like it?"

"It's worth more than I have in my savings," I admit as I pace around my apartment, which doesn't take more than a few strides given how small the place is.

"Ah, the price shouldn't have been on there. It's a gift," he says coolly, like a dress that has four digits on the price tag is no big deal. Perhaps it isn't for him. He probably spends triple this amount in a day. I'm not sure I'm comfortable with a gift this expensive, though, mainly since Nik and I are in the very early stages of getting to know each other. He must sense my discomfort, because he adds, "Just wear it, and I can return it tomorrow."

I consider this for a moment. It's a lovely dress, exceptionally elegant, and I do require something to wear tonight. But I also know he won't return the dress tomorrow, and can I truly begin to accept gifts from a man I don't intend to have anything serious with?

I'm overthinking. "Okay," I finally say, hovering my fingertips over the smooth material of the dress.

The event is a fundraiser to raise money for children who come from abusive homes. It's a respectable cause, but it's mostly for high-profile businessmen and women to make connections. It's a reason for politicians, lawyers, journalists, and CEOs to dress up, have a few drinks, and entice each other into business deals that many will regret the following day. It all screams uncomfortable and rich. Not my type of scene, but I better get used to it if I ever want to see the inside of any of the top news companies in the country.

Nik invited me as his date, and I'm not stupid enough to say no. It's a perfect opportunity to get my name out there, to network.

"I'll pick you up at six." Nik ends the call.

When it's just before five, I take a shower and apply some makeup. My job requires me to look presentable, and even though my sleep has improved in the last couple of years, I still have nightmares at least once every couple of weeks. The day after one of them, I appear to have risen from the dead.

I glance in the mirror at my terrible endeavor at a smoky eye and attempt to fix it, but it's as good as it's going to get. I complete the look with glossy, nude lipstick. Running a curling wand through my hair, I yelp when it touches my ear. "Shit."

The dress fits tightly. It's designed to cling to a woman's curves, and I stand on my tiptoes in front of the mirror, scrutinizing myself from every direction. It does look good—I look good. I draw a breath and stand taller, straightening my posture. I own a few pairs of heels since my job contract explicitly states I wear them. Jennifer, my boss, is all about presentation.

In my wardrobe, my eyes land on a pair of nude strappy heels that appear identical to Louboutin. The difference is they cost one-tenth of the price. When I slip on the second heel, there's a knock at my door. I glance at the clock on the wall above the dusty blue counter in my kitchen. Six on the dot.

I click the lock and pull the door open. The man in front of me stands six feet tall in graphite slacks and a light-blue dress shirt. His tie is the same color as my dress. I give him an approving smile. "You look rather handsome. I think I like you in blue."

He doesn't reply. Instead, his liquid-steel eyes roam my body methodically, and I feel naked under his gaze. Heat rises to my cheeks, and I tuck a loose strand of hair behind my ear.

"You look..." He clears his throat.

"That bad, huh?" I joke to conceal my nervousness.

Nik shakes his head, causing his short, midnight-black curls to sway. "Calla, I regret getting you that dress. All eyes are going to be on you."

My gaze travels to his and holds it. "Afraid that I'll take the spotlight from you?" I smile, tilting my head to one side.

"Definitely." Nik places a soft kiss on my cheek. "Shall we?"

Once outside, Nik opens the passenger door to his impressive Audi R8, and I carefully climb in. I salute him for having the courage to leave his three hundred-thousand-dollar car in this neighborhood. I'm surprised it's still here and without a scratch.

"How was work?" I ask when he gets into the driver's side and presses the button that brings the car to life.

I lean my head back into the seat and observe as his shoulders tense.

"There's a client trying to…fuck with me. Nothing that can't be handled," he adds, placing the car into drive and taking off down the street.

I distract myself from the twenty-minute drive by maintaining the conversation. I ask Nik about his trip and question if he takes such long trips often.

"More often than I like," he replies.

Even though I can now be a passenger in a car at night, I'm still nauseous every time. It's been six years since the dreadful accident that took away my mom, and each day gets easier.

Easier to breathe.

Nik turns into a long driveway and follows the road for a few minutes before stopping in front of tall metal gates. He presses a button to wind the window down, and before he has time to speak, there's a voice on the other side of the intercom. "Good evening, Mr. Stryker. Please drive forward." The gates gradually slide open, allowing us to pass.

As we crawl, following the road, I stare out the window. The cobblestoned driveway is curved with tiny bright lights. Lanky trees—blossoming with vibrant flowers—stretch from either side, forming a canopy above us. In each direction I glance, there's something ornate to see. From the manicured and shaped hedges to a wide fountain with an immense crystal sphere rotating above water. This place is classy and luxurious. Everything I expected and more. Much more.

We pull up to the front of a traditional building. It's massive and white with a dark-blue roof that stands out like the sea on a summer's day. My gaze trails the guests already ascending the grand marble stairs. I feel underdressed, as crazy as that sounds. I've only been to a couple of these events, and I can already guess this is by far the biggest one.

I reach for the door when Nik puts the car in park. He meets me and extends his hand when I climb out.

Nik hands his keys to the valet and retrieves a bill from his wallet. He passes it to a young gentleman as we ascend the steps to the entry. Security is positioned in front of the doors, but they don't bother checking Nik for ID. Instead, they grant a slight nod of their head.

We are immediately stopped by a group of three men and one older woman. "Stryker, what a surprise. I take it you're back from London."

"Really? You don't say," Nik replies with an arched eyebrow.

"And you have already managed to find a date," a gentleman with a sinister mustache remarks, disregarding Nik's comment.

Nik's lips curl into a smile. "This is Calla Maven," he introduces me. Four pairs of eyes train on me.

Nik must sense my unease and gives my hand a reassuring squeeze.

I plunge into a conversation with an older gentleman who enquires about my connection to Nik and asks what I do for a living. In the midst of explaining who I work for, Nik leans to me. "I'll be right back," he whispers into my ear and waits for my approval.

I give him a tilt of my chin. I'm perfectly capable of taking care of myself. Although I admit, I'm more comfortable with Nik around.

"I'm the founder of this foundation," Mr. Boulke tells me, and I nod in acknowledgment. He's a short, round man that looks to be in his sixties.

"I'm very grateful to be able to contribute to this cause," I say, hoping he doesn't ask me exactly how I'm contributing. Luckily, he smiles and turns to the others.

"There's someone I'd like to introduce to everyone. The man who organized this event and who wrote out a personal cheque of five million dollars to our foundation," Mr. Boulke announces.

Five million dollars.

That's a considerable amount of money, even for someone here. A piercingly familiar face emerges next to Mr. Boulke. A wave of adrenaline courses through me, and the blood streams to the tips of my fingers, deriving in hot waves.

"Ace Blackwell."

I have thought about this moment countless times—thought about him.

Ace.

It's challenging to keep my mind from drifting when he's on every single billboard on my way to work, in every single headline in magazines. He's the most talked about person in the country.

The last time I saw Ace in person was four years ago. He's the first guy I've ever loved, and still, no one has come close to making me feel even a fraction of what I felt when I was with him. Memories from the last time I saw him flood back like it was yesterday.

Calla, I'm so sorry. I'll do anything. I'll turn myself in…

You and me, we are real.

I love you.

I couldn't look at him without thinking of my mom, and I certainly couldn't stay with him. So I walked away—I *ran* from

Ace, leaving him on his knees pleading for forgiveness, and I didn't turn back.

That would have ruined both of us.

He tried to contact me on more than one occasion. It was grueling to ignore him, to pretend he meant nothing to me, when in reality, he was everything I never thought I needed. In the end, I blocked his number and avoided him like the black plague. How can you look at someone—be with someone—who took away the most important person in your life? I tried to tell myself it would get better, and it gradually did.

It wasn't until one and a half years ago that I began seeing him on the news and in magazines. It's like he became famous overnight after taking the boxing championship title.

Ace Blackwell, the undefeated boxing champion, was spotted with yet another female companion.

Ace Blackwell, the young billionaire, is looking to retire from his boxing career at twenty-three, a close source says.

I read every single article about him for the first couple of months, but it overwhelmed me, and I mentally restrained myself from Googling his name.

My thoughts fly back to the days when Ace used to fight for an illegal underground club. I guess going to Palm Valley University, the most prestigious university in the country, had its perks. That's what Ace did a few weeks after I left him.

Walking out on him was the hardest decision I've ever had to make and staring into the eyes of a broken boy who wanted nothing but forgiveness had made it much more difficult.

However, standing in front of me now isn't a boy. Instead, his shoulders are broader, his chest is resplendently muscular even underneath the clothes, and a dark, neatly trimmed stubble coats his prominent jawline. Did he get taller? His arm muscles swell underneath his white dress shirt, and I'm able to make out the outline of his tattoos. Does he still have the one he got for me?

I feel my own tattoo, a small *A* with a heart underneath it—Ace of Hearts—heating up underneath my dress. It's crazy to recall how in love I was with him back in college, even though I never admitted it, not even to myself.

Hanging off his arm is a woman around the same age as me—maybe even younger. Her hair is styled in voluminous curls that stretch well below her breasts. Ace always had a thing for dark hair. Perhaps that's part of the reason why I got highlights to make mine lighter. To leave that fragment of myself behind.

The woman's golden-hued dress streams down her body, highlighting her thin figure, leaving nothing to the imagination. I've never been the envious type, but perhaps, at this moment, I am. My chest adopts a bizarre emptiness.

I hardly notice Nik's return. He hands me a glass of champagne and rests his hand on my lower back. The gesture that felt comforting a few minutes ago is now burning a bottomless hole through me.

My eyes meet Ace's, and I've forgotten how intense they are. An infinite cosmos bursting with mesmerizing darkness. He stares back at me, but only for a second. For that second, the whole world stops, ceasing to exist. I drown in the starlight hues of blue, gray, and green. And for that second, I wonder what it would've been like if I didn't walk away from him that day.

Ace's expression is blank, almost hollow.

"Angus, I feel privileged to be able to give back to the community," Ace says to Mr. Boulke. His voice is deep and confident. A stellar smile appears on his mouth, but it seems forced. Perhaps it's just my imagination.

Mr. Boulke looks like he's about to get on the ground and kiss Ace's feet. The way his voice rises when talking to Ace is unbelievable.

Ace directs his attention at Nik, not giving me any sort of acknowledgment. It's like I'm not here. Like I don't exist.

"Nik, what a surprise."

"Ace, you didn't mention you would be attending this evening," Nik answers with a clipped tone.

"I could say the same about you."

"I try to keep my private life...private."

Ace smirks. "For obvious reasons, I'd imagine?"

I have no knowledge of what they're talking about, but one glance in Nik's direction reveals he does. His jaw is fixed in an unforgiving line, and he glares at Ace. "Are you implying something?"

"Now, why would I do that?" Ace arches one of his thick brows as if to challenge Nik.

Nik isn't a fool. He won't react in a public setting with so many influential people around, even when someone's pissing him off.

"Now, now, gentlemen. How about we make a toast?" the older woman in our group proposes. Her gold bracelets glisten underneath the lights as she raises her champagne glass with her slender fingers.

"You know Ace?" I ask Nik, keeping my expression neutral.

"He's one of my clients. The one we discussed earlier," Nik replies in a low voice so only I can hear. He gives a departing nod to the other gentlemen in the group and leads me away from them.

"Ah," I say, understanding. The client who is trying to *fuck* with Nik.

I wondered who was game enough to play a dangerous game with the Stryker. From what I've heard, Nik is the last person anyone would want to get on the wrong side of. He's ruthless when it comes to business and always gets what he wants. I've never seen that side to him, and I'm not so sure I would like to.

We barely make it five steps when someone else stops Nik for a business discussion. After a couple of hours of chatting to men who keep glancing at my breasts and women who wonder if I'm here to sleep with their husbands to fast-track to the top, my head begins to pound.

My thoughts wander to Ace throughout the night. I prevent myself from scanning the room for him on multiple occasions. The tightness in my chest returns, and I struggle to breathe. I excuse myself and stride toward the back door, requiring fresh air. My chest shouldn't ache, although it does. Ace acted like I didn't exist. But what did I expect?

I lean against the glass rail on the terrace. It's tranquil and windless tonight.

We are strangers in this life—in this city.

Strangers.

Four years is an awfully long time, I repeat, until the tightness in my chest loosens. I glance up and wish I could spot at least a single star, but the sky is thick with an invisible blanket.

Footsteps shuffle behind me, and my heart hastens.

"Ready to go, sweetheart? I'm sorry for bringing you here. You look utterly bored."

My shoulders droop as disappointment scurries through me. I compose myself, ironing my dress with my hands before turning to face Nik. "Just a bit lightheaded from the champagne." Not really a lie, I am lightheaded, but it's not from the champagne.

"Do you want me to take you home?" The hesitation in his voice hints that he's hoping I'll offer to spend the night with him. Under typical circumstances, I would have, but this night has already provided me with more than I bargained for.

"I think that would be best."

Nik nods, interlocking our hands. He leans down and kisses my cheek, brushing his stubble against it. "Of course."

On the way back to my apartment, silence surrounds us. My mind dives years in the past, back to a time where I knew Ace.

I'll never forget my first love. It was innocent but powerful as it swept me off my feet. It came unexpectedly, and I was entranced by how earth-shattering it was. I became intoxicated—drugged—unable to imagine a life without him. I questioned how I ever existed without him, without his voice, his touch, without...*him*. It was a fervent addiction.

First love only happens once, and if you're one of the few lucky ones, it's your last. But for many, like me, a breakup often follows. Whether it's amicable or not, it's a breakup like you never imagined. Mine was heart-wrenching. It felt like my soul was lit on fire, and I was unable to extinguish it. My dreams haunted me, and the sleepless nights were full of anguish. But with time, the pain faded, not wholly, but to a bearable level.

Once we're at my apartment building, Nik follows me to the entrance, and even though he's adamant on walking me up, I insist that I can manage.

I fumble with my key in the darkness, struggling to locate the keyhole. My hands shake more than usual, and I wonder if it's from how this evening's events unfolded or from the fear a hooligan might sneak up behind me at any second.

This stupid damn lock. "Shit," I curse, dropping my key. The door next to mine flies open, and Betty, my neighbor, rushes out of her apartment. The woman is in her late seventies, thin and frail, but with the baseball bat in her hands, she could run an army.

The gray bun on top of her head is so tight it draws her skin back, delivering a strained look. Her sharp eyes scan the hallway, and her face mellows when she realizes it's only me. She lowers her bat, placing her hand on her chest as if to calm herself. The poor lady was probably about to give herself a heart attack by assuming someone was trying to break into my apartment.

"Calla, dear, I thought you were spending the night with that handsome gentleman that picked you up." She eyes me up and down, searching for any signs of distress.

"Were you spying on me again, Betty?"

Betty Piggins is the only person in this entire apartment building who doesn't give me the heebie-jeebies. When I first moved in here a year ago, I spotted her struggling with her groceries and offered to help her carry them up. We live on the fifth floor, and our apartment building doesn't have an elevator. From that point onward, I've been doing her groceries once a week at the same time as mine and taking out her garbage. She thanks me with containers full of choc-chip cookies that are soft and gooey in the middle. Sometimes, when I'm lucky, she even cooks me a homemade meal. It's a win-win situation. However, I can't say the same for my waistline. It's good there are those five flights of stairs to keep me in shape.

"Spying? I wouldn't say that. Just keeping an eye out."

"I decided to return early. I wasn't feeling well."

"Care for some tea?" Betty offers. "And you can tell me all

about what happened," she adds, not buying my lie about not feeling well.

Betty's husband died a few years ago, and it's clear to see she misses him dearly. When you spend your whole life with someone, that person becomes your best friend, and losing your best friend is like losing a piece of yourself.

"I'd love some tea."

3

Avoiding Fate

Calla

Oreo's rough tongue on my cheek wakes me. His midnight-black paws knead my chest, and he meows when I open my eyes. The early morning sun seeps through the worn curtains, a promise of a sunny day. I cover my eyes while they adjust to the light.

"They didn't say having a cat would be like having a child," I remark, my morning voice sounding croaky. I stroke Oreo's head, he nudges my hand, and I sigh, lazily scratching underneath his snowy chin.

I reach for my phone on the bedside table. The table, along with most of my furniture, is secondhand. People lay furniture they don't want out on the streets, and there's some decent stuff there if you look hard enough. It's certainly better than spending thousands of dollars that I don't have on brand-new furniture.

Seven-thirty. My eyes widen. "Shit."

Shit. Shit. Shit.

My meager weekly income will convert into no income at all if I don't get to work in the next thirty minutes. Unfortunately my boss is far from empathetic. Even though I've never been late before, she won't hesitate to dismiss me on the spot for arriving late.

I couldn't sleep last night. Moreover, I might have made matters worse by searching Ace's name on the internet. I spent hours staring at commercials and advertisements he's done, watching some of his recent fights, and reading articles about him.

I couldn't shake the one common factor through all of that—his stone-cold eyes. It's the same way he looked at me at the fundraiser. There's nothing familiar about them, nothing in them that remind me of *my* Ace.

Last night, I found myself on the Instagram page of one of his recent flings, Cassidy Torrio, after reading an article titled: *A close source says Cassidy and Ace are getting serious. Could an engagement ring be on the cards?* A vague aching seized my chest, and I slammed my laptop closed but laid awake for hours after. I must have fallen asleep around five in the morning and neglected to set the alarm.

I rush toward the bathroom. The checkered tiles are cold beneath my feet, and I slip in a puddle of liquid that wasn't there before I went to bed last night.

"OREO!" I'm lying in a puddle of cat piss, and I'm going to be late for work. This day is off to a great start.

I only adopted Oreo a few months ago, and even though he's been good with potty training, using his litter box most of the time, he still manages to pee on the floor now and then. I throw an old towel on the tiles to cover the puddle. Then, hopping in the shower, I brush my teeth simultaneously, managing to finish up in under two minutes. Once I get out and cover my body with a towel, I open the bathroom window, hoping the smell of cat urine will air out while I'm at work.

The nippy air brushes against my face as I dab concealer under my eyes to hide the dark circles resulting from not sleeping. I've been trying to tell myself it has nothing to do with *him*. It's just a coincidence. But I can't seem to shake that my thoughts have been mindlessly circling him since Friday night.

Oreo meows at my feet. "So you piss on the bathroom floor, and now you demand food. Amazing life you have, huh?" He rubs his head against my ankles, and I almost trip over him, gripping the door for support just in time.

A migraine etches its way into my head and pounds with every step I take. I manage to get ready in ten minutes, setting a record.

I scurry out of my apartment, lock it behind me, and dash down five flights of stairs, clutching my heels in one hand and my bag in the other. Before I step outside, onto the lively streets of Brooklyn, I grasp the door handle and slip my heels on.

Swinging the building door open, I step forward, prepared to hurry toward the subway station, but I come to a halt when I discover Nik's black R8 parked in front of me. Even through the tinted windows, I notice his head is down, and he's busily tapping away on his phone, sending emails, I suppose. He's always working, no matter what time of day it is. So it's no surprise that at twenty-eight years old, he's already a partner in a firm, blatant evidence that hard work does indeed pay off.

He winds his window down with a bright smile. "Morning, sweetheart."

Nik is in his usual workwear, a custom-made suit with a striped tie. I doubt there's anyone that can look as good as he does in a suit. Even if I haven't seen him naked, I'd still be able to know he's in shape from the way the expensive material embraces his upper body.

"What are you doing here?" I glance at the time on my phone. Nineteen minutes to get to work, or I better start looking for a new job.

He examines my blouse. “I’m here to take you to work.”

I track his gaze and discover I’ve missed a few buttons. A flush creeps along my cheeks. I sincerely hope I don’t smell like Oreo’s pee.

“I’m late.” I fix my blouse.

Nik smirks. “I know, sweetheart. I’ve been waiting here for the last thirty minutes. I thought you were starting later today.”

“I don’t think you’ll be able to get me to work in twenty minutes. I’ll be better off taking the subway.” New York traffic is a disaster, especially at this time of the morning.

He looks at me, raising a heavy brow. “Is that a challenge?”

I roll my eyes, glancing in the subway’s direction and then back to Nik’s car. I decide to take my chances. “Twenty minutes. Otherwise, I’ll be out of a job.”

“You know, I might be looking for a secretary.” He presents me with a cheeky grin.

Anything would be better than working for Jennifer, but there’s no way I’m going to accept a job from the guy I’m sleeping with. I don’t mix business with pleasure. “Twenty minutes,” I repeat and scamper around to the passenger side.

“Yes, ma’am.”

Nik pulls up in front of my work building in a record time of fifteen minutes, providing me with enough time to get a coffee for both myself and Jennifer from the café inside.

The fragrance of coffee is rich and elevating as I stride through the glass doors. Inside, the day has already begun, mayhem surrounds me as people frantically race past with folders underneath their armpits and coffee cups in their hands.

I set the coffee on Jennifer’s desk at exactly eight a.m. on the dot. Her brown-caramel hair is styled in gentle waves, and I'm mind-blown she has the time to curl her hair in the mornings.

"I have scheduled you in for an interview with Mr. Blackwell at eleven this morning," she informs me without lifting her gaze while her red-painted fingernails tap on her phone screen.

"M-Mr. Blackwell?" I stutter.

She unhurriedly looks up. "Yes. Ace Blackwell. I assume you can manage that? I've been trying to organize this for the last couple of months. The man is hard to get a hold of."

"Uh—"

Jennifer's phone rings, and she glances down at the caller ID before giving me a slight flick of the wrist. "You're dismissed, Miss Maven."

I wander to my desk, striving to come up with something, anything that could get me out of this. My insides churn at the possibility of having to interview Ace.

Jessie, one of my co-workers, busily types away an article on her computer with her back to me, clueless of what I'm about to ask her. She rolls her neck, and her short, bouncy ponytail mimics the movement. Jessie was hired at the same time as I was, and we've become close. I don't have many friends around here, and it's nice to have someone I can talk to occasionally. Not that I'm comfortable confiding my deepest, darkest secrets to anyone.

"I'll take over your workload for the day if you take Ace Blackwell's interview," I propose, leaning against the side of her desk, choosing not to beat around the bush.

She stops working and looks up at me, her small mouth gaping.

"Plus, I can get you an interview with Nik Stryker," I add before she can reject my offer. Even Jennifer hasn't been able to get an interview with Nik. He says they're a waste of time, but I'm confident I'll be able to sway him, one way or another.

Jessie's eyes light up. "Let me get this straight...you want me to interview Ace Blackwell..." She clears her throat. "And you're going to convince Nik to do an interview for our magazine, which will put me in the top books with Jennifer. Are you feeling okay, Calla? Not sick or anything? No chance of a potential brain tumor affecting your thinking abilities?"

Nope. I just don't want to deal with an ex who unintentionally took my mom's life and now roams every woman's dreams. "Personal reasons."

Jessie raises a shaped eyebrow. I detect she's curious about what personal connections I could hold with the famous champion.

"So is that a deal?"

"You drive bargains I can't say no to."

I grin at the small victory. For the rest of the morning, I finish a few articles that Jennifer assigned to Jessie. Around lunchtime, my phone vibrates with a text from Nik.

Nik: ***Have dinner with me tonight.***

It's not a question.

Me: ***I'd love to.***

Two seconds later, my phone vibrates again.

Nik: ***I'm looking forward to dessert.***

I scan the room, ensuring no one's paying attention to me. Then, out of the corner of my eye, I notice Jessie walking into the office, and I slide my phone back into my bag.

"How was it?" I prompt her when she gets closer.

"Umm..." She looks down at the black folder in her hands. "There was a slight problem."

Before she has the chance to explain what happened, Jennifer strides toward us from her lunch break. Her emerald bodycon dress sits snugly around her figure, and she pushes up the long sleeve to glance at the time on her watch.

"Miss Maven, my office. Now." Jennifer's tone is icy as she walks past me, her red stilettos clicking down the long corridor. Her gaze never falls on me, and that's when I realize she's in one of her foul moods.

The last time she was in one of these moods, half of the office lost their job, resulting in the rest of us taking over the workload until we found replacements. As a result, we spent close to twenty hours a day in the office for a whole week.

Jessie shoots me an apologetic look and tucks a loose strand of hair behind her ear as she takes the seat in front of her computer.

Inhaling a breath, I smooth my skirt and follow Jennifer into her office. "Is there a problem?" I ask, knowing very well if there isn't a problem, there's about to be one.

"You sent Jessie to interview Ace Blackwell when I gave *you* that task. Is there a reason for that?"

"I, uh—" I clear my throat, formulating the best speech of my life.

"Actually, I don't care. I specifically told you to do it, and you disobeyed my instructions. You should be grateful I even considered you to be able to handle such an important interview."

I understand where she's coming from. This is the most eminent interview our magazine has landed. While I don't see a problem with Jessie doing it instead of me, I'm not going to voice my opinion.

"I have gotten off the phone with Mr. Blackwell, and he's very adamant you come to interview him. He made it quite clear if it's not you, there will be no interview."

Oh.

I envision Ace picking up the phone and crafting absurd requests. How did he even know I work at *Satire Times*? I doubt Jennifer mentioned who would be interviewing him in the first place.

"I'm not sure why Mr. Blackwell wants you to do the interview or how he even knows your name, but you seemed to have caught his attention."

I have a reasonably good idea of how I've caught his attention.

"So you'll do the interview tomorrow, and if you try to palm it off again to someone else, don't bother coming in."

There's a tightness in my throat like there's something lodged in it, and I can't speak.

"Miss Maven?"

"Yes, Jennifer?"

"Sleeping with my ex doesn't guarantee you a spot in my company. I rarely give second chances, consider yourself lucky." She slides her black-rimmed glasses over her eyes, an apparent gesture that this conversation is over.

That went remarkably better than I thought it would.

4

Old Friends

Calla

It's surprisingly warm today, the beginning of summer nearing. The streets are walled by high-rises filled with influential firms. Across the road, tiny pastel-pink flowers cover the branches of the trees, and if it weren't so busy, the sound of birds chirping might be audible. Every step that hauls me closer to him instigates a fire to spark deep inside the pit of my stomach. I feel as though I might unexpectedly combust at any given moment.

Circling my mind are all the reasons why I shouldn't do this. There are plenty. But I can't afford to be jobless, and Jennifer made it clear that I could very well be on the streets if this interview doesn't happen.

Even though this job isn't ideally what I want to do for the rest of my life, it's a beginning. I've worked hard to get where I am. From the day I started college, my sights were set on this city. Mr. Howley, the college chancellor, steered me toward my dreams. Although Jennifer isn't the easiest person to work for, I'm glad she took a chance on me. All I need to do is stick my head down, work hard, and hopefully, one day, I can be a writer for a significant news company, or perhaps even run one of my own.

I come to a halt in front of a building that stretches to the clouds. Blackwell Enterprises. A bulky security guard with his arms crossed over his chest eyes me up and down. I flash him my ID, and he nods, stepping aside for me to pass through the grand glass doors.

The sound of my heels clicking on the silver-veined marble floor echo through the lobby as I navigate to the elevators. My nerves are getting the better of me, and I smooth the black blazer dress that adheres to my body and stops at mid-thigh. I'd be lying if I said I didn't wear this dress for him, because even after four years, my chest hums with anxious excitement.

The elevator doors open on the thirty-fifth floor, revealing a large chandelier hanging from the high ceiling and polished, bright floors. In front of me is a curved reception desk, where a light-haired woman greets me with a wide smile.

"Good afternoon. I'm here to see Ace Blackwell." My voice fails me, emerging unsteadily. I clear my throat, endeavoring to get myself together. He's just a man.

A man that made you feel like no one else has.

Yeah, made. He's a stranger now. I've moved on.

I shake my head, clearing the ridiculous inner dialogue that's inched its way into my mind.

"Do you have an appointment with Mr. Blackwell?"

"Yes, my name is Calla Maven. I'm from *Satire Times Magazine*."

"One moment, Miss Maven." She checks the schedule on the screen in front of her. "Yes, I can see we have you booked. Mr. Blackwell is waiting for you in his office. The last door on your right." She points me in the direction.

My hands shake, and I clench them into tight fists until my

nails dig into my palms, forming moon crescents. The only thing I'm aware of is the sound of my heart throbbing against the cage of my chest, like a hummingbird hankering to escape. It's not until I sense the metallic taste of blood that I realize I'm also chewing on my lower lip.

I straighten my posture and raise my chin higher before squeezing my eyes shut. My knuckles meet the wooden door. Once. Twice. Three times.

I wait.

"Come in," a calm voice booms from the other side. His voice.

Opening my eyes, I twist the handle.

I avoid glancing at him right away, dreading to meet the iciness, which could freeze an entire ocean. Instead, I peruse his office. It's bigger than my entire apartment, with a gray color palette throughout. A dark wooden built-in bookshelf stands to the side of the room, full of autobiographies. He was always into them. Floor-to-ceiling windows cover the back wall, offering a view of the city below buzzing with life, and to the side, by the bookshelf, is a low, leather couch.

My eyes finally land on Ace. He sits behind an immense desk that occupies the better quarter of the room, observing me inquisitively. The sleeves of his white button-down shirt are rolled up to reveal more of the black ink that weaves from his hands to his forearms.

"Calla." The richness of his voice fills the room, covering me, like a veil of serene nightfall.

"Ace." My gaze meets his, and the universe explodes. I've forgotten how strong our connection was, how many words could be spoken with our eyes alone.

Ace's face is older, more mature. His dark hair is shorter, yet the faint curls I've grown to love are still somewhat there. I'm reminded of how it felt to thread my fingers through them and to hear the grunts of his satisfaction when I did so.

His gaze flickers down my body in a lustful caress, consuming me further each second it lingers. My body quivers in response, and I draw on my lip.

"Please, sit." He motions to the leather chair in front of him.

I occupy a seat opposite Ace and rest the notepad on my lap, out of his view. Jennifer emailed me a list of questions I must ask him for the magazine article.

"Why did you want me to do the interview?" I'm confused by the change of his demeanor from the fundraiser till now, but then again, he's always been hot and cold.

"I'm sorry for the way I acted at the fundraiser. I wasn't expecting to see you."

I mull over his answer, wondering if that's genuinely all it was. "I guess we were both not expecting each other. Do you mind if I ask some questions? It won't take long." I don't meet his gaze. It makes it difficult to concentrate.

Ace doesn't owe me anything, and even though there's a lot to say after four years, I can't find the words to begin. So instead, I sweep the personal aspect of this situation aside and treat this as any other interview.

"Take all the time you need." He fixes his Rolex, all the while, I feel the power of his gaze on me.

"There are rumors you may be retiring. Can you shed some light on that topic?" I begin.

He has a boxing match coming up in a few weeks. It's been all over the news, but there have been speculations it will be his last one. How accurate are those statements?

"There's no one worth a fight," he replies casually.

"Awfully cocky, aren't you?" I remark out loud and bite the inside of my cheek after my thoughts have seeped into the open.

There's a slight twitch of his mouth as if he finds me amusing. "I'm twenty-three, and no one has lasted more than two rounds in a ring with me. Skills like that do miracles for a person's self-confidence, wouldn't you agree?"

He's staging an act. This is how he portrays himself to the world. Cocky, confident, and a ladies' man. But this isn't the real him, or at least this isn't the Ace I used to know. Has he changed? Or is this indeed just an act?

"You're a self-made billionaire at the age of twenty-three. What keeps you humble?" Who wrote these questions? Surely not Jennifer. They sound like they have been picked from a generic list.

"Donating to charities, especially children's organizations," he answers as if this is all rehearsed, like he's said this all a million times before.

He donated five million dollars to children from abused homes at the fundraiser. Does it have anything to do with his past? Does he feel the need to help other children because no one's helped him?

"Is it because you can somewhat relate…from your childhood?"

A shard of roughness penetrates his exterior, and I assume no one's asked him that before. Perhaps because no one knows about his past, he does an excellent job of masking it.

"It hits close to home, yes." He doesn't elaborate.

I don't push on the topic further, yet I can't help but wonder what his father thinks of him now. Has he tried to reach out to Ace to fix their strained relationship?

"What do you do in your free time?" I read off the notepad.

He sits silent, and my gaze flicks to his. "Go out with me."

The pen I'm holding slips from my fingers, I catch it just in time and bite the inside of my cheek. "What?"

"Let me take you out. Catch up."

He rests his large hands on the wooden desk, restraining me with his demanding stare. Nerves clatter in my stomach. Does this work with women? Does he think this will work with me?

I toy with the pen in my hand. "Do you really think this…" I motion to his flirtatious posture and continue, "…will work on me? It will take more than *that* to make me fall at your feet. I would have thought you knew me better."

"I'm not even trying, Calla," he challenges as my name drips off his tongue, like sweet honey trickling off a spoon.

It would seem cocky coming from someone else. However, he's highly confident, which incites a distant spark inside of me. I have the urge to accept the invitation, but I don't—I can't.

"Don't mistake me for one of your one-night stands."

He acts unbothered, as though he expected my answer. Leaning back in his chair, he places his hands behind his head. His muscular arms strain underneath the white fabric so much so that I wonder if the material is strong enough to hold them in.

What would it feel like to run my hands down his arms and feel him touching me once more? There have been articles from close sources claiming he's a "sex god" in bed. If our old times are anything to go off, I know he lives up to that title, perhaps even exceeds it.

As if he recognizes what I'm thinking of, his lips twitch into a wicked smirk. My cheeks heat, and I quickly look down at my notepad and deliver a question without thinking. "Do you have any regrets?"

He inhales in a ragged breath, and our minds advance toward a dark place, toward memories that still haunt me to this day. "Calla—"

"You don't have to answer that. I didn't write the questions." I should have looked over them, but nerves got the better of me.

"Are you seeing anyone, or is the boxing champion single?" I read the next one. God, these questions are ridiculous.

He raises an eyebrow. "Who wants to know?"

"Apparently, every woman who reads our magazine."

"Single."

"What about Cassidy?" I quiz without thinking once again.

That isn't in the notes, but it is public record.

"Casual." His smile brims with amusement.

Casual? What is that supposed to mean? Casual fucking or casual dating? There's a significant difference between the two.

"How long have you been with Nik for?" he asks.

"Not long. We're *casual*," I explain, using his term. I resume, not giving him time to respond, but not without noticing the way his eyes narrow and his jaw tightens. It could be my eyes playing tricks on me. Why would he care?

"You're both a famous champion boxer and a businessman. Which do you prefer?" I continue.

"I do like getting hot and heavy with my opponents." His eyes glimmer with playfulness.

I bet you do.

I close the notepad in my lap. "What do you like most about boxing?"

"The adrenaline. The high. The power and satisfaction that appears after a win."

I nod, somewhat understanding. "How does it feel to be undefeated?" I prompt on my own accord.

"Truthfully? I feel unchallenged, like the only person that can test me is myself."

I can't even imagine how much supremacy that induces in a person. "What would you do if you choose to retire from your boxing career at such a young age?"

"I'd continue building Blackwell Enterprises. I'm not afraid to admit that I'm hungry for power. And if I feel as though my boxing career isn't challenging me the way I desire it to, I will pursue that mental or physical stimulation…elsewhere."

His focus on me doesn't flail as he speaks, and I begin to question if we're still talking about the same thing.

"I think I have everything I need for the article." My voice appears smaller than I expected.

"Go out with me. Please."

He's pleading, and I bet he doesn't do it often. Ace is the type of man to take what he wants without so much as blinking, and I bet people are more than happy to oblige him. "Ace…" I begin to tell him it's not a good idea.

"Old friends catching up," he says nonchalantly, like it's not a big deal.

Old friends catching up.

If only it were that simple. But he gives me that lazy smile, the one that feels like nothing has changed between us, even though the whole universe has shifted. Almost half a decade has passed. This is still work for him—like it is for me—but it seems like he's willing to knock down a small barrier if I agree to this.

"Okay, like old friends." I stand from the chair. I need to think about this, and I have learned it's always easier to agree in the moment and then cancel later.

He rises from his seat as well. "I'll walk you out."

"That's not necessary."

"Calla, I'll walk you out." He hovers his hand on my lower back as we make our way out the door. He's barely touching me, but I sense every soft brush of his fingers like it's the only human contact I've had in years. My insides ignite with fire, yet I maintain a composed expression.

Ace always was highly persistent and liked to be in control of every situation. It doesn't look like much has changed. "You know, black looks good on you," he notes, referring to my blazer dress while we're walking toward the elevators. "But red is rather… enticing," he drawls, triggering my legs to tremble beneath me.

Nothing could have prepared me for seeing Ace for the first time in four years. We're older, and we have different lives, but the way he looked at me when I walked into his office made it clear that many things remain the same. At least for me they do. And that's precisely why I can't go out with him, not even as *old friends*—whatever that means.

Before we have the chance to organize a day and time to catch up, one of Ace's business partners interrupts us in the main lobby. I use that as my chance to leave, not failing to notice the look of irritation that spans across Ace's face when the older man dives into a discussion about terms in a contract.

I guess it's a cowardly way to leave, and Ace doesn't have my current phone number, but seeing him again will cause more damage than good.

✦ ✦ ✦

"Nik," I moan his name while his head is in between my legs, his hot tongue precisely where I need it. I arch my back and tilt my head, permitting the high to distract me from everything.

Orgasms are more intense when someone else gives them to you, much more satisfying than using the vibrators I keep in my nightstand drawer. They get the job done, but it gets rather dull since there's only so much you can do with them. Sex with Nik has never left me unsatisfied. I guess that's the only thing that matters when you're sleeping with someone regularly. Even though he's only twenty-eight, he's more experienced than anyone I've ever been with.

"You never told me why you and Jennifer broke up?" I ask when he's lying on his back, and I'm draped over his naked chest.

Some would say it's wrong to bring up ex's right after sex, but the arrangement Nik and I share allows for honest questions and discussions. I'm never anxious to ask him anything, and I only hope he feels the same way.

"You never asked before."

I glance up at him as if to say, *I'm asking now*. His stubble needs a trim, and the gloomy circles underneath his eyes suggest that work has been keeping him busy. He chuckles, shaking his head at my persistent glance before answering. "She wanted kids."

"And you don't?"

"I'm twenty-eight, and I've been focused on my career for as long as I can remember. I haven't had the time to think what *I* want." He circles my bare shoulder with his fingertips. "I asked for some time, and she wasn't willing to compromise. She shouldn't have to."

I don't know how old Jennifer is, but she appears to be in her mid-thirties, so I understand why she wants children now. Nik and Jennifer dated for a couple of years, and to this day, they remain friends.

"Have you always had relationships with older women?" I ask, unable to help myself. It doesn't bother me, I'm not seeking to have a relationship with Nik. I'm merely curious.

He sighs. "Yes, but it's not something I set out to do." He pauses and then adds, "You're the first woman I've slept with that's younger than me."

"Hmm, really?"

"Are you surprised?"

"Well, yes. I thought you would have slept with people younger than yourself at least once."

He shrugs. "You're different. You're headstrong and more mature than other people your age."

"Does it bother you?"

"That you're young and know what you like? Of course not, Calla. That's what drew me to you when I first saw you."

The night we first met, I was a little more confident than I usually am—a few glasses of wine do that to a person. I caught Nik watching me all night, and long story short, his witty mouth impressed me in more ways than one.

"I'm going for a shower. Want to join?" He suggestively wiggles his eyebrows.

At first, I thought he wouldn't be able to keep up with me. Lately, I have a high libido, but this man has the stamina of a horse. "I don't think I'm ready for round three," I reply, and he chuckles before steering for his bathroom.

Nik and I are on the same page. He made it clear he isn't looking for a serious relationship, and a serious relationship isn't on the cards for me, either. They are too complicated, involve too many feelings, and too many people get hurt. I cut connections with a few previous partners because I felt them becoming too attached, and I knew I couldn't give them what they wanted. It has always been just fun for me.

My therapist is convinced I have some underlying issues with letting people in, specifically men, and I force myself not to have feelings for them to avoid getting hurt. It's not true, but I do see where she's coming from. I genuinely haven't had any emotional connection to the guys I've slept with—not that there have been many—and I plan on keeping it that way. I don't have time for a relationship. I'm focused on my career. I don't have enough sanity to work for Jennifer all my life.

I can't help staring at Nik's wardrobe. He seems too good to be true, too perfect. No one can be that perfect. What skeletons is he hiding in his closet?

Maybe I can take a peek, I'm the one sleeping with the guy. What if he's a mass murderer? I know that's very unlikely for a lawyer who's a partner at a law firm. However, you can never be too sure. After all, *Dexter* worked at a Police Department.

The water is still running in the bathroom. I climb out of his enormous bed and tiptoe across his room to the walk-in closet. His apartment is impressive, right in the heart of Manhattan, and I can't even begin to imagine how much it must have cost to purchase.

His walk-in closet has every possible combination of dress shirts and ties, all color-coded. I open a few drawers and glance inside—socks, T-shirts, and more ties.

He even folds his underwear—who does that? I'm about to leave when I spot a black safe out of the corner of my eye. The safe has a six-number combination lock, and my mind considers all the things that could be in that safe. You know, things like guns, drugs, and cash. *Blood slides.* I watch too many movies.

What the hell am I doing? This is precisely the sort of thing my therapist told me not to do. I shake my head and walk back into his room. *Relax. It's probably just essential files.*

"I was thinking..." Nik emerges from the bathroom with a white towel draped around his bottom half. His upper body gleams with water droplets. "A close friend of mine works pretty high up at *The Times*. I could have a word with him."

Something about the way he says that causes me to scrunch my brows in response. I don't need a man to get me to the top. This is what I've been trying to avoid since we began seeing each other.

"I don't need a free ride just because I'm sleeping with a reputable lawyer, Nik." I'm irritated he's brought this up right after we have sex, like it's something he owes me.

"It wouldn't be a free ride, just a meeting," he says softly, treading cautiously.

I collect my clothes from where they lie scattered around the room. "I should go." I've never spent a night at a man's house. It's not something you do when you're just sleeping with a man, at least, it's not what *I* do. And it assists in keeping things simple.

"Think about it, sweetheart. You're a smart woman, and I don't doubt that you can make it to the top without my help, but once in a while, you should take a shortcut."

I wonder if he got to the top at such a young age by taking shortcuts.

Stopping at the grocery store on my way home, I check the list Betty has given me. It's not much, but once I pick up a few things that I need, it ends up being two full bags. By the time I walk just under a mile to my apartment building and climb five flights of stairs, I'm out of breath.

"A young gentleman was here. He's even better looking than the other one. Covered in tattoos, striking eyes, looked like a real piece of work. You certainly know how to pick them," Betty reveals when she opens her door.

My pulse quickens dramatically. I hope it wasn't who I think, but there aren't many people who match that description.

"Did he say what he wanted?"

"He was going to leave a note, but I told him he shouldn't bother. I knew that note wouldn't survive with Oreo for more than five minutes, and I didn't know when you were going to be home." Betty opens the door wider for me. Her apartment is even smaller than mine, but she claims she doesn't need much.

"He said he'll pick you up on Friday at six."

I turn to her, my eyes wide.

"Did he by any chance leave a name?" I set Betty's groceries on her rustic kitchen counter.

"No, dear, but his motorbike was rather loud, that's why I rushed out to see what hooligan was trying to break into your apartment this time. Can never be too careful. You should have seen his face when I ran out with the baseball bat."

5

Facing the Past

Ace

Once I descend the stairs, a genuine grin spreads on my mouth, even though an old lady with a baseball bat was inches from taking me out. Distracted, I almost miss the man leaning against the side of the orange-brick building.

He approaches me as soon as I step foot onto the walkway. He's practically bald. Ripped jeans and an olive T-shirt hang loosely off his square-built body. His face is unshaven, with a mustache tickling his upper lip. Logan Harding is the spitting image of his father.

"Long time no see." He matches his strides with mine.

"Not long enough," I mutter under my breath.

"Is that how you treat an old friend?"

I've known Logan for most of my life. We used to ride bicycles together when we were ten. His was bright green, mine electric blue. When you're that age, you don't think about the future. When you're that age, you feel invincible.

What have we turned out to be? Logan is mixed up with criminals, and I'm no better.

Logan has always looked out for himself, no matter what. He's tried to reach out to me in the past, but I can't look at him without thinking back to the night that changed everything. He gave me the alcohol. He offered me the keys. I don't blame him for that. I blame him for convincing me to hide it, not to come forward because he was afraid. I blame him for using my family as an excuse when I was ready to give it all up to clear my conscience.

He was always thinking of himself.

I've always resented him for his lack of feelings. Over the years we've been friends, I've noticed he has the traits of a sociopath. He breaks the rules and makes decisions without any guilt.

"What do you want?"

"Let me fight," Logan says.

"No." I continue toward my bike.

He follows me. "Six years later, and you're still obsessed with her." Logan glances toward the brick building, his eyes turning into a malicious shade of gray.

My jaw sets. "You touch her, and you're as good as dead."

"Must be nice to be rich and a killer," he taunts beside me.

The words tumble through me, forming ire in their wake. I don't allow it to show—it will only boost him higher. My trainer's motto echoes loud and clear, *never reveal emotions to your opponents. They will use them to lay you to rest.*

"Come on. You know I won't disappoint in the ring. Not all of us are as lucky as you."

"If it's money you want, I'll give it to you, but I'm not letting you fight."

"It's not about the money. I want the rush. I want the adrenaline. I want to feel powerful. You—" he jumps in front of me and stabs his finger into my chest, "—out of all people, should know that it's not about the money. It never has been."

People say it's not about the money, but we're governed by it all our lives. Some of us would kill for it if it came down to it.

"You're out of luck. Find somewhere else." I sidestep him.

Dean kicked Logan out of the club back in Idaho because he was hungry for blood. He almost killed a guy at the last fight, and there was no way Dean was going to recruit that burden. Neither am I. It's the last thing I need when the whole world already has eyes on me.

"There's no one else. Dean kicked me out, and you own the rest."

"No," I thunder with finality. I send Denzel—my driver—a text, tug the helmet over my head, and start my bike. The noise of it cuts through Logan's protests. When I pull out onto the street, I speed dial Denzel.

"I've sent you my recent GPS location. Make sure the silver car that's parked out the front of the building is gone. If it's not, I need you to go to apartment nine. If there's a man there, make him leave. Make sure he doesn't come back."

"On it, sir."

Denzel is technically my driver, but he's more than that. His qualifications are impressive. He takes care of any task I set him without any questions asked, and most importantly, it's all confidential.

✦ ✦ ✦

"What's gotten into you?" Josh slaps my head as he shoves a slice of greasy, extra-cheese pizza into his mouth.

The way Josh eats, you'd think he would be a hundred pounds by now, but he's always had a fast metabolism. Tall and lanky, he could eat fast food for every meal and would still look like an athlete.

I observe him with envy and then glance at my dinner. The plate in front of me is filled with pasta, vegetables, and chicken for a source of protein. I'm mere weeks away from a fight, perhaps my last fight, I haven't decided yet. It gets dull and monotonous when no one's able to provide me with a challenge. I've won every fight since beginning my career. Nonetheless, I take my training and diet seriously during this time.

"Hmm?"

"You've been zoned out for the last ten minutes. The hell is going on with you?"

"Nothing, just thinking about work."

Josh eyes me with caution. "Yeah, right."

Once a month, we catch up, usually at my apartment, and watch the game.

"If you're thinking about work with that look on your face, then you're more driven than any other man on the planet."

He's right. I was thinking about *her.* I haven't been able to stop since the fundraiser. Then when she showed up at the interview in that fitted dress, it fucked with my head further.

"Beer?" Theo asks, lifting the non-alcoholic bottle.

I shake my head.

"Oh, right, sorry. I forgot you don't like 'empty calories' before a fight," he quotes me.

Theo and Josh used to work for a company back at home, but using my connections, I was able to get them a job with a top tech-engineering company here. It was a no-brainer for them when the company offered them triple their previous salaries.

I've recently started working on projects with them. Our latest one involves integrating both of their fields to build a computer system that mimics real-life business decisions based solely on tactics, returns, and potential opportunities without involving human emotions that cause biased judgments. We're still in the early stages of it. However, it could provide significant benefits and land us major deals with international companies if we do it correctly.

"How fast can you get me into someone's phone. Tracking calls, texts, the whole lot."

"Who?" Josh questions with a raised eyebrow.

"Stryker."

"You want me to tap a lawyer's phone illegally? Are you out of your mind? Do you know how much shit that can land me in?" Josh asks, not questioning what I need that information for.

My friends know I like my privacy, and most of the time, I try not to get them involved in stuff that could land them in shit. I do all that myself or outsource to others who are more than willing to get their hands dirty for the right price.

"I'll find someone else," I state. It was selfish of me to ask him, knowing it could land him in serious trouble if someone finds out, but he's the one I trust most with matters such as this one.

"Hey! I didn't say I wouldn't do it."

6

The Planetarium

Calla

My phone rings with a number I don't recognize, but I've been expecting this call since Betty mentioned she gave Ace my number.

Out of breath from my afternoon run, I stagger inside my apartment and jerk the door shut behind me before answering my phone. My therapist suggested exercise, and I discovered that running in the rain is soothing—so much so that it's become a habit now.

"I hope you didn't forget about tonight, Calla," Ace says as soon as I press the phone to my ear. His voice is rich, like bourbon, and the way he says my name reminds me why it doesn't sound fulfilling coming from anyone else.

"How can I forget when you tried to break into my apartment to remind me?" I don't ask him how he knew where I lived. I doubt I'd get an answer.

He chuckles, and my stomach somersaults. "Your neighbor made sure I wouldn't try that again."

Betty has made it clear if I have one more good-looking guy

come to the front door, she'll take him for herself.

"Is the undefeated champion not as fearless as everyone thinks?"

"We're all afraid of something."

It's so easy to fall into conversation with Ace. It's like we haven't spent four years living completely separate lives. "I don't think it's a good idea. Us going out tonight," I clarify.

"Would you prefer another night?"

I sigh, internally rolling my eyes. "You know what I mean."

"I'm afraid I'll need you to elaborate."

Kicking my shoes off and padding toward the window in my living room, I toy with the curtain. "Do you really think this is a good idea? I haven't spoken to you in four years…and it's just unexpected." Not to mention, inadvisable considering our past.

"All the more reason to catch up."

I pause, unsure of what to say. Uncertain of what he *wants* me to say.

"I understand if you don't want to. Fuck, I know I shouldn't even be asking this of you after everything, but…there are things I'd like to say to you that I didn't get the chance to the other day."

I consider my options. There's no denying that an irrational part of me wants to see Ace again, it's persuading me to say yes, but there's also a realistic part of me telling me to stay away. Do I follow my head or my heart?

"So where are we going tonight?" My heart prevails.

I hear a faint puff of air on the other side of the line, so light I think it's just my imagination. "I'll be at your place at six." Ace ignores my question. He's always liked to be in charge and full of surprises. "I'm looking forward to it," he adds before the line goes silent.

I know this is a bad idea, and I shouldn't be this anxious to see him. Nothing can come of it—only closure. Seeing an old friend after no contact for four years makes everyone nervous, I assure myself.

As soon as I get off the phone with Ace, I Facetime the only person who knows everything.

"What happened? Did you have another bad-dick appointment?" Mia questions when she recognizes my pouting face. She's lying in bed, her hair sprawled across the white pillows, makeup smudged around her eyes, causing her to look like a raccoon—all the remnants of the night she must have had.

After we finished college, Mia packed her bags, and with all the money she'd saved up from working at her uncle's café, she followed her dreams and has been traveling around Europe. She loves every day of it. I'm getting concerned she'll never come home, but there's no telling where home is for her anymore.

"That was one time."

I called her one night after I met up with a man at the bar. We went back to his house, and it took him half an hour to get it up. It was a hard kick to my self-esteem. He blamed it on the alcohol, but he only had one beer. That wasn't even the worst part. His phone kept blowing up with his mother's calls, and he had the nerve to answer it when he was still in me.

"I'm going out with Ace tonight." I get to the point before Mia passes out.

"Like Ace Ace?" She's wide awake now.

"How many Aces do you know?"

I fill her in on everything, including the interview, since I haven't had the chance to call her the past week, and it was a long conversation to have over text. Mia has been careful not to bring Ace up the last couple of years unless I mention his name first, which only occurred once before.

"*Old friends*," she scoffs when I mention that part. "Old friends that want to screw each other's brains out."

"Mia!"

"Was that insensitive?" Her face scrunches up in thought. "You know, since…" Her voice trails off, but I know what she means to say is *since he was the cause of everything I sought to leave behind.*

"No… Uh… I don't know," I admit.

"What's the worst that could happen?"

Nothing. Everything. It could go either way, and it's a considerable risk to take.

"He's hot, rich, and apparently a sex god," she quotes the articles about him.

Oh, trust me, I know. He's evidently the whole damn package.

"I can't have sex with him." I sigh, get up from the sofa, and head into my room.

"Why not? You already have."

"Four years ago!"

"I'm sure he'll exceed your expectations this time around," she tells me, and when I don't say anything, she raises her eyebrows. "*Sex god*," she quotes again. "It won't kill you to find out. Isn't that what you do now? Fuck and leave when they begin to have feelings?"

I roll my eyes at her bluntness. Mia has always been the one to say it how it is with no sugarcoating, and most of the time, she's right.

"Or are you afraid you'll break his heart again?"

That couldn't be further from the truth. Perhaps, the other way around.

At precisely six, after I've changed my outfit multiple times and finally decided on my best pair of jeans and a low-cut top, there's a knock on my door. With shaking hands, I manage to undo the lock. The smell of his masculine cologne drifts toward me. It's phenomenal, and he looks even better.

I take the time to drink him in, gliding my gaze over him quickly but meticulously. From his plain cotton shirt to his designer sneakers, he wears all black, looking dangerous and enigmatic.

His lips curve into an approving smile, which influences my heart to leap. Something about the way he looks at me indicates that he's not afraid to take what he wants, and at this moment, there's no mistaking what it is. Me.

Sex god. Won't kill you to find out.

It just might.

"You look..." He clears his throat. "Nice, Calla."

Nice. I don't bother telling him how *nice* he looks, I'm sure he already knows. "Are you going to tell me where we're going?" I ask instead.

"You'll see. Impatient as always?" He raises his eyebrow.

"Controlling as always?" I dare to ask.

His eyes glimmer with what seems like a challenge. "Eager to find out, love?"

We're both aware we're playing a dangerous game, one that could end in more ways than one. Ace runs his tongue over his bottom lip, dampening it.

"Let's go." I halt my sinful thoughts in their tracks before they have the chance to emerge.

Ace grins like he knows what I'm thinking. I lock the door behind me, and he waits for me to walk in front of him before placing his hand on my lower back in a safe but captivating gesture. For once, I'm glad there's no elevator in this building. The tension between us is already present without us pressed into a small space.

I'm not shocked to see a motorbike parked in front of the building while the smell of rain still lingers. Ace always preferred bikes to cars, and I sense it has everything to do with the crash.

I spent days, months, years thinking about it and wondering if I can ever forgive Ace for what he did. It was an accident, but he shouldn't have been driving drunk. There's never an excuse for putting someone's life in danger by getting behind a wheel under the influence. There's never an excuse for committing a hit-and-run, especially one that has fatal consequences. Still, I don't feel any anger or frustration toward him, even though sometimes I wish I did. It would make things easier in a way, but all I feel is the emptiness that engulfs me when I think about it.

His bike is midnight black and lethal, an expensive upgrade from his old one, and it resembles something *Batman* himself would drive. When Ace stands next to it, I understand why he chose it. There's nothing that would suit him better.

I track my hands along the leather seat and look up at him. "Well, Ace, take me for a ride."

His face lights up with a wicked grin that propels goose bumps down my legs, and he motions for me to climb on.

The night is cool, and a coat of moisture screens the roads. Once we leave my apartment block, the brilliant city lights welcome us. We race through the busy streets, the motorbike's tires flicking up water as they skim through the puddles. Ace's body is warm and firm underneath my hands. I hold them still, not daring to move, not even the slightest bit. Every single muscle underneath his shirt tenses when we sharply turn the corners. Everything about this moment is so surreal, like we've gone back in time to when everything is simple—when we were just teenagers in love, when I was oblivious.

I focus on our surroundings instead of thinking of the past. My eyes water from the wind as I endeavor to hold them open. Crowds fill the sidewalks, people either hurrying home from work or already on their way to dinner.

After a short ride, we come to a halt in front of a large building, and I recognize it immediately. It's made of glass and rectangular on the exterior, while an immense sphere is located inside with dark-blue neon lights illuminating it from all angles.

The city's planetarium.

It's incredibly fitting that Ace brought me here since that's how we used to spend our time together—watching the stars and the timeless universe above us.

He removes his helmet and grins like he knows what significance this possesses, and he's satisfied with himself for choosing such a suitable setting.

Does he do this often, take women on dates? Or do they jump straight into bed with him?

"Is this part of the Ace Blackwell experience?" I blurt, unable to help myself.

He watches me intently. "Depends, Calla. Are you looking for the *full* experience?"

I turn away without answering, not wanting him to notice that I'm falling apart under his gaze, under the celestial spell of his words. Ace seems utterly composed, which renders me even more flustered. It's a foreign feeling for me, especially around men, but certainly not around him.

We stroll toward the breathtaking building. It's wholly deserted, silenced by the serenity of the night. Did Ace book the whole place out just for me? For us? He's a celebrity, someone that gets noticed, so I'm surprised there are no paparazzi following his every move.

"I used to come here a lot when I first moved here," he discloses when we enter the building. The lights are already on for us, illuminating the space.

When I first arrived in New York, I often found myself longing for the stars. "Why New York?" I ask. Ace could choose to live anywhere in the world, yet something brought him to New York. I can't help but believe fate is at play again, and I'm not prepared to uncover what it has in store for me this time.

"I could ask you the same." He observes me with curiosity, as if trying to read my thoughts. When I don't disclose them, Ace leads us past the entrance, and I slow my pace to absorb the setting before me.

Large and different-colored planet models hang from the high and vast ceiling above us, precisely mimicking every single shadow and curve of the eternal universe.

"Isn't it the dream? To live in New York and become a journalist?" I finally answer rhetorically.

"Is it your dream?" he prompts.

"I'm working toward it. Unfortunately, some of us aren't as lucky as you."

His eyebrows crease like he disagrees with what I said. "I wouldn't say that."

"No? Being a millionaire at this age and having every woman at your feet… I'd say that's every man's dream."

He halts and turns to face me, a cunning smirk plastered over his face. "Do I have *you* at my feet?"

His ego hasn't decreased in the slightest. On the contrary, I'd say it has expanded. I rest my hand on his chest, and his smirk widens, his eyes glistening with conviction. "As I said, don't mistake me for your one-night stands, Ace."

I don't pause to observe his reaction before treading toward a Milky Way model in a large crystal ball at the center of the room. Iridescent shades of purple and blue glimmer from it, casting a glow on my skin.

"There's something different about you," Ace remarks, following me.

"Four years does that to a person. I could say the same about you." He's clearly changed. He's a different person now. Yet I can't help but notice everything he used to be seeping through his persona.

"Hmm," Ace mulls over the idea. "You changed your hair."

I conceal a smile that intends to inch its way onto my face, and before I'm able to form a reply, he adds, "I like it."

Unsure of how to respond to his compliment, I settle for a smile. "You've changed yours, too." Gentle dark curls that touched the tips of his ears are now transformed into a short style. It's a more virile look and suits him remarkably well.

Ace leads us toward a room designed somewhat like a cinema. Sofas spread throughout the area, and the ceiling is covered in stars—more than you could ever imagine, more than you would ever see in a city such as this one.

My mouth gapes in awe. No wonder he used to come here often when he first moved. There's a distant sense of wistfulness about it.

"Drink?" Ace pulls a bottle of champagne from the bucket of ice that I overlooked.

"Sure," I reply, unable to peel my eyes off the ceiling. I knew this place was here, but I've never visited. I didn't think it would be this incredible. I recognize the torn band of the Milky Way. Sirius and Orion gleam against the blackness of the ceiling, almost radiating the whole space themselves.

Ace hands me a glass of champagne. He didn't pour one for himself. He never used to drink, and I wonder if he's had a sip of alcohol since…

"This is what the sky looked when our paths collided for the first time," he enlightens me.

A few minutes later, he presses a few buttons on the computer that controls the entire room. The room goes dark, and then it suffuses with stars again. It doesn't look much different from the first one. However, this time there are a lot more stars, if that's even possible.

"And this?" I sit in one of the sofas, looking above in amazement.

He removes his jacket and deposits it on the seat next to us, and I feel his body next to mine. My gaze drops, and that's when I notice the small tattoo of a moon and stars on his arm among other black ink. It was the tattoo he got for me.

My eyes coast to his. He gives me a look that says it all—*the night on the lake, our first time*. His face is so close to mine, and if I were to move, our lips would meet. Instead, I hold my breath, afraid even to exhale. My cheeks bloom, and I detach my gaze from his intense one. Instead, I concentrate on the contents of my drink, swirling the bubbly liquid mindlessly in the glass.

Ace chuckles, casting a low sound through the silent room.

"How are Ellie and your mom?" I probe without thinking. It's been so long, and I regularly find my mind wandering to the beautiful face of the little five-year-old girl I met so long ago.

Ace's body stills. "They're fine." He changes the conversation too quickly for me to understand why. "How have you been?"

I know what he's asking me, something we've chosen not to talk about until this point. "It gets easier every day." It's not a lie.

"I think about it all the time, Calla. I regret it every day."

Grief and anguish stream through his iridescent eyes, not leaving anything in their wake.

It takes me aback for a second. Over the years, I've strived to get better. I did get better, and I continue to do so. But did Ace? Or does he still condemn himself? It's a colossal burden to carry, and a path for self-destruction.

"I wish I could go back in time. Change the events of that night. I'm so sorry."

"I know, Ace. I know."

We don't talk about it for the rest of the night, even though it's the sole reason why I agreed to see him tonight. Perhaps that's what I convinced myself. But, in reality, seeing him at the fundraiser pushed me onto a path I've been trying to avoid.

There's so much to say, yet it feels like it has already been said. And it seems pointless to waste our only time together talking about such a heart-wrenching event in our lives when we can't change anything about it. Some would say it's like moving backward instead of forward.

I lose track of time. We order pizza and talk about everything else. I notice Ace doesn't have a slice. Instead, he watches me eat. It feels like nothing has changed between us, but things couldn't be more different.

I ask him about our friends from college. "Are you still in touch with Theo? Josh? Zach? Liv?"

I haven't seen them since college finished, and I barely spoke to them during the college years after Ace and I broke up. I couldn't bring myself to look at them without seeing everything that had gone wrong, everything I desperately tried to forget.

"Theo and Josh, yes. They work together not too far from here. I'm actually working on a project with them," Ace explains. "Zach and Liv broke up after college. Zach is traveling the world. I keep in touch with him every so often."

"They broke up?" This completely takes me by surprise. "They seemed so...sturdy."

"I guess their time together had an end date."

So did ours, I think to myself. Occasionally, I feel Ace's fingers brush my leg, and I lose all track of thought for a moment.

"There's something I wanted to give you." He stands, retrieves a piece of paper from his jacket, and hands it to me.

I don't understand at first, but then my eyes skim the words, and I can't halt the smile that graces my face. "You named a star after me."

"I didn't have the chance to give it to you four years ago."

This can't happen, nothing can happen. I can't let anything happen. "I have a feeling tonight means something else to you than it does to me."

"What does it mean to you, Calla?"

"It doesn't change anything."

There's an emptiness in his eyes that I witnessed the night of the fundraiser and in his office, part of the exterior he masquerades for the whole world. "I didn't think it would," he replies without any hint of emotion.

It's easy to fall back into this thing Ace and I had before. Too easy. The man standing in front of me still took my mother's life, unintentionally or not. The pain in my chest sharpens enough that breathing becomes challenging.

"Ace—" I begin, not knowing what to say.

"It's fine. I didn't expect anything different," he assures me. But he did. I can sense it in his tone. "Shall we? Or would you like to stay longer?"

I stand from the seat, and we make our way out.

Ace pulls up in front of my apartment building fifteen minutes later, and I don't linger. Instead, I climb off and hand him the helmet. "Thank you for tonight."

"I want to see you again," he states as if the conversation we had before didn't happen.

I give him a small, bittersweet smile. "Goodnight, Ace." I walk toward my building and don't allow myself to look back at the man who still holds a piece of my heart.

Goodbye, Ace.

7

Deal with the Devil

Calla

Torrential rain veils the streets of New York for the remainder of the weekend, it's thick and melodious against my windows, but all the rain in the world is incapable of washing away the thought of Ace. I'm ensnared somewhere between trying to forget everything about him and an invisible force that keeps aligning our paths. Thinking about him is going to ultimately drive me insane. I should've never agreed to go out with him. It did more damage than good—just as I thought it would.

In an attempt to keep my mind engaged, I spend the weekend cleaning my apartment until there's nothing left to do. When my apartment is spotless, I head over to Betty's, requiring a distraction. She makes us risotto and bakes brownies, pervading the house with a mouthwatering chocolate aroma while I vacuum and mop her floors. She doesn't pry, even though I presume from the side glances she casts me that she knows something is bothering me, but I don't have any inclination to talk about it. I want to forget. Forget about everything, especially him.

On Monday morning, I unlock my apartment door, ready to

dash to the subway, and I discover Nik with his hand raised like he was about to knock. "Morning, sweetheart."

He's dressed in a tailored suit that clings to his muscular body. Even with the busy job that keeps him up most nights, he still manages to find time to work out.

"You don't have to drive me to work every morning."

A crooked smile arises on his mouth, and he hands me a take-away cup of coffee. "It's on the way."

I roll my eyes. It's not on the way. My apartment couldn't be farther away from his.

"Plus, I'll take any time I can get with you," he adds with a grin.

He takes my coffee after I have my first sip and sets it on the counter behind me. Then without warning, he lifts me, and I encase my legs around his lean waist, sensing his slacks already straining from his thick erection.

Nik was in Florida for business over the weekend, otherwise, he would have been a great distraction. He kisses me with urgency, and I reach for his pants, unzipping them quickly. We're on limited time. Nik perches my ass on the edge of the sofa and slides my dress up with one hand while supporting me with the other.

It's not long after that I'm fixing my dress and hair while rushing out the door. I settle into the leather seat, and Nik reaches for my hand, squeezing it. "A friend of mine is getting married on Sunday. I would love it if you came with me."

"Like a date?" I ask and face him. It sounds like a date, and I don't want to cross that boundary. Attending the fundraiser with him already pushed the limits, but I've overlooked it since it was business for both of us.

He glances at me briefly, detecting my hesitation. "It can be whatever you want it. Don't overthink it."

I look out the window and at the pedestrians streaming across the busy streets of Manhattan. Buildings soar determinedly toward the cloudy sky, and the traffic stretches for miles at this time of the morning.

I don't say anything as I contemplate what I should do. On the one hand, I enjoy Nik's company, and we're both on the same page, so it shouldn't be an issue, right?

"See me tonight," Nik offers, pulling up to my work.

"I'll text you." I need to think things through. Perhaps I'm worrying over nothing. Nik is the last person I'd expect to want something more from our arrangement, especially since he recently emerged from a long relationship. The thought of anything even remotely more than what we have now terrifies me to the point of withdrawing a little.

I step into the building, and a few familiar faces bid me a nod as a way of greeting. I take the elevator and use the mirror to smooth out my appearance. It doesn't make a difference. I still look like I've just been fucked.

"Hey, a few of us are going for drinks tonight. You should come," Jessie invites me when I stride past her with a coffee for Jennifer. As Jennifer's assistant, it's part of my job to fetch coffee for her every morning.

"Drinks on a Monday night?" I ask.

"Starting the week off right." She sends me a wink.

I let her know I'll think about it before advancing into Jennifer's office. She's typing on her computer. The ticking of her nails on the keyboard sends a shiver up my spine. I place the takeaway coffee cup on her desk and plaster a smile on my face. "Good morning, Jennifer."

"The article on Mr. Blackwell—" Jennifer begins without

looking up to acknowledge me, her lips set in a thin line.

I shift to one foot. "It'll be done by today."

She smiles at me, a scarce sight, and waves her hand like she has something else circling her mind. "Mr. Blackwell called just before and made a suggestion that will skyrocket our magazine reads this month," she continues.

Oh, did he now?

I sip my coffee and sit across from Jennifer, preparing for what I'm about to hear, since there's a good chance I won't like it.

"He suggested you shadow him for two weeks, follow him on his day-to-day business arrangements. Essentially, get the inside scoop."

I almost spit my coffee. I clear my throat, attempting to keep my expression blank and fail miserably. "What?!"

"I know! It's an amazing opportunity for *Satire Times*. As you know, Mr. Blackwell is an extremely private person. We know only what he wants us to know, so this will change everything. We'll be the first magazine to have this kind of information. How great is that?"

I can't believe what I'm hearing. Is this a joke? Ace has gone too far. If this is his way of persuading me to see him again, he's going about it the wrong way. It's apparent that Ace will do anything it takes to get what he wants. However, it's a new low, even for him, to bring my job into a very personal aspect of my life.

"Jennifer—"

"I know, I know. This isn't part of your job description. I'm willing to offer you a twenty-five percent pay rise for the two weeks you spend with Mr. Blackwell, and we can discuss your position further after the two weeks."

It doesn't seem as though I have a choice. Jennifer won't let me decline. If I do, I'll be without a job. It's as simple and as complicated as that. There's nothing I can do to escape this, and I'm positive Ace knew of the outcome when he made a deal with Jennifer.

Asshole.

Though a twenty-five percent increase in my pay will make an extreme difference, maybe I can buy a ticket to see my dad earlier than I've planned. I haven't seen him in months.

Jennifer's gaze is fierce as she waits for confirmation that I won't make her life complicated by refusing. I provide her with a minor, reluctant nod, and she narrows her gaze, struggling to unravel me. I assume there aren't many people, particularly single women, who would pass up this opportunity.

I have the abrupt urge to text Nik and take him up on his offer to arrange a meeting with someone from *The Times*. I wouldn't have to deal with Jennifer and the constant fear of losing my job if one hair gets out of line. I also wouldn't have to write exposés and articles on New York's most notorious bachelors, which is the last thing I want to do with my career.

I want to make some sort of difference globally, and this isn't the way to do it. Yet we all must start somewhere. Last month, I wrote an article on why there aren't many women in leadership roles and how to change that. I posted it independently on my personal website. It caught the attention of many people, and topics like those remind me why I pursued this career. This month, I'm researching the topic of euthanasia in my free time.

"If I didn't know any better, I'd say that man is infatuated with you. But of course, men are men. They all only want one thing," Jennifer comments, bitterness rippling through her tone.

Before I exit Jennifer's office in defeat, an idea pops into my head, and I turn to her again with a scheming smile. "How about we make this interesting then?"

"What do you mean?" She slides her black-rimmed glasses down to her nose and looks up at me.

"Mr. Blackwell is known as a womanizer. He's known for sleeping around." I'm unsure of how accurate my statements are. It's been reported in multiple articles, but nine out of ten times, it's only speculation. "Let's strike a deal with him. He must go these two weeks without sex, and if he can't manage… Well, I'm sure there are lots of things that Mr. Blackwell can do for our magazine."

From marketing campaigns to public statements, the limits are endless. I'm a freaking idiot for suggesting this to my boss. It's unprofessional and petty, but I can't help myself. He thinks he has a one-up on me, and I'm desperate to turn the tables.

Two can play at this game, Ace.

"And why would Ace Blackwell agree to that? The man is doing us a favor by offering this opportunity to us. This seems absurd!" Jennifer's eyes narrow as if my idea is completely ludicrous.

"More exposure for him. Every magazine will be talking about it." Although I'm not quite sure Ace wants more exposure. "Trust me, he'll do it. Just tell him we won't be taking his offer up unless he agrees to this," I tell Jennifer, confident in my bargain. I'm anticipating it will piss Ace off and compel him to drop the deal altogether, but I doubt it. That would be too easy, and I've heard he thrives off a challenge.

"The request could cost me a major opportunity. Do you know what this deal could mean for *Satire Times*?" she begins to ramble, becoming frustrated with my idea and the possibility of Ace pulling out of this.

"Jennifer, I assure you. He'll agree."

The rest of the day passes with me going over a few articles that

Jessie wrote, but I'm unable to concentrate on the words in front of me. Instead, my head is all over the place, leaping from one place to the other. Finally, I take my phone and make an urgent appointment with my therapist in two days. I'm not due for a visit for another two weeks, but a lot has happened in the last few days to surface memories from the past, and I need guidance, clarity.

After Jessie and I arrive back from our lunch at a Mexican restaurant, spending our time stuffing our faces with all-you-can-eat tacos, Jennifer calls me into her office for the second time today. She motions for me to take a seat. From her expression, I gather she's pleased with the news she's about to convey.

"Mr. Blackwell has unenthusiastically agreed to the offer, and to make sure he keeps his end of the bargain, he suggested you stay with him for the two weeks."

Stay with him for the two weeks.

Definitely not. This cannot be happening. "Oh, that's not necessary."

"I think it is, Miss Maven. How else would we know if he keeps his end of the deal? Men are deceivers, and you'd be lying to yourself if you think any of them are different." Jennifer clearly has an issue with men, and I have an idea of why that may be.

"I think I need a drink after all…or ten," I tell Jessie when I'm back at my desk, wondering how the hell I managed to dig myself into a deeper hole. But most of all, wondering how the fuck I'm going to claw myself out of it.

There's no way I'm spending two weeks with Ace. I'll lose every bit of sanity I've desperately been trying to keep intact.

It's a little past eleven when I stumble into my apartment, almost tripping over Oreo on my way to the bedroom. I drank one too many cocktails. Tipsy and seeking company, I retrieve my phone from my bag and type a short text to Nik.

Me: ***Come over, handsome.***

I don't wait for him to respond. He's never passed up an opportunity with me, and I'm not sure why it would change tonight.

Taking my time in the shower, I wash my hair and shave. Then I brush my teeth, eliminating the bitter taste of alcohol from my mouth before sliding into my most expensive lingerie.

There's a knock, and I stand a little taller in the black lingerie that emphasizes all the right areas, from my boobs to my ass. I'm aware I'm a little more confident with alcohol buzzing through my system. I doubt I would have done something like this without it.

I open the door, anticipating Nik's reaction, only to receive a shocking surprise.

"I did say I prefer red on you, Calla."

Leaning against the doorframe is the man that ruined me—the devil himself. He's dressed for the part, too, in his usual dark clothes. A black T-shirt grips his muscular body, and he runs his fingers through his tousled hair, something I've been dying to do. Ace looks like he just left a damn photoshoot. How can someone be *that* handsome? It's unreal.

His observant eyes—the ones that can render anyone weak from either fear or desire—scan my body, not once but twice. Every part of me heats in response, like a billion burning suns.

"This is not for you." I cross my arms over my chest, maintaining my voice even while the rest of me swelters.

"Shame, I can make you come in more ways than you're able to imagine."

It takes me a second to register the words that emanated from his mouth. Filled with intent, they circle me like a predator around its prey. My mouth gapes open at his blunt arrogance, and my legs tremble beneath me at the thought of it. I can't halt the sensation that begins to build in my core without him even touching me. It's like a fitful flame licking at the edges, scraping its way inside. How can he still make me feel like this?

"What are you doing here? Where's Nik?" I snap.

I'm pissed off at Ace for the shit he pulled today, involving my job in a personal aspect of my life. I strive to keep them separate, and I'm even more pissed off at myself for being somewhat glad he's here.

"Nik? Who's Nik?" Ace has the nerve to ask, strolling past me without an invitation. I grab a knit cardigan hanging on the kitchen chair and cover myself, wrapping it tightly around my body.

My head buzzes with the alcohol streaming through my blood. I'm sure I texted Nik and not Ace. I don't even have Ace's number saved. I scan the room for my phone, but I fail to find it.

Ace ambles toward the sofa, scanning the place, taking it all in. His tall, broad-shouldered figure causes the space to feel smaller than it really is.

"About today—"

I don't want to hear it. "Why are you here?" I interrupt.

"Can't I stop by to see a friend?" A smirk plays on his delectable mouth.

I furrow my eyebrows, not understanding. "What game are you playing?"

"Game? I didn't realize we were playing a game." He moves to stand directly in front of me. "If you're talking about the deal I proposed to your boss today, it's strictly a business venture," he says. "But you, on the other hand…" He takes a step closer, and my breasts respond by swelling. He tenderly skims his knuckles across my cheek. "That wasn't very professional, love. Do you really think I can't keep it in my pants for two weeks?"

"Can you?" I challenge.

My eyes travel to the clock hanging on the living room wall. It's just after midnight, and a thought solidifies in my head. The deal with Ace begins today, and this is the perfect opportunity to make him lose before it even starts.

Stepping closer toward him, I open my cardigan, revealing the set that's underneath. I route my hands down his chest slowly while keeping eye contact with him. He doesn't stop me until my hand progresses down to the waistband of his jeans, and I gently dust my fingers over his stiff erection.

"What are you doing?" he growls, grabbing my wrist and jolting it back up, keeping his fingers wrapped around it.

Nice to know I still have *some* effect on him, but so do the other women he sleeps with regularly. The thought of that makes me sick…and it shouldn't. I shouldn't feel anything for Ace. He's just a thought—a distant memory I sometimes look back on. That's all.

But now he's here in front of me.

I ignore my feelings. They always seem to do nothing but cause mental turmoil. Instead, I focus my full attention on him. "Don't you want to fuck me, Ace?" I tilt my head to the side and look up at him, waiting for a reaction.

His eyes widen, and it's my turn to smirk. He clears his throat. "What?"

"Do you want to…fuck… me?" I pronounce the words slowly and skim my free hand down my own body, teasing him.

His body stills. He appears at a loss for words. Well, that's a first for Ace, because he *always* has something to say.

"No. Yes." His jaw tenses like he's unsure of what the correct answer is. "Calla, can we talk?"

I ignore his question. I don't want to talk. I have nothing to say to him, and there's a good chance I'll like him better with his mouth doing other things. The thought of *that* mixed with the alcohol-induced frivolity causes me to neglect all rationality.

"No? Are you sure about that? Isn't that what you want from me?"

I push him down on the sofa and take his hand, guiding it over my body—over the delicate material of the lingerie that barely leaves anything to the imagination. He grips the back of my thigh with his other hand. His hands are rough and demanding on my smooth skin. It's everything I need and more.

"Prove it. Make me come, Ace. Or are you just all talk?"

His eyes turn malign at my challenge. I climb on top of him, settling my knees on either side of his body. My heart pulses in my chest as my mind grasps that I'm with Ace.

I set both of his hands on either side of my waist and roll my hips toward him. A harsh groan escapes his throat, then he shadows his fingers down my back, along my bare skin.

Oreo senses the change of atmosphere in the room, jumps off the kitchen chair where he's been sleeping for the last half an hour, and pads his way to my bedroom.

"Fuck… Calla…" Ace jerks me closer toward him. With only a small amount of clothes between us, his hardness is evident under me.

I'd be lying if I said I didn't dream of this moment at least once in the last four years. Dreamed of the way his hands would feel exploring my body. The way he'd gaze at me with longing and irrefutable desire. And now that it's happening, it's like a drug, and I'm a desperate addict.

His eyes never leave mine, and everywhere he touches me burns with the need for more. His mouth is inches away from mine, but I don't let myself close the distance. I can't lose control. I can't forget that this means nothing. Instead, I run my fingers down his arms, detecting the way he tenses under my touch. My fingers glide down, over the firm ridges of his stomach and tug at his jeans while I look up at him and run my tongue over my teeth.

He catches my fingers in his hand. "You're playing a dangerous game."

I lean in and whisper against his neck, my lips brushing over his skin. "And what are you going to do about it?"

He tightens his grip on my wrist, an indication that it was the wrong thing to say. He closes his eyes—his downcast lashes sweep against his cheek—and releases a ragged breath, like he's trying not to lose control with me, too.

My other hand veers for his jeans, fumbling with the zipper. Before I have the chance to realize what's happening, Ace grabs me and pins me beneath him.

He holds my jaw and runs his thumb down my throat. I refrain from moving, breathing, swallowing. I'm utterly still as he leans down and brushes his lips where his thumb rests—up the hollowness of my throat, toward my ear.

"I know what you're trying to do, and it's not going to work." His other hand grips my thigh, and with each word, it moves inward. "As much as I want to fuck you senseless right now until the only name you'll ever say again is mine—" his voice sends goose bumps down my legs, "—I'd rather take the two weeks with you instead of this."

He loosens his grip and sits up.

I can't think straight, and it's not because of the alcohol. I stand and move away from him as I search for answers. "Why? Why are you doing this?"

He's not allowed to come into my life after four years when it was so easy for him to give up on me. Two weeks. It took two weeks for him to stop trying, to move to a different city and forget how much pain he caused me.

I needed time to process it, but not nearly half a decade. Now, it's too late for whatever this is.

"Because I know you still want me," he says nonchalantly.

Is he trying to get a reaction out of me?

"Couldn't be further from the truth," I declare with anger building inside of me, nibbling at the edges. He's still an arrogant asshole. Clearly nothing has changed.

"Who are you trying to lie to? Yourself or me? I see the way you look at me, and by the end of the two weeks, I *will* have you at my feet." He uses my own words against me with a wily smile tugging at his lips.

Without thinking, I collide my palm with his cheek. Our ragged breathing is the only sound in my small apartment. I'm stunned at my outburst, but Ace doesn't seem fazed. It's like he expected it all along. Like he wanted me to do it. Like he needed a reaction out of me.

Everything feels wrong. I need him to leave, to give me space to breathe. "Get out."

"Calla…"

"Get the fuck out."

He walks to the door and turns around, presenting me with a wicked grin. "Be ready at ten tomorrow morning," he says, slamming the door shut behind him.

This couldn't have gone any worse. "Ugh." I collapse on the sofa and bring my knees up. My head spins with the alcohol, or is it the thought of Ace?

What an asshole. Has he always been like this, or has the fame and money made him think the sun shines out of his freaking ass?

A few minutes later, there's a knock at the door, and I ignore it. I can't deal with him anymore. I haven't even spent an entire day with him, and I'm already losing my mind. Going insane. However, he doesn't give up.

I storm toward the door and swing it open, ready to vividly tell him what he can do to himself. Perhaps, I didn't make it clear that I want nothing to do with him.

"Did I miss something, or did you and Ace just fuck each other's brains out?"

And just like that, my night changes from terrible to not so bad at all.

8

Mia

CALLA

I can't decipher whether it's my drunk mind playing tricks on me or if it's genuinely Mia at my door. A low-cut white dress with a pink cherry print adheres to her tapered waist and shows off her European tan. Her catlike velvet-black eyelashes blink slowly as she looks me up and down. Mia has always grounded me, and I'm unaware of how I've been spiraling down these last couple of years without her.

We spoke a few days ago, but she didn't tell me she was coming back. She dyed her hair as blond as white sand, and it's almost silver under this lighting. She kept the famous pastel pink in her bangs, but they've now grown out and are swept to the sides. A strand has escaped and found its way across her button-shaped nose.

"Well?" Her blossom lips form into a pout.

"I missed you so much!" I slam my body into hers. She drops her suitcase and hugs me back tightly. The smell of jasmine mixed with cigarettes coils around me. We embrace like that in my doorway until I realize it's probably unsafe to be doing it at this time of the night in this neighborhood.

"How was Italy?" I shut the door behind her. She's been all over the world but has rented a small place in Milan for the last few months.

"Amazing! Wild nights and great food. What more could you want?" She collapses on my sofa. Everyone seems to love that damn sofa.

"Sounds like the dream. What made you come home?" Once the words leave my mouth, I'm not sure where her home is.

"Realized there's only so much fun you can have without your best friend," she admits, and a smile grows on my face. This night has been a roller coaster of emotions.

For the rest of the night, we chat about everything and enjoy each other's company. She tells me about a girl she met. "Sex was incredible. She was a bit of a psycho, though. I had to get the hell out of there before I found myself tied up in a basement or something."

My eyes widen at how casual she relays that, like it's just another day in her life. It's understandable. Mia's life is the complete opposite of mine. She's wild, untamed, and there's nothing I would change about her. Whereas I like to have at least some sort of normalcy—a routine.

Mia takes a shower, and I sit in the bathroom on the toilet seat as she recalls stories from her travels. We've talked regularly over the phone, but it wasn't the same. I missed this. I missed her.

Finally, we fall asleep in my bed in the early hours of the morning, after the sun begins to rise, trickling light from under the curtains. Unfortunately, the comfort of that soon subsides, and I'm jolted awake.

"What's that awful noise? It's the middle of the night!"

"It's ten." I check my phone, roll out of bed, grab a silky robe, and drape it over my shoulders.

"Middle of the night," Mia reinforces when I smooth my bed hair and stifle a yawn against the back of my hand.

I open my apartment door to find an older gentleman standing in front of me. He's wearing an impeccably crisp dark-green suit that complements his skin tone. His face is unlined, with a pair of deep-set eyes and a square jaw. "Hello, my name is Denzel. Mr. Blackwell has sent me to collect your belongings and to drive you to his apartment." His accent is the result of a Maori heritage mixed with an American crossover.

At his words, memories of last night come flooding back. Ace on the sofa with my hands all over him. Wanting him. What was I thinking? How far would I have advanced if he hadn't stopped me? I don't have the answers. All I know is it can't happen again.

I don't know what game Ace is playing. Last night, after he left, I checked my phone, and I was right. I texted Nik, not Ace. But somehow, it was Ace who'd ended up at my doorstep, and Nik hadn't shown up or replied. Strange.

"We'll be ready in fifteen minutes," Mia tells the driver as she appears behind me in a floral nightgown.

"Both of you? Mr. Blackwell informed me there'd be only one." Denzel glances from me to Mia, visibly confused and uncomfortable to be in this situation.

"It's a package deal. Tell Mr. Blackwell to take it or leave it." Mia doesn't wait for confirmation before grabbing my hand and dragging me back to my bedroom.

Once there, I turn to face her. Has she lost her mind? I'm meant to come up with a way out of this deal, and here's Mia leading us straight into the devil's den.

"Babe." She looks at me and smiles, her grin the epitome of

scheming. "Ace thinks he can have anything he wants, and he wants you. He's playing a game, and you have to show him you can play it better than him."

"Why now? After four years?"

"You're asking the wrong person. Clearly, you two have a lot to talk about."

"I don't think I can do this. I'll lose my mind."

"Better than losing a part of yourself like you did four years ago."

I sigh. "I can't ignore the past. There's too much baggage between us. Plus, he's not the same person. He's changed. We both have."

"Two weeks. Forget about the past for two weeks and see where it takes you. If you still don't want anything to do with him after two weeks, at least you'll have closure," Mia convinces me.

"I'm not going to fall at his feet like every other woman."

"Did you forget everything I taught you?" She smiles. "Babe—" she places her hands on either side of my face, "—you're going to play his game, but on your terms. And you're going to enjoy every bit of it."

Fifteen minutes after Mia has helped me throw two weeks' worth of stuff into a bag, we make our way down the stairs. I stop by Betty's to inform her I'll be gone for two weeks, but I'll still return to check up on her.

Denzel strides in front of us, carrying Mia's suitcase while she holds Oreo in a crate.

"You know, I'm not a fan of cats," Mia announces when we're almost outside, not speaking to anyone in particular. "I do hope Daddy Ace doesn't mind, though," she adds, turning toward me and suggestively wiggling her eyebrows.

"Mia!" I shoot her a look, hoping Denzel didn't hear that. Mia has a unique way with words.

New York is the worst for traffic. Moving from a smaller town to one of the biggest cities in the world had been a shock at first. To this day, I can't say I've gotten entirely used to it. The cabbies speed through the crowded streets like their life depends on it—it's terrifying. So on the rare occasion that I choose to take a cab, I force myself to zone out instead of gazing out the window.

However, right now, my anxiety is peaking for an entirely different reason as my mind recklessly spins with thoughts of how these two weeks with Ace will pan out.

Two weeks with a man who put me back together and broke me again.

"Stop overthinking," Mia says, extracting me from my self-destruction. "Maybe Ace can release some of that tension."

"The deal—"

"We can work with the no-sex thing. I'm sure there are a million other ways he can have you screaming his name. Plus, you can always make him wish he never made that deal in the first place."

God, I missed her and her lack of filter so much.

We drive for twenty minutes before coming to a halt in front of an apartment building that radiates lavish extravagance. The sun reflects off tinted windowpanes, forcing me to squint my eyes from the brightness.

Denzel gets out to help us with our bags.

"Leave that one in the back," Mia tells Denzel, referring to her suitcase.

"You're not staying?" I ask her, puzzled.

"Oh, no." She grins. "I would never intrude like that. I just wanted to see where my girl will be staying for the next two weeks, and it's still just as fun to mess with Ace as it was four years ago."

She beams at me, aware that Denzel would have already reported the complication to Ace. She runs her fingers through my hair, fixing the front and tucking a few loose strands behind my ear.

"I'm going to check up on Brody, but I'll be back in a couple of days, and I would like to take you up on your offer."

I grin when I realize what she means. "My place is yours for as long as you need."

Denzel leads us inside the apartment building. A doorman in an emerald coat greets him. We step into a private elevator, which can only mean one thing—we're on our way up to the penthouse. Denzel enters a bunch of numbers into the keypad, and we begin to ascend.

I glance in Mia's direction, and her eyes are wide. "Wow," she mouths.

"Zero, five, two, zero," Denzel notifies me. "Mr. Blackwell instructed me to acquaint you with the codes and to provide you with appropriate keys to access the apartment since you'll be using it regularly over the next couple of weeks."

My mouth gapes open, the code is the date of my birthday. It has to be a coincidence. Why would he use my birthday after all this time? It doesn't make sense.

Stepping into the private hallway that's only used for the penthouse, I admire the walls' lavish trim, high ceilings, and decorative embellishments. We trail Denzel as he unlocks the only door on this floor.

I'm not sure what I expected, possibly something along the lines of the devil's bachelor pad, but this is far from it. The penthouse is contemporary and minimalistic but still has a homey feel to it. The open-plan kitchen is connected to the living room, and there's a smooth white sofa in front of a glass fireplace that provides a sense of comfort. The color palette is neutral, with white and gray tones throughout, except for the floor, which is dark hardwood. It's exceptionally spacious, with floor-to-ceiling windows covering each side that boasts skyline views and brings a soft hue of sunlight. A grand staircase is situated to the right of the entrance that must lead upstairs to where the bedrooms are located.

I saunter toward the back of the apartment, to the windows, and glimpse down. The city below is so far away, it's like another world. I used to be afraid of heights, but I learned there are far greater things in life to be fearful of.

"Mr. Blackwell had a meeting this morning. He's on his way back. Make yourself at home." Denzel heads toward the elevator, leaving us alone in Ace's *very expensive* penthouse.

Mia sits on Ace's kitchen countertop with her feet dangling while she takes the place in, *oohing* and *aahing*. I release Oreo from his crate, and we keep an eye on him so he doesn't mistake furniture for his toilet box.

"So, you gonna tell Nik about Ace?" Mia asks.

"I'm sure it'll come up in conversation. Plus, I don't want Nik thinking I'm hiding anything, especially when Ace is one of his clients. Not that I owe him anything. We're not…like that."

"Mm-hmm," Mia hums.

"What's that supposed to mean?" I glide my hand over the cool marble countertop. Intricate veins spread across it, and I track the lines with my finger.

"Oh, nothing."

Mia focuses on something behind me, and I slowly turn around, knowing *he* will be there. Still, it amazes me how handsome he looks in his business clothes. A white dress shirt clings to his upper body with a couple of buttons undone at the top, revealing the sharp lines of his collarbone.

"Well, I better get going. Leave you two to it." Mia hops off the countertop. "Ace, I'm stealing your driver for half a day. I hope you don't have anywhere to be."

Ace holds his eyes on me as he says, "Take all the time you need."

His stare is intense as he drinks me in like I'm a fine liquor, and color rises to my face. I take a step away from him, putting space between us.

"I have training tonight. Come with me," he says once the sound of the door closing echoes through the apartment. It's not a question, more of a demand.

"Sure," I agree, because that's why I'm here. To follow him on his daily routine and make sure he keeps his end of the deal.

"I have to take care of some paperwork in my office. I shouldn't be long. Pick a room. My bedroom is upstairs on the right." He shoots me a wink before heading for what I assume is his home office.

I trudge upstairs and select a room the farthest away from Ace's. I call Nik. I don't want to keep anything from him, and even though I don't owe him an explanation, he's become a friend to me.

"Hi, handsome. Do you have an hour to spare for lunch?"

"For you? Always."

I tell him where I am and state that I'll explain everything in person before he asks any questions.

"Did you get my text last night?" I ask when I get in Nik's car, surprisingly managing to escape Ace's apartment building without him noticing.

"What text?" His eyebrows groove in confusion. I change the topic since I've obtained the answer I needed.

Nik drives us to a small café not too far from Ace's apartment. I order a coffee and a sandwich since I haven't had breakfast yet. I tell Nik about Ace and how we used to date in college. For obvious reasons, I omit the part of why we broke up. I also don't elaborate on the depth of our previous relationship.

"This doesn't change anything between us?" Nik questions, not looking bothered, but instead wanting clarification on where we stand.

I shake my head. It doesn't, does it?

"Good. I like spending time with you."

Nik states he must get back to his office for an important meeting. "Be careful with Ace." He places his hand on top of my thigh when he's driving me back.

"What do you mean?"

"He's not who he makes himself out to be. He's…dangerous."

"Why do you say that?"

I focus on Nik, and he shrugs, maintaining his eyes on the road. I gather he's not going to give me any more information, whether it be attorney-client privilege or just something he doesn't want to share with me.

I don't pry, even though I have the urge to fire a line of questions.

"You know that meeting you said you could get me with *The Times*?"

He glances at me and flashes me a wholehearted grin. "On it, sweetheart."

✦

The prospect of coming back into Ace's penthouse unnoticed disappears as soon as I shut the door behind me. I turn around and almost bump into him. It's as if he was waiting for me. Cold hues of green, blue, and gray pierce through me.

He's changed into black shorts that hang dangerously low on his hips, and his top half is bare. It's no secret that he has the body of a Greek god. The way his muscles tighten with every move is impressive, and I discover myself ogling him with no shame whatsoever.

I'm here, aren't I? Might as well get the full show.

Ace has always been considerably good-looking. However, the fact that his career is now based around him being fit has its perks. No wonder women lose themselves at the sight of him. Who wouldn't?

His presence, especially so close and shirtless, has me powerless. The way his arm muscles strain when he runs a hand through his hair causes me to envisage all the ways he can put those arms to good use.

There's no denying the physical attraction between us. It's always been there, but I wonder if that's all there is. I'm trying to take Mia's advice and not think about the past for the next two weeks. However, that's *all* I can think about. The past has a way of seeping maliciously into my future.

I still don't understand what game Ace is playing, and the fact that he decided to mix my work and personal life just because he can pisses me off. He's going to know about that.

"Where were you?" he snaps, towering over me. I'm stunned by his tone. It's understandable why some people are intimidated by him. But I had my fair share of temperamental Ace previously, and I'm not here for it.

"Out." I retain the same tone as him.

He narrows his eyes at me. I don't need to explain myself, especially not to him of all the people. I really should have pushed Jennifer for a fifty percent increase in my pay if I'm going to have to handle Ace for two weeks.

Before he snaps at me again, his phone buzzes in his hand. He glances at the caller ID. "We're leaving in thirty minutes."

He strides toward his office, and I admire the view from behind. It's just as good as the front. Muscular back, toned ass—maybe I could get accustomed to this, but we'll have to work on that irritating mouth of his. And that damn arrogance.

"Blackwell," he answers the call in a gruff voice, undoubtedly forcing whoever is on the other side of the line to wish they'd dealt with the problem themselves.

What has got him in such a bad mood? But then again, he's always been a hothead.

I check on Oreo and realize he's made himself at home on Ace's sofa by the insane view of the Upper Westside. Ace hasn't said anything about Oreo, and I wonder if he's even noticed him.

Heading upstairs, I trail my hand across the railing. This place screams money. Ace obviously has a lot of it, but for some unknown reason, I don't feel as uncomfortable as I thought I would.

The bedroom I chose has floor-to-ceiling windows like the rest of the penthouse. Light curtains hang from the ceiling, obscuring the warm sun from heating the room. There's a bookshelf toward the side with a few books, but I realize most of them are for decoration purposes. A large gray rug is spread out in the middle of the room, and it's soft underneath my feet.

I didn't watch what Mia threw into my bag, but now that I have it open in front of me, I conclude that allowing her to help me pack was a bad idea. It's bursting with lingerie, short dresses, and skirts that I used to wear when I went through my clubbing phase.

I remind myself to stop at my apartment sometime in the next few days to pick up some clothes I can actually wear. I pluck out a short, lacy nightgown and grimace. What was I thinking when I purchased this? And what was Mia thinking about putting all this in my bag?

Deciding to work with what I have today, I slip into a plain black dress with spaghetti straps that stops just above my mid-thigh and drape a cropped black denim jacket over my shoulders. I slide a pair of white sneakers on, and my feet thank me for it, since all I've been wearing to work for the last year is heels.

I descend the stairs just in time to glimpse Ace pulling a T-shirt over his head. Even dressed as casually as he is right now, he's still incredibly striking.

He scans my appearance, but his expression doesn't disclose anything. Instead, he grabs a set of keys from the benchtop and asks, "Ready?"

We take the elevator to the underground parking, and Ace doesn't say anything the entire way down. I keep my thoughts to myself, uninterested in starting an argument in a small space, mainly because he already appears to have something stuck up his ass. Most likely, the devil's trident.

I have many questions for Ace, beginning with why he was at my apartment last night instead of Nik. I'm quite certain I'm not going to like his answer—that is, if he provides me with one.

The elevator opens, and Ace motions for me to walk in front of him. At first, I scan for his bike, but the sound of a car unlocking and lights flashing pulls my gaze to the side.

A blacked-out Lamborghini.

If I thought his bike was extravagant, then this tops the cake. I understand why he doesn't want to drive his bike during the daytime, he'd get recognized instantly, and Mia took his driver. At least this has a bit of privacy with the tinted windows, but either way, this car is a head-turner.

Ace walks over to my side and opens the door for me. He doesn't utter a word when he gets in the driver's side and starts the car. The engine roars to life, and the sound echoes through the basement.

The silence between us isn't confining, it never has been. I watch him. There's something about a man driving a car that I find appealing. Ace's hand clutches the steering wheel while the other one rests on the gear stick. Occasionally, he trails his fingers over the dark stubble that lines the lower half of his face.

Tearing my eyes from him, I glance out the window. I always wondered what it would be like to live in New York City, and now that I've been here a year, I have the urge to keep moving forward, to continue exploring what the rest of the world has to offer.

"Expensive cars and VIP experiences. Is this your usual way into a woman's pants, or do you also make time for groveling?" I finally break the silence, unable to bite my tongue.

"Correct me if I'm wrong, but you're not the type to accept groveling, and—" Ace's gaze swiftly rakes over me. "—you don't have pants on," he simply states before pulling into a parking spot by a large building. Unfortunately, his mood doesn't seem to have improved. His eyes are distant, like he's a million miles away. He shuts the engine and checks his phone before opening his door.

"Just pants, you think? What about panties? Maybe I went without them too." I wink at him before climbing out of his car, hoping to lighten the mood. But perhaps that was the wrong thing to say. Out of the corner of my eye, I notice his jaw tick and his hands tighten around the steering wheel before he follows me.

For two hours, I watch as Ace gets sweaty.

He uses the boxing bag for the first half an hour, releasing his built-up anger. After that, a man that looks to be in his late thirties or early forties approaches Ace. I recognize him from the articles as Ace's trainer. He has a stocky build, and I'm wagering he can give Ace a run for his money.

I've always loved to watch Ace in action. He's agile on his feet and calculates every move in his mind before executing it. The trainer barks out commands, and Ace fulfills them with ease.

I don't miss the glances Ace sends my way. His hungry gaze finds me now and then, forcing my toes to curl in my shoes as heat wafts against my nape. I can't help but question if he's wondering about what I said in the car. Every time he looks at me, I hold eye contact, causing him to sweat even more.

"What are you doing? Where's your head at?" His trainer taunts when he lands a hit on him. Ace grumbles something back that I don't catch, and he peels his attention away from me and back to his training.

Ace shuffles toward me once he finishes. His entire body gleams with sweat, and a violent bruise has already begun to form on his cheekbone, a consequence of being distracted by me.

"We'll order takeout at my place," are the only words he says to me the entire way back.

Clearly, the training hasn't alleviated his stress. Something is troubling him, but I feel too out of place to ask.

In the elevator back to his apartment, I finally decide to raise the question that's been on my mind since yesterday. "I texted Nik last night, and you showed up at my apartment instead of him. Can you explain that?"

"I don't know what you're talking about," he answers in a tone that tells me he knows *exactly* what I'm talking about. "But you're not going to see Nik anymore."

He has got to be kidding me. "Excuse me?"

"He's not someone you should be associating with," he states dismissively, like there's no room for arguing.

"Funny," I remark. "He said the same thing about you."

"I'm serious. He's not who you think he is."

"What are you talking about? You're not making any sense." I attempt to read him, but his expression is neutral. He's hiding something.

"He's a dirty lawyer just like all the rest of them." His voice coils with hostility.

It suddenly clicks. Everything falls into place. Ace's dad was a lawyer—maybe still is. And from what I've heard, he's not a very ethical one.

"Nik is nothing like your father." As soon the words leave my mouth, I regret them.

His jaw clenches. "You don't know anything about Nik."

"And what do you know?"

"Stay away from him."

"You don't tell me what to do, Ace," I hiss. His name is venom in my mouth.

Instantly, his hands are on either side of me, bracing against the wall of the elevator. He glares at me, but I don't withdraw. "Don't test me, Calla."

His commanding voice drives goose bumps up my legs. Still, he doesn't frighten me, and the thought of challenging him hurls an exhilarating rush through me.

Who does he think he is coming back into my life after four years and trying to tell me what to do? It's not going to work like that, and I intend to make sure he understands I'm not the same girl I was back then. A lot has changed.

I lean toward him, my lips centimeters away from his. My heart drums faster at the closeness. I look him dead in the eye and pronounce the words slowly, "Or what?"

9

Still Playing with Fire

CALLA

The silence between us is captivating—driving me insane.

Ace leans toward me, and I tilt my head back until it meets the cool steel of the wall behind me. He's barely touching me, and my body is already on fire, blistering blazes flicker beneath my skin.

The tension in this small space engulfs me, and I instinctively go to squeeze my thighs together. As if reading my mind, Ace shifts his knee in between my legs, keeping them open with ease. An overwhelming aching gushes to my core.

Ace grips my jaw with his hand and skims his thumb over my lips. His touch casts a current through me.

"I've always loved that mouth of yours." His voice is gruff and amatory.

I can't help myself, or maybe I'm just searching for trouble, looking to get a reaction out of him. I flick the tip of my tongue over his finger, all while maintaining eye contact—teasing him. He presses his body up against mine, his erection solid against my abdomen, and it takes me everything I have to keep my breathing even.

What game are we playing?

The elevator doors finally open, but Ace doesn't seem to care. His undivided attention is on me. I place my hand on his chest and gently push past him. His gaze remains on me, never faltering. And if he would stop me, I'd let him.

I stagger into his apartment. The view is breathtaking—deep orange and pinks flow through the living room and bounce off the mirrored backsplash in the kitchen. Did Ace see this view before purchasing, or was this a bonus he discovered later?

I head straight for the window, scratching Oreo's head when I pass the sofa, my legs trembling. Oreo is spread out on his back, loving his life. I observe the city below us, setting space between Ace and me, soothing my breathing and thinking of how easy it was to lose control with him.

"Hungry?" Ace asks.

Starving. But not for food.

"Hmm?"

My eyes dart across the room and meet his. Did I say that out loud? Ace's expression is blank once again, harboring his emotions. He keeps his guard up, but I'm aware of the stiffness that's still present underneath his shorts.

"Order something. I'll have whatever you do." He throws a credit card on the table and climbs the stairs.

Someone's in a mood today, and I wonder if it has anything to with Nik, or if that's just adding to his irritation. Both men are not thrilled with each other. Thus, I can't help but speculate what kind of bad blood streams between them.

A menu from a Thai restaurant is stuck to the fridge door, so I order from there since I assume it's Ace's go-to. While I wait for the food to get here, I head upstairs to freshen up. Each bedroom has its own bathroom and walk-in closet. The shower has a panel with options regulating water temperature, pressure, lights, and scents. It takes me a minute to figure out how to turn the damn thing on.

I'm not sure where Ace usually eats, but I set up the plates in front of the view of the city since it's by far my favorite thing about this apartment.

At first, I was nervous about moving to New York, but I didn't want to be stuck in a small town for the rest of my life. It's easy to flow through life in a place where you're comfortable, but I desired more. I wanted to start over somewhere far away from the place where all I know is heartbreak. I wanted to feel alive, and somehow, I felt as though New York would do precisely that.

Ace flops on the sofa next to me. His hair is damp from his shower, and he's wearing nothing but sweatpants. No surprise that even four years later, the man still doesn't know what a T-shirt is. I peel my eyes from his chest and slide his card to him.

"Keep it."

I look at him, confused. "What?"

"For the two weeks," he answers.

"What for?" I'm unsure what I would need to use it for.

"Anything you want."

"I don't need your money, Ace."

"Calla—"

"What does your schedule look like for the rest of the week?" I change the subject, not wanting to get into another argument with him since we both know how they turn out.

"My schedule?" He digs into the food.

"Yes. Anything I should be prepared for?"

He considers my question for a moment while he swallows and runs his tongue over his lips as my eyes follow.

"Mostly meetings, interviews, and training. I assume you have a current passport?"

I raise an eyebrow. "A passport? What for?"

"I have a fight coming up," he says. I already knew this since there has been news circling it. However, it has slipped my mind where the fight will be held, and Ace isn't inclined to enlighten me.

After finishing dinner, I slide onto the velvety rug, leaning my back on the sofa behind me, and stare out the window. All of this is surreal. "So, tell me…how did all of this happen?" I ask Ace as he positions himself near me, our shoulders touching.

"How did all of what happen?"

"This." I motion with my hand around us—around the vast apartment and the panorama that surrounds it. "You accomplished so much in so little time. It's impressive, to say the least."

Ace has achieved more than most people his age. He's a boxing champion, and he owns a successful company. He's attained all this at the age of twenty-three. Not many people have done that from scratch.

"After I left for Palm Valley, everything seemed to line up. The college had a good club. Although I didn't get paid as I did in Idaho…" he pauses. *In the underground club.* "It was good exposure and experience. The fights every month drew in a crowd. It didn't take long for someone to scout me," he explains.

"What about Blackwell Enterprises?" I query.

"I started Blackwell Enterprises a year ago. A boxing career only lasts so long, and the money I earned from my fights was adding up. So with the help of a financial advisor, I began investing in sporting venues, buying properties, anything that will provide a passive income in the future."

"You sound like you're fifty years old."

He chuckles. "It's good to be prepared for the future.

"It must get exhausting. I don't know how you keep up with everything."

"I like to keep busy," he confesses.

"That…I can understand."

It reminds me of myself. Busying myself has been a vital factor in overcoming the most challenging points in my life. But eventually, there comes a time when even busying yourself isn't enough to escape the vile thoughts that prowl a vulnerable mind.

I direct my attention to Ace, hoping to ask more about his accomplishments and what his ambitions are for the future, but the questions dissolve on my lips when I discover his prevailing gaze is already on me.

"Do I have something on my face?" I bring the tips of my fingers to my mouth.

Ace shakes his head and leans his back farther into the side of the sofa. Then, exhaling, he turns away from me to face the window, and I detect a brief arch of his lips. "I never thought I'd see you again, let alone have a conversation with you."

I swallow, recalling all the times I thought the same thing. The world is unpredictable, and it has a bizarre way of presenting me with the unexpected.

Ace rises when I don't reply. "I need to go over a few things in my office for tomorrow. You should get some rest."

I nod, following suit and pad toward the direction of the staircase. "Goodnight," I call over my shoulder.

"Goodnight, Calla."

✦✦✦

I drop my nightgown to the floor and bite the inside of my lip in anticipation. Then, without delay, I tiptoe toward Ace's bedroom. His door is ajar, and there's a distant sound of a shower running.

Am I losing my mind?

I shuffle on Ace's king-size bed, making myself comfortable. The sheets are soft against my bare body, and they smell like him. I squeeze my eyes closed in an attempt to control my shaking hands and soothe my erratic breathing.

I travel my hands over my stomach, and my heart accelerates when I hear the shower stop. There are only seconds before he comes into the room. Only seconds left for me to withdraw. I don't. Instead, I palm my breasts and release a light moan, just loud enough for him to hear.

Ace strolls out of the bathroom with nothing on but boxer briefs. Water droplets litter his golden chest, rolling down the ridges of his abs and past the shadows of his obliques. The man in front of me will be my undoing. He freezes when he spots me spread out on his bed. Naked. Touching myself.

Just like the old times. *Remember, Ace?*

I shut my eyes and move my fingers farther down my stomach, the aching in between my thighs grows. Then, freeing another moan, I gently thrust my hips toward my hand. I feel his weight on the bed and smell his body wash, a hint of vanilla and cedarwood.

Delicious.

"What the fuck are you doing?" His voice is gravely in the morning. Sounds like someone didn't get enough sleep. Mood killer.

My eyes flutter open and meet with his. He devours me with just a look, and the things I imagine him doing to me—with his fingers, his mouth, his efficient tongue—cause the temperature to soar.

He positions his strong arms on either side of my body, holding himself up while his face remains inches from mine. I gawk at him for a second, admiring the features that make him look so incredibly sexy and dangerous all at once. They say the devil appears in all forms.

I flash him a harmless grin and resume rubbing my wet folds, not stopping for a beat.

When he understands I'm not going to answer, he grabs my hands and pins them above my head. I swallow loudly. My body is utterly bare for him.

"Do you want to finish me off?" I raise an eyebrow, and my eyes travel to his boxer briefs, where they linger for a long second.

"Calla…" he warns me.

My toes curl. "Shame. I guess I can get someone else to do it for me." I push myself up, knowing precisely what consequence my words will bring.

Ace clenches his jaw, and the way he looks at me, like he wants to worship me in every way possible, makes me crave his touch all the more. "The fuck you will," he growls, holding me down, and I gasp when he slides a finger inside of me.

The same gasp falls from my mouth as I wake. My neck prickles with excitement as I recall the dream I just had. The heat dances between my legs, and my breathing emerges unevenly.

My eyes remain shut as I lie there, not wanting to wake from the dream. Under the silky white sheets, my hand glides up my thigh, needing some release from the throbbing ache in my core.

"Dreaming about me?" A voice originates from the doorway.

Oh my God.

My eyes fly open, and I jerk my hand far away from my thighs, clutching the blanket tightly over my body. "Ace! What are you doing here?" My voice springs higher than I intended it.

He leans against the doorframe, his arms crossed over his chest. "Don't stop on my account."

I narrow my eyes.

"You told me you have an appointment this morning. I didn't want you to be late," he answers smugly, a knowing look plastered on his face. "We'll discuss this later," he adds.

"Discuss what?" I sit up, still grasping the sheet to my chest.

"You talk in your sleep. And by the sounds of it, there's something you're obviously missing. I'm very generous. I wouldn't want to leave you…unsatisfied in my own home." The corners of his mouth lift into a cunning smirk.

I don't need to see my face to know it's a deep shade of crimson. The warmth radiates off my cheeks enough to set the room on fire. I open my mouth and then shut it again, like a goldfish.

Ace's smile grows, and his jaw becomes softer when he beams like that. "There's breakfast for you downstairs. I have training this morning, so Denzel will drive you wherever you need."

I'm quite taken aback by this. For starters, Ace didn't ask about my appointment. He was respecting my privacy, and I'm grateful for it. On top of this, he made me breakfast? The gesture is sweet, and yet I'm hesitant.

It's just breakfast. But breakfast is more than I've become accustomed to with a man. Breakfast means staying the night. Breakfast means expecting more.

This is different, I remind myself. It's my job for the next two weeks. And yet, I draw back just a little. "Thank you," I quickly reply, ignoring the argument inside my head.

Ace watches me. He gives me a nod and then turns, leaving. I stare after him, wondering if he witnessed the debate within me.

The smell of coffee steers me down the stairs and into the

kitchen. On the bench are scrambled eggs, a mug of hot coffee, and fresh fruit. I reach for the coffee. Caramel latte on almond—my favorite.

Denzel is already waiting outside by the time I stumble out. I slide into the back of the Mercedes and meet Denzel's gaze through the rearview mirror. He's dressed in his usual work clothes, a well-fitted suit with not a single crease in sight.

"Good morning," I greet him. I attempt to make small talk with Denzel on the drive there. "How long have you known Ace for?"

"Just over a year, miss."

"And do you like working for him?"

"Mr. Blackwell is very generous."

So I've heard.

Denzel pulls into the parking lot of my therapist's brick building. "Thank you." I climb out and shut the door behind me.

My therapist is a woman in her fifties, but her age doesn't show on her smooth skin. She's thin, and her long, black fingernails accentuate her bony fingers. She sits in her armchair, her raven hair cascading down her chest.

"I see you weren't due for an appointment for another two weeks. Has something happened?" she queries with her notepad in front.

She listens while I explain the sudden reappearance of a certain someone in my life. When I first came to see her, I was apprehensive talking about Ace. I'm aware therapists are required to break confidentiality in certain situations. I wasn't sure if my case would warrant that. I've never used his real name, and she's never given me a reason to believe she would report it.

"How did seeing him again make you feel?"

I consider this question for a moment, placing one leg over the other before answering. "Like nothing has changed."

Addilyn, my therapist, assesses me. "In what way?"

Her questions used to drive me insane. I considered telling her just to give me the answers instead of the endless interrogations that made me sick of hearing my own voice. But I soon realized even a trained therapist doesn't have all the answers on how to deal with my messed-up life.

"In many ways. He's still the cause of the accident that took away my mom. Yet, to this day, I don't blame him for what happened, and it scares me that one day I might."

"Because you still blame yourself for what happened to your mother's death?" Addilyn prompts.

"Yes."

How could I not? If I didn't ask my mom to turn around and go back for my journal, none of this would have happened. My mom would still be here, and Ace… I'm not sure if we would have crossed paths. But wouldn't that be better than all the suffering we've endured? Than all the blame that lurks in the darkness ready to spring at us when we let our guards down?

"Are the romantic feelings still there?" Addilyn probes.

I hesitate. "There's a lot of sexual tension." I think back to yesterday and this morning.

"What about something deeper than that?" she prompts. "We've come to find sex is like a Band-Aid for you. You use it as a way to mask your feelings and problems instead of reaching the root of them. I'm afraid if you continue to do this, especially in this situation, you'll find yourself in a detonation."

Well, that shouldn't be a problem. The deal that's in place makes sure of it. "He'll always be someone that I loved even when I shouldn't have." *My first love.* "I can't change that," I answer her question in my own way.

Addilyn nods in confirmation. "You can't. But you can choose what happens now. Do you want closure from this, or do you want something more? And if you want something more, what will be the consequences? You don't have to answer right away." She examines my cautious expression. "But it's something you should analyze and consider carefully. We can't keep going around in circles, Calla."

I feel like I haven't achieved anything in this session, but somehow, I feel lighter. I always do. Maybe that's why I continue to see her.

Do you want closure, or do you want something more? Nothing more can come out of this. Only closure.

My phone rings with Nik's number. "Sweetheart," Nik says when I get in the car, placing the phone to my ear.

"Nik." I haven't spoken to him in two days, not since he warned me about Ace. Something I still haven't solved.

Nik tells me he's been dealing with work, and I understand. I'm glad he hasn't called or texted. Unfortunately, he's not the only one who's been busy with work. I've been dealing with a real piece of work for the last couple of days, and things are about to get a lot more complicated.

"The wedding is this Sunday. I hope you haven't forgotten, sweetheart."

Oh, I have. The wedding I've agreed to go to with Nik. I made it clear it wasn't going to be a date. This was before Ace told me to stay away from Nik, but Ace is about to discover I can see whomever I like. He can't tell me what to do—I already made that clear, but this rivalry between Ace and Nik unsettles me, and I'm looking forward to finding out what the root of it is.

"I can't wait," I tell Nik.

"I can't wait for *you*."

I sigh after ending the call and dial Mia's number to check up on her.

"How's Brody?"

"He's good. I think he likes being alone." Sounds like Brody. Even when I lived with them through my college years, I barely ran into him. He always kept to himself. I guess some people just like to be in their own company.

"I'll be back on Friday. Are you up for a girl's night?" Mia asks.

"Sure. What do you have in mind?"

"Drinks? Clubbing? Anything that will end with me getting laid."

"Do you need me to buy you a vibrator?"

"Hey, not all of us have two rich men begging for our attention."

"Something is going on between them," I state and revisit the events.

She tells me she'll investigate it, whatever that means.

✦ ✦ ✦

I fall into Ace's routine with ease. His days are busy, full of meetings and training sessions that occupy most hours of his day, meaning we don't have much time to ourselves. In the evenings, when we finally make it back to his apartment, we are both exhausted. Perhaps that's a good thing.

The smell of coffee coaxes me out of bed on Friday, and I follow it toward the kitchen, where I discover a not-so-bad view. Ace is sitting at the counter with his phone in one hand, reading emails. He has dark work pants on, but his top half is bare, making the view much better. The morning sun mixes with shadows that dance inside his vast apartment and emphasize the curves of his hard muscle. I'm entranced, and I allow myself to marvel at him for a moment, taking in his distinct cheekbones and the way a faint crease forms in between his eyebrows.

"Good morning, Ace." I finally make my presence known, strolling into the kitchen.

"Enjoy the view?" He glances up at me with a grin.

I click my tongue. He doesn't miss anything. Before I can craft a remark, his eyes scan my body. Once. Twice. I look down and notice I'm still wearing the lacy nightgown, which is extremely short. It's not intentional, but it might as well be, because the look he's giving me now is like a glowing, hot liquid.

"What's on your schedule today?" I reach up to the top cupboard to retrieve a mug, sensing the nightgown marginally ride up my bare thigh. I set the cup under the coffee machine and let the brown liquid pour into it.

Ace exhales deeply before answering. "I have a meeting this morning, and then I have to go over some contracts, reply to emails, that kind of stuff."

"Are you hungry?" Without waiting for an answer, I open his fridge, hoping to repay the favor for the other day when he made me breakfast.

I've noticed he's been careful with his diet and minds what he eats because of his upcoming fight. There are containers of prepped meals stacked on the fridge shelves. I ignore those and take out eggs, ham, spinach, and mushrooms.

"Omelet okay?"

"You're going to cook for me?" He leans back in his seat.

Omelets are one of the very few dishes I'm confident making. They are quick, easy, and filling. On the occasions I have time to make them for myself, I usually use up what's leftover in my fridge.

"I'm repaying the favor." I grab a bowl from under the counter and crack the eggs into it.

"Thank you."

After mixing the eggs, salt, and pepper, I pour the mixture into the pan, place the ham, mushrooms, and spinach on top and slide it into the oven to bake for ten to fifteen minutes.

I turn to retrieve some plates for us and notice Ace staring. His molten gaze sweeps over my legs, mainly focusing on the back of my thighs, where the nightgown's material rides up as I maneuver my way through the kitchen.

Fixing the place setting in front of Ace and one next to him, I arch an eyebrow at him. "You're staring and seem surprised. No one's made you breakfast before?"

He coasts his eyes up to mine. "Not here and not like this. You're the first woman in my apartment apart from my mom and Ellie."

And Mia, but I know that's not what he means. I don't show my surprise. Instead, I ask, "How long have you had it for?"

"Over six months now."

"Hmm." I muse over that while I pour Ace another cup of hot coffee.

"What?" He leans his elbows on the bench, prompting me to elaborate.

"Is there a reason for that?"

He shrugs. "I value my privacy. This is my home. I don't feel comfortable bringing people here who won't be around for long."

"So the rumors are true then?" I set the coffee in front of him.

"There are a lot of rumors. Which one, in particular, are you talking about?"

I clear my throat. "You're a ladies' man."

He nods, not in confirmation, but merely in acknowledgment

of my words, and doesn't elaborate further.

I scoop most of the omelet into his plate and a quarter of it into mine. I don't usually have breakfast most days. Coffee holds me over until lunch.

Ace immediately digs into his breakfast, disregarding the conversation we were previously having. I pause, my fork halfway to my mouth, and watch him eat instead. "This is good…thank you," he says in between mouthfuls.

He scoffs his omelet, and I suddenly become famished, but not for food. Instead, I consume him with my gaze, wholly aware of the blatant carnal desire forming between us. When he turns to see why I'm not eating, I peel my eyes off him but notice his crafty smirk.

"Now you're the one staring," he remarks.

Once we finish with breakfast, I clean up, ignoring his glances as I work around his kitchen.

"I'll be ready in fifteen." I take myself and my unfinished coffee upstairs to get ready, feeling his gaze on me the entire way up.

Denzel drives us to Blackwell Enterprises, and we head straight into the meeting room. Ace sits back in his chair, his muscular figure making it appear almost too small for him. I occupy the seat next to him. There are ten other people around the table.

A man in his thirties with a checkered light-blue shirt stands and begins pitching his business idea to further progress Blackwell Enterprises. I try to concentrate on his presentation, taking notes on my laptop for when I must write up the article in just more than a week.

Ace skims his tongue over his teeth. He meets my gaze and smirks like he can read my thoughts. I hold his attention for longer than I intended to, and the entire room falls silent.

"Mr. Blackwell?" prompts the man who's making the pitch, soliciting my mind back to the room full of people.

"I'd like to hear Calla's thoughts." Ace keeps his attention on me.

My eyes widen. "Excuse me?"

"An outsider's point of view," Ace clarifies.

I take a second, trying to reflect on what was said before I got too busy eye-fucking the boss. "The idea for a sports venue or even a gym sounds great, but the competition in that field is high. So if you were to go ahead with those ideas, a unique approach would benefit you in the long run."

Ace leans forward in his chair, as if considering my idea. "Such as?"

I recall Ace likes to give back to the community, whether it be because of his past, something to keep him modest, or to improve his public image.

"Perhaps donating a percentage of the membership fees to a charity. It will give you an edge over your competitors, and people are willing to pay extra if they know it goes to a good cause."

Ace's mouth turns up slightly at the corners, and he nods. It doesn't seem like the idea surprises him, like he's been thinking of it himself.

Once the meeting is over, we walk back to his office. It's overwhelming how big his building is and how many people work for him.

"You should come work here."

"For you?"

"For the company."

"I'm a journalist." I don't mention all the other reasons why working for him is never going to happen.

"Sometimes we need a different perspective."

"Not going to happen."

I catch up on my work emails and check-in with Jennifer while Ace reads over files of paperwork on his desk, occasionally furrowing his eyebrows as he goes over them.

"Have you considered getting an assistant?" I question while lying on his sofa, watching him concentrate on the folder in front of him.

"Have you changed your mind and now offering me your services?"

I roll my eyes. "Seems like a lot of work for one person."

"I don't trust anyone else to handle my business affairs," he simply states.

Control freak.

"I'm almost done with this file. I'll have an hour to spare for lunch," he says.

"I'll go get us something. Do you have anything in particular you want?" I stand.

He diligently runs his gaze down my body. I suck in a breath, and he chuckles.

"There's a café around the corner," he finally replies, retrieving his card and placing it on the table in front of me.

"I'm offended that you think I can't afford to pay for lunch," I joke, leaving his card where it is and turning toward the door before he insists I take it.

This side of Ace enthralls me. I've always known that he likes to be in control, but seeing him in action the last couple of days, running the business he built from scratch, is impressive. He works too much. From his boxing career to the business aspect of Blackwell Enterprises, I wonder if he ever has downtime and what that would entail.

After only spending a few days with Ace, it's clear to see how he's so successful at this age. The man never stops. I'm too caught up in my thoughts and almost miss the woman standing at the reception desk.

A flowy, yellow dress hugs her upper body, highlighting her toned figure. She paired it with strappy, nude heels that do wonders for her slender legs.

Cassidy Torrio.

I overhear her reasoning with the receptionist as I walk past. "This won't take long. I just got back from Greece," she says. Her tanned, glowing skin is proof of that. Her dark hair falls around her breasts and bounces with every move she makes.

"Mr. Blackwell is extremely busy today," the receptionist advises her.

"Oh, I'm sure he can make time for me," she purrs.

Cassidy notices me and eyes me warily, like she's trying to figure out if she's seen me before. *At the fundraiser.* I smile at her before making my way toward the elevators.

An uneasy feeling settles in my stomach, and I try to shake it as I make my way to the small takeout place only five minutes from this building. The sunlight pours down on me, warming my skin and causing me to slow my pace to appreciate the pleasant weather. I use the short walk to clear my head and observe as people around me take their lunch breaks.

By the time I get back to Ace's building with our lunch, twenty minutes have passed. I've almost forgotten about running into Cassidy. That is, until I see her gliding out of Ace's office, closing the door behind her.

Cassidy glances at the takeout bag in my hand, smoothing out her dress. "He already had lunch."

I aim not to grimace at the unnecessary comment and maintain a smile on my face. “I’m sure by now you know that Ace has an enormous appetite.”

She scowls and walks off, her hips swaying toward the elevators. I inhale and lean against Ace’s door.

There’s a reason I haven’t reached out to Nik this week. I’ve decided to keep him at arm’s length until the two weeks with Ace are over. Except for this wedding, but I was going to make sure nothing happened between us there, either. Uneasiness trickles through me at the thought of staying with Ace and still sleeping with Nik.

Ace looks up when I walk in, but I keep my face blank as I take the food from the bag and set it in front of him. He’s still at his desk, and I wonder if what Cassidy said is true. But that’s not any of my business, although there’s one thing that is. The deal.

He brings a bottle of water to his mouth just as I ask, “Did you fuck her?”

I’m half hoping he did so that I can be done with this charade he seems to be enjoying. Unfortunately, I don’t have time for it. It’s not what I signed up for when I left my dad and moved to New York to chase my career.

By the end of the two weeks, I will have you at my feet. Not a chance.

Ace coughs, my question taking him off guard like I hoped it would. He clears his throat before answering. “No.”

“That’s all I need to know.”

“Calla—”

I don’t want to hear it. It’s not any of my business what he does. My expression doesn’t show anything as I interrupt what he was about to say. He doesn’t owe me an explanation. “I won’t be around on Sunday. I have a wedding to go to.”

"A wedding?" He reclines in his seat.

"Yes."

"With Nik, I suppose?"

I don't bother asking him how he knows. He wouldn't tell me anyway. "Who I associate with is none of your concern."

He folds his arms over his chest as his prying eyes bore into mine. "Well, I guess I'll see you there then."

10

Forgiveness

Calla

Denzel picks Mia up from my apartment. "Thank you for letting me stay at your place," she expresses as she hops in the back with me. She came back today and moved her things in.

"Stay as long as you want, really." We lived together in college, and I've missed not having her around. Her presence brings lively energy with it.

Denzel drops us off at a bar Mia has chosen, and even though it's casual, everyone attempts to appear proper in their high-end suits and attire. And then there's Mia and me, dressed like we're ready to party the night away.

Mia leans over the bar, her blond hair lying over one shoulder of her pink dress. She lolls her head to one side, pouting her glossy lips. She isn't drunk, she hasn't even sipped alcohol yet, but she likes to give the impression that she is.

The bartender is there to take her order immediately. His eyes drop momentarily to her low-cut neckline. She twirls her hair in a seemingly absentminded way and giggles before ordering two strawberry vodka tonics.

The bartender makes the drinks and sets them in front of her. "On the house."

"Wow, you need to teach me that," I state when we're walking toward a booth in the corner.

"Men are predictable. Maybe that's why I get bored of them," she admits the last part almost to herself as she slides into the booth. "That reminds me of something." She retrieves two files out of her bag and hands them to me.

"What's this?"

"This one is on Ace, and this one is on Nik." She points to the different folders. "Nothing out of the ordinary catches my eye. You know, rich and successful men that own multiple companies, but maybe you'll have a different take on it."

My eyes widen. "You researched them?" I don't know why that surprises me. I shouldn't have expected anything less from Mia.

"I had nothing else to do on the subway back." She shrugs and sips on her drink.

It's past midnight when I stagger into Ace's apartment. The lights downstairs are still on, but Ace is nowhere to be seen. I grab a bottle of water out of the fridge and head for the stairs.

My head swims with all the alcohol I've consumed. Mia scored us free drinks while men fell at her feet all night. We danced till our feet were covered in blisters and sang till our voices became hoarse.

"I'm not going to feel bad about them buying us drinks. It's part of their redemption for the centuries of oppression that women have faced," she told me.

I feel bad for people who don't have a Mia in their life. Living with her is going to be anything but uneventful.

I go to step on the stairs but recall that stairs and heels aren't a good idea even when I'm sober. I rest my hand on the glass railing to hold myself up while sliding the heels off. On my second foot, I lose my balance.

A pair of hands snake around my waist, stabilizing me, and I inhale the smell of Ace's cologne.

"Careful," he says softly near my ear, sending a chill down my back. "You alright?"

Where did he come from?

"I'm fine. I think I just need some air."

Without warning, he lifts me. His arms go underneath my back and legs, and he carries me up the stairs. I let him, wrapping my hands around his neck for support. My body is tight against his bare chest, and his full lips are set into a line.

He looks down at me. "How much did you drink?"

I hold up one finger and then change it to three. Then four. Then five. I shrug, not remembering. "I'm sure Denzel already told you." I raise an eyebrow in question.

Ace had us watched all night. After Denzel dropped us off, he stayed out the front watching us through the window. "Boss's orders," he said when I went out to tell him he didn't have to wait for us.

I noticed the drinks getting weaker throughout the night, more strawberry, less vodka, and I wonder if it was Ace's doing as well, or is it just how the clubs work here?

Ace chuckles, and his chest vibrates against my side. "I'll tell him to be more discreet next time if it bothers you, love."

"Next time? There's not going to be a next time." I hold his hypnotic gaze, and he doesn't say anything, only smiles, and that stupid dimple decorates his cheek. I don't have the energy for an argument at this time of the night, especially in my state, so I drop it for now.

Ace carries me through his immense room and out the back door to his rooftop. There's a sturdy fireplace built of marble on one side, and above it rests a projector screen. He sets me down gently on the sofa outside. The crisp breeze grazes my skin from every direction. I inhale it, instantly feeling better, and a shiver escapes my body in response.

Ace treads back inside, returning within seconds with one of his black hoodies. He stretches his hand out, handing it to me.

"Thank you," I say. Swiftly, I slide it over my body and take my dress off underneath. The hoodie covers enough anyway. Comfort embraces me, surrounds me, and my eyelids grow heavy with every inhale.

The smell of Ace is even more penetrating. I tilt my head back, looking up at the sky. Ace sits next to me, his arm brushing against mine. Lifting my legs, I bring them in front of me on the sofa and drop my head onto Ace's shoulder, too weary to hold it up.

There are no stars here. The lights of the city seize them, dulling them into barely visible distant specks in the sky. So instead, I gaze straight ahead, getting lost in the beauty of the city lights glowing red, yellow, and blue.

I'm unsure of how long we sit there watching the world around us.

Seconds.

Minutes.

Hours.

With each breath I take, I become more clearheaded.

Occasionally, he smoothes his hand down my arm in a

comforting motion, but it's anything but soothing when it sends a thousand lightning sparks through me.

"The view here is beautiful," I observe, finally breaking the silence.

When I turn to face Ace, he's already looking at me. The corner of his sensual mouth faintly twists up as he continues to consume me. I drop my gaze to where his hand is draped around my waist and outline his knuckles with the tip of my forefinger. I trace every line of the black ink, still sensing the scars beneath them. My chest tightens as vivid memories flash before me of how the scars came to be.

I sense Ace scrutinizing my every move, studying me. "Ask whatever you're thinking." He stills my fingers with his. How does he know?

Sucking in a deep breath, I try to acquire the right words. I lift my gaze back up to his. "Have you… Do you still have your episodes?" I finally ask the question that's been on my mind for days, weeks, even years. The episodes are the result of his post-traumatic stress disorder from the accident.

A memory of Ace shattering a mirror with his bare hands because he didn't want to witness the monster in front of him torrents through me. The guilt of what he did ate at him. Destroyed him. Wrenched at his conscience.

"The last time I had one was a year ago." He tightens his hold on me.

I exhale a breath of relief. It feels like a small weight is lifted off my chest. Ace wraps his hand around mine and brings it up to his mouth, silently brushing his lips against my fingers.

How can such a simple gesture make me feel like the universe is falling apart? Like there's nothing left except us against the world.

Turning to face him completely, I place my hand on his cheek, gently tracing my thumb over his mouth. His ungodly mouth. My hands quiver.

"Calla…" He catches my fingers in his hand once again. God, the way he says my name is invigorating.

My head spins. Swirls.

"I'm sorry." His beautiful eyes are full of guilt and pain.

The person in front of me isn't the dangerous, undefeated boxing champion or the notorious bachelor who has women falling at his feet. Instead, he's a man with a troubling past that still haunts him today. A man who's fighting his demons inside his head. A man who grew up with an appalling father figure and still attained all his dreams. Not everyone sees Ace the way I do. He doesn't allow it. He wears an imperceptible mask, presenting the world with what they want to see instead of what is.

"Ace…" I shake my head, trying to find words.

"Don't interrupt." He brings our hands down in front of us, and I stare at our fingers intertwining while he talks. "After that night, I hated myself for what I did," he begins. I wonder how many times he prepared this speech in his head. "When you walked into my life two years later, I thought I was being punished. I had to look at you every day and be reminded of what happened that night."

He tightens his hand around mine, and I don't move. My heart erratically pounds in my chest at the flashbacks, at the memories filled with aching and suffering.

"I endeavored to make you hate me because I couldn't deal with any kindness you gave me. I didn't deserve it, but you didn't stop giving it to me."

He was so set on believing he was a bad person because of what happened, and even then, I saw the good in him.

"I didn't know how to tell you… I tried so many times. The night when we first—"

"The night on the lake," I recall the best memory I have of us. The night when I conclusively understood how greatly my feelings for Ace were. There was no backtracking after that.

He tried to tell me that night but couldn't get it out. And I was too enthralled in him to care about what he did in the past, not knowing that it involved me as well. Involved everything I was running from, everything I tried to escape.

I don't regret any of it. I've never regretted the months I had shared with Ace. I've never regretted falling so damn fiercely for him that I didn't know whether I was in living in reality, a fantasy, or somewhere in between. But even love isn't always enough. And just because I let him go, didn't mean I wanted to.

He narrows his eyes at me for interrupting but nods. "I fell in love with you while trying to push you away."

My heart stops. That word on his lips perilously slithers its way into my chest, tugging at every string.

I shake my head. "You can't love someone when you don't even love yourself."

I always wonder about the words he said when I left him. *I love you.*

Had it just been a way to get me to stay? Because someone who hates themselves as much as Ace doesn't have anything left to give.

"I don't believe that," Ace grumbles, shaking his head. "I've never loved myself. Never. Especially not after that night. But you… Fuck, Calla. I've loved you so much that I forgot what it was like to hate."

His eyes glisten under the bright city lights. I can't stop myself when I bring my hand back up to the warmth of his cheek.

"I'm so fucking sorry," he reiterates, piercing my heart with his words. "I'd give my own life to rewind the clock. I'd do anything to alter the events of the past. I'd pay the price in any way I could if it meant going back and not getting inside that fucking car."

We both bear anguish. We're both damaged from the moment our paths chose to collide. Tears spill on my cheeks, gliding across my skin in hopes of washing away the sorrow. But the tears don't alleviate it. Not even the entire ocean would be capable of such a thing.

"I don't think I've ever blamed you, Ace."

I look into his eyes, hoping he can see my compassion and find absolution. Rendering myself bare in front of him, hoping he will understand that I don't blame him for it. I never have.

I place my forehead against his and one hand on his chest. We remain like that until I can't tolerate it anymore. Until even the small distance between us feels like we're miles apart. Internally, we're fighting for more contact. More touches.

Just…more.

He finally closes the distance, casing his arms around me, drawing me closer into his chest, condensing the space between us, so there's nothing left.

All I can smell is him. Ace's body faintly shakes.

"I forgive you," I utter, wrapping my arms around his waist.

He envelops me tighter. For the rest of the night, we stay on the rooftop listening to each other's silence, because it has so much to say. More than the words exchanged between us ever can.

My nightmares have always been a reminder of what happened six years ago. They've improved over the years, became less frequent, sometimes less intense, but I still get trapped in the memories I'd rather forget.

I used to avoid them by keeping myself awake until I was so drained I couldn't dream of anything but the darkness. Now, I don't mind. At least I see my mother's face again in the dreams, even if it breaks me.

My eyes adjust to the brightness of the sun glimmering through the curtains. My breathing evens with each second from the nightmare. It's one of the few I've had this year. They aren't always exact replays of the night of the accident. Sometimes it just feels like I'm caught in the emotions, unable to claw my way out. The feelings of fear and helplessness, but most of all, of grief.

It takes me a few seconds to recognize I'm not in the room that I picked. I'm in Ace's room—in Ace's bed. The hoodie that I wore last night is still on me under the blankets, but there's no sign of Ace or any indication he slept next to me. And I can already feel the apartment is empty without checking.

Oreo meows in my face, asking to be fed.

"Isn't it a little early for you to be asking for food?" I grumble, throwing a pillow over my head. Oreo keeps nudging me with his head and paws. I finally give in, throwing the blanket to the side.

On the bedside table is a drink that looks like Oreo threw up in. There's a sticky note stuck to it.

For your head.

A memory floods my thoughts. Ace and I used to communicate with sticky notes in college. He remembers.

I grimace at the murky-green color in the glass, almost throwing up in my mouth before even smelling it. Death in a glass. The pounding in my head worsens as I climb out of bed and reach for the drink.

It doesn't taste too bad.

Ace's bedroom is vast and immaculate. The bed is situated against a black granite feature wall, and an ottoman rests on the floor at the foot of the bed. To the left is a generous walk-in closet, and next to it is the entry to the en suite bathroom. To my right, a large bookshelf wraps around the entire wall.

I wander toward it and aimlessly read the titles. A book with stars on the binder catches my attention, and I reach for it. The bookshelf slides to the left, revealing a door with a digital panel to enter a code. My mouth gapes open in disbelief. Who has a hidden door in their freaking bookshelf? And what the hell could be behind it?

Overwhelmed and shocked, I put everything back and go downstairs. Once I make my way into the living room, it confirms what I already knew. Ace isn't here. He's got to be kidding me. So much for shadowing him at all times. I make a coffee, needing it before I deal with Ace. I dial his number, but it goes straight to voicemail.

For the rest of the morning, I catch up on a few work emails and do some research for my personal articles while waiting for Ace to grace me with his presence. When that's done, I catch a cab back to my apartment to pick up a few more things that don't leave my ass cheeks hanging out.

I begin to overthink again. Is staying with Ace a bad idea? My life was simple, but since I encountered Ace at the fundraiser, everything has gotten complicated.

I spend the rest of the day in my apartment and then head to Betty's to check up on her toward the evening. After thirty minutes, I spot a black Mercedes through Betty's window and excuse myself.

"Do you know where Ace is?" I ask when Denzel greets me

from the driver's window.

"He's at one of his clubs, miss."

Clubs? He left me in his apartment to sit and wait for him while he does who knows what. Wasn't part of this whole deal to shadow him?

"Perfect, I'll be back soon."

By this point, I'm fuming. Does Ace think my whole job is a joke? Even though being Jennifer's assistant isn't ideal, I still love the essence of my job. I'm not going to get anywhere by sitting around waiting for him all day.

I put on one of my favorite dresses from my clubbing days when I first moved here. It's scarlet red, too short for my current liking, and sparkly. It will, without a doubt, catch Ace's undivided attention since it's his favorite color on me. I coat my face in makeup, using what I have here since most of my cosmetics are at Ace's apartment.

Out of breath, I slide in the back of the black Mercedes, glance at Denzel in the rearview mirror, and say, "Take me to him."

"I don't think that's a good idea, miss. He's in the middle of something."

He'll be in the middle of something real soon. "Did he ask you not to take me to him?"

"Well, not exactly." Denzel shifts uncomfortably in the driver's seat. I have no intention of getting the poor man in trouble, but Ace is a downright pain in my ass.

"Well, I guess Mr. Blackwell won't mind then." I give him a wicked smile.

Denzel seems to consider this for a moment. Finally, a sigh stems from within him, and he pulls out onto the street without another word.

A small victory for me.

I focus on my phone instead of the road, but that causes a faint headache to form in my temples. Since when did Ace own clubs? I guess I should have done my research more thoroughly or read the files Mia compiled for me. I'm going into this completely unprepared.

In my attempt to relax and alleviate my headache, I don't realize we've arrived until Denzel pulls into a parking spot. I glance around, absorbing my surroundings. I barely distinguish a two-story, plain cement building in front of me through the utter darkness.

Denzel gets out of the car, and I follow suit. He leads me to a red metal door toward the side, tugs on the handle and holds it open for me.

The thrilling music penetrates my eardrums as I step inside. "Where is he?" I shout over it. Vivid strobe lights rapidly disco from wall to wall, triggering me to grow dizzy.

"He has a meeting," Denzel answers, tight-lipped.

"Where?" I persist.

"Upstairs, miss." Denzel nudges his head toward the staircase to the right of us. Luckily, not many bodies linger on the stairs, perhaps afraid to tumble down them in a drunken stupor.

Glancing around once I'm upstairs, I immediately spot Ace. He's next to four other gentlemen in a private booth. Two burly security guards stand on either side of the booth. Both are on alert, sweeping their half of the room for potential risks. Some of the men Ace is with have women on their laps. Ace doesn't. My eyes dart to the drink in his hand. It's as though he senses my presence and tilts his chin up. His gaze roams over my body and then locks on mine. His jaw tightens in irritation.

Ace is dressed in all black—a button-up with the sleeves rolled up and jeans. The tattoos on his arms are visible as I stare at the glass in his hand. A glass that contains amber liquid.

He mutters something to the gentlemen, sets his glass on the table, stands and walks toward me. His tall figure moves with precision—a lion that's found its prey. Within a second, he's towering over me.

A raw, busted lip lingers, and murky shadows of bruises form around his cheekbones. There are more bruises than there were yesterday after his training. And the busted lip…that wasn't there last night. I didn't hear him leave this morning. Has he been out since last night?

"Is everything okay?"

His brows tense with a peculiar expression, but he ignores my question. "What are you doing here?" His voice is low.

His gaze is clear, profound as ever, with no signs of intoxication. Snaking his arm around my waist, he leads me farther away, not to draw attention. Out of the corner of my eye, I spot the security guard following our every move, following Ace.

"My job," I finally answer him. Did he forget he was the one who wanted this?

A bartender passes us with drinks on her tray. Ace takes the one that's lighter in color compared to the rest. He watches me as he does, but I keep my face blank.

"Non-alcoholic. These men prefer to mix business with pleasure. Better for business if I have a drink with them."

Or act like he is. Ace has the upper hand, a clear mind to make calculated decisions. Smart.

"And what kind of business are you doing?"

He studies me before answering. "I'm looking to expand." He motions around us with his hand. "They are interested in franchising. You shouldn't be here. I'll be finished soon. I'll meet you back at the apartment," he dismisses me.

Excuse me?

I attempt not to show my disappointment. Instead, I nod and walk away. But I didn't come here just to be told to leave, and he's mistaking me for someone else if he thinks he can tell me what to do.

I'll wait for you instead.

I follow the curve of the stairs down to where the music is so loud I can't hear my mind running a million miles an hour. I order a shot from the bar, and the liquid burns my throat and warms my insides. It's the boost that I need. Fixing my dress, I head to the middle of the dance floor, picking a spot where Ace would have an incredible view.

I don't look up to seek him out as I sway my hips to the beat of the song. My hands glide all over my own body, into my hair. I try not to think about his authoritative eyes on me, the way his jaw will strain when he sees what I'm doing. I'm staging a show specifically for him.

How long will it take for him to admit defeat and lose our bet? I doubt it will take the entire two weeks. Then I can return to my job and cease playing games with Ace like we're still in college.

A guy approaches me, and I cape my arms around his neck. He's kind of cute—blue eyes, blond hair, not my type, but he'll do.

Only then do I raise my head, looking Ace straight in the eyes. I tilt my head to the side and smirk as I dance with the stranger. Ace's expression is nothing short of threatening.

I turn and place the stranger's hands on my waist, and he slides them to my ass. I drive my heel onto his foot, and he curses under his breath. I lean my head back onto his shoulder so he can hear me. "Do that again, and my heel will be somewhere else."

His hands instantly shoot back up. *That's what I thought.*

My hair clings to me from the perspiration, but I continue dancing. I lift my eyes to glance at Ace one more time, but he's not there.

Shortly after, I sense his presence behind me before he grumbles, "Get your fucking hands off her or I'll remove them for you." And replaces the stranger with himself. He pulls my back into his hard chest. The scent of his cologne is all around me, and I sharply inhale. My stomach clenches with an undeniable craving, making it difficult to believe this means nothing to me.

"I'm beginning to think you have a fixation with pissing me off. Do you get off on it or something?"

Wouldn't you like to know?

Ace's rough hands travel along my side to the hem of my dress. The music pounds in my ears, coercing my entire body to pulse to the beat of it while the adrenaline vibrates through my veins.

"Or something," I reply breathlessly.

I bend down and grind my ass on him. He grips my waist, instantly yanking me up. "Calla, we're leaving," he commands in my ear, sending a thrill through me. "Now."

Perfect.

Turning me toward the door, his chest presses against my back protectively as we make our way out. His breathing is deep, and his hands grip my waist tighter with every step.

Denzel is waiting for us outside. He's an older gentleman in his fifties, and there's fear in his eyes. "Mr. Blackwell—" he attempts to apologize for bringing me here.

"Do a few laps around the city," Ace snaps, pulling me into the back of the Mercedes with him. Denzel shuts the door behind us, letting the darkness lead us to each other.

The privacy partition goes up, and my heart rate follows.

I straddle Ace. My knees on either side of his sturdy figure send my dress sliding up my thighs. The air conditioning surrounds us, yet the heat scorches against my skin.

My fingers drift to Ace's face, tenderly touching the bruise forming on his jaw. "Who gave you this?"

"An amateur business associate."

Without thinking, I allow my fingers to trail up toward his delectable lips. Thoughts of how pleasant they would feel against my own, cloud every rational thought. I'm dazed. There's no other excuse to explain my actions.

Ace captures my fingers with his hand, and my stomach swims with butterflies. I'm heaved back in time to four years ago when we were in this precise position on the pier with the tranquility encircling us. How everything has changed. Yet my memories remain clear as day. At this moment, the only thing left between us is the anticipation of his lips on mine.

An invisible force pulls us together, and there's no fighting it this time. I'm craving to taste him. I have been since I saw him again, and I can't seem to stop myself tonight.

He laces his right hand with mine, softly brushing his thumb over the back of it. With his other hand, he reaches to loop his finger around a strand of my hair that loosely hangs out of the corner of my eye. "You're so beautiful, Calla," he murmurs, bringing his mouth closer to mine.

My heart drums against my chest, but there's nowhere for it to escape as Ace's lips brush against my own. The tip of his tongue sweeps against my top lip. It's subtle at first, like he's relishing the moment, becoming accustomed to all we lost when we went our separate ways. Then I part my lips to let him in, inviting the urgency of a firestorm.

It's all I remembered it to be and more. So much more. I'm captivated, addicted to him. I forget everything—our surroundings, the fact that we're in a moving vehicle with Denzel just an arm's length from us. I forget that we haven't been around each other for the last four years because it seems like no time has passed. Our lips move in sync, and all I know is him.

Ace places a hand on my thigh and the other one on my nape, luring me closer. It's as though he also can't get enough. "The dress, Calla… You wanted my attention. You have it. All of it."

His thumb traces my cheekbone, moving toward my jaw, and his gaze doesn't leave me. I'm burning underneath it.

Burning.

Spiraling.

Plummeting.

My body floods with endorphins. I tug on his thick hair, threading my hands through it, returning his lips to mine. The taste of him makes me delirious, unable to think clearly. I grind my hips against him, and he groans, drifting his hand underneath my dress, closer to where I need him to be.

"I need you," he drawls against my ear, dusting his thumb lazily across my panties, and I move my hips to meet it.

I take a breath. "Have me."

Ace is hard beneath me, and we're both fighting for air—both trying to coerce our bodies to slow down but not having enough willpower to do so. Being around him is overwhelming. I thought I'd be able to control myself, but that has proven to be impossible.

"No, Calla. I need more with you."

An upsurge of shadows washes over me. I instantly stop, pulling away from him so I can try and understand what he's implying. What does he mean by more? There can't ever be more. I can't give him more.

"I can't."

He takes a deep breath, calming his breathing before looking at me.

There are so many reasons why that's not possible—our past, I'm mentally unstable, I have trust issues, my dad. How can I be with Ace and introduce him to my dad? I can't lie to him for the rest of my life. He's the only family I have left.

I squeeze my eyes shut to suppress the pounding headache arriving at full speed. "Even if it weren't for our past, I wouldn't suit your lifestyle. I'm *not* going to sit back in your apartment and do what I'm told. I'm not about events, red carpets, and clinging to your side."

I'm not Cassidy.

"I can see that." His jaw sets. "I let you leave once. I'm not prepared to do it again without a fight."

I shake my head. I can't be with him. "I'll drive you insane. You'll get sick of it."

He raises his eyebrows, accepting the challenge. "You already drive me fucking insane, and guess what? I love it."

Nothing I say will compel him to surrender, but I try anyway. "I don't want to give you false hope. It's only physical for me. It's this or nothing."

There can't be anything more. If my dad ever finds out about Ace, he'll do anything it takes to put him behind bars. I can't let that happen. It will destroy Ace and everything he's built from scratch. I can't let him suffer even more for something that already consumes him.

Even if I've forgiven Ace for what he did, my dad won't. I know him too well. No one comes before the law.

"Liar," Ace calls me out. "You can't tell me you don't feel *this* between us."

"I'm not lying," is all I'm able to say.

Ace's eyes glimmer in response, and I know he's not going to touch me again unless it's on his terms. It's either all or nothing.

Doesn't he realize that together we are nothing more than madness? We're two damaged souls who will only fall further into the den of despair. Ace is torturing the both of us by using my job to bring us together, and the more he continues this, the more difficult it'll be to walk away when our time runs out—and it will run out. It's inevitable.

11

The Wedding

Calla

It would be effortless to lose myself in the moment and face the consequences later, to allow myself to believe there's even a slight chance we could have more. But more is a privilege. People like us, with the world against us, don't get more without hurting each other and those around us.

"Stop here, Denzel," Ace orders as he presses the button for the privacy partition to slide down. Within seconds, the car slows and comes to a smooth halt.

"What are we doing?" I sneak a glance out the window.

I can barely make anything out. Ace's substantial figure covers my line of vision. My heart still pounds from the intimacy we shared only an instant ago and how easily he called my bluff. Is it possible he can see right through me? Right through the lie I feed myself whenever I'm around him?

"We're getting some fresh air," Ace grumbles, clasping my hand in his warm one and guiding me out of the car.

We step out into the night. The cool air surrounds us, and I steal a deep breath of fresh air before squinting around. Familiar surroundings come into view—cherry blossom trees under lamps shining yellow light, gentle slopes, and the distant smell of moss with the strong trace of old urine. There's no mistaking Central Park. Although it looks different at night, it's still Central Park. The heart of New York.

My body shivers when the brisk breeze greets us. Ace turns to grab his suit jacket from the back seat and smoothly wraps it around my shoulders without saying a word. The charcoal-gray material swallows me entirely and reaches just above my knees. I relish the rich smell of Ace that wafts from it and slide my hands through the armholes.

Hand in hand, we follow the path. At first glance, there's no one in sight, but the farther we walk, I decipher human shapes in the distance. Strangely, I've lived here for one year and only set foot in the park once or twice.

"How did you end up in New York?" Ace asks.

I never told Ace that coming here was my goal for as long as I can remember. I didn't get the chance to in our short time together. "Mr. Howley was impressed by my dedication to the school newspaper. He had a contact here, and after numerous interviews, I landed a job at *Satire Times*."

Ace's expression shifts into something acutely thoughtful. "I made the right decision by leaving then."

I'm not sure what he means at first, but then it clicks. "You were the editor of the newspaper before me? I should have known."

"Dean offered me the position to gain extra credit, but I'm glad the position went to you once I left. I would've never been as dedicated. It was just a chore to me."

I notice the way Ace uses Mr. Howley's first name. "Do you still keep in touch with Dean?"

"We talk every so often."

I wonder if Dean still runs the underground fighting clubs back in Idaho. How close was Ace with Dean? Did Ace rely on him as a distant father figure?

"Are you happy here?" Ace asks, tracing his thumb over the back of my hand.

I consider his question. "I don't know," I confess. Am I happy? Some days I am, other days I'm not. Is there a certain number of days in a week a person must be happy to consider themselves happy overall? Or is it a constant feeling one must have? "Are you?"

"I should be. Anyone else in my position would be."

"But you're not." I glance at him, trying to understand.

Ace shrugs. "I'm not sure I know what it means to be happy. I don't feel fulfilled or content. It's like something is missing."

That resonates with me more than I'd like to admit. "My mom used to live here…" I pause. I've never talked about my mom with Ace. It feels strange mentioning her under the circumstances.

"You can talk about her," Ace affirms as though he knows what I'm thinking. He brushes his thumb over the back of my hand again reassuringly.

"That one of the reasons I wanted to come to New York. She used to tell me about her life here. She made it sound like a dream."

"What was she like?"

"She was carefree and adventurous, particularly in her twenties." My mind travels back in time.

"I'd figured that, considering how your parents met."

My smile is distant as I recall the story of how my mother stripped in the middle of the highway, and my father took her home in his patrol car.

"She was also generous and kind. She would always find a way to give, even when she was in no position to."

Ace's steps falter, and I turn to face him. Despair and gloominess skulk in the dark shadows of his eyes. He looks down at me with regret. It's not difficult to see how much pain he carries with him every second of the day. How can I punish him for what he's already penalizing himself for?

"I'm sorry."

I take both of his hands in mine. "We all make mistakes, Ace. Some cost us more than others. You need to find a way to forgive yourself."

"Forgive myself?" he scoffs. "What I did is unforgivable."

"I understand what you're feeling. I understand more than anyone else. I used to blame myself for that night. I still do."

He shakes his head, about to interrupt me. I know what he's going to say, that he's the one to blame. While that may be true, I don't blame him. I've tried to throughout the years. It would have been the most viable thing to do—an easier option. But I couldn't bring myself to, not after comprehending the events that led him to that point. We all deserve redemption. Ace has proven over and over that he's a good person who has committed a grave crime.

"Your father left you that night. You were distraught like any other teenager would have been. You got drunk, and you weren't in the right state of mind when your best friend handed you the keys. What was *he* thinking, given how self-destructive you were?" It's like offering a junkie a hit. "I'm not making excuses for you, because that night cost me immensely, but the burden shouldn't be solely on you. Yet you carry all of it."

"How can you say that?"

I shake my head, unable to explain. "I only blame you for not telling me sooner, for not coming forward when the accident occurred." I pause.

If he turned himself in and allowed justice to run its course, would he still be this remorseful years later? Or would he believe that he paid enough debt to society and stop condemning himself? How can I compare Ace to other felons when more than half of them are only sorry for getting caught and not for the crime itself?

"I've been seeing someone for the last few years. It helps tremendously to talk about it with a stranger," I tell him in hopes it will push him to consider therapy. He's always been reluctant to seek help. I wonder if it's because he doesn't believe it will aid, or if he thinks he doesn't deserve support.

Either way, he's wrong.

"I won't be home in the morning. I have training early, and I'll go to the wedding from there," he says, turning away and following the path back the way we came, dismissing my statement just like I thought he would.

The next morning, my mind travels to the events that occurred last night. The words that slipped from Ace's mouth. *I need more with you.*

I'm unsure if he realizes the consequences of that statement. I can't take the chance that his whole life will be destroyed because of me. I can't let him suffer more for something that happened six years ago. And perhaps, I don't want to open the can of worms again after finally sealing the lid back on.

The tightness of the room suffocates my throat, my chest, and everything around me. I focus on my breathing.

In. Out.

It doesn't provide relief. My phone faintly rings downstairs, still in my bag on the counter where I left it last night. I rush down, stealing a glimpse of myself in the mirror and shuddering at the sight. Last night's makeup is smudged all over my face, making me look like a raccoon. I was exhausted after we arrived back at Ace's apartment.

I bring the phone to my ear without checking the caller ID. I already know it's my dad. He calls me every Sunday morning at ten. My eyes widen when I realize what the time is. Nik is meant to be picking me up in an hour.

I talk to my dad while eyeing the folders Mia gave me the other day, one on Ace and the other on Nik. I don't have time to even glance at them today, so I shove them farther into my bag.

"How's work?"

"Work is good. I'm busy on a project," I tell him the half-truth.

"Don't overwork yourself, Cals. I miss you."

"I miss you, too, Dad. I'm going to try to come to see you in a couple of weeks, okay?"

We say our goodbyes, and I promise to call him next week as my gaze lands on the counter where there's a sticky note.

The green one is my favorite.

Three dresses are laid out—blue, green, and a yellow-colored one. All of them look so expensive that I don't allow myself to run my hands over them.

When did Ace have the time to get me dresses? He's insane. But I'm grateful he did. I had nothing picked out for today. I didn't have the time, and I was going to run to my apartment this morning to see what I could find.

I have a shower and get ready, choosing the baby-blue dress. It fits like it was made to my exact body measurements. The buttery fabric latches on to the top half of my body and cinches my waist. The slit on the right side stops just above my mid-thigh. The dress is elegant and daring, but not gaudy. Exactly my style.

I rush to meet Nik in the lobby. I sense his eyes set on me as soon as I step out of the elevators. "You look absolutely breathtaking, sweetheart." He places a kiss on my cheek.

"Thank you," I murmur. "You look handsome yourself." Nik's three-piece formal suit seems to be custom-tailored. It's also wondrously modish.

He leads us to his Audi R8, which is parked outside the building. "You should have informed me what color you'd be wearing so we could've coordinated."

"It was last minute. Perhaps next time."

Nik opens the door for me, and I slide inside. We make small talk on the way, and he apologizes multiple times for not calling or texting me throughout the week.

"It's fine, really." I wave his apology off. "I've been busy, too."

"With Ace?" he asks, a trace of harshness pikes in his voice.

Is that envy? I try to get further clarification from his expression. However, his face is vacant, and he displays no emotion. I suppose he's used to keeping his facial expressions in check. He's a lawyer, after all.

"He has an insane schedule. I don't know how the man does it," I remark almost to myself.

"I bet he does."

I raise my eyebrow. "What's the deal with you two?"

"He's been a difficult client."

Before I have time to probe further, we pull up to the heavily guarded gates.

The wedding is nothing short of spectacular. It seems like the bride went all out. The venue itself is located by a freshwater lake that appears exceedingly clear and pure even from a distance. It reflects blues and greens from the mountains surrounding it and the sky above. There's so much security that I'm beginning to wonder who the bride and groom are.

"Do you want anything to drink?" Nik asks when we finally make our way inside.

"Just water, please."

He nods and tells me he'll be right back. While I wait for Nik, my eyes wander to the altar, which is still empty. The pink and white color scheme extends throughout the venue. When I turn around, I spot Ace heading my way.

I don't think I'll ever get over how remarkable he looks in a suit. The other women are already eyeing him and whispering to their girlfriends as he makes his way toward me. I'm surprised no one interrupts him, since he's a celebrity, after all. But I guess there are unspoken rules when people like him attend.

I notice his tie is the same color as my dress. "How did you know which one I would pick?" I ask once he gets closer.

"I knew it wasn't going to be the green one, because you're stubborn. The yellow one." He raises his eyebrow as if to say he knows that one wasn't my style.

"So I never had a choice, but you made it seem like I did."

"It's the only way with you." He sends me a charming grin, causing my heart to flutter. "By the way, it looks better than I'd imagined on you."

"I hope I'm not interrupting anything." Cassidy appears behind Ace. Her silver bodycon dress is made precisely for her body type, and her dark curls have been professionally styled. She places her hand on Ace's shoulder, and that's when I notice the massive rock on her finger. An engagement ring?

I will deny it if asked, but the truth is, seeing the diamond ring right in front of me hits a little differently than I thought it would. I haven't realized I've been slowly letting my guard down during the past week. Slowly letting Ace back in. And there's always a price to pay for that.

If I knew, then I would have never crossed a line like this. Messing around with a taken man is not something I do, no matter who he is.

I've always believed Ace and I have the same morals, but now I'm beginning to question whether we're all that similar. After all, if he has a fiancée, he sure hasn't been acting like it.

I secure a smile on my face, refusing to let the storm building inside of me show. "Not at all. Excuse me, I better go find my date."

I turn and walk straight into Nik's chest. He steadies me with one hand on my waist while holding the bottle of water for me in his other. "Hey, you okay?"

"Yes, thank you," I say as he hands me the bottle.

His attention turns to Ace, and he gives him a grim smile, his charming blue eyes cold as ice. "Ace, I didn't know we had that many acquaintances to keep running into each other."

Nik wraps his arm around my waist and pulls me closer to his side. If it were anyone else, I'd think it was a territorial claim, but Nik knows where he stands with me.

Ace smirks. "You'd be surprised."

"Cassidy, it's good to see you again," Nik addresses her. She drops her hand from Ace's shoulder and places it behind her.

Ace is watching us, but I ignore his stare. He has no right.

Nik leads me toward the assigned seats as the ceremony is about to start. At each seated isle, jasmine-scented candles hang from the tree branches that provide shade for the seated guests. Scattered down the light-pink carpet in the middle of the aisle are red and white rose petals, still fresh and moist. The groom is already at the altar, facing the tranquil blue lakeside. He keeps running his hands through his hair in what I assume is a nervous gesture.

"How do you know the bride and groom?" I ask quietly, and out of the corner of my eye, I notice Ace and Cassidy slide into the seats next to Nik. Great.

"The groom, Mason, is a close friend of mine. We met through business a few years ago but realized we have more in common than just investment companies."

I nod. "And the bride?"

"Stella. I've met her a few times. She's good for him."

The music flows, and everyone turns to look behind them. The bridesmaids and groomsmen walk down the aisle. The bridesmaids' dresses are pastel pink to match the theme. The last couple appear as though they've just stepped off the front cover of a magazine. The man is striking, tall, with dark hair. The woman only comes up to his shoulder, even with heels. Her hair is platinum blond and falls above her waistline in wavy curls. A small girl, no older than three, runs behind them with a small basket attached to her arm. I assume it's their daughter, from the similar features.

Once everyone takes their spots at the altar, the bride walks down the aisle. She's stunning. Her white dress is fitted at the top with floral details, and the bottom of the dress flows behind her. Her mousy hair has been left mostly down, only the sides swept back and pinned with clips of pink and silver. I watch the groom's expression when his eyes land on the bride, and he wipes at his cheeks as if there are tears there.

After the ceremony, we head inside for the reception. The

centerpieces have candles and a bouquet of white and pink roses. Each table has assigned seating, and it's no surprise Ace is at the same table as us. I bet it was his doing.

There are speeches from their close family and friends, followed by laughter and tears. Finally, the bride and groom share their first dance while everyone watches them. They glide across the dance floor, focused solely on each other. From where I'm positioned, I notice the groom whispering to the bride, and she tilts her head back and laughs wholeheartedly. When the song ends, another one begins, and other guests make their way to the dance floor.

Nik stands and extends his hand to me. "May I?"

I'm surprised by the gesture. I didn't take Nik for a dancer. "You may." I take his hand and let him lead me onto the dance floor, where other couples are now gathering.

"This is a beautiful wedding," I comment as his hands park on my waist, and I put my own on his broad shoulders.

"My first one."

"You've never been to a wedding before?"

"You say that like it's a crime."

I lift my eyebrows as if to say it is. "Is it because you've never been invited to any, or for other reasons?"

He considers my question, running his tongue over his bottom lip. "You're asking me if I believe in marriage?"

I nod.

"I believe that it's a meaningless concept, and tradition is the only reason many people do it. But I'm not opposed to it with the right person, especially if it's important to them."

"I think we have similar views on it. If I find someone I want to spend the rest of my life with, I would like to commit in every way possible."

"Are your parents married?" Nik questions.

Nik and I haven't talked much about our families, or anything for that matter. Come to think of it, we barely know anything about each other. "My mom died six years ago. My dad never remarried."

"I'm sorry."

"Are yours married?" I ask, not wanting to talk about myself.

He shakes his head. "My parents aren't together. My mother died when I was ten."

My eyes widen, surprised at how many similarities we share. "I'm sorry."

The song finishes, and another one starts. There seem to be more people on the dance floor now, swaying from side to side, enjoying the moment. The ceiling is covered with lights shaped like hanging icicles that change from pink to silver.

I feel a hand on my shoulder and instantly know it's Ace. "I can take it from here." His tone is full of male arrogance.

I turn to glare at him. Shouldn't he be dancing with his *fiancée*?

Nik goes to say something, but I beat him to it. "I don't think so."

Ace narrows his eyes, and I gather he's not willing to take no for an answer. "I insist."

"She said no." Nik comes to my aid.

Ace takes a step closer toward him in a challenging manner. Nik doesn't back down. Two alpha males are not a good combination, and I'm not about to let them ruin a wedding.

I sigh and lay a hand on Nik's chest. "One dance, Ace." Nik looks to me as if asking if I'm sure, and I nod in response.

Ace situates his hands on my waist, a little lower than necessary. I grab them and move them higher. He smirks condescendingly, and I narrow my eyes.

"Anything you want to tell me?" I prompt him when we begin to sway from side to side.

He furrows his brows like he has no idea what I'm talking about. "Why don't you enlighten me on what I've done. Something has obviously got you in a mood."

"A mood?" I scoff and look back to our table where Cassidy sits. Something about this situation doesn't seem right.

Ace follows my gaze, and his mouth curves up at the sides. "Are you jealous, love? Is this what it's about?"

My toes curl at the endearment. "I could ask you the same since you're the one who interrupted."

"Seeing you with other men does more than make me jealous, Calla. At least I can admit it."

"Other men, or just Nik?" I counter, trying to squeeze any information out of him that I can.

"I told you to stay away from him."

"And *I told you* you have no right to tell me who to see, especially when you're…" I trail off.

"When I'm what?"

He's clueless, and the more I think about it, the less plausible it seems they are engaged. So many things don't add up. I recall Ace telling me about his father, and how he cheated on Ace's mother with many other women during their marriage. Ace hated him for it. He wouldn't do the same, would he?

"When I'm what, Calla?" he repeats the question, leaning closer toward me, letting the warmness of his breath caress my mouth, clouding my thoughts.

"I need to use the bathroom." I withdraw from his grip and walk toward the back corner, but instead of going into the bathroom, I veer to the right and slip outside, onto the deck. I need a moment to gather my thoughts.

No one else is out here, so I lean on the wooden railing and stare out at the scenic view. The clipped grass in front of me is like a blanket of greenery, suffocating the ground. In the distance and toward my left is the lake I saw on arrival, reflecting in the sun like a splinter of glass. It's truly a breathtaking venue.

I hear the door open behind me, and the clack of heels on timber. I turn to find Cassidy approaching me. Did she follow me, or is this purely a coincidence? It can't be, she saw me walk past her. She leans on the railing, and retrieves a compact mirror followed by lipstick from her purse. Out of the corner of my eye, I notice her gaze sweep over me.

There's no denying that Cassidy is stunning. I'd be lying to myself if I thought otherwise. From her plump lips, to her flawless skin, and her vivid blue eyes, she looks like she's been airbrushed on the front cover of a magazine. How can anyone compete with that? She and Ace make a dazzling couple.

She looks me up and down in a disapproving manner. "You slept with him, and now you're attached just like all the previous women."

My eyes widen at her bluntness, and I wonder how she even got that concept in her mind. I open my mouth to speak, but she continues.

"Such a shame." She sighs, capping her lipstick. "A friendly warning—he'll be done with you shortly. No one lasts more than a couple of weeks."

The last thing I expected from her was an ambush. However, if she's engaged to him, then she has every right. But I've been studying them all day, and I don't think that's the case. They don't appear like an engaged couple.

"Are you speaking from personal experience?" I ask, keeping my face neutral.

She laughs. "Darling, I've been the only constant thing in his life for the last two years."

Two years?

"But don't worry, the ring is not from him, if that's what you're wondering," she says sweetly, lifting her hand to examine the extravagant diamond on her finger. "I have better things to do than to pine for men that don't have feelings. But the connection that Ace and I share goes beyond any jewelry or sentimental thing."

Cassidy leaves me more confused than I was before. If the ring isn't from Ace, then what sort of relationship do they have? I return to the table, questioning everything I know.

"I've passed your number on to my friend from *The Times*. He said he'll give you a call next week to arrange a time to meet," Nik says.

"Thank you, Nik." I place my hand on his shoulder to show him I appreciate the effort. He had no obligation to do this, especially considering our relationship is based exclusively on the physical aspect.

"It's nothing. If you ever need anything else, let me know."

The wedding doesn't conclude till late, and after hours of mingling with everyone, including the newlyweds, I'm ready for bed.

"I can take her," Ace says when Nik offers me his hand, ready to leave. "Since we're going back to the same place anyway," he adds.

Cassidy shoots Ace a look. "I thought you were taking me home."

Ace shrugs. "I'll get Denzel to drive you."

On the drive back to the apartment in Ace's Lamborghini,

both of us are quiet. Ace reaches out and links my hand in his. I look at him, but he keeps his eyes on the road. I'm too tired to say anything or pull away, so I just let it be. It's nice. His warmth radiates through me, and I tilt my head back against the seat and close my eyes.

We seem to be slowly crossing lines into dangerous territory. What will happen once the two weeks are over?

"Why do you have a driver?" I question, not knowing if it's just a regular service one gets when they have enough money.

"I prefer not to drive a car, and the bike isn't an appropriate option at times."

I nod in understanding.

Ace's phone rings back at the apartment. He answers it and strides into another room. I have a shower while he takes the call, letting the hot water stream and relax the knots in my muscles. Then, pulling a sweater and some shorts on, I descend the stairs to discover the front door closing and Ace slipping behind it.

He left. Again. Without so much as telling me he was going out.

It's as if he doesn't remember why I'm here, even though it was his idea. I'm meant to be following him to all his *arrangements*, but he seems to think it's only when it suits him. Where could he be going at this time of the night?

Cassidy?

I quickly grab my bag off the counter and follow him. I watch the elevator go down to the basement, but instead of following him there, I head to the lobby and out the glass doors. The doorman gives me a quick once-over and a curt nod.

There's a cab sitting out front, and I open the door and slide into the back seat. "Good evening. There's a black Lamborghini that's about to come out of the basement. Follow it, please."

12

Seeking the Truth

Calla

It's midnight, and I've barely slept in the last forty-eight hours. The red brake lights from the cars in front of me blur. I coerce my eyes to stay open. Keeping myself awake is second nature to me. I know how to do it. I've done it for years so I didn't have to endure the nightmares that tried to invade if I surrendered to the temptation.

I retrieve a piece of chewing gum from my bag and place it in my mouth. The minty taste deceives my mind into staying awake and offers me something to do instead of grazing on the skin around my nails or chewing on the inside of my cheek—bad habits when my nerves are at their peak.

The files Mia provided me with are burning a hole in my bag, and I take them out, sighing. I turn my phone light on and skim through them while glancing up every few seconds to ensure we're still following Ace. The cab driver maintains his distance a few cars behind.

Ace Blackwell. The undefeated boxing champion, the youngest to ever hold that title. He's invested in multiple companies, from clubs to sporting venues. However, it doesn't stop there. He doesn't just own companies and properties in New York. There are also some in other countries.

The revenue he makes per month requires me to recheck the figures, wondering whether my eyes are playing tricks on me. No wonder he could donate five million dollars without so much as blinking. This is not exactly public record, and I wonder how Mia obtained all this information.

He used the money from his first fights to begin Blackwell Enterprises one year into his career. Impressive and almost impossible, but Ace makes it seem effortless.

There's a mention of a sibling, but nothing in detail. Nothing in particular about Ellie or his mom. It seems like Ace went to extreme measures to exclude them from the public eye. But why?

Next, I open the file on Niklaus Stryker. He grew up in Massachusetts and attended Harvard Law School. Impressive. After graduating from law school at the age of twenty-three, he moved to New York and began working as an associate. Two years ago, he was made a partner at the corporate firm now called Stryker & Portman. He's never lost a case, and that's what makes him so well-known.

Nik has purchased a few properties, one in London, which doesn't surprise me since he often travels there for work. There's nothing about his family or siblings, only that his mother raised him alone and passed away suddenly when Nik was ten. His father wasn't in the picture until four years ago. No names, nothing I can search up.

We've been following Ace for twenty minutes throughout the city, driving to the point where I feel like we're going around in circles. He doesn't seem like he's going anywhere in particular. I'm beginning to think this is a waste of time and quite a bit of my money. Maybe there's something on his mind, and he needs to clear his head. I close both files and toss them back in my bag. I'll look at them more thoroughly another time.

I'm about to tell the cab driver to take me back to the apartment when a feeling in my stomach influences me to wait a little longer.

Finally, Ace turns into a narrow, dark alleyway, and I instruct the driver to stop after it. From the back seat window, I observe another car waiting for him.

I squint my eyes and press my nose against the window to get a better look. Ace and the driver from the second car get out simultaneously and swap vehicles. Ace gets in the G-Wagon, while the other man, whom I don't recognize, takes the Lamborghini expeditiously and without hesitation, like they've done this many times before.

Ace is taking precautions, but is it because of the paparazzi or something else? I glance around to see if anyone else is following him, I don't detect anything out of the ordinary. Over the last week, I've observed that Ace doesn't get noticed if he doesn't want to be.

Even though it's past midnight, it's also the weekend, meaning the streets are still lively with traffic. We continue to follow him, this time routing onto the highway and out of the inner city. After another twenty minutes, Ace comes to a halt in front of a large house. From what I can see under the dim street lamps, the neighborhood itself is quiet and prestigious. Each home has a security gate at the front of the driveway, and the houses themselves are beyond spectacular.

Ace doesn't park in the driveway. Instead, he pulls over near the curb on the side of the road and strides toward the white three-story house on foot. He's changed into black jeans and a plain black T-shirt instead of the suit he wore earlier tonight. He's a shadow in the night.

I get out of the cab and pay a hefty fee. We've already been driving for close to an hour, and cabs aren't cheap. I'm not going to wait in the back seat while the meter runs. I maintain my distance on the other side of the road where Ace won't see me.

The large front door opens, revealing a woman behind it. The light on the porch is bright, but I can't see clearly enough to distinguish her features even with it on. Ace disappears inside, and the door shuts behind him.

A heavy feeling flows through my chest, and even though I expected this, it still manages to surprise me. I try not to jump to conclusions, because things aren't always as they seem with Ace.

Drops of water speckle my hand, and I look up. A blanket of dark clouds covers the sky. I curse under my breath. This is just my luck. I shuffle under a tree, weighing up my options. How long is Ace going to be there? And what am I to do when he comes out? I can't approach him and have him know I followed him here.

As I contemplate my options, I don't notice when someone comes up behind me and covers my mouth with their hand. My breath hitches in my throat like cotton, but I would recognize those hands anywhere.

Ace heaves me closer toward his hard chest, into his warmth like he's trying to shield me from the rain. "If you thought you could follow me without me knowing, you're mistaken, love."

"Just doing my job," I mumble against the palm of his hand.

Did he know all along I was following him?

"I didn't realize that included being a pain in my ass." He removes his hand from my mouth and instead positions it on my hip.

The hardness of him digs into my back. "Is that a gun, or are you excited to see me, Ace?" I twist myself around to face him, pressing my body into his, and scan him, confused.

His body stills. I know Ace is *well-equipped* down there, but this… This is something else.

"Calla…" he warns, grabbing my wrist before I can reach for it. He casts me a look that tells me to drop it, but he's dreaming if he believes I'm going to. He should know me better by now.

I narrow my eyes, piecing everything together. "Why do you have a gun?" My voice leaks out steadier than I thought it would.

Ace doesn't answer. Instead, he takes my hand and leads me toward his car. I allow him only because the rain is getting heavier, drenching my clothes.

Ace turns to me when we approach his car across the road. He considers something, his expression softening just for a second. "Do you want to drive?"

"It's fine. You drive."

He nods, opening the passenger door for me, and I climb up. The step is high, and Ace holds my waist for support. I don't say anything when he begins driving, hoping he'll explain, but he doesn't. I stare absently at the road in front of me, not noticing we aren't going toward his apartment until Ace speaks.

"I need to run another errand. It won't take long." He tightens his hands around the steering wheel.

I get the impression he's not too thrilled I'm here. Perhaps he should have thought about that before he suggested the whole shadowing thing to my boss.

"Errand?" I question.

He steers the car into a small parking lot behind a structure. There aren't any lights here, nothing to indicate where we are. I can only just make out the back door to the building and the uninviting essence of it.

Ace parks but leaves the engine running and turns to me. "Stay in the car."

"Are you going to explain why you have a gun?"

I don't bother asking about the secret door in his room or who the woman he just visited is. Those are conversations for another time. I'm aware he's hiding something. History repeating itself, reminding me why I can't ever trust him. But I shouldn't expect him to tell me anything, I'm only temporary in his life.

He ignores my question and hands me his keys. "If I'm not back in ten minutes, leave."

I stare at the keys in my hand and then look back at him. "You have to be kidding me?"

"Just for once, do as I say, Calla."

I have the urge to argue with him, but his stone-hard expression signifies I should obey. Instead, he offers me a look that says he'll explain everything later.

"Fine," I snap.

"Good." He shuts the door harder than necessary as he gets out.

I recoil in response and watch as he disappears behind the metal door, my eyes boring through his back—*if looks could kill.*

Five minutes go by, and I can't stay still. I bounce my legs while staring out the window, waiting for Ace to emerge from that stupid door. Something about this doesn't feel right, and my worry threatens to bubble over.

Eight minutes go by, and my hands begin to shake. I chew on the bottom of my lip, lost in thought. The time doesn't slow down as I wait for Ace. On the contrary, it speeds up. Ten minutes feel like one. When fifteen minutes go by, I drum my fingers on the center console. I can't leave him here. If he has a gun, this isn't just an errand.

I open the center console, unsure what I'm doing or searching for, but my eyes widen as they land on another gun. "What the fuck, Ace?" I hiss under my breath.

Getting out of the car, my shaking hands grip the gun, not knowing what the hell I'm about to get myself into. Never in my life have I been more thankful to my dad for teaching me how to use a pistol. Hopefully, all of this is a misunderstanding.

I shut the passenger door behind me. The rain is heavier now, and I have no inkling as to what I'm on the verge of walking into, but I'm not going to abandon Ace. He may be able to take care of himself, he may have done this for years, whatever the hell this is, but I won't be able to live with myself if I leave him and something happens.

I use all my weight to open the metal door, and I run into Ace's chest when I finally push it open. His jaw ignites with a twitch, and his dark eyes narrow down at me. It's clear he's pissed. So freaking pissed that if this were a cartoon scene, I'd see steam streaming from his ears.

"Sixteen minutes. You should be gone," he snarls in my ear, gripping me by the waist with his strong arm and turning me around, back toward the car.

Bossy.

I do a once-over of his face and then skim the rest of him, checking for fresh bruises, blood, anything, but there's nothing of the sort. What is he into that requires him to carry a gun? Multiple guns. It can't be good or legal, for that matter.

"I wasn't just going to leave you."

"You think I can't handle myself?" he asks tightly.

I scamper, trying to match his strides when he loosens his grip around me. "I thought you might need help." I grit my teeth, getting frustrated with all his lies and secrets.

"What the fuck were you going to do?" His eyes zero in on the gun in my hand, and he shakes his head almost to himself, like he's not even shocked.

I climb into the car, returning the gun to the center console where I found it. Ace watches me with irritation. When I'm done, he starts the car and reverses out of the car park, his arm muscles flexing on the wheel as he does.

Water droplets strike the windows as we drive. A blanket of gray covers the sky. It's so heavy I can barely tell the difference between the sky and clouds. Despite feeling nauseous in the passenger seat, especially at this time of night, the rain calms me as I observe the raindrops spill down the windows.

It took me six years to be okay with riding in the passenger seat at night. I knew I had to overcome that fear of mine, and my therapist pushed me toward self-healing. At first, I began taking cabs at night, just around the block. The first few times were horrible. I had to ask the cab driver to pull over to throw up on the sidewalk and walk the rest of the way. Eventually, it got better. I got better.

I turn to Ace as he drives, expecting him to start talking, explaining something, anything. But nothing.

His mouth is set in a pale, grim line. His eyes focus on the road, but his mind seems like it's elsewhere. I continue to watch him, not caring if he notices me gawking at him or not.

There have always been secrets with Ace. Nothing has ever been simple. Maybe that's why it's challenging for me to let someone else in. It's hard to trust again when all you know is why you shouldn't. In the past, we both broke each other's trust. Him, by hiding the truth, and me, by leaving when he needed me to stay the most, but I'll never blame myself for that. I did what I had to, and I would do it all over again.

"What?" he demands, still looking straight ahead. His elbow leans on the open window. Half of his body is drenched from the rain, but he makes no effort to wind the window up, and I choose not to say anything about it.

"Nothing."

"What do you want to know? Just ask, Calla. Fuck!" His voice blares through the silent car, and the breeze peppers my legs with goose bumps.

I open my mouth and lock it again. There are an endless amount of questions that require answers, and I'm unsure where to start. I close my eyes and fill my lungs, my mind churning with thoughts, not knowing how to piece them together.

I open my mouth again, this time letting the words speak for themselves. "Why now, after four years? The gun? The secret room? Was that your mom? What do you have against Nik?" I finally ask, unable to stop myself once I start. "You want me to give you *more,* but you can't even give me the truth. I don't want to start from lies again." I don't know where it's all coming from. I don't remember when I allowed myself even to consider giving him more.

Ace's expression is bare, yet his hand stiffens on the gear stick. He doesn't answer me, doesn't say anything at all. Instead, he turns the radio on. Why did he even bother telling me to ask him if he's going to give me the silent treatment when I do?

I usually don't mind the silence between us—but this, not knowing anything and imagining everything, is driving me insane. Or maybe it's the lack of sleep. Either way, I'm heading into a delusional state of mind.

I stifle a yawn as Ace pulls into another parking lot where his

Lamborghini waits for him. A younger man with tattoos covering every visible part of his body except for his face gets out, and Ace provides him with a nod as we walk past. Ace doesn't speak when he opens the door for me or the whole thirty minutes back to his apartment. It's not until we're parked in the basement that he discharges the constraining silence.

He runs his hand over his stubble, not making a move to get out of the car, finally turning to me. "I spent the last four years waiting for you when I should have been fighting for you instead. That's why now."

His words catch me off guard. They were the last thing I expected, and their impact expels all the air out of me.

"Ace—" I'm unsure of what to say as I contemplate his words. There are still so many things I don't know, things he won't tell me.

"I'll explain everything else. Tomorrow," he assures as if reading my mind.

He must notice the hesitation on my face. "Tomorrow," he promises and places his hand on top of mine.

Tomorrow seems like a thing to say when you don't want to talk about something. Tomorrow never comes.

I'm tired and overwhelmed as we make our way to his apartment.

I lie in bed after having a shower, unable to sleep. Sonorous thunder followed by a bright flash of lightning fills the room. Ace's words dance through my head on repeat.

I spent four years waiting for you. I should have been fighting for you.

Ace has a place in my heart that no one else can ever have. I've always known that, and I've always wondered if somehow, in a twisted way, we were meant to cross paths to find each other.

Fate. I've heard it's cruel and unfair.

I climb out of bed and head for Ace's room, where the lights are dimmed. I stand at his door as the thunder, deep and ceaseless, throbs through the walls. I fold my arms around my body snugly.

Ace sits on his bed, his solid back positioned against the charcoal headboard while his laptop rests on his thighs. I drink in the marvelous sight. His bronzed skin is much like the blaze of dawn, beautiful and inviting.

"Can't sleep?" He tilts his head toward me, looking up from the screen.

I shake my head. Seems like both of us can't. Maybe it has something to do with what he said in the car, but then again, I've never been one to have a good night's rest. Neither has he.

I wander to his bed and sit on the edge, observing him as he reads an email, his eyebrows furrowing at some parts. Gazing at the man in front of me, I don't think I've ever gotten over him. Ace isn't just someone you get over.

"You work too much."

He doesn't answer for a while, and I begin to think he's not going to at all. "Is there something else you'd prefer me to do, love?"

Oh, I can think of a million things I would rather you do. To me.

"Is that so?" He raises an eyebrow, closes his laptop, and sets it aside.

I don't know whether I said it out loud or if he read my mind, but warmth settles between my legs. At the same time, I stifle a yawn. How long have I been awake?

Ace chuckles, the soft and low sound rendering me so weak that I'm glad I'm sitting down.

"I should go to bed." I rise, unsure of why I even came here in the first place.

"Stay."

That word makes me pause. It holds more meaning than I'm

ready for. I shift from one foot to the other, weighing up the options and consequences in my mind.

Ace reaches for my hand and pulls me toward him. "Stop thinking for once. Stop fighting this thing that wants to bring us together."

"Your ego?" I joke.

He grins lazily. "Something like that."

Ace lies back, pulling me with him, and I let him. He turns the light off, and I rest my head on his chest. He trails his fingers up my arm, his touch affecting me in more ways than I'd like to admit.

His heartbeat penetrates the silence, steady and soothing. For a minute, I forget what's happening around us. I feel safe from the things that hurt me inside, and it's the best feeling in the world.

"Do something for me."

It's never a question with Ace. "Hmm?" I ask anyway.

"I will tell you everything. Everything that no one else knows. Give me a week before you discard the idea of us."

Maybe it's the lack of sleep or the way he makes me feel high on his presence and ready to disregard boundaries. I'd agree to anything when he's this close, this vulnerable. What's he doing to me?

"Okay."

You can feel two different things at the same time with one person. I feel like I'm fighting a constant battle within myself. I want to let go and move on, but at the very same time, I want to work things out and stay. I'm afraid of the latter one. I'm afraid if I choose to stay with Ace, it will indicate that I'm okay with his actions *that day*.

And I can only hope I figure out what to do before I destroy myself even more.

13

Secrets

Calla

The odd feeling of being watched prickles my spine. "Are you watching me sleep? You know, some would say that's a little bit disturbing," I mumble into the pillow.

"Like I said before, you talk in your sleep. And snore," Ace's voice originates clear as day.

"I do not." I squint my eyes open and peer up at Ace. He's hovering above the bed in olive-green exercise shorts. "Have you been out?"

"I had training."

"Why didn't you wake me?"

A warm smile glides over his mouth. "You were out like a log, mumbling something about not getting enough beauty rest."

Yeah, right.

"But if you want to see me get sweaty, I'll gladly recreate the scene for you." Ace winks.

What time is it? It's too early for me to be blushing.

He chuckles, the sound gentle and infectious, before heading toward the shower. I admire him from behind as I bury myself deep inside the sheets, reluctant to get up.

It's after two in the afternoon when we leave Ace's apartment. He hasn't told me where he's taking me, but he never does. It's a constant guessing game with him. Just like last night, we stop to switch cars. I suppose it has everything to do with not being recognized—not being seen or followed. What does Ace have to hide? He promised he'd explain everything today, and the anticipation interspersed with my nerves is like a bank of clouds hovering above me.

We arrive in front of the same house I followed Ace to last night. During the daytime, it's even more extravagant than it seemed at night. A lush garden that I overlooked yesterday stretches in front of it. It's delightfully intricate with luscious roses and fragrant pink cotton-candy flowers just beginning to bloom.

Ace takes my hand in his, stabilizing me when I jump from the steep step of the G-Wagon. He doesn't release my hand when we make our way toward the opulent house. Instead, he tightens his grasp. The lines are becoming blurred between us. It's naïve to consider that I can spend time with him and walk away at the end without my mind going to war with my heart.

As we approach the white-columned front porch, my gaze roams the exterior of the house in awe. Sumptuous green vines eddy up the columns and swathe the railing.

Ace presses the doorbell beside the contemporary oak door. We don't have to wait long before it's swung open. I instantly recognize the woman on the other side of it. I would know she's Ace's mom even if I haven't seen her before. There's an uncanny resemblance. Dark, dense hair, turbulent eyes, razor-sharp features, and that magnificent dark skin tone. However, my attention is immediately drawn behind her, where a small girl stands.

Ellie.

Her picturesque eyes, the same as Ace's, that previously lit up a whole room, are now dull in color and energy. Her hair is considerably shorter and sparse. It's still the distinctive, dark color that runs through the family, but it's lusterless. Yet she still manages to smile when she sees us. A jaded smile that seems like it demands a considerable amount of effort. She's nine now, but she looks small for her age. Almost fragile.

My heart breaks when the realization hits me. Ellie is sick. I can tell from the manner she moves in, like every shift of her body takes too much effort. The way she smiles as if she's holding on to the last thread of hope. There's one kind of sickness that can make a person like this, and it's the most horrible type.

I don't look at Ace for confirmation, but he gives my hand a light squeeze to reinforce my thoughts. It's incredible how we can communicate in small actions such as these. It's as though our minds are interwoven, running on the same wavelength.

"This is—" Ace begins to introduce me.

"Calla." Ellie looks at me.

My eyes widen. I didn't think she'd remember me. I only saw her a couple of times four years ago.

His mom smiles at me. "Don't look so surprised. Ace hasn't brought a girl home since you."

This bewilders me even further. I don't know how to feel about that. Four years is a long time. Not that I have ever brought a man home to meet my dad, but that situation is a little different.

"He talks about you all the time," Ellie adds, her smile growing wider.

Ace doesn't seem pleased that both his mom and sister have called him out.

"Ellie," Ace warns her.

She sticks her tongue out at him, and he shakes his head. She still has him wrapped around her little finger, and it's the cutest thing. I've always wanted a sibling, but I guess my parents had enough after one. I glance at Ace and raise an eyebrow to ask if what his mom and Ellie said is true. He shrugs.

"It's good to see you again, Ellie. Your home is beautiful," I tell Ace's mom.

"Thank you." She looks over to Ace with gratitude and pride as she answers.

Reese, Ace's mom, leads us toward the living room and kitchen. There's a large ornate glass-and-crystal chandelier hanging above us in the hallway. Countless family pictures scatter the light-silvery walls, mainly of Ace and Ellie. Some with their mom, too. One catches my eye. Ellie is about two and is held by a man I can only assume is Ace's father from their resemblance. I peel my eyes away from the photo as we walk farther. The hatred I have for the man is extreme, and I haven't even met him.

The living room space opens to an undercover outside area with a manicured garden and a clear turquoise pool to the side. "I'm going swimming today," Ellie announces. "Do you want to come?" She glances at me and then at Ace.

The weather is warm today, with summer nearing. Ace looks at me, but I shake my head. I don't have a bathing suit or a change of clothes. "I'll put my feet in."

Ace grins, takes his shirt off, and throws it on the table as he heads outside. It's refreshing to see him around his family, to see another side to him.

I sit on a wooden deck chair next to Reese's mom while Ellie and Ace swim in the pool. The fervent sun heats my skin. I inhale the balmy air as I tilt my head back against the cushion and watch a game of Marco Polo in the pool. Ace is gentler with Ellie. He's careful not to push too far while they're playing, like she's fragile.

"Ace didn't tell you about Ellie?" Reese asks. She must have noticed the shock I've tried to mask.

I shake my head. It might be because we weren't in touch for four years. Guilt suddenly gnaws at me. "How long has she been sick for?"

"Two years." Reese keeps a smile on her face, for Ellie's sake, I assume, but there's sadness in her voice. Reese was a nurse when I last saw her, and I wonder if she still works or if her full-time job is looking after Ellie.

"How bad is it?" I ask, hoping everything isn't as dreadful as it seems.

"She's getting better every day."

My shoulders relax at that statement, but the anxiety still lingers in the pit of my stomach. I'm unsure of the extent of Ellie's sickness or what the word *better* means for her.

I rise to go to the bathroom. At the same time, Ace climbs out of the pool. His eyes turn toward me, and a mischievous grin graces his mouth.

Oh, no. "Don't," I warn him. His steps don't falter as he moves toward me. I retreat, taking a step backward. "Ace…" I try again, but he's not listening.

His wicked smile only grows wider as he grabs me by the waist, soaking my clothes with his body. Ellie laughs loudly. I can hear his mom in the distance, telling him it's not a good idea. I'm glad she's on my side. However, Ace doesn't have a care in the world. His sights are set on me.

He leans down to lift me and whispers in my ear so only I hear.

"I think you should get a little wet today, love. Hmm?"

Before I have the time to form a reaction, warm water from the heated pool engulfs me. It seeps through the material of my clothes, weighing me down. I'm going to kill him. I rise to the surface for air, but Ace is nowhere to be seen. Then I feel a pair of hands on my waist, gripping me from behind.

I twist and splash him. "There *will* be payback."

"Of course. I'm looking forward to it." His eyes glimmer with a challenge.

"I'll get you a change of clothes, and you can have a warm shower," Reese offers as I climb out of the pool, my only clothes now soaked.

"Thank you," I say. I shoot Ace a look that says I'll deal with him later.

When I descend the stairs in the Nirvana T-shirt and a pair of black leggings, Ace and Ellie are at the coffee table in front of the TV. They have set up a chess game, and Ellie seizes Ace's chess pieces without blinking. Ace isn't surprised, like this happens more often than not.

"Stay for dinner," Reese offers.

Ace makes his move, and Ellie grins at him before taking another one of his pieces. I glance at Ace to see if he heard his mom, and he gives me a look that conveys it's up to me.

"Yeah, I'd love to."

"I'll go get started." Reese heads toward the kitchen.

"I'll help you," I offer, leaving Ace and Ellie to play another round. Ace presents me with a heartfelt smile.

Reese asks me to wash and cut the vegetables while she prepares dough for the lasagna.

"I'm sorry," she says when we put the filling in between the lasagna sheets. She stops preparing the dish and wipes her hands on the ruby apron around her waist. "I'm sorry my son's actions have impacted you in a way I could never begin to imagine."

I look at her, puzzled for a moment, while she stares back at me with penitent eyes. It takes me a while to understand what she's apologizing for. "You know," I say, almost to myself.

She nods. "I was working at the hospital when they brought you in. You were unconscious. Not long after, Ace came rushing in," she recalls. Her eyes are distant, as if she's stuck in the memory of that night six years ago.

"He kept asking about a girl that was in a car accident. You were the only one that came in that night after a car crash."

The memories from that night are still clear as day, and the dull aching in my chest is something that will never fade when I remember it.

"He couldn't have known about a car accident unless he was there. I've had my suspicions since that night. I chose to remain ignorant, not wanting to believe it, but he told me the truth two years ago."

Ace didn't tell me he went to the hospital to look for me after the accident.

"I know he must have apologized to you, and I understand that nothing will ever make up for the consequences of his actions. But as his mother, I also carry the weight of his mistakes, and I'm deeply remorseful for the events of that night. There are days where I wonder if there was anything I could have done to prevent it. Any speech I could have given him about drunk driving that would have made him think twice about getting behind a wheel in his state."

I stare at Reese, unsure of what to say. I've been thrust into a conversation I wasn't ready for. Ace's mom knew of the accident from the start. But how can I even begin to condemn her for not saying anything, not taking any action? Her husband left without a trace, and her family was already broken. How could I expect a mother to go against her son, especially for a stranger?

"I'm forever indebted that you chose not to turn him in. His life would be very different right now if you had, and you had every right to. You still do."

Reese stands beside me. Her motherly eyes are bright and sorrowful.

"That wouldn't have achieved anything. He's remorseful. He hasn't touched a drop of alcohol since. He's going to live the rest of his life knowing what he did. I think that's punishment enough, but I know some people would disagree."

What would putting him in jail attain, apart from my own revenge? In a way, I've strayed against everything I was taught and taken the law into my own hands. They say love is an illness, and that statement couldn't be more accurate in this situation. It blinded me and shifted my morals.

"What's taking so long?" Ace wanders into the kitchen.

His sudden interruption startles me. Was he eavesdropping, or did he just happen to come in at the wrong moment?

"Are you over getting beaten by your nine-year-old sister?" his mother asks him, and I stifle a small laugh, still shocked by Reese's confession.

We eat dinner at the heavy table in the dining room. The lasagna is impressive. I'd ask for the recipe if I had the time to spend hours making dinner, but I usually don't spend more than fifteen minutes in the kitchen at a time. We have apple pie with vanilla ice cream for dessert while Ellie tells me about their trip to Disneyland earlier this year. It's so easy to pretend everything is okay in the hopes that one day it will be.

It's a little past eight when we say our goodbyes. I had to reassure Ellie I'll be back to see her.

Ace begins driving back in silence. I understand that Ace talks about things in his own time, so it's pointless to try until he's ready. He requires an interval to go over it in his head first. I guess we're similar that way.

We swap cars back to his Lamborghini, and I'm beginning to realize the need for privacy. For him and his family.

"Ellie got diagnosed with leukemia two years ago and went through treatment. She was in the maintenance stage. We thought it was over, but then she relapsed. This time it was more aggressive. She went through her last phase of treatment this week. The doctors say it's looking good, but it's killing me to see her like this." He grips the steering wheel. "Today was one of the good days."

Guilt consumes me. I should have been here for him, and if not for him, then for Ellie.

"I'm sorry." I place my hand on his, where it rests on the console between us. "I'm sorry I wasn't there for you and Ellie before."

Ace flips his palm, intertwining our fingers. "You don't need to apologize, Calla."

He turns into the basement and parks the car. I don't move, and neither does he. Being in Ace's company is soothing. When we're together, we drift through time and space without anything in our way. Only when we pull away do I realize how dangerous it is.

He draws me toward him, like the distance between us in the already small interior of this car is too significant. "Come here."

I glance at him like he's lost his mind. The car is not exactly spacious, and at first, I don't make an effort to move onto his lap like he wants me to.

"Calla."

I straddle him while he's in the driver's seat. He places his hands on my waist, bringing me closer. This car is not meant for this. We're so close together that I feel every rise of his chest.

The empty look in Ace's eyes affirms that he blames himself for this too. He blames himself for Ellie's sickness like it's some sort of punishment for his previous mistakes.

"It's not your fault." I bring his face up to look at me. His eyes are clearer than ever before, with speckles of blue through the iridescent green.

"Then why does it feel like it is? Why does it feel like I'm getting punished through Ellie?"

I don't have an answer for him. Maybe it is punishment. A merciless, heartless punishment that I wouldn't wish on anyone. Ellie doesn't deserve this. She's only a child. And Ace… I can't even begin to fathom what would happen to him if he lost Ellie.

"She'll get through this. She's strong, and she'll come out even stronger."

"What if—"

"She'll get through this," I repeat, because there's no other option worth considering.

Ace exhales a deep breath, and I'm not ready for the words I suspect are about to come out of his mouth.

"I need you."

Those three words seep into my heart like a sweet but pernicious tonic.

"I'll be here for you," I comfort him without thinking about the consequences. Without thinking about anything except how vulnerable Ace is at this moment.

No matter what we are or what we'll be, I care too much for

him just to leave again, especially when he needs me so much to stay. And I don't care if it will ruin me in the end. I guess I'll have to deal with that when the time comes.

He wraps his arms around me even tighter, and I rest my head on his shoulder, threading my hands through his hair.

"I can't even begin to explain what I'd do for you," he declares.

I can't shake the feelings he incites in me. He causes my heart to beat faster. He makes me dizzy with just his presence. But that's not what scares me the most—he makes me feel like everything is okay when nothing is. It never has been with us. Maybe I was trying to avoid this, trying to avoid Ace because seeing him and spending time with him brought back the feelings I've struggled so hard to forget.

Ace grasps my hand, not letting go as we go up to his apartment, and he tightens his grip when we ascend the stairs to his room. He removes the book with stars, and the bookshelf opens, revealing the secret door I saw previously.

Ace looks at me briefly, like confirming I'm still here, and then he turns to type in the code. He presses his thumb to the pad, and I assume it's another security measure, like the secret door and pin isn't enough to keep someone out. The tunnel of anxiety deepens inside me with each second.

This could go a few different ways. My mind churns all the things that could be behind the door, but nothing compares to what I find when it opens.

It's the same size as an average-sized walk-in closet, but everything about it screams illegal. Guns hang on the walls—lots of them, all different kinds. Pistols, shotguns, rifles, revolvers. On the floor near the back are bags with cash. It's like Ace has too much and doesn't know what to do with it all, so he threw it in here.

Scanning the room in shock, I then turn to Ace, who is watching me intently, like he's waiting for me to run. I'm thinking about it. *What is all this?*

I don't move and continue waiting for an explanation, worried that whatever he says will have the power to change everything.

"I own the biggest underground fighting clubs in the world."

14

Needing Her

Ace

A deafening ringing builds in my ears from Calla's silence. The dim-yellow light that shines from the ceiling casts a golden tinge on her smooth hair. I need her to say something. The silence is haunting me.

"For how long?" she finally asks. Her voice emerges steady, but my eyes land on her small, shaking hands. She keeps her distance from me. I hate every bit of it.

"Two years."

"Why?" she asks.

"I needed money for Ellie's treatment," I explain. I don't want to keep secrets from her. Not anymore. At least not this one. "After I moved to a different college, I didn't earn a lot of money from my fights because they stopped being illegal. I tried to get my life back on track. My mom worked long hours, but she could barely afford to pay the bills on her own. I gave her everything I had left after I paid my own bills."

Calla's big green eyes with speckles of gold throughout urge me to continue.

"There was a man that came to my fights, a friend of Dean's—his name was Marcus. He watched me for months. Finally, he approached me a week after Ellie got diagnosed." When I was at my lowest, when I would have agreed to just about anything. When Ellie's face was filled with so much fear and dread after the doctor told us she had cancer. Her life got turned upside down within the blink of an eye. There wasn't anything I could do to fix it.

"I didn't know what I was getting myself into. It probably wouldn't have mattered anyway. I would have done anything." I have crossed so many lines without a second thought, and I'd do it all over again for Ellie. For my family.

Calla pads over to me slowly, her expression smooth and indecipherable. I can usually read her like a book, but she's closed herself off, buried herself away from the monster standing in front of her. I've already ruined her life in more ways than one. It's a miracle she can stand to be around me. Maybe this is the final line.

I can't take my eyes off her. She runs her hands over the guns that hang on the walls, picking up the Desert Eagle 0.5 with a fitted silencer and turning it in her hand.

My favorite gun. I don't particularly have use for them, but there are precautions I must take. All the guns in this room are always loaded. Owning underground clubs comes with dire responsibilities.

I considered getting rid of the business, but some of the younger fighters are there for the same reasons I was. They either need the money, or they need a way to deal with their demons. Like I did. Dean offered me that opportunity—that escape. I'm here to offer it to them. If only it were that simple.

"And these? What's all this for?" she asks about the guns.

"It's not like the clubs I fought in back in college. A lot of money is involved, many debts need to be paid, and the people involved go to extreme measures to get what they want. Consider it a security measure I must take."

Calla runs her trembling fingers over the barrel as she takes time to consider my explanation. To assess whether she wants to stick around or whether this is all too much for her. I wouldn't blame her if she left. I'm not good for her, but it doesn't stop me from wanting her, needing her with every ounce of my body.

It's like the farther apart we were, the easier it got to convince myself it was for the best. Seeing her with Ellie and my mom today flicked a switch in me.

I'm so fucked up for forcing her to stay with me for two weeks, but I already knew that. I didn't see another way. I was desperate and acted in the heat of the moment.

The freckles on her face form constellations, and it's as if they are the only stars in the entire universe. Her chest rises and falls in a way that implies she's trying to calm her breathing.

Seconds feel like hours. I hate waiting, patience isn't my strong suit. If this were anyone else, I would have lost my shit by now. But for her, I'm prepared to wait as long as it takes.

She hangs the gun back on the rack and finally turns to me. I never wanted more with anyone. Not until I met her. I drop my gaze, anticipating the worst.

She moves closer toward me, and her entire existence prospers around me as she lifts her hand and rests it on my cheek, inviting me to look at her. I lift my head. Her eyes meet mine, and I almost drop to my knees.

"You did what you had to." *I understand*, she seems to say. "It was to support your family, Ace. Other people would have done the same."

I scoff. "I doubt they would have gone this far."

She shakes her head. "Probably not, but you did what you thought was right. You did *more* than other people would. I admire that about you. You don't think about the consequences *you* will face when it comes to the people that you love."

Fuck…at this moment, I know that it's her. It's always been her, and it always will be. There's no one else for me in this fucked-up world. She understands me more than anyone else will, understands the lengths I'd go to protect my family.

On instinct, my hand goes around her nape, and my thumb rests on her throat. Her skin is soft and radiant. I set my forehead to hers. "Calla," I say her name for no reason other than to hear it.

A delicate breath escapes her lips, and I can't resist her, she holds all the power over me. I pull her closer, and my lips connect with hers. Her mouth is gentle and sweet, like the vanilla ice cream from earlier, and the intensity of my longing for her deepens with each second. The smell of her, the taste of her, hypnotizes me beyond any reason.

She parts her lips, and I claim her mouth like there's nothing else worth savoring. Her body trembles against me as I slip my tongue inside her, my mouth working powerfully against hers.

Calla laces her hands in my hair as she clings to me. I groan low in my throat. She wraps her legs around me as I gather her in my arms and press her against the wall. Her lips are flushed pink and already swelling with need.

I trail my mouth down her jaw, down her throat, reacquainting myself with the feel of her skin against my mouth. I tug on her shirt, demanding to feel her bare skin. She understands and quickly removes it.

There's nothing underneath.

I trace the delicate line of her collarbone with the pad of my finger. She sucks in a breath, and her eyes follow my thorough movements, her dark lashes sweeping down. Her hair drapes like a curtain over her breasts, and I reach to tuck the strands behind her ear.

"Enticing," I murmur as I bow my head and capture one of her plump breasts in my mouth while I cup the other one in my hand. My eyes settle on that fucking tattoo, my mark on her—a memory in the form of an imprint.

I dart out my tongue, licking and sucking gently on her nipple, which hardens further in my mouth.

Calla moans, a gentle, artless sound. I love hearing her while I devour her. My cock strains against my pants, and I reach down to adjust it. She places her hands on my shoulders and tilts her head back, giving me access to all of her.

"Take your shirt off. Now," she commands. I obey with one hand while still pinning her to the wall with the rest of my body.

She trails her fingers up my chest and places her mouth on it, scattering kisses. Tugging on my waistband, she looks up at me. Pleading with me. Wanting me.

Fuck. "Not yet." Not tonight.

"Why?" She unwraps her legs from my torso, and I place her down.

"I need more time with you."

I must pay Jennifer one hundred thousand dollars for her new marketing campaign if I can't stick to our deal. I bet she's pulling that number out of her ass, but I don't give a shit, since I earn triple that in a day. Money isn't the problem. What will happen after the deal is over is. I need more fucking time. I need more time to prove myself to her. She's back in my life now, and there's no chance I'm letting her walk away without fighting for her. I learned my mistake.

"Then let me," she murmurs, puts her hands around my waistband, and pulls it toward herself. "Let me take care of *you*."

I swear my cock fucking twitches as anticipation fills me. Jesus fucking Christ. *Let me take care of you.* Does she know what those words do to me?

Calla pulls my pants down, and my hard dick springs out. She licks her full lips deliberately, keeping her expressive eyes on me, and I'm a goner. "Calla..."

Smiling, she drops to her knees in front of me and scrapes her teeth over her bottom lip. As soon as she wraps her hand around my pulsating cock, all my self-control dashes out the fucking window. My entire body shudders when she grips me tighter, accustoming herself to the size of me. The way she looks at me in her hands, as though she's starved for me, drives me feral.

Calla leans in and meticulously runs her tongue up the side of my cock, leaving me gleaming wet with her saliva. I buck my hips as the carnal pleasure surges through me, and pre-cum trickles from my head. A devious smile forms on her exquisite mouth, revealing that she's enjoying this just as much as I am. She skims her delicate tongue over the tip, followed by her lips like she's making out with it—expelling breathy moans.

With one hand, I grab the metal table behind me, and I use the other to trace my fingers over her jawline, struggling not to fuck her mouth, letting her set the pace on her own.

"Fuck," I groan and grind my teeth.

Inch by inch, she draws more of me in, leaving additional wetness along my entire length. My chest pumps rapidly as her hands twist on the base of my cock, and her head bobs down, taking as much as she can while her hands work the rest of me.

Where the fuck did she learn this?

"Look at me," I command.

She takes her mouth off me, looking up at me innocently while her hands continue stroking me, maintaining an exhilarating tempo. "I've been dying to do this. I love having you in my mouth," she declares and wraps her beautiful lips around me again.

Fuck, fuck, fuck.

No one's ever been able to finish me with their mouth, but two minutes with her, and I'm grappling with self-control, attempting to bid more time.

"I fucking love your mouth."

I fucking love you.

"Mm-hmm," she hums, propelling vibrations through me, and her silky tongue kneads the most sensitive spot on my shaft.

I groan, trying not to blow my load in her mouth after only two minutes. She keeps steady eye contact and focuses mainly on the tip, twirling her tongue against it.

Teasing.

Driving me fucking insane.

My entire body tenses.

I want to claim her in every way possible, ensure everyone knows she's mine. She's off fucking limits.

Calla takes me deeper into her mouth, gagging. I wrap my hands around her hair to keep it from her face, desiring to see her. Her wet lips slide over my veins, and she flicks her tongue over the ridges. All the blood in my body rushes to my balls, which she massages.

She rests her hands on the back of my thighs, her nails digging in my flesh, and tugs me closer, taking all of me. She looks up at me, finally permitting me to fuck her perfect mouth.

I attempt to be gentle at first, moving slowly, but with her hands on my thighs, she's sucking faster, and my thrusts become relentless. I grip her hair tightly, and she moans, encouraging me to continue.

"I'm going to come," I warn, but she doesn't stop.

She persists to deep throat me, her eyes watering and her cheeks hollowing like she's desperate for my release. Her tongue continues to massage the perfect spot, and my forehead dampens. A guttural groan escapes my throat, and I tilt my head back as I come down her throat.

She doesn't stop sucking me until she swallows every single drop. Her cheeks glow with color when she stands, and her lips are round and swollen.

Not wasting any time, I lift her and carry her to my bed, wanting to worship her all fucking night.

"Ace, I'm not expecting anything in return," she tells me when I place her on the bed near my headboard.

"I *want* to give you everything I can," I pledge as I prowl toward her.

I mean every word, and I hope she knows it's not limited to sexual favors. I will give her everything in more ways than one.

Beginning on her stomach, I trail wet kisses down her body, occasionally grazing my tongue across her bare skin, showing her what I'm capable of doing. Her eyes widen as she takes a ragged breath.

"Yes or no?" I tug on her pants.

"Yes."

That's all I need to hear. I pull her pants off and kiss her thighs, taking my time while I meticulously inch my fingers toward the inside of her legs. I lick her through the smooth material of her panties, tasting her.

She arches her back off the bed with a moan, raising her hips to my mouth.

"Greedy, are we?"

She sighs in response, causing me to chuckle at her impatience.

My cock grows again as I pull her flimsy panties aside and reveal the pink, waxed skin beneath them. A harsh groan builds in the back of my throat. She's absolutely flawless. Covering her clit with my mouth, I suck her, swirling my tongue against her sensitive skin as I observe the way her body responds.

She tastes so fucking tempting, better than any memory I have of her.

"Oh…Ace." She twists, trying to scoot up on the bed.

I grab her thighs, opening them wider and holding her in place. My tongue moves back, gliding over her soaking entrance, dipping inside, and appreciating the way her mouth marginally parts in pleasure.

Her hands locate their way into my hair, and she pulls at it. I missed the way they thread through it and tug when I skim my tongue over her delicate skin, the way she thrusts her hips into my face when she craves her release. I slide a finger inside her tight pussy and spread the slickness over her clit. She's responsive and needy, shimmering wet with arousal.

"Ace, please," she whimpers, begging me as she matches the thrusts of my fingers with her hips—brazenly fucking my hand.

"Please what, love?" I tease her, circling her clit with the tip of my tongue, not entirely giving her what she wants.

Before I realize what the fuck she's doing, she flips over and sits on my face, surprising me with her eagerness. I place my tongue on her and allow her to do the rest.

She clings to the headboard while riding my face, her perfect, round tits bouncing with every thrust. Witnessing her in control and taking what she wants from me is alluring. She swells, becomes hotter, and I grip her thighs in place with one hand as my tongue laps her folds while she's on the pursuit for her release. Then, gliding a finger inside of her, I begin pumping her to the rhythm of her thrusts.

Her body tenses and shakes as she cries out my name when the climax hits her. "Ace!"

I slow my pace, but I keep licking her, sensing her tremble around my tongue while holding her up by her waist.

15

Girl's Day

Calla

Ace makes me feel things I never thought existed, things I never believed in until I met him. But the more he makes me feel, the more inclined I am to pull away—to distance myself from him to safeguard myself.

His steady breathing fills my right ear, and he drapes his warm arm across my abdomen. I resist the urge to run my fingers through his soft, scruffy hair. The memory of tugging on it earlier is prominently embedded into my mind.

He sleeps peacefully, and I watch the precise movements of his chest. You wouldn't imagine he has a room full of weapons and is involved in something illegal.

I've lost count of how many times I lost myself beneath his touch last night and couldn't get enough. I craved more of him. I wanted him in every way possible, but he made it clear it wasn't going to happen. I wonder what deal he made with Jennifer to have this much self-control. I make a mental note to ask my boss what Ace will lose if he breaks it.

Ace's phone rings on the nightstand, disrupting my thoughts, and he groans, reaching for it, barely opening his eyes. He checks the caller ID before answering it. "Blackwell," he grumbles into the phone. His morning voice is more profound than usual.

A woman begins apologizing profusely. "Mr. Blackwell, I'm so sorry to call you so early. I have someone at the reception desk demanding to be let up."

"Who?" His tone is clipped, and I feel sorry for the person on the other side of the line.

"Her name is Mia. I told her you don't allow visitors unless they have been preapproved, but she demands—" the woman rambles, nervous of how Ace is going to react.

Ace moves the phone away from his ear and raises his eyebrows at me. I shrug, remembering Mia said she'd come over this morning to return my apartment key since she made her own copy. I glance at my phone. It's past ten in the morning. I'm not surprised we slept this long, since we didn't do much sleeping all night.

"Let her up." Ace hangs up without another word.

I make a move to get out of bed, but Ace tightens his grip around me. The white blanket covering his body has drifted down to his torso, only *just* concealing his crotch.

"I thought I'd have more time with you in my bed this morning," he murmurs in my ear, making his intentions *very* clear.

"Hmm, is that so?" I maintain my voice steady, even though I'm struggling to keep my breathing from accelerating.

"I can show you exactly what I had in mind, love." His fingers skim down my shoulder, delivering goose bumps in their wake.

"Mia is waiting," I say breathlessly. I search for the T-shirt that I wore last night before things got heated, but I don't recall where it ended up.

"We're leaving in a few days," Ace states with his hands behind his head, flaunting his biceps muscles.

"Leaving? For your fight?"

He nods. "Paris."

I reach for one of his button-up shirts and roll up the sleeves. It's white and comes up to my mid-thigh. Good enough.

"Paris," I repeat. I've never been to Paris.

Ace's gaze roams my body, and I don't miss the way his tongue grazes his teeth intentionally. The things that man can do with just his mouth are incredible.

"Done staring?" He smirks.

"Are you?" I counter, aware that his eyes haven't left me.

"No."

"Too bad." I leave his room, swaying my hips a little extra to tease him.

He inhales sharply, and I giggle without turning around.

I open the door to Mia standing in the doorway, she pulls me in for a hug. We haven't seen each other much over the last week, both of us have been busy. She's moved into my apartment and has been attending job interviews. She told me that trying to settle into one city after traveling for so long isn't easy.

"I can't believe you didn't put me on the guest list. Oh, and we'll talk about this later," she hums in my ear, and then gives me a knowing look.

"I didn't know there was one." I pull away and shut the door behind her as she continues into the kitchen. I should have known, since Ace likes his security. From his family to his illegal business activities, it's clear why he would want discretion.

I can't begin to imagine how someone with his status can be involved in something like that without the whole world finding out. But Ace is Ace. If he doesn't want people knowing, they won't.

The last one and a half years have proven exactly that.

"Are you busy today? I was thinking we can have a girls' day. Go shopping. Have lunch," Mia suggests, sinking into the seat at the kitchen counter.

I place a mug under the coffee machine and press a button. The hot liquid streams and fills the kitchen with a strong fragrance.

"Uh, I'm meant to shadow Ace at all times for the magazine."

"Take the day off. I have some errands to take care of." Ace stands to the side, already dressed in his business clothes—one of his many white button-down shirts and charcoal slacks with an immaculate tie to match. I didn't hear him come down the stairs, and I have no idea how he managed to get dressed this quickly.

He scans his phone screen as if reading something before pocketing it.

I raise my eyebrow at him. *What kind of errands?*

He doesn't answer my questioning gaze, but I'm guessing I know the gist of those errands since he doesn't want me accompanying him. Instead, he says, "Take your time. I won't be back till later."

We haven't thoroughly talked about what he revealed to me last night. I'm not even sure if I want to know the details. It's another secret I have to keep from everyone—from my dad. But I understand why Ace did what he did. I know he would go to extreme measures to protect the people he loves no matter what it costs him in the end. Wouldn't other people do the same for their families?

He's always been like that, and it's one of the many things about him that drew me in. Ace is selfless—a man who will take care of you no matter the consequences.

Ace retrieves his card from his wallet and drops it on the table in front of me. "Take it."

I open my mouth to tell him again that I don't need his money, but Mia reads my mind. She shoots me a look of disapproval and smiles at Ace. "She'd love to."

Ace grins. I narrow my eyes at both of them. Why is he so adamant I take his money? From a young age, my mom taught me to take care of myself, to never depend on a man for anything, especially money, and I've been building my career from scratch.

"Do you want to take my car or for Denzel to drive you?" Ace provides me with a choice. Very unlike him, it makes me feel like he finally understands he can't tell me what to do. However, I can't think of anything worse than driving an expensive car in New York traffic. So I go with Denzel.

I head upstairs to have a quick shower and get changed. Mia is waiting for me near the front door when I return. Ace is nowhere to be seen, but somehow, I can feel he hasn't left yet.

"Hold up. I'll just grab my bag," I call from the kitchen.

When I rush toward the front door, Mia is frozen in place. She slowly turns to me, and her face is flushed red, her eyes as wide as saucers.

I glance behind her to better look at what or *who* might be the cause of this. A broad smile spreads on my face. Standing in the doorway is a tall, well-built man wearing a dark-gray suit with a briefcase. He stares at Mia, dumbfounded. He looks like he did in college—brown hair and muddy coffee eyes, reminding me of a grizzly bear. Theo. Mia's college boyfriend and one of the few people who made college bearable for me, especially after Ace.

I've never seen Mia act this way and especially not for a man. If I didn't know her any better, I'd say she's flustered.

"Theo! Hey!" I try to diffuse whatever is going on between my best friend and her ex-lover. It's been years since I have last seen him, and by the looks of it, it's the same for Mia.

"Uh, Calla, hey." He glances at me and then back at Mia.

"We have to go. We'll be late for the appointment." Mia panics.

What appointment? What has gotten into her?

She forces me out the door. Her nails dig into my hand that she's clutching so hard I think she might leave permanent damage.

I turn back to glance at Theo, and I don't think he even notices me. He's too busy ogling Mia's lean legs, which look great in her black mini skirt.

"You never did tell me why you and Theo never worked out." I break the silence after Denzel has been driving for ten minutes.

"I'm not into men."

That's a lie. She doesn't meet my eyes and plays with the strap of her bag.

"Are you sure about that?" I convey her a look, saying I know that's not the case.

Mia has always been open about her sexuality, and she doesn't have preferences. She likes what she likes, and there's not much else to it.

"It wasn't the right time. I wanted to travel, and he wanted to focus on his internship," she explains, not bothering to elaborate further.

Another lie. I bet Theo would have dropped everything and followed her anywhere if she asked him to. It was clear from the way he looked at her. *Still* looks at her.

"Maybe now is the right time," I suggest.

"He's married."

"What?"

"Married, Calla. He's married," she pronounces *married* like she also can't believe it. I allow that to sink in for a moment. I want to ask her how she knows, but one glance in her direction tells me to drop it for now.

Denzel drives us to Fifth Avenue, as per Mia's orders.

We enter a store, and my eyes widen at the luxurious feel of it. I don't need to check the prices of the clothing to know everything is expensive. Too expensive.

"Have you not read Ace's file? You could buy this whole store, and I doubt it would even make a difference to his account." Mia searches for my size in everything I glimpse at, while I'm too afraid even to touch the clothes.

"Doesn't mean I should. I'm fine with Target."

She scowls in response, sliding the red lingerie I glanced at off the rack. I reach to take it from her. I certainly don't need it for that price. It's more than one of my paychecks, but she swats my arm away.

"Have you fucked him yet?"

Only Mia can go from one extreme to the other. "No, he's pretty set on the deal."

She rolls her eyes. "He's pretty set on *you*. He doesn't want you to leave."

"I already told him I wouldn't. At least not completely."

"Well, maybe the man has trust issues since the last time you said that you left him on his knees begging for you."

She's a little blunt after running into Theo this morning. Even though she's trying not to ruin the day, her mind is elsewhere.

"You had every right. I'm not saying you didn't," she adds.

It's a little past four in the afternoon when I'm on my way back to Ace's apartment with a car full of shopping bags. Mia asked Denzel to carry them for us when we couldn't hold any more on our arms. He was more than happy to oblige. He must get a very substantial paycheck.

I don't even want to know how much money we spent today—Ace's money. I can't explain why it makes me feel uncomfortable, but it does.

Mia avoided all conversation about Theo and was ready to gauge my eyes out when I called her out on still feeling something for him.

"He's a married man. Who do you take me for?" She glared at me, evidence that she does still have feelings for him.

I wonder if Ace is at the apartment or if he's still running his *errands*. I retrieve my phone to text him, but Nik's name pops up on the screen.

"Sweetheart, I need to talk to you."

✦ ✦ ✦

I'm in front of Nik's apartment door, shifting from foot to foot. My feet are a little sore from the heels I wore today and the endless walking from one store to another. I bite the inside of my cheek hard enough to taste blood. Another nervous gesture.

Nik said he wanted to see me, and it couldn't wait. He seemed nervous on the phone, something I'm not used to. Usually, he's calm and grounded, or at least, good at acting like it. The man is experienced at that since his job requires it.

The door swings open, and I absorb his outfit—a light-colored T-shirt and some drawstring sweatpants. His dark hair is swept back, and it's eerie to see him in ordinary clothes when he's usually in a suit or naked. Both states are equally as pleasing to look at.

"Nik, is everything okay?"

"Of course, sweetheart." He leans toward me and places a kiss on my cheek, his way of greeting. Although he's trying to compose himself, I notice his body's tautness and abrupt movements. Did something happen at work?

I was going to let him know we can't continue sleeping with each other, but perhaps this is not the time for it. The least I can do is listen to him.

He opens the door further, and I enter his apartment. My shoes click through the silence of the room. I've been here a few times, but I haven't stayed long enough to appreciate it. It's smaller than Ace's but still ten times the size of mine.

Nik turns to me. His blue eyes, like the remnants of a storm, pierce into mine. He cuts straight through the bullshit, a trait I have come to appreciate about him. "I can't do this anymore."

"Hmm? This…as in us sleeping together?" I ask, seeking clarification. If so, then this is the first man to break off our arrangement, and I'm totally fine with not being the one to do it.

He places his hand on his forehead, his thumb rubbing his temple. "I have feelings for you."

I freeze as my lungs twist with uneasiness, transmitting the feeling throughout my body.

"Nik—I…" I'm lost for words. This is the last thing I expected.

He seems to understand he caught me off guard and takes a step toward me. "Calla…"

I cut him off before this escalates any further. "I can't. You know that," I remind him. I've told him multiple times. I thought he understood.

"It's him, isn't it?" he asks, no emotion present in his voice.

Ace? Yes. No. It always has been him, but things always seem to get more complicated with him, too. Am I ready for that?

"I don't know." I shake my head.

It doesn't matter anyway. I don't have feelings for Nik, and I'm not going to lead him on. He deserves better. This thing we have needs to end now that I'm aware of his feelings.

"I can't give you what you want." I fiddle my fingers with the strap of my bag, holding eye contact with Nik. "God, I didn't even think you wanted that, Nik. You just came out of a relationship. I didn't think you'd want to jump into another one. What happened to finding out what you want?"

He walks toward me, and I refrain from taking a step backward even though my body impels me to do so. "I have. I want you. I want everything with you."

This has become a lot more complicated than I'd like it to be. "Where is all this coming from?" I don't recognize what has changed in the short time between the wedding and now. We were on the same page then, weren't we?

"I have liked you from the first time I saw you. I would have agreed to anything if it meant spending more time with you in hopes you would change your mind."

I'm left entirely blindsided by his revelation. I've spent more than two months sleeping with a man who has feelings for me. Sleeping with a man who hoped one day I could provide him with a relationship—something that I'm uncertain if I'll ever be ready for.

"I'm sorry, I don't feel the same way." It's cold and harsh, but it's the truth. And the truth is the only thing I'm able to offer him at this point.

He nods, a grim expression glazing his face. "I see."

My chest tightens with guilt. It makes it even worse that he's so understanding. There's nothing left to say, and the obstinate silence seeps from every direction. "I'm sorry. I should go," I say uncomfortably, and he gives another nod of his head.

Nik might be every woman's dream. Successful, handsome, and a gentleman. And yet, I can't force something that's not there, feelings that perhaps will never be there.

Approaching him, I brush my lips against his cheek before looking up at him. "Thank you for everything. You're an incredible man, and I hope you find someone that can give you what you're looking for."

"You, too, sweetheart. If you ever need anything, I'll always be here." He grasps my hand in his.

It's in this moment that his guard comes down, and I catch a glimpse of the pain behind it. I've broken it off with many men, but it never gets easier. It's never something I'll become accustomed to doing. I leave his apartment, close the door behind me, and lean against it.

Ace isn't home when I arrive. I busy myself with unpacking the bags of clothes I bought today, keeping my mind off Nik and his wounded expression. I try not to question if I did anything to give him the wrong idea. I made it clear from the start what we were, and he agreed. Where did it go wrong? Was it the wedding I decided to go to with him? The fundraiser?

I tread to Ace's room and lie on his bed, waiting for him. Without any distractions, I wonder if he's okay. My mind swirls with everything that could go wrong. Without a clue where he is and when he'll be back, I shut my eyes, unable to think about anything else. Grueling images envelop my defenseless mind.

Is it always like this with him? Finally, unable to bear any more worry, I grab my phone and call him. He answers on the first ring.

"Calla." His voice is steady and calm.

I emit a sigh of relief. "Ace," I breathe into the phone.

"Is everything okay?"

"Yes, I…" I feel stupid for calling him. He's been doing this for two years and doesn't need any distractions.

"I'm kind of in the middle of something, love." I hear a distant scuffle followed by a grunt of a man and then cursing. Is he fighting someone? "I'll be home soon. I hope I satisfied you enough last night so that you won't be inclined to seek it elsewhere."

He's busy but has the time to banter with me? I graze my bottom lip with my teeth. Did he give in last night because he thought I would pursue my needs with someone else if he didn't? "Let's hope so," I tease.

"Calla, I swear if you let another man touch you while you're staying with me, I'll make sure they never forget what it cost them."

I swallow loudly. "Jesus, Ace. Don't go caveman on me."

"I'm dead fucking serious. We'll discuss this later if you like. I have to go."

"Stay safe."

"Always.

The bed shifts, and I open my eyes. It takes me an extended moment to adjust to the darkness, but I recognize Ace is here from the smell of his shower gel. I squint my eyes open to glance at the time on the bedside table—it's past one in the morning. I must have fallen asleep waiting for him.

"Sorry for waking you."

I'm too tired to reply. "Mm-hmm," I hum, closing my eyes and finally drifting into a deep sleep, knowing Ace is here—safe with me.

✦✦✦

When I wake the following day, Ace isn't in bed, but I hear his voice, stern and cold. He's on the phone, and it's clear he's discussing business matters, either legal ones or something *else*. I'm not quite sure which. Does the man ever sleep?

"Deal with it," he snaps.

He enters the room with his business slacks already on but his chest bare. My gaze roams his body—his abs, his muscular chest, his tensed shoulders—until finally settling on his face. It reminds me of the sea on a stormy day, with murky shadows prowling under his eyes and the edges of his jaw sharp as lightning.

"If I knew you'd have that look on your face when you woke up, I would have stayed in bed." His voice is softer now, filled with a hint of impulse, and a smirk appears on his mouth.

"What look?"

"The look that makes me want to do very indecent things to you, Calla."

I roll my eyes. A little less than a week left with Ace, and he's still adamant about keeping his end of the deal. The man has more willpower than I've given him credit for.

The better half of the day is crammed with business meetings, some face-to-face, and some over the internet. I shadow Ace, observing the man that's skilled in more ways than I could have ever imagined. He's in his element, in control, sitting at his desk discussing a deal with investors in an online meeting, his final one of the day.

"Mr. Blackwell, I just wanted to inform you that we'll be proceeding to the final stage of the project next week. Unfortunately, we've been having issues with the approvals for the specifications of the program…" the man on the other side of the line speaks, his voice coming out gravelly from the laptop speakers.

"You said that last week. In fact, you *informed* us everything would be finalized today. I was hoping this meeting would bring pleasant news, but I'm afraid your company's time-management skills seem to be lacking. As a result, we're beginning to question whether you're a suitable fit for us." Ace's voice is calm but deadly.

I approach his desk and perch my ass on the edge of it, making sure the other people in the meeting can't see me. Ace's gaze falls on me, and he raises his eyebrows, questioning what I'm doing.

Trying to ease your stress, Ace.

"We're doing everything we can, Mr. Blackwell…we're not in charge of the approvals, but we're trying to push them through as quickly as possible."

I brush my foot against Ace's thigh, spreading my legs marginally, providing him with a glimpse of the white lace underwear I'm wearing underneath my skirt today.

Ace clears his throat before speaking, reluctantly tearing his eyes away from me. "You haven't notified us of any issues until just now. You sent an email last week, which pushed the date back without an explanation. I've been more than understanding, Blake, and gave you the benefit of the doubt. Companies are lining up for us, ready to provide us with a prompt turnaround, and nothing is stopping us from finding someone that's more…efficient."

Ace talking business is one of the hottest things I've ever seen—power surges off him in relentless waves. My foot lands on his pants, where he hardens against it. *Game on.* Ace wraps a hand around my ankle in warning, and I flash him an innocuous grin.

"You'll have to start the entire process from scratch. We have already completed most of the work. All I'm asking for is a week, at most, to get these approvals pushed through."

Ace's jaw clenches, whether it be from the frustration of the meeting or…other matters. "Three days. I hope there won't be any more delays. Your company is already breaching the terms of the agreement, and it would be a shame if I have to spend my valuable time in court and then in search of replacements because of your incompetence."

Without waiting for a reply, Ace shuts his laptop. His assertive eyes set on me. "Fuck, Calla. If you're trying to distract me, it worked."

"Good, you work too much. Is everything okay?"

"The project Theo, Josh, and I are collaborating on is taking longer than we accounted for." Ace shakes his head. "If we weren't already late, the things I would do to you right now…on this desk…" He grasps the tops of my thighs with both of his calloused hands, forcing them farther open to emphasize his point.

"What are we late for?" My voice is uneven as I focus on his rough hands on me and how my pulse increases tenfold.

Ace smiles. He knows why I'm trying to move my legs back together, but he doesn't allow me to. Instead, he brushes his thumb over my panties, coercing a small moan to tumble from my parted lips.

He chuckles and stands from his desk, leaving me hot and bothered, losing my own game again.

"We're going to stay at my mom's tonight," he says. "She's going out, and Ellie is going to have a movie night with a friend."

I pack a small bag for the night. The drive to his mom's house is quiet. I can see that something weighs on Ace's mind from how the line in between his eyes deepens. Working too much is going to kill him, and I wish I only meant it rhetorically. I don't know much about what Ace's other job entails, but I'm guessing there's no room for error in that field. One mistake can cost him everything.

"Thank you for coming. I've ordered pizza, and it should arrive soon. Ace, I've made dinner for you, it's on the middle shelf in the fridge," Reese tells us when we arrive. She looks at me and then at her son, and a smile shapes her face. She leaves shortly after.

Ellie and her friend, Bella, wear matching pink pajamas, and their hair is plaited the same way with a matching rose-gold clip on the side. "Calla, come see!" Ellie clasps my hand and drags me eagerly outside.

The backyard is transformed into a glamping wonderland. It's every nine-year-old's dream. A large screen is set up in the middle with white blankets and cushions all around. Fairy lights and pink bubblegum-scented candles hang from the broad trees, converting the backyard into something out of a fairy tale. To the side, two teepees rest on the clipped lawn. Ellie and Bella huddle together and discuss which movie they want to watch.

"You saw Nik yesterday," Ace states, his voice emerging harsher than usual. Perhaps a hint of jealousy present?

I begin to wonder how he knows, but the answer is clear. "Denzel." He's exceedingly loyal to Ace. I should've known he'd convey my whereabouts to the boss.

Ace nods.

I open my mouth to explain that Nik and I are done, that whatever it was we had is over, but the faint sound of the doorbell ringing interrupts me. Ace doesn't move to answer it, and the doorbell rings again.

"I'll get it," I say, guessing it's the pizza Reese ordered earlier. I rise, conveying Ace a look that says we'll have this conversation later.

I open the front door, prepared to take the pizza boxes, but in front of me is the man I've come to despise. He's the spitting image of Ace, but older and without tattoos.

Cocking his head to the side, he studies me for a moment. "You must be the nanny. Is my wife around?"

16

Daddy Issues

Ace

The famous saying goes, *if you want something done, do it yourself,* and it couldn't be more accurate. It's challenging not to have direct strings to the underground fighting business. I employ other people to take care of it, especially when it comes with significant responsibilities, but some of my employees can't follow simple instructions. How hard is it to retrieve information from someone? Cops showed up at the last fight, which means someone must have ratted, since the locations aren't announced until the day of the fight. I have my theories—one of them is Logan.

I head inside to check what's taking Calla so long to get the pizza and instantly hear her voice.

"Wrong house." Her voice is too calm, the way it is when she's anything but. The anger radiates off her, and I'm not even near her yet. Whoever is on the other side of the threshold better start running the other way.

I round the corner and notice her closing the door with urgency, a hand grips it and forces it back open. I'm going to break that fucking hand, and I'll find pleasure in doing it.

"I don't think so, darling," a man says. It's a voice I've hoped I'd never hear again.

I clear my throat. Calla turns her head toward me with a panicked look. Her eyes are my favorite color, light golden brown, like warm honey with a hint of springtime green.

"Ace, my boy, you're here," my *dad* says. My fucking father. A pathetic excuse of a human being. What the fuck is he doing here?

My hand twitches and forms a fist at my side. I have the urge to knock his teeth out, preferably one by one.

Calla observes me cautiously, like she doesn't know how I'm going to react. A soft brush of her fingers against my hand makes me assess the situation, and I flatten my fist against the side of my thigh. The man in front of me obliterates everything that comes before him. He's fucked up my family in more ways than one. I'm not going to let it happen again.

Wearing a gray button-up shirt and a pair of trousers, he leans on the doorframe. Gray hair scatters through his dark curls, and he looks ten years older than his actual age. He's usually put together, but standing in the doorway, he seems weakened. The arrogant look on his face hasn't diminished, which gives me more reason to want to get rid of it and him.

Not in front of Calla. I won't lose my temper in front of her. Instead, I smile at my father. I'm good at the smart-ass act, too. Pissing people off with my words occurs intuitively.

"I thought the next time I'd see you would be in the realms of Satan."

"That's no way to talk to your father." He gives me a disapproving look, the way he used to when I was young and did something to displease him.

I scoff and clench my fists at my sides again, hard enough that they begin to shake. Most things I did displeased him, like going out with my friends instead of putting effort into my schoolwork. My father always wanted a son to follow in his footsteps, to become a lawyer just like him. But after I witnessed what that entailed and what kind of man it forced my father to become, I wanted no part in it. The turning point was when I told him I wanted nothing to do with it. After that day, I was no longer his son. He made that abundantly clear.

Calla's arm brushes lightly against my own again, and I know it isn't accidental. She's telling me she's here for me. Her touch causes me to take a second to calm down, to see reason.

"I got this," I finally say once I believe I'm not going to do anything stupid. But what I mean is for her to watch Ellie and Bella.

She understands. She always fucking understands. She gives me a nod before turning on her heel and heading toward the back door.

"What the fuck are you doing here?" I growl, keeping my voice low so the girls don't hear. I can't have Ellie coming in here. If it weren't for the photos on the walls, I doubt she'd even recognize him. Mom told her he's gone. I bet she thinks he's dead or something. I want to keep it that way, since she's better off without him. We all are. It's not as though he's ever made an effort to contact her, and today isn't the day, either. There's always an ulterior motive with him. Give it two minutes, tops, and the bastard will reveal it.

"Can't an old man visit his family?" His voice emerges raspy. The alcohol on his breath percolates through the air, and his bloodshot eyes indicate that isn't the only thing in his system.

He's high as a fucking kite.

"You don't have a family here. I thought I made that clear the last time I saw you." Every word comes out ragged, the anger is brewing inside of me like a summer storm.

The last time I saw him was one year ago when he came requesting money. I gave it to him to make him disappear. I didn't need more problems, especially when Ellie was at her worst, and I knew he'd use my mom and Ellie to get to me.

We're outside on the driveway now, with the darkness upon us.

"I need money."

Straight to the point. I figured that's why he was here. Where the fuck did the two hundred thousand go?

A cruel laugh emanates from my mouth. "Why don't you ask your son." I spit the words at him, especially the last one. His *other* son—the only son that matters to him. But he won't, because he wants to act like the perfect father figure to one while showing his true fucking colors to the other.

A duplicitous smile crosses his face. He isn't aware that I know about my half brother. We all have secrets. Some of us are just better at hiding them. "You know—" he sucks on his tooth, "—you two would get along."

We don't. "Next time you come here, you *will* regret it," I drawl the words, making sure he grasps the promise I'm making.

"Are you threatening a lawyer, boy?"

"You lost your license to practice six months ago," I state with a feral grin. I know, because I made it happen. It was too easy.

He examines me, piecing the puzzle together. "Come on, *Dad.* I thought you would have realized sooner."

The look on his face is invaluable, but he composes himself rather quickly. "Do me a favor, son? Give me the number of the nanny. She seems like a good sort."

It takes me a moment to register what the fuck he just said. A moment to understand who he's referring to. And once I do, the restraint I had two seconds ago vanishes into thin air.

My hand retracts while simultaneously forming a first. It collides with his jaw.

Once.

Twice.

Three fucking times.

Quick but brutal—just how I like it.

"She said fuck off," I spit and leave him on the sidewalk, knowing he won't be stupid enough to come near the front door again. At least not tonight.

I'll have to get security to guard the house around the clock from now on. Who knows what the fuck this piece of shit has gotten involved in. And he'd come here to get to me, to get more money out of me. I'm not giving him another cent.

As if on cue, the pizza man pulls into the driveway. A scrawny-looking guy gets out of the car, his eyes widen as the scene unfolds in front of him. He hands me the pizzas with shaking hands.

"Thanks," I grumble and give him a hundred-dollar tip. I stride inside, adrenaline still propelling through me.

Calla is distracting the girls. A Disney movie plays in the background while she brushes the braids out of their hair. She laughs at something Ellie says. The sound is soft but melodious and has the power to bring any man to their knees. How I survived four years without her is still a mystery to me.

"Pizza is here."

Three heads turn toward me. Calla meets my eyes and then looks at my hand, the knuckles on my right hand are busted. She stands, takes the pizza boxes from me, and sets them up on the blanket in front of the screen.

I sit farther away in an attempt to get my head in a suitable space before going over there. My blood is still simmering with anger. He'll keep coming back, if not now, then later. I need to do something about him. There's no chance I'm letting him near my mom or Ellie. Or Calla.

Calla makes her way over and takes my hand in hers, examining the damage. I watch her. She's silent for a moment, but I can hear her thoughts running through her mind. Her fingers are velvety, and she traces my knuckles, barely touching them, like she's afraid she'll hurt me.

A strand of wavy dark hair falls, masking the right side of her face. I reach for it, tucking it behind her ear. She finally lifts her head and searches my face. She's so fucking beautiful.

"Nothing happened with Nik yesterday."

Nik. Another problem. In more ways than one.

I have his phone tapped, every call, every text. It's all tracked. Someone's messing with my business, and I have an uncanny feeling it's him. Something about that fucker seems off, but I have no evidence yet.

Fucking lawyers.

"Nothing happened?" I ask.

I'm ecstatic nothing happened between them. I don't know how I let him put his hands on her for so long, how I let anyone put their hands on her.

She shakes her head, a smile emerging on her bow-shaped lips. I can't help myself, I lean forward and press my lips to hers. It's brief but says everything that needs to be said.

"Don't let it get to your head," she says when she pulls away, glimpsing over at Ellie and Bella. They are too engrossed with themselves and the movie to notice what's going on.

I can't wipe the stupid grin off my face. "Never, love."

We sit behind the girls and watch the movie they picked. I zone out for most of it, thinking about how that piece of shit had the nerve to come here. What if I hadn't been here?

"Ace," Calla begins. "Did you have contact with your father previously?"

I glance at the girls, confirming they're still immersed in the movie before answering. "He came back asking for money a year ago."

"Did you give it to him?

"I had to. It was the only way to get rid of him without eliminating the problem altogether." I grit my teeth. "I don't want him anywhere Ellie or my mom."

"Has he ever…" She sucks in a breath, and I know what she's going to ask. "Has he ever laid a hand on you?"

I stare straight ahead, not meeting her inquisitive stare. "Twice. The first time was when I told him I wasn't going to be a lawyer. The second time was the night he left."

Both of those memories are clear as day.

17

Paris

Calla

Have you ever thought that maybe everything is destined to happen the way it does? Perhaps I was meant to be shattered into a million glass shards and then forced to locate every fragment. Perhaps I was meant to meet Ace four years ago and run into him again in the future. Is everything predetermined by preceding events? Or is *fate* just a redundant word that we use to cast meaning into unlikely coincidences?

I can't help but wonder if and how there'll ever be a normal with Ace. Can I overlook everything? It's not just the past that's haunting us now—it's the future and what it contains. Will I ever be able to introduce him to my father, knowing that if my dad knew the truth, he would feel betrayed for more reasons than one? Telling him the entire truth won't help anyone. How would that conversation go down? *Hey, Dad, I met a guy. He runs illegal underground fighting clubs, and he's the one who caused Mom's crash. Oh, and I have kept this from you for the last four years.*

It doesn't sound good. And if it doesn't give my dad a heart attack, there's a good chance he'll go into permanent shock.

"I need to get a few things from my apartment," I tell Ace when we drive back from his mom's house the following day. He didn't mention his father making an appearance to his mom this morning, and I doubt he will. "And I need to check up on Betty," I add.

"I'll take you there." His eyes are on the road ahead, but his thoughts are elsewhere.

"The lady next door," I remind him who Betty is.

He cocks his head, and an amused smile crosses his face. Most likely remembering how he almost got swiped with her baseball bat.

My phone rings with a number I don't recognize, catching me off guard. I answer reluctantly.

"Hello, Miss Maven?" a male voice says on the other line.

"Yes?"

"My name is Timothy Kline. I'm from *The New York Times*. Nik passed me your number, and I'm calling to organize a time for us to meet."

Even though I've been aware that this call would come, I had my doubts, especially after how things ended between Nik and me.

"Thank you for calling and agreeing to see me."

"Nik is a good judge of character, and if he says you're the person we need, I trust him."

I feel even worse about the situation with Nik. Why couldn't he be an asshole instead of a gentleman?

"How about next week? Say Wednesday, two o'clock?" Timothy suggests.

It grants me time to prepare, and the two weeks with Ace would be over by then. My life will hopefully have returned to reality, whatever that is. "That's perfect. I'll see you then."

Ace raises his eyebrows as if to ask what that was about when I end the call.

"Nik helped get me a meeting with someone from *The Times*."

"A meeting?" Ace scoffs under his breath. "I could get you a job offer."

I narrow my eyes. "You're not going to."

Ace pulls up near my apartment building. He turns to me with the engine still running. His eyes are brighter today. I'm guessing last night was the first night he slept adequately.

"Why? Why can't you let me do things for you?" But I know he's asking why I let Nik and won't let him.

It's not like that. It's really not. "A meeting is one thing. I want to know that if I get this job, it's because of me. Not because of a man, not because of someone else."

I have no doubts Ace could pull some strings. The man can do anything. But being put on a pedestal is one thing, while being given a free ride into the top company is another.

"Calla—"

"Promise me you won't get involved with this." I can't let him meddle with my career any more than he already has. I don't want a free ride. I never have.

He doesn't appear thrilled by my request but mutters something along the lines of, "Fine."

"I have some things to take care of. Denzel is on his way," Ace tells me.

I get out of the car and progress around to his side. His window is already down.

"Will you be out late?" I crane my head to face him, worried about what kind of *business* he will be taking care of. Has it got something to do with his father?

"I will try to be quick for *you*." Ace winks and stretches out, placing his lips to mine, surprising me by the gesture.

His lips are warm, and I part mine to allow his fiery tongue to slip inside. I clasp my hands on either side of his face, getting lost in the moment. Warmth blossoms in my chest, my core tightens, and I withdraw before I get carried away.

Ace grins widely and presses his foot on the gas, taking off down the street.

I roll my eyes with a smile on my face as I make my way toward the building entrance. There are times like these where he acts like such a boy. However, I'm quickly reminded that *boy* is the wrong word for Ace.

I unlock the front door to my apartment. Mia, dressed in a baby-pink dress that matches her bangs, sits stiffly on the sofa. She glances behind her to the bathroom door.

With a guilty look, she presses her lips together before mumbling, "Theo is here."

"What?!"

"Shh." Her gaze darts to the bathroom again, where there's the sound of water running in the sink. "Theo wanted to talk, but I didn't answer his phone calls. Ace told him I was staying here. I'm going to kick his ass," she hisses.

"I'd love to see that."

She sneers, her eyes twinkling at my words.

Before I have the chance to ask anything else, Theo emerges from the bathroom. He's wearing jeans with suspenders and a striped, blue T-shirt that outlines his broad frame.

"Theo," I greet.

His eyes widen, and then his mouth forms into a goofy grin. "Hey, Calla! Good to see you. Nice apartment," he rambles.

"Thank you," I reply, although "nice" isn't the appropriate word to describe it.

I glance from Theo to Mia. Well, this is highly uncomfortable. I've walked in on something I shouldn't have in my own apartment. "You two…continue." I wink at Mia. She glares at me before I slip out.

I head over to Betty's apartment. She opens the door and begins informing me about the last couple of days.

"Is there anything you need?" I ask her, remembering she had some prescriptions she needed to fill. "Groceries, medicine?"

"No, dear, the gentleman is doing just fine."

"The gentleman?"

"Tall and dark, calls himself Denzel."

"Oh, I see." This is Ace's doing. I say my goodbyes to Betty, informing her I'll be back in my apartment next week.

Denzel waits for me downstairs in the Mercedes. "Why have you checked up on Betty?" I question as I slide into the back seat.

"I do what the boss tells me to," Denzel states as if it's that simple. I'm afraid to ask how far he'd go for his boss.

It's a breezy afternoon, and there isn't a cloud in the sky. I can't help but think about Mia and Theo. So I decide to text her.

Me: *Tell me everything.*

Mia: *He's still here. We're going to dinner.*

Mia: *Apparently there's too much to explain without a drink.*

I shoot her another text, advising her to keep me updated and toss the phone back into my bag. Denzel drives through the underground parking that provides direct access to Ace's penthouse without going through the lobby.

I step into the apartment at the same time Ace descends the stairs fresh from a shower. I didn't expect him to be here. My eyes land on the black designer suitcase near the entryway. "We're leaving tonight?"

He nods, assessing my reaction to the news. I didn't think it would be this soon. He loves his surprises, doesn't he?

"How long are we going for?" I ask, needing to know how much to pack.

"We'll be back on Tuesday."

"Okay, I'll go pack."

A smile surfaces on his mouth. "I have a couple of emails to reply to before we go. We'll leave in an hour."

When I enter the room, there's a suitcase like Ace's, but red, near the wardrobe. I run my fingers over it. All of this is so surreal—spending time with Ace, accompanying him on trips. We're playing with limited time—we both know it.

How will everything be after this is over?

I pack the suitcase, stuffing it with all the clothes I have here. It doesn't even fill it, but I doubt we'll have time to stop at my apartment again. So this will have to do for a few days.

After a quick shower, I text Mia explaining everything.

Ace drives us to the airport in his G-Wagon. He has his window down and leans his elbow on it while holding the steering wheel with the same hand. His other hand rests on my thigh.

It shouldn't make me feel the way it does—giddy and excited. It's as though I've known Ace all my life, when in reality, I've spent less than five months with him in the last four years. I guess the quantity of time doesn't matter, because there's always been a sense of familiarity between us that I've never had with anyone else.

I'm not sure what I expected, but a private jet wasn't it. Behind the dark-gray plane is the ferociously red sunset, causing the sky to appear on fire.

We're on our way to Paris. And it's meant to be the city of love.

I guess I find modes of transport more comforting than my bed. I sleep the whole way to Paris. Seven hours, perhaps a record time for me.

Denzel, who I didn't even notice on the private jet, is already expecting us when we get off the plane. He's standing near a Bentley in his usual navy suit.

As we drive to our hotel, I gaze out the window in awe. I've never been to France before.

The narrow streets stretch in front of us without distinct lanes, and the sturdy buildings on either side contain intricate details that are utterly picturesque. Denzel knows how to navigate through the unfamiliar roads without the need for directions, an indication this isn't his first time here. Pedestrians step off the paved curbs without looking for oncoming traffic, causing Denzel to slam on the brakes frequently. We follow the cars in front of us in a steady stream, and I marvel at the sophisticated architecture. At the same time, my legs crave to step onto the cobblestone sidewalks and explore the hidden café's, the local life, and the popular tourist attractions.

Ace is next to me, one hand on my knee, the other scrolling on his phone through an endless amount of emails. Dark circles blossom under his eyes, making it obvious he's barely had any sleep on the way here. He needs an assistant. The amount of work he does in a day is extraordinary.

"This is not your first time," I observe.

He pockets his phone and looks at me before answering. His bright eyes have more green to them than usual today. "I come here now and then for business."

"You've never come here for leisure?"

He shakes his head. "Some projects required me to stay here for a few days or a week, but I've always been occupied with business."

It's afternoon by the time we check into the hotel. It's beyond extravagant. I didn't expect anything less with Ace. The place has a modern feel to it, even though the exterior architecture is ancient. Our room is on the highest level and opens onto a balcony with a daybed and a fantastic view of the Eiffel Tower. I linger by the window, gazing out in admiration. I'm in Paris with a man, and not just any man.

I'm in Paris with Ace.

Ace stands beside me, his presence igniting a thrill within me. "There's an event tonight."

"Hmm? What kind of event?" I question, unable to get enough of the view. Ace has made himself comfortable by taking half of his clothes off.

"Fundraiser. Well-known and reputable business associates are going to be there. It's also part of the publicity surrounding the fight tomorrow. So my presence is required." He steps closer toward me. "Go with me."

"Are you asking or demanding, Ace?" I turn and raise my brows.

A playful smile matures on his mouth, and my eyes instantly dart to it. "Did it sound like a question? Because if it did, perhaps I have to rephrase it."

I shake my head at his cockiness, and even though I hate to admit it, the authority in his tone renders me weak at the knees.

"I don't have anything to wear." I brought dresses with me, just nothing to attend something like *that*. If it's anything like the one Nik took me to, it's going to be considerably over the top.

He smirks, appearing pleased with himself, like he was hoping I'd say that. "I have a dress for you."

Of course he does. I've always adored when a man takes control. It's contradictory, since I also can't stand a man who tells me what to do. But there's a time and a place. Or maybe it's just Ace.

As if on cue, there's a knock at the door, and Ace unlocks it, revealing Denzel with two garment bags. One with a suit and the other with a dress, I assume.

Ace takes them and drapes them over a chair to the side. "Hungry?" he asks, and without waiting for a response, he picks up the phone to order room service.

He never fails to surprise me. However, never in a million years did I expect him to start speaking French while ordering room service for us. My mouth drops open. Is there anything this man can't do?

I never imagined he could become any more attractive, and I know his mouth is a gift from above that can do unholy acts. I'm almost embarrassed to admit what I want to do to him right now while he's ordering freaking croissants. Squeezing my thighs together and hoping the aching tension will pass, I force my thoughts to drift elsewhere.

"You speak French?" I question as soon as he gets off the phone.

"I've learned some phrases here and there." He shrugs it off like it's nothing. That wasn't a few phrases—it was the whole damn menu.

Room service arrives within twenty minutes. Fresh baguettes, croissants, seasonal fruit, and cheeses. My stomach grumbles as I carry the tray onto the balcony where a dainty table stands. Ace settles across from me. His lofty figure is almost twice the size of the wooden chair.

"What will this fundraiser be like? Will there be lots of people?" I sink my teeth into the buttery croissant as I wait for Ace to answer. The rich taste of it explodes in my mouth.

He reaches for the baguette. "More than there were at the last one," Ace replies. "Perhaps we can go as a couple."

I cough, the crumbs of the croissant heading down the wrong way. "A couple?"

"I realize I have a reputation when it comes to…entertaining women. I don't want anyone thinking it's what I'm doing here," he adds, motioning his hand between us.

"You don't seem the type to care what people think." I swallow before looking at Ace, and I notice he's watching me. His expression is acutely thoughtful as if he's expecting me to shut him down immediately.

"I don't, but *you* do."

"So you want to go to the fundraiser and pretend to be an official couple? With me as your girlfriend? Won't people talk?"

"They always talk, Calla. It's either they talk about this, or they find something else. It's always good to be in control of the media."

I take another bite of the croissant while thinking about it. It now tastes too dry. *Girlfriend. Couple*. The words feel distant to me. They are everything I've been endeavoring to escape for the last four years. I know my dad doesn't follow this type of news, so there's a limited chance he'd see anything. But there are other things to consider. How would it affect my career?

"Tell me what you're thinking," Ace prompts.

"I'm thinking about how this will impact my job. I'm meant to be getting insight on you, not cozying up. Do you know how that will look?"

"Jennifer will know it's for the media, especially at an event like this. Think about how the public will react to a magazine article about me straight from the mouth of *my girlfriend*? I don't think you should be worried about Jennifer."

Ace has a point, yet the uncertainty lingers. We're taking things too far, too fast. We're pretending, but even that is dangerous territory. And every day with Ace feels like a candle burning beneath my skin.

"You don't have to agree to this. Just tell me I'm stepping out of line, and I'll drop it."

But even though the doubts continue to loiter, I recognize this will be good for Ace. It will take the prying eyes farther away from his family, farther from the things he's trying to hide. However, he doesn't want to hide me from his public life. I'm unsure if that's a good thing or not. He seems to conceal everything he cares about.

I'm overthinking again. "No, you're right. We'll go as a couple."

Ace cocks his head, observing me, looking like he's trying to understand what's running through my head, but even I'm unsure of how I feel about this. It's not a big deal, I attempt to convince myself.

We finish eating in silence and begin getting ready.

I'm thankful I brought a curler with me. My hair falls in waves, but I accentuate them with the help of a curling wand.

The dress is beautiful, and the honeyed fabric licks against my skin. It's red, for apparent reasons. I wonder if Ace was infatuated with the color before I accidentally sent him the lingerie picture back in college. Or was that the turning point?

With floral embellishments all over and tiny diamanté's scattered over the material, this dress fits me like a tight glove. The front is a straight cut made of a mesh material, dipping moderately into the curves of my chest. It covers everything that needs to be covered, but it still has a sensual feel to it.

"Zip me up?" I ask. Ace wears a white button-up shirt that's still unbuttoned and dark-gray trousers with his feet still bare.

My gaze skims over the red tie loosely dangling around his neck. It matches my dress impeccably. His suit jacket hangs on the back of the dining room chair. Ace shuffles toward me, and I sweep my hair to the front so he can zip my dress. His fingers dust my bare skin, electrifying me.

I wonder whether it's the sexual tension between us that's been building for too long or the fact we're in Paris. Whatever this thing between us is—it's unbearable.

He slides his hands to my waist, and I lean into his chest. We're facing the rooftop, where the sun is setting in incredible vibrant scarlet hues. The Eiffel Tower is visible—the lights have already been turned on and are sparkling in the distance.

Ace's hands travel from my waist to my hips. He leans into me, his breath warm against my neck. "The dress is beautiful, but all I can think about is you out of it."

My breath hitches in my throat, and I steady it. How can he make me feel like this with words alone?

He chuckles, obviously knowing he'd get a reaction out of me.

Oh, Ace, how the tables are about to turn.

Ace buttons his shirt up and fixes his tie. I steal glimpses as his muscles strain with each movement. Beneath the red dress, I have a corresponding red lace garter belt that extends just above my thighs. It's unnoticeable unless you know it's there, and I plan to make sure Ace is paying thorough attention.

I set my leg on the chair to buckle my strappy nude heels. I take my time with them, skating the dress to the side to reveal a glimpse of the seductive lingerie.

In my peripheral vision, I see Ace turning to me, and I allow his menacing gaze to linger for several heartbeats.

I gradually turn my head, and our eyes unite. Heat fosters inside me, flowing with an aching hunger. I wore this for *him,* and he damn well knows it. My intentions are exceedingly obvious. His expression falters into something insatiable, only for a second, and then he composes himself.

"Ready?" Ace offers me his hand, blatantly ignoring what I revealed.

He leads me out of the apartment toward the elevators. A red Porsche is parked outside the building near the front entrance.

"I think it matches your dress, yes?" Ace asks and smiles, the shadow of a small dimple peeking through.

"Ace Blackwell is coordinating with his date. Who would have thought?"

"Only for you, love." He opens the car door for me. I climb inside, careful not to muss the fabric of my dress.

From my dress to his tie and now the car, Ace has gone all out. It's easy to forget that this is my job. I'm getting paid to be here and spend time with Ace. I try not to think about what will happen once all this is over, but it keeps dangling at the back of my mind, haunting my thoughts from time to time. Whatever this is between Ace and me, it's too good. We're not facing reality. We're just brushing everything to the side to deal with later. I'm dreading later.

"How did you get so involved with the fighting clubs? You said a man called Marcus approached you, but how did you get from there to running them?" I probe as we drive.

A second is a whole hour when I watch the way Ace's hands tighten and then relax on the steering wheel. It's as though he's considering what to tell me. He told me about the underground clubs, but I bet it's only the tip of the iceberg.

Finally, he exhales. "Marcus sought me out because he had a

terminal illness. He didn't trust his daughter to take over. She's careless and self-absorbed, too young and not ready for this… lifestyle."

"But you are?" I interrupt.

His shoulders tighten. "It's more than that. I needed the money, and Marcus knew I was desperate. So he taught me the ins and outs and left me in control of everything. The only catch is I have to give fifty percent of the revenue to his daughter."

"But you don't need the money now, do you? Why are you still involved?" I try to understand the situation better.

"Some of the guys there are in the same position I was in back in college."

"So you feel responsible for them? Even though they don't know who's behind this?"

"I guess. It's not only that. Do you think people who know I'm involved in this will let me walk away? Take Marcus's daughter as an example. She's getting a weekly income without putting her ass on the line, and there are others like her. Not many, but a few. If I choose to walk away, how long do you think it will take them to want vengeance on someone like me? They think I have everything. If this all falls, I'll be the first person held accountable."

I allow that to sink in. Ace couldn't walk away if he wanted to. Is that what he's saying? And if so, where do we go from here?

My mind is everywhere as we arrive. I meant it when I said I'm not going to leave again, but what are my options in this situation? I never thought I'd want stability until now. Not knowing where Ace is most nights and thinking about if and when everything will collapse isn't how I want my future to be. Once again, I sweep the thoughts to the back of my mind, not wanting to deal with them until we return from this trip.

There's a wide red carpet flowing toward the building entrance, where colossal vintage double doors open. The paparazzi are snapping shots of everyone who enters, coercing the guests to twist their bodies a certain way for the perfect picture. How big is this event? There's no doubt in my mind that my photograph will be in the magazines tomorrow, but I'm optimistic it won't be the front cover.

Ace notices my reluctance and squeezes my hand before getting out of the driver's side. I open my door, and Ace is already there. He extends his hand for me to take. It gives me the consolation I didn't think I needed. We make our way inside, briefly pausing for our picture to be taken.

The interior is already crowded with men in suits and women in beautiful dresses. My eyes widen at how many people I recognize, some of them well-known celebrities.

Ace leads us to a group of gentlemen standing near a table. They are significantly older and emit a powerful atmosphere.

I figure Ace must be well acquainted with them. "This is my girlfriend, Calla," Ace introduces me after greeting them.

Even though we agreed to this, I'm still shocked when he comes right out and says it. I offer my greetings, and they dive into a conversation about business. The gentlemen own a successful technology company, and Ace has been working on a project they seem to hold interest in.

Once everyone has arrived, we take our seats for dinner. Ace and I sit at a table with the gentlemen and the women who I presume are their wives. A waiter brings glasses of champagne over, placing them on the table in front of us. Somehow, I manage to turn and knock Ace's untouched glass with my elbow, spilling the drink over Ace's pants.

I gasp. "I'm so sorry." I grab the napkin in front of me and dab his pants with it. It's a good thing no one's paying attention to us.

"Calla, it's fine."

God, how much did this suit even cost? And I've ruined it with my clumsiness.

"Calla…" Ace warns, placing his hand on top of mine to halt my actions. His voice is hoarse, and I lift my head. He clears his throat. "It's fine."

I press my lips together, suppressing a smile after noticing the swelling in his pants and realizing what I've been doing. We have a long night ahead of us.

For dinner, there's a variety of dishes served. Salmon timbales, fondant potatoes, duck confit with red-currant sauce, and for dessert—a salted caramel mille-feuille, which is layers of buttery pastry combined with caramel custard. I take small portions of everything, wanting to try all the dishes.

There are speeches made toward the end of the meal, and the host thanks everyone for their donations.

"Would you like to dance?" Ace offers.

I look at him like he's insane. "No one is dancing."

"They will if someone takes the lead." He extends his hand, urging me to take it.

The expression on his face is light and wholehearted as I lift my fingers to his palm. He leads us to the middle of the dance floor. A band performs to the side, and the music streams softly. It fits in with the event's theme and allows the conversation to flow smoothly throughout without people having to yell over the music.

I case my hands around Ace's shoulders while his proceed around my waist, and he draws me closer to his chest. We fall in step with the song. I let Ace take the lead, and he permits the tempo to control his movements.

"Everyone is watching," I whisper, glancing around us.

He tips my chin, soliciting my attention, and his hand brushes across my cheek. I tear my gaze from the hundreds of eyes and look at his handsome features. The neatly trimmed stubble softens his sharp jawline, and his eyes catch the golden ambiance from the chandelier above us. I get lost in the endless constellations in front of me.

It's as though I'm the only one in the room worth his attention, and everyone else is merely a trifling distraction. No one's ever looked at me like that.

"You know, I wasn't always an asshole or full of myself," he finally notes, tilting his head to the side.

"Really? One would think you came out of the womb with an elevated ego."

He chuckles, but it fades quickly. "Rather the opposite, actually. For more than half of my life, I sought validation from the one person who would never give it to me."

I bite the inside of my cheek. Ace rarely opens up to me on his own, and for him to admit this, is significant.

"For as long as I can remember, I always looked up to him. And I convinced myself he could do no wrong. Perhaps, that's why I ignored the signs that were in plain sight. I didn't want to believe the man I held in high view was capable of such things."

There are many things Ace holds himself accountable for, one of them being his father's unfaithfulness to his mother. Ace believes he should've seen the signs—the secret cabin, the extended business trips. But he was only a kid. He shouldn't take that burden onto himself.

"I grew up with people who had their fathers around. Logan's dad wasn't a saint, but he spent time with Logan, took his family on business trips and holidays. Theo and Josh's father was an unfaithful man, but he too accepted both of his sons without forcing them to live up to unattainable standards. With my father, I always felt like I wasn't enough. I was always trying to prove myself to him, fighting for his attention daily when all he cared about was his job."

My heart breaks for him. I can't even begin to imagine what that must have felt like. Ace still carries it with him, and he always will.

"The first time my father laid a hand on me was when I told him I didn't want to pursue law. The second time was the night he left. I still wonder if the outcome would have been different if I'd decided to follow in his footsteps. Would I have finally gained his approval? Would he still have left?"

My grip tightens on him. "Jesus Christ. You must know that wasn't your fault, and you can't keep wondering what if. Your father is a horrible man. You can't hold yourself accountable for him leaving."

He nods. "Even though I know that, it still lingers at the back of my mind. I think that was a pivotal moment in my life. After that, people's perceptions of me didn't matter anymore. It was like a switch was flicked, and I didn't care how much of a disappointment I was. The only thing that mattered was that I didn't end up like him."

Ace snickers under his breath. "But I guess that went out the fucking window too. I'm just as bad as him, if not worse. He took the law into his own hands and bent it for himself. I'm no different in that regard."

I shake my head, refusing to believe it. In a way, I disregarded the law too, and I don't think that it makes us bad people. We're just people who made terrible decisions.

I place my hand on his cheek. "Ace, you're anything but a

disappointment. If my opinion counts for anything, I think you've become an incredible man. You put on an act, but underneath it, you're selfless, kind, and anyone would be a fool to think otherwise once they got to know you. You're nothing like your father."

A grin flirts at the corners of his mouth. "It counts for everything."

He leans down while tilting my chin to meet his remarkable mouth. The kiss is thorough and fervent, and his tongue darts out to sweep my bottom lip. I can't help but smile during it, placing my hands around his neck and greedily pulling him in.

Our chemistry is a lustrous flame, igniting brighter by the second, withstanding even the most catastrophic downpours.

When we come apart, I realize no one's paying attention to us anymore. There are others on the dance floor, not many, but more than I expected there to be. I appreciate that Ace shared a vulnerable part of himself to make me at ease.

The rest of the night, Ace discusses business with some significant investment partners. Again, I find myself feeling out of place, but I knew it would be like this. I'm merely a journalist in a place full of entrepreneurs and well-known celebrities. An outsider in many aspects.

One moment, I'm standing next to Ace, and the next, I turn, and he's not there. I scan the room and spot him striding toward me. How long has he been gone? I was too busy watching the women to the right of me who are having some kind of disagreement.

Ace drapes his arm around my waist and tugs my back closer to his chest. "There you are," he murmurs, his warm breath tickling my neck.

I *inadvertently* brush my bottom against him since we're already so close, and my pulse hastens at the feel of him.

I have a drink in my hand, and I turn to Ace. While keeping my eyes on him, I remove the olive that's floating on top and place it in my mouth. I suck on it and then extract it by the toothpick, still whole, making a *pop* sound with my lips. No one notices except for him. Teasing Ace with my mouth has become effortless now that he knows what I can do with it.

"Excuse me, I need to use the bathroom." I smile before placing the empty glass on a waiter's tray.

Walking past the women who are still in the midst of an argument, I sense Ace behind me. He snakes his arm around my waist, constricting his grip and guides me toward a shadowed corner of the hallway, where a tall potted plant obscures everyone's vision of us.

"Is something wrong, handsome?" I ask in the most artless voice I can muster, batting my eyelashes for the full effect.

His beautiful eyes pierce mine while his jaw grinds in irritation. "Yes, we're leaving."

"Already?" I pout. "But I was having so much fun with you." I travel my fingers to his chest and twirl his tie between my thumb and forefinger.

He seizes my hand with his. "We'll have more fun alone."

I don't doubt that.

Ace grasps my jaw with his other hand, skimming his thumb over my lips. "By the time I'm done with you, the whole city will know my name."

I'm aware I'm playing in a perilous territory, but trouble has never felt so damn tempting—especially when it looks like *that*.

Ace has removed his suit jacket and rolled up the shirt sleeves, forcing his strong biceps muscles to strain against his shirt. My thoughts race with everything he's capable of doing, and my hands sweat.

I didn't think tonight was going to be any different. Ace made it clear that sex was off the table, at least until the deal was over. Has that changed?

"You're quiet. Was it something I said?" he questions with a cocky, deliberate grin. His hand rests on the gear stick, occasionally shifting it as he drives.

It's everything he said. And if his words alone can make me feel like this—hot and bothered—I can't even begin to imagine what the rest of the night is going to entail. He's a man of his word, and if he makes a promise, he'll keep it.

The anticipation mixed with a raw desire for him delivers heat to settle between my legs. Though his ego is getting the better of him, and the smug look on his face is driving me insane.

"I'm just thinking of *all* the things I want you to do to me, Ace. But first, I want to suck every single inch of *you*." Again.

I've never thought much about going down on a man before. It's always been for their pleasure, and it didn't do much for me. But with Ace, it's different. I *want* to please him. I want to see the hazy, half-lidded look on his face when I take all of him. I want it to be all he thinks about until I do it again. And again.

"Calla…" he warns, but his grin doesn't falter. As much as he's trying to act like that didn't affect him, his body stiffens.

Good. "Was it something I said?"

He chuckles and shakes his head. The light from the streetlamps illuminates the inside of the car, and I notice how his mouth curves.

"I like this," he declares.

"What?"

"You and your dirty mouth."

Oh, I bet you do.

Abiding by the speed limit, Ace drives through the narrow streets where people are only beginning to emerge from their apartments and hotel rooms, ready for the night ahead of them.

There's an entire city in front of us to explore, but we're craving to explore each other instead. We have lost our minds. Being apart for so long, trying to fill the empty void with others but never being fully satisfied, has left us starved for each other.

I place my hand on his thigh, unable to keep any distance between us. He inhales sharply. My fingers travel up, and I already feel him hard underneath my fingers. A satisfied smile colors my face.

If we weren't already pulling up to the hotel, I'd love to see how much self-control Ace has when my mouth wraps around him in a moving vehicle. Instead, I palm him through his pants, and he grunts, clenching his teeth.

"Calla, I don't have much control left, and if you keep doing that, I won't hesitate to take you in the car."

I gulp loudly. Every word that manifests out of his mouth makes me wetter. I squeeze my legs together but maintain my hand on him.

He parks the car in front of the hotel and climbs out, drooping his jacket over his arm to cover the stiffness in his pants while handing the parking valet the keys. In a heartbeat, he's next to me, resting his hand on my lower back, guiding me toward the elevator.

Every step we take feels like a waste of time, time that can be spent doing something we have both been waiting too long for. Ace must be having the same thoughts, because he quickens his pace toward the elevators, and his jaw ticks in annoyance when an elderly couple enters behind us.

The elevator isn't vast, and we stand toward the back. Ace cups my ass, as though silently claiming me. He leans down and brushes his lips against my nape before murmuring, "I've wanted to taste you again, to feel you writhe beneath my tongue. But most of all, I've been dying to fuck you, to be inside you…"

My eyes widen, and I glance toward the elderly couple, sincerely hoping they don't hear his vulgar language. My brain stops functioning, and I have nothing to say as the thrilling fervency dances beneath my skin.

The asshole has left me unequivocally speechless.

18

The Release

Calla

When we reach the top floor, Ace interlaces his hand with mine. He scans the keycard, unlocking our suite. I walk toward the kitchen and set my purse on the counter with shaking hands. The room is chilly from the air-conditioning we must have left on, and goose bumps scatter along my skin, from my legs and up my spine. Why am I so nervous?

Ace steps behind me. I don't turn around. Instead, I grip the benchtop for support. My legs are weak, like I've been running laps around Central Park. I swallow hard as my heart drums in an unwavering beat.

"Don't get nervous on me now, love."

He wraps his hands around my waist, and his calloused fingers brush against the delicate material of my dress. The room shrinks, urging us together while my sole focus is on keeping my breathing even.

"I'm not nervous."

Ace moves his hands upward. Every part that he touches catches fire, and the blazes ripple through my skin like an inferno. His fingers tentatively graze my ribcage, and his thumb brushes underneath my breast, precisely where the dress turns to mesh.

"No?" he muses as he drags his fingers up my arms and toward my back, where they hover above the zip of the dress. "May I?"

"Yes." I squeeze my eyes shut.

With my permission, Ace sweeps my hair to the side and unzips me, allowing the dress to pool at my legs. The cool air greets my body's heat, but it doesn't provide any sort of relief.

"What did you say in the car? You want to suck every inch of me?" he drawls against my neck, letting my hair fall down my back again.

My teeth scrape my lower lip as the arousal pools in between my legs.

"Turn around," Ace instructs without waiting for a response.

I turn to face him and see the ravenous storm building behind the shadows of his eyes. My top half is bare, and my nipples pebble with each passing second. I hold my breath as Ace traces his forefinger around one like he has all the time in the world.

"Do you want to fulfill your promise?" he asks as he circles it again, unhurriedly, using only the tip. "Or would you rather I show you what I've been dying to do?" he refers to what he said in the elevator.

I exhale, and then I'm forced to sharply inhale when Ace flicks my nipple before moving on to the other. I can't think. I can't speak. I whimper as I try to form a sentence, a fragment. Something. What has gotten into me?

"Words, Calla. I like words," Ace informs me with a delighted smirk as he rolls my nipple between his thumb and forefinger.

"You," I manage to elude.

He chuckles darkly. "Gladly."

Ace closes the distance and puts his mouth over mine. I instantly part for him and allow him to kiss me with hunger and permanency. The kiss is everything I hoped it would be and more. It captivates, tugs me further in, and propels bolts of electricity through me like I'm an active circuit.

Ace's tongue is hot and teasing, showing me what he's capable of doing in other places, and I gently tug on his lip with my teeth. My legs tremble, and I steady myself by grasping his sturdy arms.

Breathing becomes arduous as I battle with the desire to consume him entirely. He supports me with one hand, and with the other, he clears the bench, sweeping everything that was on top of it onto the ground. Paper rustles. Glass shatters. He lifts me and positions my body on the kitchen counter. Cool stone meets my bare ass.

Ace drops to his knees in front of me. The image is quite extraordinary. He's still fully dressed, apart from his jacket that's draped over a chair. He gazes up at me, insatiable desire clear in his expression, like he's been waiting for this all his life.

He places his large hands on my thighs and searches my face for permission. It's *this*—the way he asks for consent even though he knows damn well I need him makes me vulnerable. Ace is a gentleman who knows how to be dominant. God, I love that. I love—

"Please," I beg, needing more contact, more of his touch before I go insane.

Ace chuckles once again. The deep, low sound permeates the quiet room. He lowers his head and places his lips against my inner thigh, softly kissing it. I feel everything—the way his mouth sucks gently on every spot. The way his stubble brushes against my smooth skin, forcing me to crave him that much more.

His finger goes in between the thin waistband of my garter belt, he pulls it and releases it abruptly. The unexpected sting makes my eyes widen, and I part my lips as a hiss escapes them.

Ace places the pad of his thumb gently through my lacy underwear. He's barely touched me there, but the tension is already building inside. I buck my hips forward, wanting release. The friction of his thumb and my panties heighten the pleasure, so I do it again.

He grins and looks up at me. "You're so fucking wet, love."

Without warning, he dips his head and kisses me through the sheer material. The flick of his warm tongue against my sex is just enough to drive me crazy.

"Ace," I moan his name and tilt my head back, parting my legs farther. Then, I feel a rough tug followed by a *snap* as he tears my lacy panties off, including the garter belt that costs more than my monthly salary. I look down at him, narrowing my eyes. "Ace! They were expensive!"

"I don't care. I'll buy you more. You should know better than to wear this around me. I prefer you with nothing on." He draws me closer, resting my legs over his broad shoulders, and adjusts his pants as his erection grows.

Out of habit, my hands reach for his hair, and I tangle my fingers through the softness of it.

Parting my folds with two of his fingers, Ace's expression is nothing short of haughty and animalistic. Without warning, he drags his tongue up my center, licking it up as if he intends to devour all of me. It's gradual and concentrated. I lose all sense of place and time as my yearning builds deeper, passionately swirling in my core. With just a simple movement of his tongue, my head spins, and my legs tremble.

The entire universe shatters.

"Sweet—" he murmurs against me, "—like butterscotch."

His tongue sweeps where I need it the most, and I gasp when he unrelentingly sucks on my clit. There are no words to explain what he does to me, but it's nothing short of incredible. My breathing quickens when he continues to form an astounding pattern with his tongue, slow at first, but his speed increases with each passing second.

Ace knows my body better than I do, and if he desired to, he could make me come within seconds, but he holds off. Instead, he takes his time, gliding his tongue up and down my entrance—curving the tip of it inside. He isn't sloppy, on the contrary, it's impressive how skillful his strokes are. Slow and teasing, he pays attention to every tender spot and drags out my pleasure.

A moan with his name on it spills from my lips when he slips a long finger inside of me, and I tug on his hair.

"Tell me no man has ever made you feel the way I do."

There's been pleasure with other men, but nothing like this. Nothing has come close to the earth-shattering feeling that's ascending in me now. Whether it be the familiarity or perhaps something considerably more, Ace marked my heart a lifetime ago. He inked it permanently with his existence in a thousand ways, and there's no way to erase him.

"No one. Only you."

"Good." Ace slips a second finger inside me, curling both of them to reach that sweet spot. The male arrogance glows vividly on his expression as I *beg* him to take me on the kitchen counter while I shamelessly grind my hips on his face, and he pumps his fingers in and out. If I weren't so turned on right now, I'd be embarrassed by the sounds saturating the room—my frantic moans, the apparent noise of my slick wetness.

Ace's pumps are accurately in sync with his hot tongue, and my toes curl as the orgasm consumes me. It bursts through me, an explosion of shimmering fire unfolding throughout my body. I grip his hair with one hand and his shoulder with the other. Ace groans, and the sound vibrates against me, elongating my detonation as my body quakes from the aftermath.

I don't have time to recover as he lifts me from the kitchen bench and carries me toward the balcony. I wrap my legs around his torso and bury my head into his shoulder, still high from seconds ago.

"I meant what I said, we're not done. Everyone's going to hear that you're mine."

I always thought being possessed by a man wasn't for me. I never wanted to be anyone's. But with Ace, it's different. I want to be his. Every part of me craves to belong to him.

Out on the balcony, fresh air loops around us, the weight of it snug against me. Ace sits on the daybed, and I position my legs so my knees are on either side of him—my body utterly bare for his perusal. The whole world is below us, yet he's focused exclusively on me.

Taking my time, I move my hands to the buttons on his shirt and work them open. The urge to feel his skin increases until there are no more buttons left, and I slide the shirt from his squared shoulders.

The night is dark, but the Eiffel Tower's luminosity hazily glows upon us, revealing the outline of his shape. Ace has been training for hours every day for his fight tomorrow, and it shows prominently on his physique. Muscles contour his chest and abdomen, and his obliques lead into a deep V line.

Only we can make out each other's lines, curves, and marks.

Others would just make out two shadows from afar, at best.

Ace observes me as I lean in and place my lips on his skin in a light kiss, flicking my tongue over the coolness of his chest like I would with his cock. He winces, gritting his teeth.

"Pretty little mouth." He softly lifts my chin with his fingers, skimming my lips with the pad of his thumb as he leans into me. Then, swiftly, his tongue parts the seam of my lips, diving into my mouth with need. I taste the remnants of myself on him as he roughly engulfs me, stealing my sanity.

I reach for his pants, undoing the leather belt, which results in a grunt from Ace.

"Have you done this before?" My voice is jagged as I catch my breath.

"Had sex?" he asks with an arched brow while his mouth treks along my jawline, grazing his teeth against the smoothness of my skin.

"Had sex on a rooftop," I clarify breathlessly. It's clear he's had plenty of sex before. One doesn't become this skilled in the field without practice. A lot of it.

"No, this is a first for me."

I drown in his words as his mouth locates a sensitive spot on my neck. I tilt my head back, closing my eyes, and his mouth travels down my chest, taking advantage of the access I'm providing him with. Ace takes his time, even though I can sense his stiffness below me.

"Does that arouse you? That I haven't done this with anyone before?"

"Yes, extremely so." It sends multiple waves of gratification through me.

He bows his head, capturing my nipple in his mouth, groaning in contentment as his tongue skims the tip of it. Ace sucks on it with an impeccable amount of pressure, grazing his teeth against the swollen skin, and I swear he could make me shatter without so much as touching me down there. "Fuck!"

Fumbling with the button of his pants, I finally undo it. "I want to feel you. Just you." I hope he understands what I'm saying, what I'm asking of him. I want the rawness of him in me.

Voracious eyes that are full of power land on mine. I want to feel *him,* without anything between us. However, the gnawing feeling that he might have done this with others is unsettling.

"I've always used a condom. Always, Calla. I'm clean," he reassures me. I don't believe Ace would lie about this. So this will be another first for us.

"So have I." Even though I'm on birth control, I've never been comfortable having sex without a condom, especially since I've never had a relationship with a man. I've always been vigilant about practicing safe sex with my previous partners.

Ace's grin widens with masculine dominance like he's ecstatic no one has ever had me like that before. "Way into my heart." He flips me onto my back.

His mouth is on me everywhere—my chest, my lips, my neck—like he can't get enough. Neither can I. I sketch his body with my fingers, storing every bump and contour in my memory. The way his muscles contract when I glide over the spot above his heart, the way his breath becomes tattered when I graze his hips with my nails. Time ceases to exist, permitting us to discover each other in a sacred manner.

Tugging at his pants, I ache to feel every part of him. Ace kicks them off. My eyes stray down, past the rugged ridges of his stomach and toward the deeply bronzed skin of his lower half.

He hovers above me in his prime. "Tell me you feel this. Tell me I'm not the only one who's grappling with self-control." As his words spill, he nudges me with the broad crown of his cock, covering it with the slickness present in between my legs.

"You're not." I'm dying to feel him. I arch my back to meet him as he rubs himself up and down my entrance.

"Greedy," he murmurs as he continues the movement.

I shudder, still sensitive from the earlier orgasm on the kitchen counter. My hands grip his shoulders as I brush my mouth against his ear. "I want you without limits. I don't want you holding back with me."

Ace uses his hand to guide himself. The tip of him—only an inch—enters me. Blazes erupt. How many times in the last week alone have I thought of this moment? How many times has my imagination run wild, envisaging all the ways he would take me?

I stretch around him. His size is extensive, truly large, and if it weren't for the fact that I already had him, I would question if I'd be able to take it all.

"Calla," he drawls my name as he inches farther in.

Framing his face with my hands, I pull him toward me. I let our mouth connect as the rest of us does. Bit by bit, Ace continues to inch himself in me. Just before he fills me entirely, he retracts. His mouth fiercely rages against mine, finding a duteous beat. I part my lips farther, eagerly requiring his absolute possession.

As he plunges his tongue inside my mouth, he does the same with his cock, filling me, forcing the satisfying pain to prosper into indulgence.

"Fuck, you feel amazing," he grunts, holding himself up with one hand and grasping the curve of my hip with the other. He halts as I get accustomed to the fullness of him, and when I dig my fingers into his chest, he does it again and again. With each profound thrust, he succeeds in hitting the same sensitive and receptive spot.

I glance to the side, trying to locate something I can muffle my screams with. I reach for the pillow, but Ace spots what I'm doing.

He grabs my hands and pins them over my head. "No. Did you forget what I said? I want to hear you while I'm fucking you, love. Loud and clear."

He slides out slowly, making sure I can feel every single inch of him, and oh my—

How I ever went without this—without him—is a mystery. We stabilize each other in every way imaginable. The link between us is immaculate. The way he takes control and seizes me entirely and unconditionally makes me believe that I belong to him and no one else.

At this moment, as we move through space and time, I become addicted to his scent, the way he tastes, the way he looks at me greedily and with pure, demanding desire. But most of all, to the way he anchors me.

I lose myself beneath his wonderous touch.

Ace releases my hands and lifts me by my waist. I pull myself on top of him in a sitting position.

"How many times have you pictured this? Me on top of you?"

He cups my breasts and molten liquid tunnels under my skin. "More times than you can ever imagine, but my mind has never done this justice."

Pleased with his answer, I wrap my hands around his neck. Our tongues meet as I tangle my hands in his hair, trying to draw him closer even though there's already nothing between us. Ace guides me with his hands, plunging me up and down his length. Every move is deliberately calculated. My head rolls back against my shoulders as he persists in thrusting into me. The sweat on our bodies makes it hard to keep a tight grasp on him, so I dig my nails down his back, which fuels a groan from deep inside Ace's throat.

"Look at me." He snakes his fingers around my neck.

My eyes fuse with his, and the intensity within them prevails. I'm unable to look away. All I see are two bright stars.

I tremble around him as the light splinters through me. Igniting me. Ace slams himself into me one more time, making our climax spiral out of control while I cry out his name over and over. I've never experienced anything like this. It's beyond anything words could ever explain.

He spills his release inside of me, and traces of it trickle down my thigh. My breathing is jagged, and my heart thuds inside my chest, alongside Ace's.

He's still inside me when I rest my chin on his shoulder. "What changed?" I mumble against his warm skin. "I thought you were set on the deal."

"I'm set on you, Calla. I couldn't give a fuck about the deal. It's always been you."

I realize what he's saying. He knew there was a chance of me leaving after we had sex. But here…in a different country, I have nowhere to go. In a way, it's manipulative, but in the end, we both get what we want.

He trails his thumb against my parted lips, down my jaw, and to my neck.

"That was…mind-blowing," I say softly, and he hardens inside of me at the sound of my praise.

✦ ✦ ✦

Ace and I didn't get much sleep last night. We were too preoccupied with what we have been missing out on for four years, what *I* have been missing out on.

I thought I haven't done too bad with my previous partners, but Ace makes them seem less than the starters before the main meal. The way Ace fucks is exceptional. I don't know what I expected, but he exceeded everything. It's not that he wasn't good in college. He was. But there's a different side to him now, a side so confident in his actions. He lives up to his title, surpasses it, and so much more. The man has endless stamina and is outstandingly equipped.

Ace rolls over to my side and wraps his arm around me. "Not a morning person, love?"

I peek through the gap of the blanket. He looks at me intently, like he's trying to figure something out. Figure out how I'm going to react after last night? Well, I can't exactly go anywhere, can I? And if I could, would I leave?

There are issues we need to sort through. Things we need to talk about if we ever want this to work. But for the first time in my life, I'm not inclined to run.

Reaching out with my hand, I drift my fingers over his cheek, stroking the prickle of his stubble. The corners of his mouth turn upward in a mischievous smile, and my fingers trace his bottom lip.

"I'm not running, Ace."

He grasps my hand, brings it up to his lips, and kisses it softly. Balminess streams inside and reminds me of the days back in college.

"It would shatter my ego if you did."

His eyes glint under the warm sun. His eyes are my favorite thing about him. From the first time I saw him, they captured me in more ways than one and spoke a thousand words.

Ace places a quick kiss on my mouth. "I'm going for a shower." He tosses his half of the blanket over me, and the smell of sex wafts toward me. He stands, completely naked.

My gaze roams over his body, and I try to keep my mouth from opening. Will I ever get used to this view? To him?

He places his hands behind his head, stretching. *Show off.*

"Join me." He turns to amble inside without waiting for a response while I stare at his behind.

I climb out of the remarkably comfortable daybed and look at the mess we created last night. The pillows scatter over the balcony floor, and so do the remainder of our clothes. Some of the pot plants are broken, but I don't recall how that happened.

Padding toward our room, I realize how sore I am today. The pain in between my legs is uncomfortable but bearable. Nevertheless, it's something I expected after a night like that with Ace.

I search for my phone, wanting to check for text messages. The last twenty-four hours have been a blur, but I'm reminded Mia went out with Theo, and she promised to keep me updated. Finally, I locate my phone in my bag by the window, but it's dead.

Searching for a charger, my mind spins with all that could have happened with Mia and Theo. I know her well enough to know she wouldn't sleep with a married man, but I've never seen her look at a man the way she looked at Theo that day in Ace's apartment. It was almost as if she wasn't herself.

I plug my phone in, ensuring the battery symbol comes up before leaving it on the bedside table and heading into the bathroom where Ace is waiting for me. The shower is already running, and the mirror is steamed, so I'm unable to see my reflection, but I bet it's something unpleasant that will make me grimace.

Ace smiles as I step under the hot water and tilt my head back to wet my hair. He breathes in deeper, and before I have the time to reach for the small shampoo bottle, Ace is already squeezing it into his hand.

I turn, and he lathers my hair. It feels so good that I lean my head into his hands, appreciating the intimate moment between us. After he's finished, I do the same for him. He faces me and bows his head as I squirt shampoo into my palm.

"I hope you're well-rested. You wouldn't want to be worn out for your fight."

"You know, they say that sex before a fight helps with performance."

"Well, your performance is going to be outstanding today," I remark as I rinse the last of the conditioner from his locks.

"It always is." His tone overflows with self-assurance.

Does that have a double meaning? Does he mean he always fucks before a fight? Is that part of the reason why he yielded after resisting for so long?

I check my phone. It's ten in the morning, and we need to leave for Ace's fight shortly. It doesn't start until three, but he's required to be there by midday.

There are a few texts from Mia on my phone. I skim over them, trying to get the gist of what happened. The essence of it is that she slept with Theo. However, the kicker is that Theo told her he's in the middle of a divorce. Typical man. But Mia should know better than to believe something like that.

I step onto the bustling streets of Paris with Ace. He takes my hand in his and traces his thumb over the back of it. Denzel waits for us by the car and greets us with a nod when we get closer.

"Mr. Blackwell, Miss Maven. I hope you had a nice night."

My cheeks flare, recalling exactly how *nice* the night was.

"We did, Denzel," Ace replies without so much as blinking and slides into the car, pulling me in with him.

"Your mom doesn't come to your fights?" I ask as we drive.

"She comes to most of the home ones, to my dismay."

"You don't want her attending?"

He sighs. "I think you've noticed I try to keep my family as far from the media as I can. It's hard enough on them without prying eyes and ill intentions."

"I understand. I'd do the same."

Ace takes precautions, he calculates every decision. Perhaps it's because he hadn't in the past. He's learned from his mistakes, and now he weighs every risk in his head.

We arrive outside an ancient building. The pale stone exterior contrasts with richly colored glass panels that catch the sunlight, and I have to squint through the glare. The parking lot only has two other vehicles, which makes me wonder whether Denzel has mistaken the location. But then I realize this must be the back entrance to the main building.

For the next couple of hours, I observe as Ace prepares for his fight. He doesn't train or work out. He saves that energy for the main event. Instead, he consults his trainer, getting final guidance and insight on his opponent. He then listens to music, he tells me it's his ritual. "Everyone has a customary routine before a fight. This is mine."

When there are only forty-five minutes to go, Ace begins his stretches and a warm-up. His trainer then wraps his hands in strapping tape. I sit on the black leather sofa, watching the scene unfold in front of me. From the moment we arrived here, Ace hasn't acted nervous. No edgy gestures, no tension present in the way he carries himself.

He's confident. He's a man that hasn't lost a match.

When the time for the fight comes, I sit with Ace's trainer at the front, getting a full view of the ring. The venue is bigger than I thought it would be, and it's full. Everywhere I look, there are bodies upon bodies waiting for the action to begin.

Ace's opponent, Raphael, is a similar size to Ace. Perhaps a tad shorter. He's stocky and almost as impressive. It must be an honor to fight the champion. Is he already expecting defeat? Or does he think he has a chance?

Ace and his opponent touch gloves, and it begins.

At first, it's like two predators circling each other, waiting for the other to show their weakness. Neither of them takes their eyes off each other.

Raphael attempts to gain the first hit, swinging for Ace's exposed side. I bite down on my lower lip in anticipation, but Ace evades the attack and drives his fist forward with power. The crowd becomes wild, cheering, and Ace's trainer shouts words of encouragement beside me. Raphael stumbles back from the hit. He spits out blood but recovers promptly, stepping into his fighting stance once again.

I concentrate on Ace, witness him calculate the speed at which his opponent moves. He scans Raphael every time he attempts a blow. Finally, on the third attempt, the glove grazes Ace's cheekbone. Yet he doesn't recoil. They continue this game for the first round—three minutes. Ace on the defense, simply perusing, and Raphael endeavoring to obtain a good shot. When the bell announces the end of the round, they turn and head back to their corners.

From here, I witness a nasty bruise forming on Ace's cheekbone. The medic applies ice to it for the duration of the brief break.

Ace's trainer leans into me. "Ace is trying to figure out what

Raphael's weak point is," he yells just as the second round is about to start.

"What if he doesn't have one?" I yell back over the roaring of the crowd.

"Everyone has a weak point."

"What's Ace's?"

His trainer raises both brows as if to say there's no way he's telling me the pivotal information about the most successful champion in the world. I respect him for that.

I return my attention to the fight as Ace and Raphael are given the go-ahead. This time, Raphael wastes no time, eager to use the element of surprise. He swings for Ace's face, and Ace effortlessly takes a step back. At the same time, he watches Raphael's left shoulder. I follow his observation.

Ace has uncovered his opponent's weak point. Each time Raphael swings, there's a minor flinch of his shoulder. A previous injury, perhaps. It's unnoticeable if you don't know what to look for.

A feral grin coats Ace's face. The fight is over just as quickly as it began. Ace rounds his prey, ducks at the appropriate moment to avoid another gloved fist flying his way. The panic is abundantly present on Raphael's face. He knows the end is nearing just by looking at Ace's stance.

This is nothing like Ace's fights back in college. He was a leopard then. Now, he's evolved into a lion. Rampant, unpredictable—such a wondrous creature. He stalks his prey to the ropes and unleashes the beast.

19

Craving Chaos

Calla

Ace is in the living room, perched against the edge of the kitchen counter, dressed in a cream cotton T-shirt and black shorts. I don't know whether I prefer him in a suit or like this. Both forms are marvelous.

"We're leaving today?" I ask when I notice his suitcase by the door.

"After breakfast."

I didn't get to see much of Ace last night. After winning the fight, he had publicity conferences and interviews. By the time everything concluded, I couldn't keep my eyes open. The previous night of not sleeping, and a full day out, caught up to me.

"Is Theo married?" I question Ace when we're driving through the narrow streets, our suitcases packed and in the trunk.

"He is."

"Is he getting a divorce by any chance?" I hope Theo wasn't lying and, I'm inclined to give him the benefit of the doubt.

"Not that I know of. He's only been married less than a year."

I close my eyes and exhale. The situation is more complex than I anticipated. "Would he lie to sleep with Mia?"

He considers my question before asking his own. "Did he sleep with Mia?"

"Yes."

At this, he shakes his head in disbelief, and his entire mood shifts—married men and infidelity strikes close to home for Ace. So perhaps bringing Theo up today was an awful idea. I hope it doesn't ruin the rest of the day for us.

I rest my hand on his in reassurance. "Maybe it's a misunderstanding," I reason, even though the uncertainties swimming in my head say otherwise.

Ace doesn't reply. Instead, he interlaces our fingers and silently stares out the window. Although I can't hear his thoughts, I can sense them. The irritation is plainly written on his expression.

Denzel pulls up to the dock, and I realize we're going on a boat on the Seine. When Ace said we'd be going to breakfast, I didn't think it would be on the river with the finest views of the Eiffel Tower.

A picnic is laid out for us toward the back of the boat with fruit, croissants, cheeses, and macarons. "This is amazing."

"I thought this would be the best way to see Paris in an hour."

The boat glides through the river at a steady pace, and my gaze leaps from side to side. Luscious foliage trees on either side peek in the distance, forming a boundary around the banks. The famous Eiffel Tower, made of iron and woven like lace, stretches to the cloudless sky. The views surrounding us are truly breathtaking, and the fact that I'm in Paris with Ace still feels surreal.

You'd never think of Ace as a romantic, but he persists in surprising me every day. "I have something for you," he admits once we're stretched out on the blanket.

"Hmm?" I swallow the mouthful of flaked pastry and lift a

takeaway cup of hot coffee to my mouth.

"Close your eyes," he orders, and I roll them before doing as he said. No point arguing with Ace. He always gets his way.

Ace takes my hand, and a cool metal object touches my skin. "Open."

A rose-gold bracelet hangs from my wrist. My heart soars out of my chest. It's a Cartier love bracelet covered in diamonds, one of the ones you need a screwdriver to unlock. It has something to do with sealing your love. I twist my hand, examining it in awe as it sparkles under the glimmering sun.

It's probably worth more than my whole years' salary. "Ace… It's beautiful but—"

"Calla," he interrupts, grasping what I'm about to say. "I have more money than I know what to do with. Let me spend it on you."

There are many reasons why I feel uncomfortable taking expensive gifts from men, but the reason with Ace is different from everyone else. With him, it's as though he's trying to make up for the past when he doesn't need to. It's already enough that he's here.

"Consider it an early birthday present," he adds, probably noting the unsure look on my face. My birthday is in two days, and of course, he remembered.

"Thank you. It's beautiful." I'm unable to take my eyes off it. I wonder if he gave it to me knowing the whole meaning behind it.

"I have taken the rest of the week off. So it's going to be just you and me," he reveals, and my heart beats faster at the power that phrase holds over me.

You and me.

"Are you going to tell me where we're going?" A smile forms on my face.

He echoes it. "Somewhere warm and sunny with a private beach."

Being with Ace is like breathing. It's tranquil and feels like second nature. However, occasionally breathing becomes difficult for me, and I begin drowning inside.

For the last four years, I've been numb. I've gotten used to just living and not feeling. I guess in some ways, it was easier like that, not caring enough to be disappointed or hurt, having men fall at my feet because I'm not the one who gets attached. We all know men hate commitment—well, at least until you won't give it to them. Men want what they can't have, it's as simple and as complicated as that. But maybe it's not just men. Perhaps it's the entire human race.

Then Ace came into my life again, flipping everything upside down, making me understand why no one can make me feel the way he does. I've tried to run from it, but a part of me craves him. I crave the chaos that makes me *feel*. I crave him. There's no other way to describe it except that it's like an addiction. The more I get, the more I want, even though I recognize it's foolish and detrimental.

Staring out the small window of the jet, my mind wanders to the things we probably will never understand. Is everything interconnected? If a specific event in my life didn't happen back then, would I be where I am today?

We're flying above the clouds to somewhere sunny with a private beach. That sentence has never even crossed my mind, but here I am.

Ace sits across from me with his laptop on his knees. Running his fingers over his stubble, he furrows his eyebrows a few times as he scans the information displayed on the screen.

"Anything I can help with?" I recline in my seat after takeoff. I always get anxious when a plane takes off and lands because most plane crashes occur on the runway.

Ace glances at me, and I see the flicker in his eyes like he's considering giving me a generic answer but then changes his mind. Instead, he says, "There's a client who owes me a lot of money. He's been gambling at fights and not paying up. I'm currently conducting some research on him."

"What happens now?"

"He'll be taken care of." His voice is low while he notes my expression. Ace places his laptop to the side, stands, and moves toward me.

"By you?" I probe when he braces his hand against the back of my seat, towering over me. He smells like the cologne I've gotten used to over the last couple of weeks, and it's alluring.

"Something like that." He doesn't break our eye contact. He's opening up, showing me glimpses of what no one else sees. Revealing what's underneath the guard he's put up in front of the rest of the world. "Does that make you uncomfortable?" Ace questions, but I know he's asking if it makes me uncomfortable with *him*.

"No, you're not a bad person." I knew that from the start. Even though he acted like an asshole the first time we met, he was fighting his demons. And the more I got to know him, the more I understood.

He chuckles coldly. "Some would disagree."

"They don't know you."

He shakes his head and takes a step back. "You've always tried to find the good in me. What if there was none to begin with? It's like you're blind to the crimes I've committed, to the burdens

I live with…"

"You've always tried to convince me you're not good, but every decision you've made up to this point has never been just about you." Instead, everything has been about his family, about Ellie. From his illegal fighting to help out with money when his dad left to doing what it takes for Ellie's treatment.

I doubt he's even blinked an eye over what this all means for him. He did what he had to do. Sacrificed more than most people would risk. And yet, he's so set on thinking the worst of himself.

Does it have anything to do with his past? The accident? His father?

Denzel drives us through Sicily's streets, and I watch as we pass the architectural buildings. In the span of a couple of days, Paris and Italy have my head in a daze. After about an hour, Denzel draws to a halt in front of an incredible villa towering over the seaside. We pass through a set of black gates, and Denzel parks the car near the entry.

The villa is whimsical and luxurious. It's three stories and has what appears like the best views in the whole country. On top of that, white stairs lead to a private beach, just as Ace promised.

I stand on the balcony and look out into the distance. The brilliant water sparkles with the reflection of the sun. It's the most electrifying blue I've ever seen and clear—crystal clear.

"I need to take care of a few things here. It shouldn't take long." Ace appears behind me. "If you need anything, Denzel will be out the front until I get back."

I twist to face him, and he props his arms on either side of the glass rail behind me, his body inches from mine.

"What if I need something else?" I rest my hand on his chest and gently tug against the collar of his shirt.

Mischief lights his face, and I can't take my eyes off him. I step on my tiptoes and press my lips against his. They're soft but possessive, and in an instant, his hands are on my hips, pulling me closer toward him. He tastes like everything I never knew I needed.

"Calla…" he murmurs against my mouth. "I'd thought you'd prefer indoors this time."

"Outdoors has always been our thing."

"I won't be long," he reassures me again, gripping my hips. "Dinner after?"

"Sure."

"Good." He pulls away but pauses near the balcony doors and turns. "And, Calla?"

"Hmm?"

"I'm having *you*," he says casually and walks inside toward the front door.

I lean against the rail, and my heart races with anticipation, but that feeling is quickly replaced when I hear the door shut. Every possibility churns through my mind. What does Ace need to take care of in Sicily?

Plane rides make me feel tired and dirty, and I need to take my mind off the constant worry, so I take a bath. Sitting in the living room afterward, I dial Mia's number, but it goes straight to voice mail. It's not that unusual for Mia. She's able to go days without picking up her phone, but the fact that the last time I heard from her was when she was with Theo doesn't make me feel better.

I decide to try Mia again later and call my dad instead.

"Hey, Cals, is everything okay?" My dad asks when he answers.

His voice directs a feeling of nostalgia through me.

"Yeah, everything is fine." I tread toward the balcony in my white bathrobe. I don't bother explaining anything over the phone. It's a conversation for another time, for when I can figure out how to bring it up.

The fact that I'm in another country with a man would be enough for him to have a heart attack. I've never brought a man home to my dad, apart from Nate, but he's more of a family friend than anything else.

"I was thinking about coming up next weekend if you don't have any plans." I haven't seen my dad in a while, and after these two weeks with Ace, I need to clear my head, put space between us to see how we'll work when we're not together most hours of the day.

Telling my dad about Ace, about who he is, has crossed my mind more than once. I still haven't decided whether I'm going to. I guess I'll have to make that decision soon. Eventually, I'll have to introduce Ace to my dad. It's inevitable if we choose to stay in each other's life.

The question is, can I keep this secret from my dad for the rest of my life, or should I put everything on the line and hope he understands just to relieve my conscience?

"It's perfect. I'll organize a late birthday dinner. Maybe invite Nate and his dad? And Uncle Dave?"

"Yeah, that sounds good. I'll let you know my flight details when I book it."

Ending the call, I glance around, not sure what to do. I'm on a beautiful island, and I'm not going to spend my time cooped up inside. I slip on a white cotton dress, which is perfect for this weather, release my hair from its bun, and track a brush through it.

"Miss," Denzel addresses me when I step out the front door.

"Denzel," I greet him. "Call me Calla, please. I'm going for a walk. I noticed shops by the beach when we were driving past." I explain.

"Okay." He gives me a nod.

Okay? That was easy. I don't know why I thought it wouldn't be. I begin walking along the cobblestone pathway, but I turn to the sound of footsteps behind me. Denzel halts when I do.

We hold eye contact until he speaks. "Uh, the boss made it clear that I'm to stay within close range to you at all times."

Ah, of course he did. "Well, I guess *we're* going for a walk, Denzel."

I stroll through the streets and toward the main beach. Denzel doesn't make an effort to catch up to me. Instead, he mimics my pace and keeps his distance. I cross the boardwalk toward the beach. Removing my sandals, I amble barefoot on the sand. Even though it's around six, the sun is still out.

I stare into the distance, and my head whirls with endless thoughts. I came here to get my mind off things, yet here I am doing the complete opposite.

This thing with Ace, whatever it is, feels too good—almost unrealistic in a way. The last time it was like this, everything came crashing down within the blink of an eye. So I'm preparing myself for that again. Some would call that catastrophizing, my therapist would call it anxiety. I call it saving myself from disappointment.

A bird captures my attention, and my gaze follows it as it glides over my head and lands on the boardwalk. Maybe it's some sort of sign. An omen. Or just the universe highlighting my doubts, reminding me that nothing can stay good for long.

Because that's when I notice him.

Ace sits at a restaurant table across the narrow boardwalk. From a distance, I notice how he tilts his head back a little and laughs at something the woman in front of him said. I instantly recognize her. Cassidy.

Her dark hair cascades in small curls down her face, and she leans across the wooden table, stroking her hand over his. My chest crams with a heaviness I'm not accustomed to, and everything halts for an extended moment.

It's not that Ace is with another woman that bothers me the most, although it's something that pains me as well. What bothers me the most is that he didn't enlighten me he was doing this. I thought we were past the lying and the half-truths.

I thought wrong.

If the situation were reversed, and I was having dinner with another man without telling Ace, I could only imagine what his reaction would be.

I'm not going to make a scene, but I'm also not going to go back to the villa and pretend like I didn't see this. Instead, I head toward the bar in need of a drink. Or five.

20

She Owns Me

Ace

Cass twirls the champagne glass in her hand and raises it to her broad mouth. She sips on it slowly and swallows, smacking her lips together. Finally, her impossibly vivid eyes land on me.

"I need you to handle something." I cut through the shit and get straight to business. Time is money, or in this case—time is Calla.

It's not a coincidence that Cass is here in Sicily. It's a beautiful island, and Cass is fond of keeping tabs on what I'm doing like it's her fucking business.

Each second at this table feels like a waste of fucking time. However, this dinner will inevitably take longer than I'd like it to. Cass has always enjoyed playing games, and I used to play them with her. For a while, it was the only thing distracting me enough not to succumb to the most sinister part of my mind. Cass demonstrated how to draw a line between my inner shadows and sanity, but her line is a twisted vine.

It's apparent why her father had his doubts and eventually decided she wasn't a suitable candidate to take over the business.

"Ah, I thought you'd at least let me order dinner before asking me for favors." She picks up the menu and scans it deliberately.

"It's not a favor. You know that." My voice is low with authority as I lean back in my chair.

"I've been thinking, and I've decided we should expand our… business," she motions around with one of her hands while still holding the menu with the other, pretending to peruse it. I know she already decided what she'll have within the first three seconds of glancing at it.

"Expand?" I prompt.

"We're not exactly protected. The cops are on our asses. They have been for the last couple of months. We've had…offers to join with some of the most influential people in the world and expand, make more money. We have the manpower, and we'd get protection from everything, including the law."

I shake my head. Cass has been on my case about this for the last few months, and I'm not interested. She's itching to get involved with the world's most powerful criminals, but I stay as far away from that as I can. "That's not something I want to engage in."

"Of course you don't want to. If all of this goes to shit, it won't affect you. What about for people such as myself?"

She has no fucking idea that it will affect me more than I'd like it to. If everything goes to shit, I sink with it.

"You do whatever you like in your free time, Cass. Just don't get me involved in it."

She glares at me, her bright eyes turning into slits.

"Back to what I'm here for. I know Logan has been fighting, and I know it's you who permitted him to. Take care of it. I don't want him anywhere near the clubs."

"No," she states.

My jaw ticks as irritation builds in me. "No?"

"Logan is a moneymaker. Didn't you wonder why we were up more than twenty percent last week?"

"I don't care. He's more trouble than he's worth."

"I'm prepared for the risk," she says.

"You're involved with him." I should have known Logan would sample other methods when I turned him away on more than one occasion.

Her answer is a simple shrug. "A woman has needs, and since you're not fulfilling them anymore…" she travels off. "But perhaps there are ways to convince me," she purrs, tilting her head to the side.

"I'm not interested."

"What a shame. We used to have so much fun."

I turn my head, done with this pointless ordeal, and that's when I see *her.*

Calla is at the bar with her back to me, but I'd recognize her anywhere. Light-brown hair flows down her back, and she laughs at something the man next to her says. The man's hand shifts to rest on her back, and I tense in my chair.

"Fuck," I mutter under my breath, and Cass follows my gaze.

A malicious smile develops on her face. "Ah, have you found us—"

"No," the words spill out of my mouth sharply before Cass finishes her sentence.

"No?" she asks, pouting her lips. "You always liked to share, Ace." Her hand glides over mine, and I glare at her.

I shake her off and cross my arms over my chest. She laughs at my reaction. Games. Her fucking games.

Cass has been talking, I know that by her expression. She's waiting for me to answer the question she's just asked. I didn't hear her, and I don't give a shit. Instead, I place my hands on the armrest of the chair, ready to stand. "Take care of Logan," I command Cass, not in the fucking mood for this.

"Oh, maybe I can ask her myself," Cass says and moves to stand.

I have no idea what she's talking about, but she won't be stepping a foot anywhere near Calla. Within a second, I'm towering over Cass, I brace my hands on her chair.

"No, you won't," I say, mirroring her smile. "However, you'll go home and take care of Logan. I'll get Denzel to drive you to the airport."

Her smile doesn't falter. "Not even going to lend me your jet?"

"No."

"Shame, I remember the time we—"

I turn, not bothering to listen to what manifests out of her mouth next.

My eyes scan the place, and I spot Denzel to the side. I should have been more precise with the instructions I gave him. I ordered him to always be within thirty feet of Calla. However, I should have articulated that no other man was to go within that range, either. My mistake.

My gaze settles on the guy whose hand hovers against her back. My teeth clench together, and my fists curl at my sides. I take long strides toward her, not bothering to glance back at Cass. I meet Denzel's eyes, and I flick my head in the direction of Cass. *Take care of her.*

He nods, striding toward her table.

I reach the bar and stand behind her. "Calla."

She laughs at what the man next to her said, something I missed. Then, finally, she turns her body toward me. Her smile disappears, and her eyes ignite.

My eyes roam her face and then her body. The white dress she's wearing barely leaves anything to the imagination. Her breasts are accentuated under the thin, almost sheer material, and I have the urge to throw her over my shoulder and haul her to the villa.

"Eyes up here, Ace," she snaps with annoyance.

My eyes land back on hers. She's pissed off, she has every right to be. I should have informed her about Cass. And now she's making a point, displaying exactly how it felt for her to see me with Cass, to be left in the dark. Point taken. I fucking hate it.

The bartender sets a drink in front of Calla, and she reaches for it, but I take it before she can. "No more."

The light above us reflects the orange tones through her hair, and her amber eyes sparkle with fury.

"You." She points her tiny finger at my chest. "Don't have the right to tell me what to do." She retrieves the drink from me and sips it through the straw.

Her round lips suck on it while she looks up at me through her dark downcast lashes. She knows exactly what she's doing, and I love it. The confidence radiates through her.

I grin, because she thinks she's got me. It's like she's forgotten what I can do to her with words alone. If she needs a reminder, I'll give her one.

Positioning my hand on her waist, I twist her in her chair so she faces me directly. Inclining toward her, my senses heighten. She smells like strawberries and alcohol. The heat sears off her body.

"If I have to carry you out of here, you won't be able to walk for a week."

"Ace!" She gasps, and her face turns red. She quickly twists to ensure no one else overheard, and I snicker under my breath.

She crosses her arms and leans back, away from me. "You have to do better than that." She smirks, twirling the straw through the drink.

"Calla," I warn her. She's testing my patience.

The idiot that's sitting to the side of us, watching the scene unfold, intervenes. "Hey, the lady said she's not interested."

I sneer before facing him. My hands curl into fists at my sides, preparing to eliminate the problem with one precise movement.

Calla must sense this and positions her hand on mine, granting me a slight shake of her head. On instinct, my shoulders relax, she has me wrapped around her fucking finger.

She faces the man. "Thanks for the drinks, but my *boyfriend* is here now."

An unavoidable grin pierces my face. Seizing my hand, she leads me through the restaurant and toward the paved boardwalk. The air is cooler here, and the sound of the sea against the shore alleviates my mood.

"You're grinning like a Cheshire Cat," she states. "A dangerous action when a woman is pissed off."

I case my arm around her petite waist, luring her closer toward my side in response. "I'm sorry."

"I'm not the same girl I was in college," she expresses, but what she implies is she won't tolerate me keeping her in the dark as I did back then, too.

"I know, Calla. Fuck…I know."

We stroll along the beach toward the villa, the streetlamps flicking on one by one in the distance. There aren't many people out tonight, at least not yet.

"Cassidy. Have you been with her?" she asks. From the tone in her voice, I sense she's not jealous. She's curious. I would be, too, if it were her having dinner with a man—in fact, I'd be more than curious.

My jaw clenches.

"How many times?"

I don't say anything. I can't provide her with an honest answer because it was too many to keep track of.

"That many, huh?"

"She's Marcus's daughter," I reveal, not knowing what difference it makes.

"Mixing business with pleasure, Ace." She shakes her head.

"I need you to trust me," I say.

"With what?"

"Everything."

She looks at me like I'm asking the world of her, and I understand because I am. I'm asking her to let me take the lead. I need her trust for this to work.

21

Timing is Everything

Calla

The delicate white curtains in our room flow in the cool morning breeze. Outside, through the balcony doors, the gentle waves crash against the shoreline. I could listen to the sound all day. It's therapeutic. However, I'm distracted by Ace tightening his grip around my lower waist and drawing me toward his bare chest. The smell of his body wash, fresh and masculine, causes my head to swim, and not just as a result of my very low alcohol tolerance last night.

It took me less than twenty minutes to become tipsy at the bar, and by the time Ace approached me, I was in the confident and talkative stage. Luckily, I didn't say anything I regret this morning. At least, I hope I didn't. And given that I was somewhat drunk, I'd forgiven him too quickly for the stunt he pulled last night.

Ace's arm presses on my stomach, and I realize I need to use the bathroom. I shift his hand off me slowly, but he doesn't move. The man is built like a slab.

"I need to use the bathroom," I whisper, not knowing if he's awake or just stirring. He groans groggily against my shoulder and gently grazes his lips against it. The feeling of his stubble on my bare skin impels a shiver through me.

I reluctantly climb out of bed and head toward the bathroom, skimming the tips of my fingers against the wall for support. This is precisely the reason I hate drinking—the morning after.

I check my phone while simultaneously brushing my teeth. There's a text from Mia. One text, even though I sent her about a hundred.

Mia: *I will explain everything when you get back*

Great. She couldn't be vaguer if she tried. That's Mia. Over the years, I've come to understand how to communicate with her, but without any communication on her end, I have nothing to work with.

I rinse the toothpaste from my mouth and attempt to FaceTime her, but she doesn't answer. There are two possible reasons. Theo's kidnaped her, or she just doesn't want to talk. I'm hoping it's the less insane option, but I worry anyway.

Running a comb through my hair, I realize I look better than I have in a long time. The dark circles that have previously resided under my eyes have faded to mere shadows, and my skin is clearer than it has ever been, forcing the tan freckles on my nose to become blatant.

"Mia isn't picking up her phone." I sigh as I head back into the room. Ace is still in the bed, but he's sitting up against the headrest, holding his phone with one hand.

"Theo isn't either," he says sharply.

Ace isn't thrilled about those two. If Theo weren't married, the situation would be very different. There are always two sides to every story, and I'm willing to give them a chance to explain, especially since this is out of character for both Mia and Theo.

I stand in front of Ace, and he sits up on the edge of the bed, with me in between his legs. "Let's not worry about them." He sets his hands on the backs of my thighs. "I'll get someone to check on her if you want. But I want to spend the last couple of days with you." He glances at me as if he wants to say something but then changes his mind.

"You can tell me anything. You know that?" I remind him.

"Trust me," he says those two words like it's that simple. Like they explain everything. They don't.

"Show me that I can." I situate my hands on his shoulders. What's a relationship without communication? There'll always be misunderstandings and arguments.

He sighs, pulling me down to him and covering my mouth with his.

I hate that there's still this barrier between us. There are things he can't trust me with or just won't tell me—like last night. It's ironic, considering he expects me to trust him.

Ace has always been secretive, always kept things to himself. It has everything to do with the fact he's never had anyone to please, anyone to answer to. I'm not asking him to answer to me, but keeping secrets is what ruined our relationship previously. There's only so much I can take.

I overthink. I'll drive anyone insane with the number of trust issues I have. There's a reason why I haven't dated in the last four years. It's not because of the candidates—some of them ticked all the boxes. The main reason is that I couldn't give my all to a relationship when I didn't even give my all to myself.

"Let's do something today," I suggest, wanting to get out of this mindset. That's all I've been doing this trip, putting everything to the side. What are a few more days?

"What did you have in mind?" he wiggles his eyebrows, returning to his playful mood.

Last night, we ended up watching a movie back in the villa. It was a relaxing change since we've been on the go the last couple of weeks, either trying to jump each other's bones or attending to business matters.

"We can go sightseeing," I propose.

"Sightseeing?"

"Mm-hmm, it'll be fun. I'm sure I can come up with a disguise for you." I run my hand through his disheveled hair and tug on it gently. He groans in satisfaction.

I'm surprised that the entire time I've been with Ace, we've never had an issue with him being a public figure. However, we've barely been out in public apart from the private events and Ace's fight. The small number of times we have been out were at night. I have noted people seem to stare more than usual, but I guess that's the least of his worries.

"Role-play? Interesting kink, Calla." He journeys his hand up my side and sweeps his thumb over the thin material of the nightgown, skimming the side of my breast.

I gasp.

He laughs at my reaction. Rising from the bed, he places a kiss on my forehead. "We'll go sightseeing. Get ready, love."

✦ ✦ ✦

Taking one last look in the full-body mirror, I glide my hands down my white billowing skirt. It has a split down the side, and the matching long-sleeved top completes the outfit.

In the living room, the balcony door is open. Ace is talking to someone on the phone. His tone is neutral, but I gather he's discussing business from the blunt, clipped replies.

Tiptoeing barefoot on the cool hardwood floors, I step through the white panel doors. Outside, the smell of saltwater and warm sand circulates me. I breathe in deeper, relishing it. It's something I could get used to, and so is the view.

In front of me is silvery-blue water and a sky without clouds, the perfect day to be a tourist in an unfamiliar city. But it's not the scenery that takes my breath away, it's the man who's in front of it. With his back to me, he courses his hand through his morning hair, tugging on it. The muscles beneath his shirt stir with each shift.

I stand there for a moment, wishing I could stop time. Wanting this to last forever, but the pessimist inside me tells me nothing lasts forever.

I pad behind Ace, he detects me and turns. His gaze roams my body in admiration and lust. The way he looks at me like I'm the only person in the world is both a blessing and a sin.

Running my hands up his chest, I note the way he strains under my touch. As I turn to leave and allow him to finish the call, Ace catches my wrist. He draws me into him and wraps his free hand around my waist with a snug grip. I raise my brows at him, and his mouth coils into a smile.

"We'll have to discuss this later. I have something that requires my urgent attention," he says into the phone while grinning at me.

I noticed over the last couple of days that Ace appears more relaxed, less stressed. He needed this, needed to take a step back from work. Even though it's a small step, it's made a big difference to his overall mood.

Ace ends the call and slides his phone into the pocket of his shorts. "You look beautiful, Calla."

No matter how many times he compliments me, my heart still quickens, and my cheeks heat in response. I never thought much of compliments. They usually make me uncomfortable, and I don't know what to say in return. However, Ace causes a serene humming in my stomach.

"I'd be careful with what you say. There's this guy I'm kind of seeing… He's jealous and extremely impulsive."

He laughs, a wholehearted sound I'll never get sick of. "Lucky man."

Lucky me.

Hand in hand, we explore the historic streets of Sicily. We stop at a discreet café to order takeaway coffees. A few people take second glances at Ace, but they keep to themselves.

It's not until we've been walking for ten minutes that I notice Ace's sense of direction is extremely precise, like he knows where he's going. He leads us toward the harbor, where yachts and powerboats are stationed.

My mouth drops open. "This is not what I had in mind…" I utter, mind blown that he must have had this planned before I suggested sightseeing. It's proof he knows me better than I realized.

"You'd rather do something else?"

"No, this is amazing."

"Perfect." He lifts me from the dock and sets me on the boat, only taking his hands away when he's sure I have regained my balance.

The boat takes us about an hour from the shore to a tiny island where we can swim, snorkel, or just appreciate the scenery. The entire way there, my attention flickers from Ace to the horizon, where the sea blends in with the sky.

I'm afraid to admit it, but a part of me already knows I never stopped loving Ace. I lied to myself repeatedly over the years, so many times that even I started believing it. But the lies can't hide what I feel when he looks at me in admiration.

Once we arrive at our location for the day, I notice other sailboats gliding in the distance. The azure sea stretches around us, sparkling below the balmy sunrays. The water is clear, and if I concentrate, I'm able to make out the bottom.

Ace removes his shirt and stands on the edge of the boat, as if asking to be pushed in.

Without waiting for him to determine what I'm about to do, I lean into him. "I think you should get a little wet," I drawl, using his words as I push him into the sea.

He rises for air and flicks his head before setting his gaze on me. "Get in the water."

I shake my head with a smile.

"Calla, don't make me come over there." Even though he has a wide grin on his face, I discern the way his voice drops. It's the way he talks when he wants something—with authority and strength.

And when a man like Ace wants you, there's no room for arguing. My toes curl at the thought of it. I strip my clothes, thanking my past self for putting my bikini on underneath.

Instead of jumping in, I perch on the edge of the boat and slide my feet in. It's the end of spring, and the water is still chilly as it laps against my ankles. Ace is instantly in front of me, placing his hands on my waist and pulling me into the water with him. It's deep enough that I can't touch the bottom, but Ace can. I wrap my legs around his waist and put my hands on his shoulders for support.

He brings his mouth to mine, tasting like the sea, and I tug him closer. "Calla," he murmurs, teasing me with his tongue, tracing it against the seam of my lips.

We don't remain longer than five minutes in the water, it's freezing. So instead, we spend what seems like hours lounging at the front of the boat and talking about the last four years. About the parts of each other's lives we have missed out on.

Out in the middle of the sea, there are no distractions. Just us.

"I'm going to see my dad when we get back to New York," I tell Ace when we're sitting at the front of the boat having a picnic.

He's quiet for a moment. I almost think he isn't going to say anything. "You should," he finally replies.

There is an understanding between us. I still haven't decided what I'm going to tell my dad, but seeing him is a start. I'll decide the rest later.

"I feel like this is the calm before the storm," I state, meaning it literally and metaphorically. The sea is too quiet, and the sky that was cloudless this morning now darkens.

The thought of going back to New York is something I haven't come to terms with yet. Something doesn't feel right, and the closer we get to the end of this trip, the more this feeling intensifies.

"No matter what happens, remember that for me, it's always been you."

No matter what happens, he says that like he's aware of something I'm not. I can't find the words to ask what he's implying. Perhaps I'm afraid that his explanation will taint the remainder of our time together.

Once we return to the villa, I wash the salt out of my hair and sand out of places I didn't know it could get into.

Ace sits on the edge of the bed when I enter our room. "I want to ask you something."

"Hmm?" I'm unprepared for what's about to come.

"How do you feel about trying something?"

"Trying what?" A knot forms between my eyebrows.

My eyes drop to the black belt in his hands tied up in a way that resembles handcuffs. At first, I don't quite understand, and then it hits me all at once, like a tidal wave. He wants to tie me up when we have sex?

Oh, no.

"Ace." I shake my head.

This means everything. It's not about the belt in the form of handcuffs. It's the meaning behind it. I know what he's asking of me—my entire trust, vulnerability, and everything in between—it scares me to give this much of myself to a man, and he's fully aware of that. If I let him do this, there's no coming back. All my safeguard barriers will be erased.

"Trust me, Calla."

If he thinks I'm going to let him put that around my wrists, he's dead wrong. Being tied up in my most vulnerable state is unsettling. He's pushing me too far, too fast.

I almost drowned when I was five. My mom and dad took me on vacation to the beach. My dad told me not to go too deep, to stay in the shallow while they watched from the shore. But I misjudged what "shallow" meant. One second, I was ankle-deep playing with my sand bucket, and the next, a wave had tumbled me over and kept pulling me in.

Maybe that's when it all began, the constant panic of needing to have control of every situation. I've never been a fan of drinking or taking anything that would, in hindsight, make me feel like I couldn't think. Anything that would make me turbulent in my own body.

Then, when I was sixteen, I watched my mother die in front of me and couldn't do anything about it. I was trapped next to her for hours, unable to call for help. Unable to save her.

From then on, I desperately tried to keep away from situations that required me to give a part of myself that I couldn't.

Everything changed when I met Ace. For the first time in my life, I let someone see even the most broken parts of myself. The details I've kept hidden. The features I was afraid no one could ever understand, but he did. He broke my barriers down one by one, and I let him without even realizing it. I thought he was helping me heal. But, in reality, I was setting myself up for the most explosive destruction yet.

Everything that I was afraid happened.

"I can't do this." I shake my head again. I'm not ready to give him all of me. Why is he trying to push this? It's been only about a month, perhaps not even that, since we reconnected. More than half of that time I spent trying to convince myself we couldn't be together. I've only just come to terms with the possibility of us.

Ace drops his eyes to the floor. I wrap my hands around myself.

I stand between the bathroom and Ace for what seems like the longest time, waiting for him to say something. His face is blank, how he usually keeps it when he doesn't want me knowing what's toppling through his mind.

At times like these, I feel like I don't know him at all.

He finally lifts his head, observing me like he's trying to figure me out, like I'm the biggest mystery he's ever seen, when in reality, he's the mystery. "Why?"

Are we doing this now? After spending a fantastic day together, he wants to discuss why I have trust issues. Unfortunately, the list is too long to cover in a single night, and it's not easy to talk about.

"It's not a switch I can just flick. Give me time. Show me I can trust you instead of trying to force me, Ace."

It's not as simple as he makes it out to be. Especially not for someone like me. I've fallen to the point of no return and built a guard around myself so nothing can ever break-in.

I'll never tell him how much I cried that night. I cried more than I ever have. I felt like I was drowning, and no one could pull me back up. It was worse than anything I've experienced before.

If I stayed with Ace back then, there's no predicting how destructive we could have been together. Relying on someone to heal you never lasts.

"Time?" He snickers. "What has that got me in the last four years?"

I refrain from listing his achievements over the last four years. I'm sure that's not what he's talking about. I needed time to heal on my own. We both did.

"We're running out of time," Ace says unexpectedly, and I'm not sure if I hear him correctly.

Running out of time.

"What's that supposed to mean?" My voice comes out ragged.

He shakes his head. "Forget it."

He can't just say that and tell me to forget it. "What does it mean, Ace? You can't tell me anything, and you expect me to trust you. When has that ever worked for *me*?"

The last time I trusted him, everything blew up in flames. Quite literally. The whole sky burned amber the night I discovered his secret—our secret, in a way.

Ace pushes himself off the bed and stands. He towers over me. I barely reach his shoulders.

"I'll give you as much time as you need. But will you ever trust me? Or will there always be this barrier between us? I can see it in your face. You're unsure of us. It's like you're on the verge of running, and I'm uncertain if that will ever fade."

"I—" I want to tell him it's only temporary, but how do I know for sure? Will I ever be able to let my guard down and give him what he wants—all of me? Or have I finally built a barrier that can't be broken? Not even by him.

My therapist says to get over PTSD, I need to face the events that caused it in the first place. Where do I start?

Ace waits for a response that I can't provide him with right now.

"I guess I have my answer." He turns and leaves.

Seconds go by, and the front door slams. I'm left alone in the empty villa, stuck with my thoughts, questioning what he meant when he said we're running out of time. My lungs twist, cutting off circulation, and for the first time in a year, I experience an anxiety attack.

I spend the rest of the night on the balcony breathing in the salty air of the sea below me. I stop myself from looking up at the sky, knowing it will only make me ponder things more. Sometime after midnight, Ace returns. I'm already lying in bed. My eyes are closed, but I'm not asleep.

"I'm sorry," Ace apologizes, somehow knowing I'm awake. The bed shifts, and he lies next to me. He smells like body wash and faintly of the beach. He must have walked along it to clear his head, but I wish he stayed and talked to me instead.

"Mmm," I mumble, not knowing what to say. I guess we both can't give each other what we need. I need absolute openness and honesty, and he needs trust. Both can't work without each other, and neither of us is willing to give it up first.

"I know it's only been two weeks, but it feels like I've known you my whole life," he explains.

I know the feeling, but at the same time, I don't. I only know what he wants me to. I turn around to face him. "What did you mean by we don't have much time?"

He shakes his head and brushes his fingers down my shoulder, over my upper arm, electrifying every spot he touches. "I don't know, Calla. It just came out. I wasn't thinking."

Another lie. How many more will there be?

"Okay," I resign, not wanting to start yet another argument. This is another thing we'll have to discuss eventually, but when?

Ace props himself up with his elbow, and his other hand cups my face. He trails his fingers down my cheekbones and over my lips. My eyes don't leave his face, observing him closely as he touches the freckles on my nose that I've always been self-conscious about.

"Beautiful," his voice is low, and finally, he leans down, tilting my chin toward him and places his lips to mine.

He kisses me slowly, like he's savoring the moment between us. His lips are gentle against my own, in tune, and I disregard everything I've been worrying about. I feel like I'm eighteen and back in college, kissing the guy I've fallen in love with, and everything is the way it's meant to be.

It's as though I've barely shut my eyes when I'm jerked awake by the sudden sound of sheets thrashing and a throaty grumble.

Opening my eyes, I discover Ace disturbed in his sleep. His eyebrows furrow, and sweat beads on his forehead. Words that I can't comprehend tumble out of his mouth.

He's having a nightmare. I don't shake him, knowing from

personal experience it's the worst thing to do. "Ace."

He doesn't wake up.

"Ace," I call louder, gently touching his shoulder. His eyes dart open, and his gaze focuses on me, but it's like he doesn't see me, like he's still wedged in the nightmare.

"Calla," he echoes my name as if not accepting my presence.

"It's okay. I'm here."

Ace wraps his arms around my body, pulling me closer to his burning chest. I rest my chin on his shoulder and wait until his breathing regulates.

"How often do you have these?" I haven't seen him have one before, but I've only spent two weeks with him, and in the first half, we didn't sleep in the same bed.

"Not often," he reassures me.

"Ace—"

"A couple of times a week. It's not that bad."

"You should go see someone," I advise. Has he ever talked about this to anyone before? Maybe I was wrong when I thought we'd both healed in the time apart. Perhaps he hasn't healed at all.

"No," he dismisses my suggestion.

"Why?"

"It's not for me."

"Ace…" I want to ask what the dream was about.

"Calla, we'll talk about it another time. Go back to sleep."

My head rests on his heated skin, and we lie like that until the sun rises. Neither of us moves or says anything, and eventually, I doze off on Ace's chest.

I told Ace I wanted to spend the whole day relaxing in the villa and utilizing the private beach for my birthday. We've been doing things every day. It doesn't bother me. I know Ace is a busy man. However, it would be nice to spend time with him away from everyone.

We don't wake up until later in the evening, since we fell asleep late in the morning. At least I fell asleep, I'm not sure if Ace did.

"Happy birthday, love." Ace is looking down at me when my eyes flutter open, like he's been watching me sleep.

"Ugh, don't remind me." I pull the blanket over my face.

He peers at me. "You don't like birthdays?"

"I don't like getting old."

"You're the same as me now." He grins. His birthday isn't until November.

I raise my eyebrows as if to say precisely my point. Even though Ace is twenty-three, I'd assume he was in his early thirties if I saw him on the street. It has nothing to do with the way he looks, it's the way he carries himself. Knowledge and a life full of lessons make him appear older than he is.

"Come out when you're ready. I have something planned." Ace brushes his lips against my forehead. He jumps off the bed and flashes me a grin before heading out of the room. He's in a good mood today.

This is our last evening before we fly back to New York tomorrow. The thought leaves an unnerving feeling inside of me.

I follow the smell of tomatoes and onion cooking into the kitchen. Ace is wearing a loose button-up T-shirt unbuttoned, revealing his sculpted chest and red shorts, far from his usual dark attire. It's in these rare moments that he truly looks his age and not far older.

He's standing by the electric cooktop with his back to me, tomatoes and onion cooking in one pan, and in the other, water boils with pasta.

This is the best thing he could have done for my birthday. Any man can take you out to dinner, but a man who cooks for you is a man worth keeping.

"What are you making?" I ask. He turns and scans me, from the short red sundress I'm wearing—matching his shorts—to my bare feet.

"Bucatini all'amatriciana," Ace answers, and I raise my eyebrows. What's sexier than a man cooking Italian for you, and not just any man, but Ace.

"I've left you speechless, Calla. Are you impressed?" He grins playfully, teasing me.

Walking toward him, I laugh. "Yes, very. I mean, I should have known you cook from the first time I saw you making pancakes."

His grin widens at the memory, and he winks. "My specialty."

"I'm still waiting to try those," I remind him. The last time he made them in college, I didn't get the chance to taste them. Instead, I smacked him with one.

"Tomorrow morning," he promises and turns back to the stove.

"I could get used to this. You cooking for me in a kitchen overlooking the Mediterranean Sea. What more could a girl want?" I permit my fingers to skim his lower back before leaning against the counter behind him.

"We could live here."

"Hmm?" I ask, waiting for him to give me a sign he's just kidding, but he turns to me again, a serious expression coating his face.

"We could live here. Buy this, or any other villa that you want, and start our lives."

But our lives have already been started in another city. What would I do here? I'm not just going to sit here and look pretty while Ace works. *Works*. And I sit at home like a housewife.

I don't tell him how ridiculous that idea is right now. Instead, I smile and say, "Maybe, one day."

Ace retrieves an envelope from his pocket and hands it to me. I take it, staring at it in confusion.

Inside are two tickets. "Tickets to see your dad," Ace clarifies.

There are two tickets. At first, I think Ace is implying he wants to come with me. But then he says, "I thought you might want to take Mia with you. But you don't have to use the second one."

"Ace, you didn't have to. When I said I was going to see my dad, I wasn't hinting at anything."

"Calla." He turns and braces his hands on the granite countertop on either side of me. "I wanted to. Let me do things for you."

"You've *done* enough." I glance down at the very expensive bracelet that's dangling off my wrist. "But thank you." I rise on my tiptoes and press my lips against his.

His strong hands case around my waist, and he lifts me, positioning me on the smooth counter, making it easier for me to explore his mouth with my own. I slide my hands over his chest, and his tongue teases my lips.

"Fuck, Calla." He pulls away. "I did plan on having proper food before having you."

My core tenses at his words, and the need for him intensifies, but my stomach grumbles, and I'm reminded I haven't had food in almost twenty-four hours.

"Where did you learn how to cook?" I change the subject.

"I know the basics. I taught myself when my mom was at

work, and I looked after Ellie," he says. "Never quite got the hang of baking."

I recall the day he took me to see Ellie for the first time, and I briefly zone out to four years ago, to Ace driving my old Mazda while the Arctic Monkeys were on.

Tugging myself back to the present, I watch Ace serve up the pasta and take our plates outside. I grab some forks and napkins and follow him. Out on the balcony is a table overlooking a magnificent sunset. The warm-orange shade gleams over the sea as the waves lash against the sand below us.

"This is so good," I comment after I have a forkful. The different flavors burst in my mouth, and Ace grins, gaining an even bigger head.

"I want to tell you something," he begins cautiously when I take another forkful of pasta in my mouth.

"Hmm?"

He sets his fork down and focuses his attention on me. "After the accident, I watched you now and then for two years. I couldn't help checking up on you. It was guilt eating away at me."

I wipe my mouth with a napkin before considering what he just told me. "That's how you knew so much about me already," I say out loud, remembering the details he knew about me back in college without me telling him.

He nods and waits for me to answer.

"Okay," I finally say.

"Okay?"

"It's in the past, Ace. It was six years ago. We were both dealing with our trauma and did irrational things."

He stares at me as if he were expecting a different reaction. I'm unsure of what he wants me to say, so I ignore his demanding gaze.

After dinner, I help Ace clean up—I stack the dishes in the

dishwasher and wipe the bench. Ace ushers me back out and trails with a dessert in his hands. Chocolate fondue with cut-up strawberries, banana, and marshmallows.

"Thank you for doing this tonight. It's perfect."

Ace dips a strawberry in the chocolate with a long fork and offers it to me. I open my mouth, but he taps my nose with it before placing it in.

"Ace!" I laugh, wiping the chocolate with the napkin.

We consume the rest of the dessert—more like put it all over each other while laughing, and my face and hands are sticky by the time we're done. So are Ace's.

Standing from the small table, I head over to the stairs that lead to the beach. I slide the dress straps off my shoulders, and the material pools around my feet. I'm left in only my underwear, with my top half entirely bare.

Ace consumes me with his gaze, drinking me in.

I'm aware of everything—the way the waves crash against the shore below me, calmly and slowly. The moonlight shines down on me, casting a shadow and accenting the curves of my breasts. Ace looks at me with pure lust and need.

"I'm going for a swim. Want to join me?"

I don't wait for a reply and turn my back to him. I descend the stairs and hear the distant sound of the chair shifting and Ace standing abruptly, almost knocking it over.

"Fuck," he mutters under his breath as he rights it and follows me.

22

The Last Night

Ace

Calla treads into the ocean while the moon illuminates a straight path for her. Her brunette hair cascades over her bare back, and her fingertips brush the stillness of the water, barely touching it.

It's frigid in the sea since the temperature drops significantly during the night.

Finally, when she's waist-deep under the moon, she turns, exposing her naked chest. "Are you coming, or are you just going to stand there and let me have all the fun?" Her mouth curves up into an angelic smile.

Never has anyone made me as vulnerable as she does. How the fuck can she do that with a simple smile? My feet move, guiding me to her like I'm a puppet on a string. I'd do anything she asked me to. She had me from the very first time I saw her.

At first, I thought it was some kind of sick obsession. After the accident, I couldn't stop thinking about her. She was on my mind twenty-four-seven, driving me fucking insane. I thought I was losing my mind. I kept telling myself it was the guilt eating at me, that it wouldn't last, but the constant need to know if she was doing okay remained.

I strived to stay away from her when she went to college, but I couldn't.

I still can't.

It's more than just a tug toward her. It's as though my whole fucking world spins for her. For the last four years, I've been existing, trying to get by the days, months, years, hoping I'd feel something for someone else, or at the very least, forget about her. But everyone else has been a distraction, and Calla is the only one who seizes my mind. It's a fucking mental illness, and there's no cure.

I encase my hands around her waist. Her skin is soft, and I brush my thumb down her bare stomach. She shudders, her eyebrows creasing together like she's churning thoughts in her head.

"What is it?" I ask.

She doesn't look at me. "Have you talked to anyone about your nightmares? Or the accident?" She traces a spot on my chest with her forefinger, apprehensive about how I'll react.

"Someone like?" I prompt, hoping she doesn't bring up a shrink again. I don't need to share my fucked-up life with a person who doesn't give a shit.

"Anyone… Theo, your mom."

"My mom?"

"She told me that you told her about the accident, but you didn't say much more," she explains.

My mom always knew about the accident, perhaps before I even told her. She was more than disappointed, and I could see that somehow, she blamed herself, too, which in hindsight, destroyed me further.

"I haven't talked to anyone." It's something I have to live with for the rest of my life, and I shouldn't get the easy way out.

"You should."

I still her fingers by taking them in my hand. "Calla—"

"I'm not trying to make you do anything. I'm just worried about you," she says defensively.

"I know. You don't need to be."

She provides me a look that says otherwise. "I can come with you to therapy if you want. Just think about it, Ace. You've been through more than other people have. Setting everything to the back of your mind continuously isn't going to make it go away."

"Why do you think I need someone to talk to?"

"Because you never talk to me. Not about anything important. It feels like you're one person with me and a different person with others. I knew you back in college, and it feels like I barely know you now. I doubt you talk about your issues with other people, either. It's not healthy."

"What do you want to know?" I cup her face, tracing the corner of her soft mouth with my thumb, and she parts her lips instinctively, only a fraction.

"I-I..." she stutters. I've put her on the spot. "Do you want kids?"

I chuckle, knowing she didn't mean to ask me that, but she blurts out things under pressure. "Are you trying to tell me something, Calla?"

She wraps her hands around my neck, shaking her head. "I want to know everything. I want you to want to talk to me. If not to me, then someone. You can't live like this...not being able to sleep and having nightmares every time you do for the rest of your life."

"I'll think about therapy," I say and lean down to meet her lips, ending the conversation. They're soft, with the flavor of rich chocolate and strawberries.

"Thank you for everything," she murmurs against my mouth. "Today was perfect."

There were a million things I could've taken her to do on her birthday. I could give Calla the whole fucking world in her hands if she asked me to. But she asked for this, and who am I to tell her no?

I lift her, barely feeling the weight of her in the water, and she wraps her legs around my torso. I move my mouth in sync with hers, slow and tentatively.

"I'm falling in love with you all over again," she mumbles. I pull away and look at her, for the first time seeing her for everything she is. The honey-colored speckles in her eyes catch against the moonlight, and a strand of hair falls down her forehead.

She always tries to see the good in everyone, no matter what. "There's always been a part of me that's loved you all these years, but I pushed it away. I tried to convince myself we're not good for each other, not suited. Because how can I love someone that—"

Someone that committed a severe crime. Someone that took a person's life.

"And now?" I prompt.

"I'm tired of fighting this. We're messed up, but…"

"But something keeps bringing us to each other," I finish for her, tucking the strand of hair behind her ear.

She looks at me, and a small, distant smile surfaces on her lips.

There's a shower outside, and Calla tilts her head back, rinsing her hair from the saltwater. My eyes don't leave her—they are *unable* to leave her. Her breasts are pebbled, and I notice the small goose bumps glazing over them, down to her silky stomach and in between her thighs where a sheer white thong covers the bare fucking minimum.

"Enjoying the show?" She raises a brow, gazing straight at me.

I grin. "When aren't I?"

I retrieve the button-up shirt that I left on the stairs' wooden rail and slide it over her body, just until we get inside. She saunters up the wooden stairs, the shirt not doing a whole lot to cover her toned ass. I inhale sharply, adjusting my pants to make room for the growth.

She tilts her head back toward me. "Perv."

I slap her ass. "I'll fuck you hard for that."

The only thing deterring me from taking her right on this beach is the potential cameras around this place. Not that I care about them filming me, but I don't want anyone else seeing Calla and the things I'm going to do to her.

Once we're inside, Calla strolls to the bathroom. She removes the shirt and her panties, abandoning the clothes on the floor like they're an inconvenience. She turns the shower on and eyes my shorts while waiting for the water to heat up.

I take them off.

She tugs me with her into the shower. "Showering with you has become my favorite thing to do."

"Is that so?" I situate my hands on the curve of her waist.

"Mmm." She hums while sliding her hands down my chest and suckling on her bottom lip.

I bow my head, catching her breast in my mouth and drawing on her nipple with a concentrated suck. She gasps, her body jolting at the sensation. I continue placing kisses down her body, my tongue darting out now and then to capture the silkiness of her skin.

Finally, I kneel on the shower floor and rest my hands on her knees, spreading her legs wide. "I wanted to do this all day, Calla." I part her lower lips, and my fingers massage her.

I glance up, and her cheeks are flushed more than usual from the steam, her breasts are already swollen with need. Just the way I want her—ready for me.

Leaning forward, I run my tongue from her entrance to her clit, and she shudders, jerking away. I tighten my grip around her thighs, keeping her in place, and a moan eludes her lips when I continue the gradual, wet strokes with my tongue.

She tastes addictive, like something I won't ever get enough of, and my tongue circles her, slowly at first and then increasing speed, building her up.

I allow myself to glance up at Calla. Her head leans against the shower wall, and her eyes are almost closed. The showerhead is positioned so that the water hits her chest directly, streaming down her body, and I reach up and roll her nipple in between my thumb and forefinger.

She drops her lower lip, and a small moan escapes them. The way she reacts to me is fascinating. I've never been with someone this responsive. I could make her come more than ten times in one night. Perhaps we need to test that theory out.

"Your mouth…" she gasps, unable to finish her sentence, and I chuckle against her, which results in another moan.

Smiling at my thoughts, I keep tonguing her, disregarding my throbbing erection in favor of experiencing her. The way she wraps her fingers in my hair and tugs on it when my tongue grazes the most sensitive spot makes the crown of my cock bead with pre-cum.

"Ace…" she moans, almost inaudible but desperate, needing me to give her more.

"Mmm, I love the way you taste," I hum against her, knowing the vibrations will drive her insane.

I push her thighs farther apart and lick her where she needs me the most, drinking up all her arousal and feeling her grow slicker with every flick of my tongue. I look up for a second to meet her eyes. They're fixated on mine as my mouth remains occupied.

"Fuck… Oh my God," she curses when I slide one finger inside her.

"Dirty mouth, love," I suck on her and add a second finger, enjoying the clench of her walls as I curl them both, pressing hard and fast. Within seconds, her nails dig into my shoulders, and I grasp her legs tighter for support as she buckles her hips toward me, giving herself over.

I wipe my mouth on the inside of her leg and rise to my feet. She wastes no time and wraps her hands around my neck, bringing me closer. My mouth finds hers—soft, hot, and wet.

"I need you inside me," she murmurs against my mouth, her tongue frantically meeting mine. "Right now."

Her words make my cock harden to the point of pain. "Patience is a virtue."

"Ace—" She wraps her hand around me and tightens her grip.

"Fuck… Calla." I focus on not blowing my load right in her fucking hand.

I lift her and position myself against her entrance, trailing wet kisses down her neck, sucking, licking, and letting the hot water course down my back.

She drives her hips against me, craving me inside her. Finally, I give in, slowly pushing myself into her with a raspy groan.

The tightness of her forces my self-control to dissolve, and I can feel in the depth of my balls that this round isn't going to last. The need to come is more intense than ever before.

I clasp her hands above her head and thrust into her, feeling every drive, from root to tip, and I'm still unable to get enough.

The urge to be deeper, to possess her, to embed myself into her until there's no backtracking—overcomes me.

Finally, releasing her hands, I use my thumb to circle her clit while she pants my name. Her walls clench around me, and her nails insistently scrape my back.

"You feel so good inside me. I'm so close. Don't stop," she mutters against my neck. She's aware of what her words, alone, do to me, and I can't resist any longer. Her words, her tongue skimming my neck, her hands around me… It's my weakness. She's my weakness.

I slide her up, almost off my cock, and then plunge her back down while she clutches onto my shoulders. My release knocks me hard, like a gunshot. Every synapse fires in my mind concurrently, and the sensation is sublime. Grunting, I spill inside her. She comes after me, trembling with deep desire, and her walls clench around me as she milks me dry.

"Fucking hell," I mutter into her shoulder.

23

Home

Calla

Waking up this morning feels unusual—almost nostalgic, even though we haven't left yet. Ace and I have been trapped in our bubble for the last few days, and it's been wonderful. It's altered everything, but we can't stay like this forever, no matter how much I yearn to.

I have a real job that, under normal circumstances, doesn't involve shadowing Ace. I like my job. I enjoy working, even if it's for Jennifer, for now. In the future, I want to be able to draft articles that matter, about important issues instead of about rich and famous men. But we all have to start somewhere, and if this is what it takes, then I'll take anything I can get.

If it weren't for this job, I wonder how many more years would have elapsed before Ace and I ran into each other. We would have, eventually. It's evident from the way fate keeps guiding us together that something here merits a chance. I'm willing to try. Perhaps I'm ready to set everything on the line one more time.

Stretching out on the vacant king-sized bed, I yawn. After two weeks with Ace, I'm not shocked he's not in bed this morning. He's almost always awake before me. It makes me query if he sleeps at all or avoids it so he doesn't experience nightmares like I used to.

Rising out of bed, I tiptoe across the cool wooden floors into the bathroom, pausing by the window to behold the hues of blue. The view of the sky and sea covers every inch I can grasp. In the distance, several sailboats glide across the glass-clear waters.

I brush my teeth in the bathroom and wash my face, not bothering to put any makeup on, only some tinted sunscreen. We're leaving soon, and it's a lengthy flight home.

Walking out into the open-plan kitchen, I locate a scene that, once again, sparks distant college memories. Four years ago suddenly feels like yesterday. I lean against the wall in awe of the view in front of me.

Ace is in the kitchen with his back to me. The balcony doors are open, and the translucent curtains are drawn back, permitting the morning sun to engulf the spacious room and reflect from the light pendants hanging above the kitchen counter.

Music trickles out of the speaker on the bench, and Ace hums to it, his voice low but filled with a softness that makes me reluctant to disturb him. It's a sight to see. I linger for a moment, absorbing it, hoping this isn't the last time I wake up to this.

When I'm finally unable to keep away, I pad over and snake my arms around his waist. "Good morning, handsome."

He doesn't flinch. It's like he knew all along I've been ogling him. "Good morning, beautiful," he turns, presses his warm mouth on mine, and pulls me closer. The kiss is soft and slow as he takes his time with me.

I wrap myself tighter around Ace's warm body when the drafty morning breeze sweeps upon us.

"You're always awake. Do you ever sleep?" I frown.

His mouth curls at the corners, and he deposits a soft peck to my nose while kneading my shoulder tenderly. "I had a few emails to go over."

"In the middle of the night?" I ask, recollecting he wasn't in bed when I woke to use the bathroom.

"I couldn't sleep," he finally admits. "I did some work instead, updated my schedule for the rest of the week, and went over some contracts that required my attention."

I trace the dark lingering loops under his eyes. He stills my fingers, and I meet his eyes. "I'm fine."

"Don't say that when you're not." I know it's what I would have said four years ago.

I hope Ace does consider going to therapy. I'm unsure of how long he can endure this before it destroys him. There's so much trauma, so much guilt still consuming him.

"Calla—"

"Ace, you need to talk to someone about this. I can see what carrying all this guilt is still doing to you, and it's hard to watch someone you lo—care about go through this without trying to help."

"You love me?" He arches his brow even though I mentioned that word yesterday as well.

I roll my eyes. "Is that the only thing you managed to get out of that?"

"I like hearing it, so, yes."

He turns back to the pan, and just like that, this conversation is over. I sigh, turning to inspect the fluffy pancakes, just like he promised last night.

He flips the last one onto the plate and serves them up with strawberries, banana, and maple syrup, topped off with whipped cream. My mouth waters looking at them. At the same time, my stomach grumbles, and I remind myself I need to get home and start using those stairs again.

"So good," I state with a mouthful, and Ace laughs.

"I told you. My specialty," he says with a wide grin.

"How's Ellie doing?" I ask in between chewing. I'm not sure when I'll see her next. I have to get back to work, and the tickets Ace gifted me to see my dad are for this weekend.

Ace shrugs. "She's getting better, but she was getting better last time too, and then she got worse again." His expression is defeated.

"She's strong. She'll get through this."

"I don't want to get my hopes up."

"Sometimes all we have is hope. We have to believe we deserve something good to happen. Ellie is the most amazing, strong little girl I've ever met, and she deserves the best. She will get through this, Ace."

He blames himself for this, too, and there's nothing I can say that will alter his mind.

After breakfast, we pack our belongings and leave the villa. The drive to the airport is jarringly silent, as though both of us are afraid of what will happen when we arrive back home. The inevitable is nearing. Perhaps another black hole.

"Can I use your laptop? I didn't bring mine, and I quickly have to check my emails," I ask Ace after takeoff.

"Sure." He passes it to me.

I click on the internet browser. The page is already open to his emails. I'm ready to press the log-out option, but my eyes linger on an unopened email.

From *The New York Times*.

Is this a coincidence, or is he meddling in my career again after he promised not to?

"Tell me this email isn't what I think it is." I look at him for confirmation, hoping it's a coincidence. Maybe he's working with them.

He glances over and exhales before answering. "It's exactly what it looks like. You deserve a position there more than most people, and I know what it would mean to you to work there."

At least he's honest, but it doesn't make me feel any better. How doesn't he understand that I aspire to do this myself? What he's doing is excessive.

"I'd rather work with Jennifer knowing I got the job because of my skills—because of me—rather than work there knowing I got the job because of you."

He sighs, staring out the small plane window. "I haven't mentioned your name yet. I just asked for a favor from a friend, and this would be their reply." He gestures to the screen.

"Good. Don't do anything else," I snap, frustrated.

"You let Nik help you. Why is it so hard for you to let me?"

"Nik got me a meeting. A *meeting*, Ace. It's an opportunity for me to sell myself to them, show them my qualifications, experience, and see if they like me for me. I'm not guaranteed a job from this meeting. It's not a free ride, which is what you're proposing." I take a deep breath, attempting not to get worked up over this, but it's difficult not to when Ace strayed behind my back after I specifically asked him not to.

There's silence between us while he thinks about what I just said. Then, finally, he looks at me. "I'm sorry. You deserve the world, Calla, and I'm just trying to give it to you."

His words are good-natured, but the fact that he went behind my back after he promised he wouldn't doesn't sit right with me, and his reasons aren't exactly convincing. I get the impression there's more to this.

"Why are you trying to compete with Nik? He's not in the picture anymore."

He drops his head in his hand and pinches the bridge of his nose with his thumb and forefinger. He's shutting me out, a habit he's become accustomed to when he doesn't want to disclose something. But keeping secrets will drive me away.

"Ace, talk to me. Please." I rest my hand on his thigh, rubbing it gently. Something is bothering him, and I want to be the person he can confide in. I want to be there for him. "It doesn't matter what you tell me anymore. I'm not running. I want to be here for you, to understand."

There's silence again. I reach for the bottle of water in front of me and take a mouthful. When I finally think he won't answer, Ace does the unexpected.

"He's my half brother."

My mouth gapes open, and all the air is knocked out of me. Out of all the things I thought he might tell me, that wasn't one of them. I stare at him like he's just told me the sky is falling, deliberating whether this is a joke. But Ace wouldn't joke about something like this, and knowing his father's history, everything somersaults into place.

"Are you sure?" My voice is barely audible.

"As sure as I can be without having a blood test."

"Does he know?"

"No."

"Shit, Ace." I scoot back in the seat and lean against the headrest. "Shit."

My head spins, and I've never had travel sickness before, but I abruptly have the urge to hurl my breakfast all over this plane.

I hold it in and take deep breaths. How didn't I figure it out? No wonder Ace has been acting this way at the mention of Nik's name.

"I had no idea."

"I know." He links my hand in his and skims his thumb over the back of it.

For the rest of the flight, we barely speak. I have too many questions, but I can't bring myself to ask them. How long has he known? Why did he hire Nik as his lawyer? Why didn't he tell me earlier? Nothing makes sense, but at the same time, everything fits together.

Sometime during the nine-hour flight, I fall asleep. However, when I awaken, I'm more fatigued than ever. My eyes droop heavily, and I zone out during the car ride back to Ace's apartment.

Ace, on the other hand, is busy with work, as per usual. He has a few calls come in about meetings, and I admire how his mouth moves as he talks with urgency and authority. It reminds me of where it was only a night ago. But now that we're back in New York, it seems farther and farther away.

Still on the phone when we arrive at his apartment, Ace advances toward his office, and I mount the stairs. I pack my bags, knowing I can't stay here. Even though I'd rather stay with Ace, it's time to go home.

Coming downstairs, Ace glances at my bags and then at me.

"I'm not running," I explain. "But I don't want to rush into things. I have my apartment, my own life…" It's impulsive to move in together.

He nods, but I suspect he was hoping for a different outcome. "Of course. I'll get Denzel to drive you to your apartment."

I move toward him. "I don't want things to change between us. I want this." My hands run up his chest. "But if it's not something you want…"

"You're all I want, all I need, Calla." He lifts me onto the counter, and my hands fly to his hair, tugging him closer. His mouth covers mine in a heartbeat.

My hands explore under his shirt as he continues kissing me. It's different from the other times and doesn't evolve into anything else. I wrap my legs around him, and he cups my face while his tongue flickers rhythmically with mine. A reassurance that we *need* each other.

Ace escorts me downstairs with one hand around my waist and the other carrying my bag. Denzel waits outside by the entrance, and he takes the bag from Ace once we get closer.

Ace inclines his head, pressing his lips briefly to mine. "I'll call you tomorrow, Calla."

Somehow this goodbye feels wrong, but I can't pinpoint exactly what about it feels wrong. I slide into the back of the car and allow Denzel to drive me home.

✦ ✦ ✦

Oreo is instantly at my feet when I unlock the front door to my apartment. Mia agreed to take care of him when I explained Ace was taking me to Paris. I hope she remembered to feed him every day, since she's been *busy* with other matters, such as Theo.

I squat down and pat Oreo. He meows, nuzzling his head into my hand. My eyes flicker up to Mia as she walks toward me from another room. "You have a lot of explaining to do, Mia."

She pushes the glass of red wine that's on the counter toward me like she's been waiting for me to come home all night. "You might want to sit down for this one, babe."

It's peculiar being in my apartment after everything that's happened in the last week. My life has changed drastically. The place seems smaller than I remember—maybe because I've become accustomed to Ace's colossal living arrangement.

The feeling of being home doesn't overcome me like I thought it would. Instead, *home* is distant, somewhere that's not here. I wonder if home isn't a place for me anymore, but the presence of a certain someone? It scares me how rapidly I've fallen back into something that shattered me once already.

Abandoning my suitcase by the door, I tread over to the laminate counter and take the wine glass in my hands. I twirl the contents, watching the rich-red liquid swirl inside. I glance up at Mia, assessing her expression. Her pale-blue eyes consider me, too. We both have so much to tell each other.

I take my wineglass to the sofa and sit by the window, glancing out at the city I've always dreamed of living in. The city that never sleeps. However, it's somehow too loud, too intolerable, and I shut the blinds, wishing this feeling would eventually subside.

"I hope you're about to tell me that you didn't sleep with a married man," I finally confront Mia as she plunges next to me.

Her silky pink nightie leaves nothing to the imagination, and her skin glows underneath the yellow bulb, but I've seen her with less on before. Her eyes widen, and her expression changes to disgust. "What!?"

"Is that a no?" I raise a brow and nurse my wine, waiting for the explanation.

"I thought by telling you that I slept with him, you'd grasp that he's separated. I would *never* get myself in that kind of a mess." She looks genuinely offended that I thought any different.

"I didn't know what to think after you ignored my phone calls and messages for days, and Ace was sure that Theo was happily married," I explain, feeling guilty for doubting Mia. I shouldn't have, but how was I supposed to know when she left me in the dark?

She sighs. "Theo and his wife separated. Recently."

"How recently?" I question.

"Two weeks ago, before we bumped into him at Ace's apartment. Theo was there to tell Ace about it, but apparently, something came up, and he didn't get the chance to."

My thoughts wander to Ace and how angry he was when he found out about Mia and Theo. I'm hoping Ace will allow Theo to explain before doing something irrational and stupid.

"His wife cheated on him, and he filed for divorce the day after. She's not very cooperative and wants another chance. From what Theo told me, it sounds like their marriage wasn't great, either. They got married in Vegas the same night they met. Theo told me they tried to make it work, but they're two different people."

I watch her as she talks. Her hair is in loose curls, bouncing with every word, and she brings her knees up to her chest, squishing her breasts.

"But they *are* separated," she emphasizes again. "He's moved his stuff into his own apartment."

I'm sure Mia is well-acquainted with his apartment and other parts of him by now.

"So are you two…?" I'm unsure of what to ask. Are they just fucking, or is something going to come out of this? I never know with Mia, but I doubt she even knows herself. It's been less than a week.

She scoots back onto the sofa and stretches her legs out again. "I never told you the real reason Theo and I broke up in the first place. It wasn't just the travel. I couldn't be exclusive with him—I'm not into monogamous relationships. I'm not ready to settle down, and I don't know if I'll ever be." For some reason, I'm not shocked.

Mia has always been a free spirit, and I can't see her being attached to one person for the rest of her life. However, I also can't see Theo ever being okay with that. I doubt he's into sharing.

"I'm not into relationships with men, for that matter," she adds. "Theo is the only guy I've ever been attracted to enough to want to bang his brains out."

I clear my throat at her vulgarness. "I'm sure you did that and more in the last few days," I remark, and she gives me a look that confirms everything and more.

"How was *your* trip?" Mia returns the attention to me when I've only just started getting to the juicy details. "I hope you got some good dick."

Her eyes land on the bracelet that Ace gave me, and she raises my wrist. "Jesus, Calla! This bracelet costs more than forty grand! How good did you fuck him?"

"Mia!"

"I wish he had a rich brother," she adds nonchalantly, admiring the diamonds embedded in the bracelet.

Coughing, I almost spit out the drink in my mouth.

"What?" she questions, her eyes growing wide.

"I only found out a few hours ago…" I warn her before continuing. "Nik is Ace's half brother."

Her mouth gapes open, and she doesn't say anything for a few elongated moments.

"Didn't include that little detail in your files, huh?" I ask.

"What the fuck! How did you manage to get yourself in that mess? Fucking brothers?" She gulps down her wine and pours herself another glass, drinking that one, too.

"An unfortunate coincidence." I narrow my eyes. "It's not like I intended for that to happen. I haven't seen Ace in four years. How was I supposed to know Nik was his long-lost brother?"

She shakes her head in disbelief. It feels disloyal leaking Ace's secret to Mia, but in a way, this affects me as well. I don't bother asking her not to tell anyone. I've been friends with her for long enough to know that this conversation will remain between us.

"Trust me. I was as speechless as you. More so since *I'm* the one who is in the middle of this."

"Did Ace ask who's better in bed?" She wiggles her eyebrows.

"Why would he ask me that?"

"Men are egotistical creatures. They like to know if someone beats them at their own game," she explains.

"Well, I'm glad to say that he didn't bring it up, and I hope it never comes."

She shrugs. "Nik can't be that good if it took you less than a week of spending time with Ace to end it with him."

I groan, covering my face with my hands. My head dizzies from the wine, but it's nice to be able to talk to Mia.

✦

The following day, my alarm pierces my ears. I didn't miss waking up early, knowing I have to deal with Jennifer today.

"What's that awful sound, and why is it right near my ear," Mia groans from the other side of my bed, hugging a pillow over her head. As much as I want to do the same thing, I push myself to get out of bed.

I get ready for work and feed Oreo on my way out. I depart my apartment building to discover Ace's black Mercedes by the curb with Denzel in the driver's seat.

Once I near it, the window rolls down, and I look inside, encountering Denzel's bright smile. "Good morning, Denzel."

"Good morning, miss—Calla," he corrects himself.

"I'm capable of getting myself to work. I've been doing it for years," I say warmly. It's not Denzel's fault he must follow absurd instructions from Ace.

"Mr. Blackwell insisted."

I draw in a breath and get in the car, not bothering to argue. A free lift to work isn't so bad. "Is Ace at work already?"

Denzel glances at me through the rearview mirror. "Yes, he had an early board meeting this morning."

The rest of the drive passes in silence, and I blankly look out the window as we crawl through Brooklyn traffic. Finally, I pull my phone from my purse and text Ace.

Me: ***Thank you for the ride, but perhaps next time I could ride you on my way to work.***

Out of all the places I've had sex, I've never done it in a car. Wildly erotic thoughts of Ace fill my head, and I slip my phone back into my purse without waiting for a reply.

"Thank you," I tell Denzel when we pull up in front of *Satire Times,* and I get out of the car.

I order the usual two coffees from downstairs, one for myself and one for Jennifer—unsure if she expects one from me but not wanting to get on her wrong side this morning.

Her office door is open, and she glances up from her computer screen when I stand in the doorway. I set the coffee cup on her desk, and she slides her glasses off her long face.

"I guess Ace couldn't hold out." Her piercing eyes meet mine.

"Excuse me?"

"I received a check from him for one hundred thousand dollars." She grins widely, clearly pleased with herself, but her tone is still icy. I didn't think Ace would bother with Jennifer. He could have simply acted like he kept the deal.

Jennifer taps her long fingernails on the table. "I still expect a full article by Thursday morning on my desk for review."

"Of course," I reply, and just like that, I'm dismissed. No other questions about Ace or how I spent my time with him. I guess she'll find out in the article, or at least what I want her to find out—which is the bare minimum.

At my desk, I briefly check my phone. A text from Ace awaits me.

Ace: ***Don't tempt me with a good time unless you're willing to put your money where your mouth is, love.***

I swear my heart drops into my panties. I squeeze my thighs together and type out a text that will distract him from whatever meeting he's in.

Me: ***Trust me, Ace. I know exactly where to put my mouth.***

For the remainder of the day, I catch up with work matters that I missed the last two weeks. It's no surprise Jennifer issued me a pile of work to finish by the end of the week, plus the article on Ace. The day flies by, and I skip lunch to get on top of all the emails and other bits and pieces.

By the time the afternoon rolls around, I've almost forgotten I have an interview with Timothy Kline—Nik's business acquaintance and one of the top people at *The Times*. He's moved our interview from his office to a nearby coffee shop. I was confused at first, but I suspect he wants to get out of his office after a long day, so I agreed.

For some unknown reason, I had a particular vision of Timothy in my head—a redhead with glasses. I also pictured him wearing a checkered shirt. However, the man in front of me is the complete opposite. At least, he's the only man in the coffee shop, so I assume it's him.

His dark-blond hair is short, leaving all his features on display. His facial hair is dark and neatly clipped, allowing for stubble to pierce through his olive skin. If I had to guess, I'd say he's in his mid-thirties.

"You must be Calla," he says when I make my way to him.

I nod. "Thank you for meeting me, Mr. Kline."

"Please, sit." He motions to the seat across from him. "Miss Maven, I'm afraid you've been brought here regarding a different matter. My name is Mark Stanton, and I work for the FBI."

24

What Did You Expect?

Calla

My breath hitches in my throat when I process what he said. I continue eyeing him, anticipating for him to tell me this is a joke. He must realize this too, because he reaches in his jacket pocket and withdraws a badge. It's not until I grant him another once-over that I catch a glimpse of a holster under his jacket.

"I wasn't sure if you'd be willing to speak to me, so I had Timothy set this up for me. Your interview with him has been moved to tomorrow. I apologize for that." He lowers in the seat across from me.

Confused and shocked, I'm unable to find any words.

"I'd like to ask you some questions," Mark continues.

"Questions? About what?"

A waitress carries out two coffee cups and sets them on our table. "I hope you don't mind, I ordered for you. Caramel latte on almond." Mark offers me a tight-lipped smile.

I swallow. He knows my coffee order, which indicates he's done his research and wishes for me to know.

Mark leans back in his seat. "You've been with Ace Blackwell for the last two weeks," he states. It's not a question but an invitation for me to elaborate further.

There's no way to escape this, and I figure cooperation is better than causing a scene in this situation. "I— It was my job to follow him around and get the inside scoop on the boxing champion and entrepreneur." I provide him with the most generic answer I'm able to muster.

"And what did you gather from your two weeks?" Mark's posture doesn't reveal anything. His shoulders are pushed back, while his face is blank.

"He's very reserved." I keep it short and straightforward.

He assesses me but doesn't prompt further. Instead, he changes the topic. "I'm aware that you attended the same college as him for a few months. What was the nature of your relationship?"

I reach for the cup of coffee and take a sip to give my hands something to do. "He was my roommate." Not a lie, but not the whole truth either. I wonder if he knows this.

"And now? Are you perhaps romantically involved with him?"

I inhale. Should I lie? Should I tell the truth? What's this about? It can't be good.

"I take my job very seriously, Mr. Stanton. I would never mix business with pleasure." Lie it is, then.

"I see." He looks out the window, and I follow his gaze. There's nothing there except for the busy streets of Manhattan.

A quiet moment lapses between us, and I aim to stay still, not to fiddle with my hands or bounce my knees. I attempt to remain unstirred, like I have nothing to hide.

"When you spent those two weeks with Mr. Blackwell, did you notice anything unusual?"

"Unusual?" I echo, maintaining my tone neutral and shift my

shaking hands off the table and onto my lap.

"Were there times where he acted…out of character?"

"Not that I noticed, but I wouldn't know what his regular behavior is." Another lie. I know Ace better than most people.

Mark nods. His coffee remains untouched where the waitress placed it.

"Can I ask what this is about?"

He ignores my question and continues with another. "During your two weeks with Mr. Blackwell, did you hear him speak of a Cassidy Torrio?"

I consider this for a moment, pretending like I'm trying to recall the information. "No, I can't say that I did."

How much lying will get me in trouble?

"How about Logan Harding?"

At that name, a ghostly shudder races up my spine. Ace didn't mention anything about him. Is he somehow involved in all this? "No."

"Ah, but you know of him?" Mark continues.

"He attended the same college as us."

My phone rings in my bag, and I retrieve it, using it as an excuse to stop the interrogation. I glance at the screen. It's my dad. I called him earlier to let him know my flight details and that Mia would be coming with me this weekend, but he didn't answer.

"I'm afraid I have to take this." I rise from the wooden chair, striving to find an escape route.

"One last question, Miss Maven."

My gaze meets his.

"What is your relationship with Niklaus Stryker?"

Pausing, I think of the correct answer. "He's someone I used to be involved with."

"Romantically?" Mark questions.

"I guess you could say that."

"Very well then. Thank you, Calla. You've been a great deal of help. If you remember anything, no matter how small you think the detail is, please give me a call. Any time." He hands me his card. I take it reluctantly and march toward the door, keeping my feet steady. By the time I make it outside, my phone stops ringing.

The moment I'm out of Mark's sight, my feet hasten on the pavement. My heart thumps boisterously in my chest, and for a while, that's the only sound I hear. I consider calling Ace, but that doesn't seem appropriate or safe. So instead, I head toward his apartment. The sound of my heels on the concrete pavement is one of the two sounds I can hear on one of the busiest streets in the city. The other sound is my heartbeat—rapid and uneven.

I'm surprised I spot Denzel in the black Mercedes as he pulls up near the curb. I get in without stalling, afraid I'll have a panic attack on the street if I don't. I don't realize Ace is in the back seat until I meet the striking eyes that have haunted me for the last four years. The power of them shatters my defenses. God, I love them. I love him. A sense of serenity washes over me. I'm safe with him. It scares me that he's the only one who solicits this feeling. It scares me because somewhere at the back of my mind, I know he may not be around for long.

Ace, still in his business clothes and annoyingly good-looking, captivates me with just a glance. The way he looks at me—with need and desire—makes my head spin, and I'm thankful the privacy partition is already up.

"You promised me a good time, Calla," he says in a low tone. His words almost make me forget about everything that just happened, but not entirely.

"Ace—" I begin, but I'm unsure of where to start. Everything that happened five minutes ago feels illusory and distant.

Ace utilizes the pause to distract me from my following words. He lifts my hips and pulls me onto his lap. I straddle him, and his mouth turns up into a playful grin. All my deliberations go out the window. It's just him and I while the entire world spins around us.

I feel *everything.* The way I'm ironed against him, the heat of his body beneath mine like a wildfire igniting. He presses his fingers into my hips, and I inhale his irresistible cologne. It renders me delirious and craving for more, craving to forget about reality, the imminent events of the future, and everything in between.

Cars pass us, and pedestrians stride by on the sidewalk, some carrying briefcases, others with faces buried in their phones. We stop at a set of red lights, and a middle-aged woman stares straight in, but I know for a fact she can't see inside due to the tinted windows.

Soft music streams through the speakers as we drive. I recognize the band, it's Ace's favorite—Arctic Monkeys. I used to listen to them on repeat, but then the memory of Ace became unbearable.

"So is that mouth of yours all talk?" Ace asks cockily, exploiting my own words against me.

His hands roam my body, vigilantly skimming my bare arms before slipping under my blouse and caressing my side. His thumb brushes against the bottom of my breast, driving an electric current through me. Throughout all this, he maintains his gaze on me, observing how I quiver beneath his touch.

If he doesn't know about the FBI and I tell him, everything may change. How long before something awful happens? If not now, then soon. I feel the dread looming above us like a tornado ready to conquer everything in its path. I need one more moment with him before my whole world collapses again, because it will. It always happens when something is this good between us.

"Took you a while." A small smile plays on my mouth as I tug on his tie, undo it, and toss it to the side. I thought he'd find me sooner, especially after my bantering texts this morning.

"My meetings took longer than expected," he explains and sweeps his lips against my neck, sucking the spot just below my earlobe that drives me senseless every time. "Too long."

My hands soar to his chest, unbuttoning his shirt with rapid speed, demanding to feel his skin on mine. Ace grins at me, and when I finally undo the last button, he rips my blouse open. Well, that's one way to do it. Under different circumstances, I'd chastise him for ruining yet another piece of my clothing, but now, I can't care less.

He raises a prominent eyebrow, eyeing my indecent black lingerie underneath. "Do you always wear things like this to work?"

I put it on this morning, predicting I'd see Ace this afternoon. I shrug. "Is that a problem?"

He orbits my nipple over the sheer material with his thumb, and it peaks. "I know it's not for me, since I told you I prefer you with nothing on." He bows his head and places his wicked mouth around it, drawing on it through the fabric.

Searing bliss gushes through me, and a moan spills from my lips before I ask, "Are you jealous?"

Ace squeezes my nipple between his thumb and forefinger, causing my stomach muscles to clench. I curse under my breath. He glances me dead in the eye. "No. I'm just protective over what's mine."

Mine.

I'll never be able to get over that word when it stems from his carnal mouth. I want to be his, consumed by him—wholly, utterly, and in every way possible.

In one hasty movement, he unclips my bra, and it tumbles to the floor of the car. He lowers his head, takes my nipple in his mouth, this time without anything between us, and sucks on it hard, grazing it with his teeth. The pain mixed with pleasure sends me into an unusual kind of frenzy.

I set my hands on his shoulders firmly and rub myself against him, turning both of us more aroused with each passing second.

"It's erotic seeing you like this, all hot and bothered," he groans against my shoulder, placing a kiss on it.

"Ace…"

"What? What do you want, Calla?" He teases me with his mouth, with his tongue, with his hands.

Oh God. This man has the power to shatter me into pieces and put me back together again.

I lure his mouth to mine, and his tongue promptly slips inside. He tastes like a drug, sweet and inviting. It's impossible to ever get enough.

A song plays delicately in the background, the lyrics inflaming the profoundness of my feelings. With Ace's rough hands on my naked body and his tongue stirring against mine—I'm propelled into a euphoric daze.

Drawing my skirt up, he caresses me through my panties with his thumb. The contact of the material and his fingers ensnare me, and I rock myself against his hand, needing more.

More of this.

More of him.

More of everything that makes me feel like an everlasting inferno when only minutes ago I was submerged in my mind.

He chuckles, the sound is genuine and charming. "I love how

needy you are."

"Only for you," I utter between ragged breaths.

"I know, love."

I reach for his belt, removing it with ease, but his slacks prove to be more challenging. The back of this car is relatively spacious, but not when it comes to undressing one another.

Ace assists me in sliding his pants off, followed by his boxer briefs. We're left naked, breathless, and with an undeniable yearning for each other.

I drop my gaze and wrap my hand around his smooth shaft. I've never witnessed a more flawless one. I run my hands down and up it, focusing my thumb specifically on the head.

"Fuck," Ace mutters under his breath.

I tease us both with his tip at my entrance, coating him in my slickness and kneading his length between my folds. Ace reaches for me, tucking a strand of loose hair behind my ear and tipping my chin to face him. His vividly glorious eyes speak a thousand words, and if I look into them any longer, I'm afraid they'll consume me entirely.

I roll my head back, closing my eyes, needing him inside of me. The connection between us is colossal, magnified by everything we've been through.

"Calla." My name surfaces from his mouth frayed. His hand progresses around my jaw, and he brings my head back to him. "Look at me," he commands, and my eyes flutter open, meeting his. At the same time, he enters me.

I stretch to welcome his thickness. The look on his face is infused with lust, passion, and everything else a woman dreams of seeing when a man looks at her. Ace stays inside of me without moving for a few heartbeats as we both catch our breath.

He guides my hips, and we move in sync. I dig my nails into his shoulders, and even though I'm on top, I allow him to take the lead, because I know he needs it more than I do right now. One of his hands remains on my hip, and the other treks toward my clit. Ace circles it with his dexterous fingers, gradually at first, but the speed intensifies with every thrust into me.

Sweat beads on his bronzed skin, glimmering like the deep sun when it sets across the infinite ocean. His lips part as he maintains speed and precision, and I marvel at his touch. It feels like a constellation of stars pirouetting against my skin.

I'm saturated with arousal, my inner thighs gleaming wet. The sensation in my core swells as he strikes a sweet spot, triggering a loud whimper within me.

"Not yet," Ace orders when he knows I'm on the verge of caving in.

He trails wet, voracious kisses down my jaw, neck, and chest—sucking and nibbling at my most receptive parts. I'm losing myself with every touch of his.

My hands roam his body, feeling the muscular figure beneath me and wondering how I got so damn lucky. Some people go their whole lives without finding their other half. I found mine at the age of eighteen when I wasn't ready for him yet, when I needed to fight my terrors before letting someone in.

I'm ready now.

I'm ready for him.

"I love you," I breathe, and it's not until he groans my name that I realize the words I spoke. I have thought them countless times over the past few days, and somehow, in my most vulnerable state, they have tumbled from my lips.

I'm earnest, and I need him to know that. I place my hands on either side of his face. "Ace, I love you. I love you so much that it hurts."

I love him like the ocean loves the shore, with unforgiving and conclusive desire.

"Calla," he drags out my name. I know he won't say it now during sex. And he doesn't have to, because I see it on his face, in his eyes. I can see he feels the same way.

His fingers are back on my clit as his thrusts become deeper. The stimulation of my clit and G-spot propels the most penetrating orgasm rippling through me, something I've never experienced before.

"That's it. Come for me." Ace presses his lips on mine, feeling me incoherently muttering his name into his mouth as I come undone on top of him, my walls clenching around his erection.

He follows soon after, reaching his own climax and spilling inside of me while burying his head in the crook of my neck. After catching our breath, Ace uses his shirt as a rag, wiping it between my thighs.

Denzel parks in the basement, and my cheeks flush a deep red when getting out of the car. Ace is left shirtless, and he sets his hand on my lower back as he directs me toward the elevator and into his apartment.

"Ace… There's something I need to tell you," I reveal when we're in his kitchen.

The curtains are open, as always, revealing the whole city. It's incredible what he has achieved at such a young age. Yes, some would say Ace took shortcuts, but the shortcuts weren't to benefit himself initially. They were for others—for his family, for Ellie. I don't want to imagine what could have happened if he didn't take them.

He fills two cups with water and hands one to me. He tilts his head and drinks, and I watch his Adam's apple bob up and down. Finally, he sets his glass down on the counter. "Hmm?"

"I was meant to have *The Times* interview today," I begin.

"How did that go?"

I take a sip of water and set the glass on the counter, too, preparing to disclose something that has the potential to change everything. "It didn't go. Someone by the name of Mark Stanton showed up instead. He said he's with the FBI."

Ace's head snaps toward me, but his expression remains unwavering. However, I know him well enough now to recognize when he's deep in thought.

"Did you know? About him?" I prompt when he doesn't provide a timely reply.

"I had my suspicions, but I didn't think they'd target you. They've been probing around."

"What do they want?" I ask, but I already have a good idea. Ace isn't exactly a saint. He's involved in things that aren't legal. Isn't this what I was afraid of all along?

"To bring the country's criminal activity down, but they don't know anything. They're just guessing."

"It sounded like he knows a lot more than you think."

"Tell me everything."

"He asked me questions about you, about Cassidy, about Nik." About Logan.

"What did you tell him?"

"Nothing, Ace. I told him that you and I aren't involved. I told him that I never heard the name Cassidy, and I told him that Nik and I used to see each other." His fists curl at the last detail.

He nods. "Good."

"Ace…he also asked me about Logan."

Ace sets his jaw at this, gripping the edge of the counter.

"Is he involved with you?" I question.

"No."

"Then why would the FBI be asking about him?"

"Cass is involved with him."

Oh. "What's going to happen?" My hands shake.

"I'll take care of it."

"What does that mean?"

"I'll take care of it, Calla. You don't need to worry about it," he vows, approaching me and placing a kiss on my forehead. He wraps his strong arms around me. "I'm sorry that I let it come this far. It won't happen again."

He tilts my chin to face him and covers my mouth with his. A promise that he'll deal with it.

"Stay with me tonight," Ace invites me once he pulls away.

I know it's unhealthy to rely on a person so much you can't be away from them for more than a day. We've been together almost every day for two weeks, but it doesn't feel like enough.

"I don't have any clothes." An excuse. One I hope he doesn't accept.

"You don't need any," he says playfully, but when I narrow my eyes at him, he adds, "You can sleep in my clothes, and I'll drive you to your apartment early tomorrow morning so you can get ready for work."

And that's all it takes for me to succumb to him, maybe because something at the back of my mind tells me that everything is about to change.

25

Clouded Reality

Calla

The next couple of days pass in a blur. I'm occupied with work, finally completing my two-page article on the famous Ace Blackwell. I'm resigned to the fact that no one will be able to perceive Ace the way I do. He's not just the world's youngest boxing champion, a womanizer, and the youngest entrepreneur in the country. He's much more than that.

Underneath the stone layer he's constructed over the years, underneath all the hurt and blame encompassing him, underneath everything he's trying to conceal, is everything I fell for.

I've tried to portray him in a unique light without disclosing anything the world doesn't already know, respecting his privacy for apparent reasons. But, to reveal glimpses of the genuine Ace, I had to dig deeper and recollect the memories that made me fall for him in the first place.

He doesn't let many people in, whether it has something to do with his past, his father leaving, or because he doesn't trust anyone. The reasons fit hand in hand with each other. However, it's one of the many things that aren't public record, and I'm surprised at how well Ace has kept everything away from the media.

Ace and I once had a conversation I still remember to this day. We were at his dad's cabin, which was in the middle of nowhere, surrounded by nature, away from every bit of civilization. We were lounging outside in a daybed attached to four posts with a clear view of the night sky. The stars were dull that night. It was perhaps the night when I understood Ace and I are more alike than I ever thought we were.

Have you ever looked at the sky? I mean, *really* looked at the sky and witnessed it for what it truly is. How can something so vast not mean anything at all? How can we go on with our lives without searching for more?

The answer is simple. We are all afraid. Afraid of what we might encounter in the process, afraid it might not be what we hoped for, afraid to leave the comfort of our minds to explore the endless possibilities of greater opportunities.

In a way, I felt that. The time I spent wishing to change the past could have been spent elsewhere. Every moment, every event led me to where I'm meant to be.

Thinking back on the memory now, it was clear what Ace was also trying to tell me that night. He was struggling to apologize for what he mindlessly took away from me. He was ready to face the consequences, and maybe somewhere in the back of my head, I knew. I just didn't let myself form the connection. The answer was in front of me. It was right there directing me to acknowledge it, but I was afraid. Afraid that nothing would be the same again. But eventually, that moment came anyway. You can't run from fate. It always finds you, and it doesn't wait until you're ready.

Jennifer seems pleased with the article I penned, or at least I assume she is. She hasn't given me that look yet—the one where she narrows her eyes with her glasses tilted downward. She also unexpectedly permitted me to finish early today after telling her I'd be flying to see my dad this weekend.

Ace, too, has been busy with work, or so he said. He's been distant ever since the FBI incident, and I wonder what's going on that he's not telling me about. The answer is evident in my head.

I don't ask him about it for two reasons. One, I haven't seen him since then, and two, I don't ask him because I'm still hoping he'll tell me himself. Perhaps it's wishful thinking on my behalf.

It's Friday afternoon, and I'm thrilled to see my dad. However, the thoughts of Ace, the FBI, and potentially telling my dad the truth about the accident during this trip home make me exceedingly unsettled to the point where I'm nauseous.

Denzel drives Mia and me to the airport. As we drive on the highway, the sun sets in front of us—a muddy crimson and orange. In a way, it appears like a flame, burning the world to the ground, leaving nothing but ashes—the night sky. The longer I stare at it, the deeper my thoughts go, subconsciously building a fire in my mind.

I'm an overthinker. Once I get a thought in my head, I allow it to spark alight like a blaze, infusing it with gas now and then until I convince myself a situation is ghastlier than it really is. I've been working on it with my therapist, striving to halt the never-ending cycle. It's more complex than it seems.

Ace suggested we take his jet even though he already bought the tickets for me, but the flight is only one hour, and it would be unnecessary to use the jet, especially when the tickets are first class.

"Mr. Blackwell sends his apologies. He's been held up at work," Denzel informs me from the driver's seat.

Ace told me he'd drive Mia and me, but I haven't heard from him all day. I haven't seen him since Wednesday morning when he drove me to work after spending the night together at his apartment. Everything appeared fine then, or as fine as it could be after discovering the FBI is after him.

Mia conveys me a look that reveals she thinks that's bullshit, and a part of me knows she's right. The other part wants to give Ace the benefit of the doubt. During the drive to the airport, I attempt to convince myself everything will be fine and focus on appreciating the moment. I haven't told Mia everything about Ace. It's not my secret to share.

Mia agreed to come home with me when I told her my dad is a fantastic cook and there'll be a tower of food for my late birthday dinner. Food is a way into a woman's heart.

Since being in New York, Mia has found a part-time job as a tattoo artist. She's only been doing small shifts now and then, since she doesn't officially start until next week. I'm proud and excited for Mia. This has been a dream of hers since college. I recall looking through her sketchbook for the first time back in college and being stunned by how realistic her artwork is.

When we land in my hometown, my dad and Nate are waiting for us outside. At first, I almost don't recognize Nate. I haven't seen him in a couple of years. The last few times I came down to see my dad, he wasn't in town. He's cut all his caramel locks and looks more grown-up, more mature.

Nate finished his college years and walked out with an engineering degree. Impressive right? On top of that, he graduated at the top of his class. Over the years, he's worked at a few companies over the country, but his heart always brought him back here. He now owns a small mechanic workshop in town. Some people never want to leave home, and others, like me, will do anything to stray as far away as possible.

"Hey, Cals." My dad greets me and engulfs me in a tight hug. My dad has never been the affectionate type, but I guess the years are turning him into a softie. He doesn't appear much different, except that he's lost some weight, and his hazel eyes have aged more than him.

"Hey, Dad, you're still looking good. Decided to finally cut the late-night snacks, I see," I joke.

He laughs. "The doc said I better start taking care of myself."

"Cals, I haven't seen you in so long." Nate's arms go around me next, and I return his hug while my dad greets Mia.

Nate's shoulders are broader and more defined, like he's been working out. He pulls away, taking the duffel bag I brought with me. I'm about to tell him I can carry it, but Nate's sights set on Mia.

"I didn't know you were coming," he declares in a more sarcastic tone.

"Is that a problem?" Mia raises her neatly plucked brows to imply that if there's a problem, he better get rid of it, and fast.

Nate takes the hint and raises his hands in front of him in a defensive manner. "No problem, boss."

Mia offers him a tight-lipped smile, visibly not impressed with how he spoke to her. You don't want to get on the wrong side of Mia. I can guarantee she'll make you regret the day you were born.

I sit in the front seat of my dad's Jeep, glad he finally chose to replace his old Holden Commodore. It was beginning to get unreliable, but Nate always made sure it wouldn't break down. I'm grateful my dad has Nate. I want someone to be here to look after my dad, but it can't ever be me. I can't stay in this town for more than a few days. It holds everything I've been trying to forget.

Mia and Nate sit together in the back, and I pray Nate doesn't say or do anything that will result in an argument or worse. It's late, and I don't have the energy for it, at least not today. Perhaps tomorrow.

It's not long before we arrive at my childhood home. It's dark, so I can't distinguish much of the exterior, but the feeling of familiarity instantly washes over me. Nate says his goodbyes and tells me he'll be here bright and early tomorrow. I appreciate his efforts not to hover.

I carry the duffel bag into my old bedroom, and Mia follows.

"I set up the spare room, if you want it, Mia. Instead of both of you cramming into Calla's room," my dad says behind us.

Mia and I look at each other, and it's Mia who answers, "Thank you, but Calla and I have shared a lot more than a bed. I think it'll be alright."

The expression on my dad's face makes my cheeks turn crimson. I offer him no explanation and swiftly head to my room, closing the door behind us and turning to Mia.

"I think my dad has the wrong idea about us after that."

"Better than him knowing who you're dating." I know it's supposed to be a joke, but my heart pounds in my chest when I think about the secret that I've been keeping from my dad for the last four years.

✦ ✦ ✦

The following day, I'm awake before Mia. It's early. Too early, but I've had one of my nightmares. I rise and tiptoe out of my room, closing the bedroom door behind me.

Walking down the hallway, I pause by a closed door. I twist the doorknob and walk into the small study. It's exactly like I remember it. By the window, a small wooden desk is positioned against the wall. I gaze out into the backyard, and memories flood through me like a tsunami. The old, rusted swing is still there, unused and falling apart. So is the sandpit. I doubt it's much of a sandpit anymore. The neighborhood cats have been using it as their toilet since I was in school.

My mom was a schoolteacher before she died. Her old books are still where she left them, untouched. Her stickers and stamps are in the second drawer. Her colorful pens rest in the blue plastic pen holder on the desk. I know my dad doesn't have the heart to move them, nor does he want to. It serves as a memory, a small space where everything of hers remains. Some people visit their loved one's graves to mourn, my dad and I visit this small room.

I sit at her old desk where she used to mark the students' homework, running my hand over the wooden top, which acquired roughness over the years. The wall in front of me is a chalkboard, which still bears her writing on it from a few days before the crash. I stare at it.

"I miss her so much, Cals."

My eyes snap up to his, and it's the only indication that he startled me while I was in my thoughts. My dad leans against the doorframe, his significant figure making the room seem smaller.

"I know. I do, too." I sigh.

"I'm sorry that we never talk about her. I'm not good at that stuff."

I can't hold it in any longer. Four years have already been too long. I've constantly attempted to avoid conversation about my mom, about the accident. I was always afraid I would say something I wasn't supposed to.

I'm done with all the lies, all the secrets. They're eating me alive.

I take a breath and look at my dad, witnessing the pain he still holds. He's never remarried or even had another relationship. I can't imagine what he's felt over the years, living in this house that's still filled with her. At least I moved out, moved on.

He hasn't.

Before I change my mind, I allow the words to surface. "There's something I need to tell you about the night of the accident."

My dad shuffles closer and takes the seat across from me. His figure swallows the small chair I used to sit in when I was younger. It doesn't look right, but nothing looks or feels right at this moment. I've been keeping a secret from him for the last four years. There were times—right after I learned about Ace being the drunk driver—that I avoided my dad altogether. I found excuses not to see him. I was afraid he'd look at me and instantly know. My paranoia and anxiety mixed into one.

My eyes drop to the desk as a way to calm myself. I focus on the calendar of 2010—the one my mom scribbled in. Her writing was immaculate, neat, and straight, the kind that all teachers have.

I sit straighter and force myself to talk before I have a change of mind. "I met a boy in college. He was my roommate. At first, we didn't get along. I thought he was rude, arrogant, and had his head shoved up his ass." For my dad to understand where I'm coming from, he needs to know the whole story—not just glimpses, not only the worst part.

"We were given an assignment that forced us to spend time together. Over the weeks that I got to know him, I discovered he wasn't as bad as I thought. He was just broken, suffering for his past, trying to push everyone away. He has a little sister, and even in college, when he should have been focusing on himself and his future, he focused on his family and worried about how to support them when they were struggling".

I inhale, and continue, "There were undeniable similarities between us, and I didn't realize it back then, but he pulled me out of the most destructive place in my life."

My dad listens without interrupting. His face is blank. He's usually an open book, but now, I can't tell what he's thinking. Maybe because I'm nervous. God, I'm so freaking anxious that my hands begin to shake, and I place them in my lap, digging my nails into my palms, forcing myself to continue.

"The same night as the accident… Christmas Eve, his dad left them without an explanation, just packed a suitcase and left. Ace…" I speak his name in front of my dad for the first time. "Ace wasn't thinking straight. He got drunk. He wasn't in the right state of mind, and his best friend offered him the keys to a Chevy. He was on the same road when mom and I were coming home from Grandma's house…" I let the rest speak for itself. There's nothing more to say.

My dad was working when it got called in, and he was one of the first officers at the scene. I can't imagine how hard it must have been for him. To not know what happened or what the next few days, weeks would hold for him.

"His name is Ace Blackwell," I utter, almost silently. There's no need to explain further. My dad would know who he is. Everyone knows who *Ace Blackwell* is.

My dad's expression doesn't change much, and I wait, giving him time to process everything I just told him. Then, when he still hasn't said anything two minutes later, my mind thinks it's a good idea to add, "I've been spending time with him over the last few weeks…"

At this, his lips set into a grim line, and he places his head in his hands. The wrinkles on them are prominent, reminding me of all the years behind us.

Perhaps it was the wrong time to add that detail. I've never brought a man home or even mentioned the name of one, and now, I've sprung everything on my poor father, all at once. But I can't tell him half a truth. It's not fair.

When he lifts his head back up, his expression is unexpected. Instead of being angry, upset, or frantic after hearing everything I've been hiding from him all these years, his face fills with something I haven't seen before.

Disappointment.

He'd never tell me that, but it's right in front of me.

Everything comes together when I see the look on my dad's face. "You knew about Ace. You knew he was the one who caused the accident."

He shakes his head. "I didn't know for sure. I spent months working on the case outside of work hours. There were minor signs—he came to see me one day to apologize for what happened and give his condolences, but so did many other people I wasn't fully acquainted with. I also traced the money he sent us, but I never made the connection. I couldn't continue with the case when all the concrete evidence was a dead end. People were beginning to question my sanity, and the time came when I had to stop pushing for answers before I would lose my job… I should've figured it out. It was right in front of me."

"The money?" I ask. "What money?"

"He sent cash and cheques. I guess his conscience was eating him alive, and he thought money would fix that."

"I didn't know…"

Ace was illegally fighting to support his family after this father left. I didn't know he was sending money to us as well. I should have known, it's something Ace would do.

He shakes his head in disbelief. "Remorse only goes so far. Remorse doesn't hold people accountable for their crimes… How long?"

I look at him quizzically, trying to figure out what he's asking. How long have I been seeing him, or how long have I known?

"We were together in college for a couple of months. I didn't know then. When I found out that it was him, I couldn't be with him. We met again about a month ago through work," I tell my dad. He opens his mouth as if to say something, but then he closes it again.

"He's not a bad person. He's never been. He's just made terrible decisions that have cost us significantly. Dad, there's a reason why I've never brought a man home, why I've never spoken about one. It's always been him… He was the first boy I ever felt something for, and I haven't felt that way with anyone else." A tear rolls down my cheek, and I look to the side, trying to conceal it.

"Jesus Christ," my dad mutters under his breath while rubbing his forehead. "I thought you just weren't into men. I never expected this."

The silent room already felt small, but sitting here with my dad in front of me feels claustrophobic. He's always been the rational one and thought a lot in his head instead of talking, so I'm letting him do precisely that. Process. There's not much for me to say, so I wait for what I know is about to emerge from my dad's mouth, preparing myself.

Even though I've been expecting this, when my dad begins talking, his words still shatter me. "I can accept the reality, and I can learn to live with it. But I don't know if I can live with the fact that the person who took away your mom—my wife—won't be reprimanded in the eyes of the law."

I resist the urge to tell him Ace has already suffered enough, that it isn't solely his fault. It won't do any good. My dad has worked by the rules all his life, and it's impossible to change one's perspective on how things ought to be done.

The morning sun rises and seeps through the curtains, and I notice the tears glistening in my dad's eyes. "I can't accept you being with him." He shakes his head, the hurt evident in his face. He can't even say his name. "And I thought you had higher standards than to go for someone who's sleeping with a different woman every week."

Of course, my dad has heard about that part of Ace's life. Everyone has. It's all over the tabloids and the celebrity news. And it may have been true before, but I know Ace is nothing like his father. I trust him, at least with that aspect of our relationship.

"He's nothing like that, Dad," I find myself defending him. But if my dad knew the truth, if my dad knew what Ace is involved with, we wouldn't even be here talking.

"If you told me this for my blessing, to clear your own conscience, I can't give you that. I can't do it, Cals." He shuts his eyes for a moment. "Your mom was everything to me. She pulled me out of some of the darkest parts of my life. It would feel like I'm betraying her."

My dad rises and strides to the door with his head hung low.

"Please…" I call after him. "Please, Dad…don't destroy his future because it will destroy me, too."

He cuts me a glance like he's unable to come to terms that I'm pleading for someone who's the cause of our tragedy. "You have no right to ask that of me. But even if I wanted to put him behind bars, the time for that has expired. I hope you can live with the conscience that comes with taking the law into your own hands."

I hear him unlock the front door and then shut it behind him, leaving me alone to wonder if I did the right thing. I know my dad, and I know he needs time to process. But, nevertheless, I question everything. The only thing that's holding me together is the weight of the following words—*the time for that has expired.*

Am I betraying my mother by choosing to be with the person who caused this? What would she think of this situation? My mom had a kind and forgiving heart. What would she want me to do? It's one thing to forgive, it's another to act like it never happened. Am I letting my feelings cloud reality?

I take my phone and do the one thing I know will ground me. I call Ace.

"Calla," he answers. As soon as I hear his voice, I relax in the chair. My nails have been digging into my palms for the last ten minutes, and now craters are embedded into my skin.

"Good morning."

"Is everything okay? How's your dad?"

"I talked to him… I told him the truth about that night." Ace exhales through the phone, and I continue, "Why didn't you tell me you went to see him?"

"I didn't think it was worth mentioning. I was a coward. I went to confess, and I backed out the very last minute."

"I told him that I'm seeing you. He walked out."

"He loathes me, Calla, and I don't blame him. I'm liable for everything that comes my way."

"He can't do anything anymore. But you knew that already, didn't you?" I wonder out loud. Ace must have guessed that after so much time, it's unlikely that the law would be able to bring any action against him.

"I have to go."

"Is there something else wrong?"

"No, I just have a lot of work to do."

"Anything I should be worried about?" I hear a voice on the other side of the line. I can't make out what they're saying or whether it's a man or woman. "Ace?"

"No, nothing you should worry about. I'll call you later?"

Before I can form a reply, the line goes silent.

26

Heartache

Calla

I remain in the same spot staring at my phone for a long moment until I hear arguing from my room. Finally, I stand and follow the sound of Nate's voice.

"There you are." Nate grins at me. Just as he promised, he's here nice and early, dressed in a blue flannel shirt and cream shorts.

"Could you tell this asswipe that it's rude to pound on a bedroom door at this time of the morning! When I didn't answer within two seconds because I was sleeping, he barged in. What if I'd been naked?" Mia crosses her arms, and a shallow line forms in between her eyebrows. Her eyes are set on the target—Nate's face.

I don't have the energy to be a mediator after the conversation with my dad, after wondering where this leaves us—leaves me.

"That would be a sight to see, wouldn't it?" Nate winks at her.

Mia attempts to slap Nate on his arm, but he follows her movements like a hawk and catches her hand smoothly. "Ah, easy tiger."

She scoffs, jerking her hand away, and slams the door in his face, leaving Nate and me in the hallway. Someone woke up on the wrong side of the bed.

"By the way, that was a compliment," Nate declares through the closed door.

"Maybe you should work on those." I lead him out into the kitchen and brew a coffee, already longing for the luxury of coffee machines and takeaways.

"So, what did you wanna do today?" Nate asks, and without giving me time to answer, continues, "We can go to the movies, or there's some kind of fair in town for the weekend. We can go to the museum. I know you always liked to go there even though it's the most boring thing on the planet…"

I listen to him list all the things we could do today. Nate is a country guy at heart. Our relationship has never changed. Even though we're polar opposites, and no matter how much time passes since we see each other, we always pick up where we left off.

I wrap my hands around his waist and place my head on his chest. "I missed you." My voice breaks, and tears spiral down my face. Too much has happened today, and it's not even eight in the morning.

"Hey…" he soothes my back. "Cals, you alright?"

Deeply sweet notes of vanilla fill my nostrils as I bury my head into Nate's shirt.

"I'm fine." I wipe my tears with the back of my hand and mumble, "Sorry," into his chest.

I don't know why I'm crying. Telling my dad went better than I expected. If what he said is accurate, and the time has indeed expired, I don't have to worry about him doing everything in his power to put Ace behind bars. But he'll also never accept that I'm with Ace, and I don't blame him. He has every right not to.

"Don't apologize for being upset." Nate's fingers brush my chin, and he lifts my head to face him. His bright eyes gaze into mine. "What's wrong?"

"I'm not sure," I reply, and his eyebrows furrow together. He's not buying it, so I continue, "Do you know that feeling when you think something bad is going to happen, but you don't know what?"

He considers my answer. His stubble is longer than when I last saw him and completely covers the lower part of his face. He nods and shifts his gaze away from mine. "I do, Cals. Anything you want to talk about?"

I shake my head. "No, I just want to get my mind off it."

"Got it." Nate pulls me in for another hug. Nate has always been comfort for me—someone that I grew up with.

Admittingly, at the start of college, I was bitter about how Nate had broken up with me, but looking back on it now, I realize it was for the best. We were never compatible in that way. He needs someone who can ground him, someone who likes country life. Someone who's the opposite of me.

Nate gently releases me and heads toward the table where the half made coffees stand. He puts two sugars in his and grabs the milk out of the fridge. I watch Nate move around the kitchen with ease and realize he must come over often since he knows where everything is. I'm not surprised. He and my dad are close. Nate has become like the son he's never had.

"Wanna sit on the porch?" Nate hands me the warm mug.

I nod.

We walk toward the front door, and I bring the mug to my nose, inhaling the rich smell of coffee. Outside, my eyes fall to the empty spot in the driveway where my dad's Jeep was parked earlier this morning.

"Did you see my dad when you came?"

"Yeah, he was leaving. He gave me a grocery list for tonight's dinner. Said that something came up at work."

I nod in acknowledgment but don't say anything else. I wonder if there was another way I could have told my dad about Ace that would have resulted in a different outcome.

"Did something happen between the two of you? Did you fight?" Nate questions.

"Something like that, but I don't want to talk about it. What have you been up to? Anyone special in your life?" I nudge him with my shoulder, cautious not to spill my coffee.

He snickers. "Haven't really been looking for that. I've been busy with getting things up and running at work."

Nate isn't a bad guy. He's intelligent, good looking and knows how to treat a woman. Anyone would be lucky to have him. He's the same age as me, and from what I know, he hasn't dated anyone since me—back in school.

"Don't look at me like that, Cals. From what I've heard, you haven't mentioned anyone either."

"I *am* seeing someone," I reveal. He'll eventually find out, whether from my dad or perhaps in a poorly written celebrity magazine.

"Oh." He faces me. "I don't suppose it's anyone I know? He better be treating you right."

"Actually, it is someone you know." I stare at the mug and the dark-brown liquid. "Ace."

His eyebrows shoot up in surprise, he brings his mug to his mouth and takes a long sip. "Ace Blackwell, huh?" He hums, swallowing. "Isn't he like famous now? I didn't even know he was into fighting when we were back in college."

Not many people did, for obvious reasons. "Yeah, he kept it on the down-low."

"So you two are the real deal?"

I shrug. "We're seeing how it goes."

"What happened in college?"

I shrug again. "He moved to a different college. Neither of us was willing to do long distance," I lie.

I'm always going to have to lie about that part of my life. It's not that I don't trust Nate not to tell anyone, or maybe it's that, too. The main reason is it's not easy to explain. Not many people would understand.

"How about we go to the town fair? They have a market there. We can look around, get the groceries, and be back in time to help with dinner," Nate suggests, changing the topic.

"Sure." I rise from the step we've been sitting on, dusting my behind with my hand.

I ask Mia if she wants to come with us, and my eyes widen when she agrees and proceeds to get ready. I didn't expect that answer from her since Nate is standing beside me.

Nate drives us in his blue pick-up truck, an upgrade from his previous one. The market is only a fifteen-minute drive from my dad's house. I sit in the front and Mia in the back.

"You don't like me, pixie. Why's that?" Nate looks at the rear-view mirror toward Mia as we drive past a field of sunflowers with the windows rolled down. The soft breeze catches my hair, and I put my hand out the window, fighting against the wind.

I suck in a deep breath, and my nostrils fill with the blossoming aroma of fresh flowers. Nostalgia floods through me. I'd do anything to go back to when I was five or ten—when everything was simple. When I traveled along this same road with my mom and dad, sing-along songs blasting out of the speakers.

I turn to look behind me at Mia, waiting for her response.

"It's not that I don't like you. I just don't like some things that come out your mouth," Mia replies.

I press my lips together, holding back a smile, and Nate shakes his head in disbelief.

The market is expansive. It stretches and covers two wide roads that are closed from six till twelve on Saturdays and Sundays. Grocery stores are only located around the block, but on the weekends, everyone prefers to come here in support of the local grocers, butchers, and small businesses.

After half a day of walking through the stalls, inhaling different types of flowers, drinking more coffee, and dealing with sly remarks flying between Nate and Mia, I'm ready to go home.

We grab ingredients for what seems like a feast, but it will only be my dad, Mia, Nate, and his dad. Uncle Dave is out of town for the weekend, and my grandma is too elderly to travel this far. I haven't seen her since last Christmas, and guilt punctures me.

My dad's Jeep is parked in the driveway when we return, and I take a deep breath before climbing out of the truck. I grab the bags with the groceries and head inside.

Depositing the groceries on the counter, I notice my dad has already begun preparing the potatoes for dinner tonight. Nate and Mia enter behind me, and I know my dad won't continue the conversation from this morning. There isn't much left to say anyway. On top of that, he won't want to do it with Mia and Nate here.

"Let me help," I offer.

He nods.

I inform my dad about *The Times* interview, the one I went to the day after meeting Mark Stanton. Timothy Kline is who I pictured him to be—a redhead with glasses, and he indeed wore a checkered shirt for my interview. It went considerably well, and

Timothy said he'd give me a call next week to discuss everything in more detail.

"That's great. I know it's been your dream for a while now." My dad rinses his hands under the sink.

The emotional distance is a barrier between us, and I wonder if it will always be like this from now. Do I have to choose between family and the person who makes me feel alive? I ponder the thoughts that fill my head with rapid speed—question after question. Never an answer.

I take a shower before Nate's dad arrives and wear a casual sundress and sandals. I felt a headache coming on throughout the day, and now it's developed into a faint throbbing.

By six o'clock, the house is full of delicious, mouthwatering food. The table is crammed with baked potatoes, mini pizzas, a roast, pasta salad, sautéed vegetables, and there's dessert in the refrigerator.

My dad went overboard for only five people. He's always been the one to cook in our household, and he thoroughly enjoys it. But unfortunately, I didn't receive that trait from him.

At the table, my dad pours champagne into everyone's glasses and raises his glass, clearing his throat. "Happy birthday, Cals."

Everyone wishes me a happy birthday, even though it was last week. Conversation flows through the room—my dad talks to Nate's dad about an upcoming fishing trip, Nate discusses how he's going to eat everything on the table since he's starving, and Mia chastises him. They behave like siblings.

I bring the glass of champagne to my lips and almost gag at the smell of it. I cover my mouth with my hand as I wait for the feeling of nausea to disappear.

"Are you okay?" Nate notices my hesitation.

"Yeah, I just need a minute." I stand from the table and head toward the bathroom. I stare in the mirror for a moment, leaning my elbows on the counter, and then take Advil for my head.

As I make my way back to the kitchen, Ace's name lights up my phone, and I'm taken aback. After the conversation this morning, I didn't think he'd call me. Slipping into my bedroom unnoticed, I answer the Facetime call. Ace is in his apartment office, sitting behind a desk. It looks like he's put his phone against his computer as he's not holding it.

"I'm sorry for earlier today. Since we got back from the trip, I've been flooded with work." He sounds drained, and he leans back in his office chair.

"I understand." I rest on my bed.

"How is it going at your dad's?"

"It's okay. We're just having dinner."

"In your room?" A sensual smile plays on his lips. I miss seeing it in person. "The room where I fell in love with you?"

My breath gets stuck in my lungs, and the memories come rushing back—the photo, Ace coming to see me here, the first intimate moment we had.

"Calla! You better not be in your room while we're out here having the time of our lives!" Nates yells through the thin walls. Way to ruin the moment.

"Who's that?" Ace's eyebrows furrow.

"Nate."

"Ah, of course." He runs a hand through his messy hair, his mouth settling into a grim line. He's never been a fan of Nate.

"Calla!" Nate's voice rings as he gets closer.

Oh my God. My bedroom door swings open, and Nate peeks inside. "Your dad is wondering where you are. He wants to give you a present."

"I'll be right there," I tell him, and he flashes me a grin before Mia drags him out and mouths *sorry* to me.

"Sorry, I have to go," I tell Ace, frustrated that Nate interrupted.

He nods in understanding, but the tightness in his jaw speaks volumes.

"Is there something wrong? Did you want to tell me something?" I prompt.

"No, I'll talk to you later, love. Have a good night."

My dad gifts me a heart-shaped golden locket for my birthday. Inside is a photo of my mom, my dad, and me. My eyes fill with tears, and I look up to the ceiling, not wanting to cry.

"Thank you," I say.

The rest of the night is lighthearted. Everyone has a few drinks except for me, and my dad's shoulders relax as he leans back in his chair, even cracking a few jokes.

On Sunday morning, my dad drives Mia and me to the airport. He engulfs me in a big hug at the terminal gates. "I love you, Cals. I always will. But I can't accept the decision that you made. It doesn't sit right with me. It goes against everything I have faith in, and I can't..."

I understand. My dad doesn't know Ace the way I do. He only perceives him as the person who took away his wife. Perhaps if my dad spends some time with Ace, he will realize... *Realize what?* Ace will always be the person who took away his wife. My dad can't see Ace the way I do. There's no way he'd be able to grasp it from a different perspective. If I knew Ace caused the accident from the start, before I fell for him, I would have never seen him in a different light.

Even though the flight back home is around one hour, it feels like nine. Mia and I catch a cab from the airport, and I instruct the driver to drop me off at Ace's apartment. I need to see him, and I assume he's home on a Sunday.

The woman at the front desk recognizes me from the week I spent here and greets me as I make my way to the elevator. Although I still have a key, I don't use it. I don't live here anymore, and we haven't discussed our boundaries. Instead, I knock and shift from one foot to another as I wait, smoothing my skirt with my hands.

The door opens, and I'm met with Ace. He's in his usual black attire. This time it's jeans and a black button-up shirt. Too casual to go to work in, but too dressed up to stay home.

"What are you doing here?" His eyes widen, and he steps outside of his apartment instead of inviting me in. He tucks his hands into his pockets, his body language unmistakably closed off. Something about him is different today.

What has happened over the last few days while I was at my dad's? Why does everything feel like it's changed from the way he's looking at me right now, with a stone-cold expression.

"I just got back from the airport." I'm perplexed by his demeanor.

Ace glances around the hallway, his eyes lingering on the elevator doors. "You need to go."

Is he waiting for someone? "What?" I try to understand what's going on.

"You can't be here. Go home," he says in a rough voice.

"What do you mean? Are you busy?" I persist.

I'm over the lies, the half-truths. I haven't had a relationship for more than half a decade, but I'm sure this isn't the way things are meant to be dealt with. Communication is vital, right?

"No. I just don't want you here."

My heart quickens, and my mind tracks through the events that could've brought us to this point. The last time I spoke to Ace, he seemed fine—*we* seemed fine. Is this because of my dad?

"Ace, what's going on?"

"Leave."

I take a step back.

A corner of his lips turns up, but the smile doesn't reach his eyes. Instead, they are cold and callous. I hate it. This isn't the person I spent the last month with. The second of silence feels like an eternity, and I continue staring at him, hoping he'll meet my eyes, but he doesn't. He keeps glancing around the hallway in anticipation of something, *someone*.

I'm not prepared for what comes out of his mouth next.

"I told you I would have you at my feet, Calla." He looks anywhere but directly at me as he heaves the daggers into my heart.

Everything stops except for the ground, which starts sliding out from beneath my feet. I struggle to swallow the lump in my throat while planting my feet firmly to the floor.

Breathe, breathe, breathe, I tell myself over and over.

I'd rather be punched in the face—twice—than to hear those words. Everything overcomes me all at once. I keep breathing, or at least I think I'm breathing. It's hard to tell when I can't feel my body.

I don't wait for Ace to say anything else, and I don't wait for him to realize what he's done to me with that sentence, although I'm sure he already knows. Without a single word and without revealing how much that hurt, I turn around.

I don't look back.

I don't cry.

The only sound is my footsteps echoing through the empty hallway and my heartbeat hammering through my chest.

Breathe in. Breathe out. This came out of nowhere. Nothing could have prepared me for it. The worst thing is, I was trying to avoid this feeling all along.

Was this his plan from the beginning? Those words keep replaying in my head like an evil curse. He said them to me at the start.

Was this all a game to him? A way to hurt me as I hurt him, perhaps? Was anything he said or did genuine? I question everything. The last hope of Ace and I, of us, of the trust that has been building—is shattered with a single sentence.

I notice a familiar face in the lobby—dark hair, blue eyes, gorgeous figure. Cassidy. My mind runs wild with more questions, but I keep forcing myself to put one foot in front of the other.

Was he waiting for her, or is this just a coincidence? It can't be.

Amid heartbreak and disappointment, my mind doesn't register another familiar face that's heading for the same elevator up to Ace's apartment.

27

Filling the Void

Calla

Numbness washes over me, over my whole body. I wish it would take over my mind, too. I closed myself off, enfolded myself in a protective layer over the last four years so I'd never feel the way I do now. Only Ace knows how to tear me apart like this. I should've never let him in.

He's the destruction I desperately sought to avoid.

As usual, Denzel is by the Mercedes when I stumble through the grand doors and onto the street, letting the buttery sun warm my skin. It's a little past midday, and passersby stroll on the sidewalk, soaking the beautiful weather.

"Let me give you a ride," Denzel offers. His tone is the same as always, with no hint whether he knows what just happened.

What did happen? I'm bewildered myself. I do know whatever there was between Ace and me is now over. That is clear—crystal clear. There may be an explanation for what he said, but I don't want it.

I shake my head and continue walking. "I think I need some fresh air."

The breeze brushes against my arms, and I continue putting one foot in front of the other. I walk to my apartment. It takes me two and a half hours, and the entire time I dissect the scenario repeatedly. From the way Ace looked around the hallway, he was, without a doubt, expecting someone. That someone ended up being Cassidy.

Once I enter my apartment, the emptiness of it engulfs me. The small space is now vast and hollow. The smell of the twelve red roses on the counter—which I can only assume are from Theo—overpower the apartment. My breathing, along with the distant sound of cars coming from the window next to me, cram the room.

There's a void inside of me driving me insane. I'm losing my mind—I love the person I'm meant to hate. I always have, but the time arises when even love can't overpower all the reasons why we can't be together. The list keeps growing awfully long.

There's no denying that something keeps pulling us together, both back in college and now, four years later. What if it's just a lesson, something to learn and move on from?

Oreo meows at my feet, and I squat down to run my fingers through his soft fur. He purrs in response and nuzzles closer, almost leaping into my lap like a dog. My eyes fall on the Cartier bracelet dangling on my wrist, and the void expands.

The sudden urge to remove the bracelet strikes me. Where did I put the screwdriver? I haven't seen it since the trip, and I don't recall unpacking it. I attempt to slide the bracelet off my wrist, but it's too small. I try it again and again. I keep trying, and each failed attempt agitates me.

I find myself on the floor in my living room, my knees digging into the hard floors, while I frantically tug at the bracelet on my wrist. I want, no, I *need* every visible reminder of Ace gone. He knew what he was doing when he spoke those words, he knew they would shatter me, and there's no coming back from that. I'm not going to be formulating any more excuses for him.

"Hey, hey, are you okay?" Mia rushes over. I didn't know she was here.

"I just need to get this damn bracelet off!" I'm hysterical now. The events of the past couple of days take their toll. First, it was telling my dad I'm seeing the person that should be our enemy. Now, a day later, everything has changed, and I'm questioning whether I made the greatest mistake of my life.

My relationship with my dad will never be the same, no matter what. I was aware of that before deciding to tell him, and I took that risk. For Ace. Am I that naïve?

"Where's the screwdriver?" Mia kneels, so she's eye level with me. She doesn't ask why I want the bracelet off or what happened. She knows me too well to realize that talking about it at this moment will cause more harm than good.

"I-I don't know." I attempt to slide the bracelet over my wrist again.

Mia stills my hands with hers, seeking to calm me. She nods and stands, taking me with her. She leads me to the bathroom and uses the shower gel to soap up my wrist.

My heart is beating frenetically, seeking to escape the reality of heartbreak. Finally, with a bit of tugging and pulling, the bracelet slides off. I hoped to get a sense of relief, but there's nothing.

Mia doesn't ask me what happened at Ace's apartment, and I don't offer her any information. I want to forget about it like a bad nightmare. Instead, we watch a horror movie. I'm not too fond of horror movies, but I can't do anything remotely happy.

A new week comes and brings chaos with it—like the events of last week weren't enough to send a sane person over the edge. I go to work as though nothing has happened. Jennifer has her plate full, deciding how to make use of the one hundred thousand dollars I acquired for her. The result is a side of her I've never witnessed before—happy. Or at least, I'm guessing she's happy. She hasn't fired anyone in over a week. We're all on edge, anticipating that the worst will come.

Mia starts her new job and subtly drops hints that she's able to cover up my only tattoo whenever I want. I haven't talked to her about Ace. I can't—not without revealing everything, and I'm not prepared for that.

Perhaps the best thing would be to forget the events of the last few weeks. Pretend it didn't happen. Unfortunately, that only seems to work when I'm occupied with something. So I stay late at work. Some nights, I work till midnight, so my mind focuses on other things—anything but him.

I've asked Mia to leave the key to Ace's apartment and the bracelet at the front desk, refusing to do it myself for fear of running into Ace. I can't look at him.

I visit Betty and do her groceries for her. In return, she cooks for Mia and me some nights. I fall back into my usual routine. I keep busy. However, there are nights when Mia stays over at Theo's that I lie in bed, unable to fall asleep. That's when my mind fills with thoughts of him.

Denzel has offered me a ride to work every day, but I decline every time. This is Ace's doing, and I'm done playing his games. So I catch the subway instead, as I did in the past.

On Thursday, I see my therapist, Addilyn, and explain what happened over the last few weeks. She stops me throughout and poses questions such as, "How did that make you feel?" and, "What did you hope would happen?"

She crosses her thin legs and leans back in her seat, sliding her glasses off and wiping the lenses before looking back up at me. Her eyes, almost as dark as the night sky, stay on me for a minute. I scoot back in my seat underneath her gaze. All therapists have that look, the one that makes you talk about your deepest and darkest secrets within two minutes of entering the room.

"Do you think this man has an ulterior motive for saying that?" she finally asks after I explain the last encounter I had with Ace.

"I think he's trying to push me away."

"Why would he do that?" she prompts.

I wonder how many clients she sees a day, and if she ever gets sick of hearing about their problems. What secrets are revealed in this room, behind closed doors, in the hope that talking about them will fix everything?

"To protect me in a way, perhaps."

I've been trying not to think about him, but nothing adds up. I know Ace well enough to know he's not a cruel person. He's not the one to seek revenge. There *has* to be another reason for him doing what he did.

"And how do *you* feel about that?"

"I hate it. It's disappointing, especially after everything we've been through. We've progressed, and I finally thought we could figure everything out. I guess not. I've been clear with him on what I need—honesty, and while he's given me some honesty, he's never been entirely open."

"You are not willing to give him another chance if he asks for it?"

"When do the second chances stop being that and become third, fourth…fifth chances? When is it the time to say enough is enough?"

She doesn't answer my question. She never does. Instead, she smiles. "Good."

Friday rolls around, and I finish up at work around seven-thirty. I walk toward the subway station with my heels clicking on the pavement and my feet swollen and aching. Every few minutes, I have the urge to take my shoes off, but the thought of walking barefoot repulses me.

The sun sets across the horizon, and it soaks the city with a soft-pink shade. For me, the day is coming to an end. For others, the night is only just beginning.

My phone buzzes in my purse, and I retrieve it to find Timothy Kline's contact from *The Times* light up my screen. I answer, putting the phone to my ear.

"Good evening, Miss Maven. I'm sorry to call you so late on a Friday."

"Good evening. That's not a problem." I've been waiting for this call all week. Unintentionally, I cross the fingers on my other hand while continuing to walk on the busy sidewalk to the subway.

"I'm calling you with good news. We want to offer you a job," Tim says, and I squeeze my eyes shut for a second in excitement.

"We have a special project for you. We've been looking for someone for this position and have concluded that you're perfect for the job. We want to offer you a position in Switzerland for eight months. You'd fly there in less than a month, and we will cover all expenses. After that, you'll have a guaranteed, full-time position with us," he continues, briefing me on the details.

The sound of a new text makes me quickly pull the phone from my ear and glance at the screen.

Mia: ***Have u seen the news?***

I barely have time to skim over the message when a new one comes in.

Mia: ***Call me when u see this!!!!!!***

I place the call on loudspeaker and head over to my social media account that I barely use. I follow the main news accounts on there. I don't have to scroll far to understand what news Mia is talking about. The first article causes my lungs to twist in agony.

Ace Blackwell has been arrested and held in custody, allegedly charged on almost ten different offenses. Is this the end of the champion's career, or has he been wrongly convicted?

My hands shake, and I can't see clearly. I can't even press on the article to read further details. The people around me turn into blurry silhouettes, and I freeze in the middle of the pathway. My worst nightmare has come true.

"Hello? Calla?" Tim calls through the phone when I don't reply to his offer. His words pluck me out of my head.

"Yes, I'm here. Can I have some time to think about this?" I manage to ask.

"Of course. I understand this is a big decision, but it is one in a lifetime opportunity, and we'd love to have someone with your qualifications and charisma on our team…"

I barely register the words coming out of my phone. All I can think about is Ace. At first, I believe this is my dad's doing, but then everything adds up. The FBI caught up to him, and if they are willing for this matter to go public, they have enough evidence against him.

"Of course, I won't make this decision lightly." My words sound distant.

Hailing a cab, I get in the back seat. Instead of heading home, I have somewhere else in mind.

Perhaps taking this job will be good for me, a new beginning in a new country. Far away from this. Focusing on my career at this age will pay off in the future. But I can't leave without doing everything I can for Ace—even if he doesn't want my help. I can't imagine how his family is dealing with this, and how Ellie is coping after going through so much.

The cab drops me off in front of an apartment building, and I stand on the sidewalk for a moment, preparing myself for the conversation I'm about to have. I've been here before, but tonight it's different. I'm unsure of what I'm walking into. This may be a big mistake, but how much worse can it get?

Exhaling, I walk through the large wooden doors. The familiar chandelier hanging from the ceiling of the lobby greets me with warm trickles of light. A light, rich palette covers the place, and it's eerily quiet—so much so, that I bet I'd be able to hear a pin drop. My dress, which during the day felt light, now weighs me down with every step I take.

Positioned in front of me is a grand desk that wraps around the back wall in a curved shape, highlighting every bit of the elegance this building contains. I've never really paid attention to it until now. I stall and take in the lobby's architecture, letting my eyes wander—internally preparing myself for the worst.

It's not until I'm in front of the door that I've walked through plenty of times before with my finger raised to press the doorbell that the reality of this situation hits me. This feels wrong and manipulative, but I have no other choice.

I press the doorbell and let it ring, tapping my fingers on the strap of my bag while I wait. These walls are soundproof, but I swear I can hear footsteps. Finally, the doorknob turns and reveals a pair of sapphire eyes.

Nik.

A very unclothed Nik, wearing only some navy sweatpants that hang off his hips. He rakes a hand over his messy hair to fix it into place.

How didn't I figure it out before? Dark hair, striking eyes, fantastic physique—the resemblance is unmistakable. If I was skeptical beforehand, now there's no doubt Nik and Ace are brothers.

The only two men who impressed me in *that department* are brothers. Great. Only I'd get myself in that situation unknowingly.

"Calla?" he asks, sounding confused, like he was expecting someone else. I'm not bothered by it, seeing as the last time I was here, he confessed his love, and I wanted nothing to do with it. Tonight, I'll be the one groveling if the situation requires me to.

"Nik, I'm sorry for coming here at this time on Friday, but I need your help." There's no time for sweet talk or building the scene.

"What is it, sweetheart?" Nik's face shows concern. He raises his arms as if to comfort me, but then he rethinks and drops them at his sides. I feel uneasiness seep in, understanding I ended things with Nik for Ace, and now I'm willing to beg Nik to do everything he can for him.

If anyone can get Ace out of this mess, it's Nik. He's never lost a case. He's the best, everyone knows that. Still, Ace and Nik haven't got off on the right foot, and I doubt Ace will want any help from Nik—or anyone for that matter.

"Have you seen the news? Ace…" I begin, but I'm unable to find the words to explain everything I've discovered in the last ten minutes.

"Yeah, I've seen." Nik shuffles into his apartment, and I take it as an invitation to follow him and shut the door behind me.

As we walk through the hallway and into the living room, I glance around his apartment. Everything is the same as it was before—luxurious and tidy.

"And?" I prompt.

"And what?" He turns abruptly, and I halt in my steps.

His body is inches away from mine. The heat off his shirtless chest spreads through the space between us. There's no denying that Nik is an attractive man, and not just in a physical sense. He's also well-educated, and that gives him another type of alluring pull.

I take a step back. "Aren't you his lawyer?"

"I'm not taking the case," he says roughly.

His eyes bore into mine, and the younger version of me would have dropped the subject right there and then. However, I've learned to deal with intimidating men, and Nik knows I'll say what's on my mind. I recall him telling me it's one of the things that drew him to me. Once I find myself set on a task, there's very little that can deter me.

"Why not?"

Until now, it hasn't crossed my mind that Nik might be the one who did this. He got me the interview with *The Times*, and that's where the FBI agent, Mark Stanton, *introduced* himself. It would make sense that Nik set it up, but my gut feeling tells me Nik wouldn't do something like that. He isn't that type of person.

"I don't take cases that I can't win," he states, heading toward the fridge behind the kitchen counter.

Oh, so that's how he keeps his zero-loss score. Quite misleading. "Have you even spoken to him?" I persist.

"I don't have to. He *was* my client. I know plenty," he emphasizes the word *was*, enough for me to understand it's not the case anymore. He pulls out two bottles of water and hands one to me. "Unless you prefer something stronger?"

I shake my head. "Thank you."

There's a knock at the door. Nik *was* expecting someone. He walks past me, and I stand in the living room, unsure whether to follow him or not. If it's female company, I don't want to risk them getting the wrong idea about this encounter.

Nik returns with two takeout bags, and it smells delicious. My stomach grumbles, and I realize I haven't eaten anything since lunch, it's now eight. I planned to order takeout on my way home so it would arrive at my apartment at the same time as I did. That was before plans changed.

"Have you eaten?" Nik sets the food on the counter.

There's Thai food, burgers, and even churros for dessert. He ordered a whole feast. The amount of food he's laid out has me wondering if he's expecting company.

"Oh, I don't want to intrude." I fix my bag strap.

"Calla, I'm having dinner alone in my apartment on a Friday night. You aren't intruding. You'll be doing me a favor." He motions for me to sit at the counter.

I should say no and go home, but my stomach protests in response, and I still haven't achieved what I came here for. Placing my bag on the empty chair beside me, I sit and inhale the smell of caramelized onion and the sweetness of the chocolate dip.

"Dinner alone? It looks like you have ordered for ten people."

He raises his eyebrow at me, and a cheeky grin appears on his face. "Are you doubting my capabilities?"

Oh, definitely not. But I don't say that. "Seems like a lot for one person."

"I had a long week."

So have I. I reach for the burger, cutting it in half before biting into it. It's the best thing I've ever tasted. The bun is warm and a little bit crispy but still soft in the middle.

"How did the interview at *The Times* go?" Nik asks.

I swallow a mouthful. "I wanted to talk to you about that..."

"Hmm?"

"It was strange. The FBI showed up instead of Tim..." I take a drink of the water and carefully examine Nik's face for any clues.

He places his fork down and looks at me, instantly understanding what I'm getting at. "You think I had something to do with that?"

I shrug. "To be honest, no." I just wanted to make sure.

"I'm stunned that you think so low of me that you'd even bother to ask that." The hurt is evident in his tone.

"We didn't exactly end our—" I pause, trying to think of the right word, "—arrangement on the best of terms."

He snickers. "So you assumed out of revenge or jealousy I'd do something like that? Calla, I have the highest respect for you, and even if I didn't, I wouldn't go behind someone's back."

"I'm sorry. I shouldn't have even thought it."

"Apology accepted," he says and stabs his fork into the pad Thai noodles.

"But apart from that, they offered me a job...in Switzerland." I change the conversation.

There's a pause for a minute while we both eat. I can't stop myself from stealing glances at Nik beside me and comparing all the similarities to Ace. Perhaps it shouldn't be such a surprise that I pursued Nik to begin with. He reminded me of Ace, even if I didn't realize it then.

"I think you should take it," he finally speaks, making it sound so simple.

The hesitation on my face must be apparent. There's no denying it's a great opportunity, but I'd have to start all over again in a new city, with no friends or family. It's not a quick flight back here. It's nine hours, and the flights home will also leave a massive dent in my wallet. The situation is daunting.

"What are you afraid of?" Nik asks.

"Change."

"Change is inevitable. There will always be change. If not now, then soon. You can't keep avoiding it and hope to get to the top just by staying in the same place. Is it not your dream to work for *The Times*?"

"Yeah, I guess it is," I reply, questioning myself. My dream is bigger than that. I will always pursue more. If I take this job, it'll only be the beginning.

"You should take the opportunity. Switzerland is a beautiful country. You'd like it."

It'll be a good change from the chaos here, an eye-opening experience. I'd be stupid to pass it up. I wait for Nik to finish eating the main meal, and it's not until dessert that I begin what I came here for. "Ace…"

Nik exhales deeply. "I can't take the case. He was a tough client, and I get the feeling we both don't like each other very much. However, I'm willing to pass it on to someone else in my firm." The finality in his voice sends a chill down my spine.

The only chance Ace has to walk out of this is Nik. There's only one thing left to do. It will alter everything, but there's no other choice. "Would you change your mind if I told you he's your brother?"

He stares at me, no doubt trying to figure out if I'm tricking him.

"Have you ever wondered why you both look so alike? Or why your dad was never in the picture when you were younger?"

"I don't have a brother," he says, but his voice is unsure.

I don't mention he may have other siblings he doesn't know about since his father is the definition of a manipulative cheater. That's a conversation for a different time.

"How does client-confidentiality work?"

Nik raises an eyebrow. "Calla, I want to be very clear on something. We are friends. You can tell me anything without being worried that it will be said elsewhere. No matter what it is. You have my word that anything you tell me will never leave this room."

My heart pounds, and the words are itching to get out. All the secrets, the lies, everything I kept inside, things that not even my therapist knows.

I tell him. I tell him everything, from the accident to when I met Ace in college, to the underground clubs and how everything is falling apart.

The entire time, he listens without interrupting or asking questions. I hate that he's keeping his expression neutral. I know it comes from years of practice, but even that falters at some points in the storyline. It takes me thirty minutes, and even then, I feel like I skipped over some bits.

"He'd never tell you, but I feel Ace is envious of you."

"In what way?"

"Your father always wanted him to follow in his footsteps, to become a lawyer just like him, but Ace wanted nothing to do with that. And here you are..." I let the rest speak for itself.

He scoffs and rubs his forehead. He opens his mouth and then closes it again. I've never seen Nik at a loss for words. He generally has a lot to say.

I give him a minute, waiting for him to process the information I've dumped on him—six years in thirty minutes.

"Okay."

"You'll take the case?" I almost jump to my feet.

He nods. "If you think that I'm going to barge in there now, you're going to be very disappointed. That's not how these things work. I'll have to make some calls before I charge in there at full speed."

I exhale and let myself relax for the first time since reading the news this evening. "Thank you. For everything."

"I don't think you should be thanking me just yet. From what you told me, this situation is very ugly, and I don't know what evidence they have already compiled on him. Go home, and get some rest. I'll start working."

I stand and grab my bag from the chair next to me. This was the most Nik and I have ever talked, and for some unknown reason, I find myself completely trusting him. I trust that he'll do everything he can to help Ace.

Hopefully, Ace will allow him to.

"Can you do me one more favor?" I try when I'm almost out the door.

He nods.

"Don't mention to Ace that I came here."

28

Repercussions

Ace

One week ago

Pacing around my apartment, I persist in glancing at my wristwatch and then to the front door. Waiting.

Five minutes.

Five minutes until everything changes—whether it be for the best or the worst, it's still uncertain.

It wasn't a difficult choice. This is the only way to be with Calla. The only way our life can be normal again, or as normal as we could ever be together. I'm doing this for her even though it may go terribly wrong. She requires stability, and I'm seeking to provide her with it by making the impossible happen. It's also the only way I'm able to get out of all the fucked-up shit I've gotten myself involved in.

I knew the FBI was closing in on me, closing in on everything I've tried to keep hidden for two years. I was thrown in the deep end without having full knowledge of the consequences, and I'll take full responsibility for that.

A man was killed at one of the fights by Logan—someone that should have never been there in the first place. Cass decided to cover it up, and now I'm paying the price for it.

That's why when Mark Stanton offered me a deal, I decided to take it. Call me an idiot or a coward. I don't give a fuck. I'm sick of the games, the risks, a life filled with uncertainty. I'm willing to give everything up, risk it all—the money, the fame, my integrity, and everything in between for a life with her.

To my surprise, Mark explained just how involved Cassidy is. She runs the show more than I do. She gets the best of both worlds, picking and choosing whenever she feels like playing the boss. This entire time, she made me believe I was in charge. She played games with me, whether it be for her sanctuary or just because she was bored and had nothing else to occupy her time with. In reality, she decided to take the position from me a long while ago without my knowledge and continued to let me do the dirty work.

It wasn't a difficult decision to throw her under the bus. She manipulated me and played me. She's lucky she's still breathing.

While the thoughts churn in my mind, making my fists curl at my sides, there's a knock on my door. I guess she's early—for once. Let's get this shit over and done with.

I'm wearing jeans and a T-shirt, but even with the casual clothes on, I'm weighed down by the wires underneath. I stretch my muscles. If she figures it out and tries to run, I'll be ready for it, and Mark will be waiting by the elevators as well. Our plan is about to be put into action.

I unlock the door, and my eyes widen. Calla is standing in front of me in a sundress. The material is loose, and her skin glows vibrantly. She lifts her gaze to mine, and her mellow eyes dance with the sunlight that peeks through the window. Warm chocolate waves fall down the sides of her face, contrasting with the caramel freckles scattered on her nose and cheeks in a T shape.

Her full mouth curves up at the corners when she sees me, and I have the urge to pull her into my arms. I haven't seen her for two days, but it felt longer than that after spending two whole weeks by her side.

If it were any other time, I'd be thrilled to see her. I'd be over the moon that she decided to come here without calling me first. But today, it's all fucking wrong. I need to get her out of here, fast.

"What are you doing here?" I step outside of my apartment, slightly shutting the door behind me, leaving a small gap.

"I just got back from the airport." Her mood is already depleting from my uninviting behavior.

"You need to go." I glance around the hallway. Cass will be here in less than five minutes, and this could go terribly wrong. The only way to get Cass here was to tell her I was interested in our previous arrangement. She was more than thrilled to hear that—almost too thrilled. It has me questioning whether she has her own tricks up her sleeve.

"What?" Calla asks, uncertainty flooding her expression.

"You can't be here. Go home," I state in a colder tone, hating myself for daring to speak to her like that.

"What do you mean? Are you busy?" she asks, and I hate the understanding that flows over her face. I don't deserve her, I knew that from the start.

"No. I just don't want you here." I know her too well. I can't tell her the truth. She won't leave if she knows Cass and then the FBI will be on my doorstep in less than five minutes, and I can't let her stay.

"Ace, what's going on?" she questions. I wanted to tell her last night, but I didn't get the chance to, and I couldn't have her worrying about me, especially when she was spending time with her family. She doesn't deserve to be pulled into this mess. My fucking mess.

"Leave."

She takes a step back as though I have physically hurt her, but she still doesn't go.

I can't meet her eyes, because I know what I must do to get her to leave, and it's going to destroy everything I've been trying to build between us. I needed her complete trust because there was a part of me that knew something like this would happen. Something that would test everything we've been working on.

The time is ticking down fast. At any moment, the elevator doors could open, and Cass could stride through them. "I told you I would have you at my feet, Calla." The words are vile and don't hold any truth.

A part of me needs her to call me out on it, to look me in the face and accuse me of lying. She should know me better, but she doesn't do any of those things. The hurt in her face is evident. She attempts to capture my gaze, but I don't allow her to.

It takes all my willpower not to say anything else. There's an intense urge to go after her when she turns her back on me and leaves, but my feet are frozen in place, and I grip the doorframe so hard that my knuckles turn white.

I watch her disappear into the elevator, and distant flashbacks from four years ago deluge my thoughts. I don't blame her. I never have. I have fucked up on more than one occasion, and it's not fair for me to keep asking more of her without being able to give her anything back.

Returning inside my apartment, rage builds inside me—everything spilling from within. I know the consequences of my actions, but I'd rather her hate me and be safe than involve her in this mayhem.

"Fuck!" My fist collides with the wall, and my whole future shatters in front of me.

Present

I sit in the interrogation room they have finally brought me into. Last week, I was under house arrest, unable to go anywhere except for my apartment or office, while they gathered more evidence on Cassidy.

I couldn't risk talking to Calla because I knew my moves, calls, and everything were tracked if I stepped out of line. I've already told Mark that Calla doesn't know anything, even though I know he didn't buy the lie. I don't need her to be used against me or to get involved in this. I don't need to ruin her life more than I already have.

"Take the deal, Ace. You testify on the stand against Cassidy and Logan, and…I'll cut you a deal of six years. Four of them mandatory," he proposes once again, standing over me like a lion upon its prey.

I've been in the same spot for hours, my body going numb from the hard chair beneath me and the cool metal desk I'm leaning my elbows on.

Mark has blindsided me. Bastard.

"You said two if I gave you Cassidy. And there was no mention of anything mandatory." I grind my teeth. The original terms would see me out in three months or less on good behavior without testifying against her on the stand. That was the only reason I took the fucking deal.

"There's too much evidence against you. You should be doing a lot more. I'm being generous here," he reasons in a calm, calculated voice. Too relaxed, like he's thinking about what he's going to have for dinner tonight when he goes home to his wife.

"If you were confident, you wouldn't offer me anything." There's a smugness to my irritated tone. I didn't request a lawyer since I thought this was going to be a clean-cut arrangement.

I didn't account for Mark's deception. I know I should have. I've been taught not to trust anyone. I was too focused on the desired result to account for everything that could go wrong.

"I'm trying to help you."

I scoff, and my hands form into fists on the table. "By going against your word?"

"New evidence has come to light. It's not my decision anymore," he says, sounding bored and dismissive.

"What kind of evidence?" I inquire.

"You know I'm not permitted to disclose that."

"Because you don't have shit," I grumble underneath my breath even though the odds aren't in my favor.

He braces his hands on the table in front of me, his dark sleeves are rolled up, and I raise my head to meet his animalistic stare.

"That's the only deal I'm able to offer you. After I leave this room, there won't be any more handouts. Six years. She'll have protection, so will your family, and you will too when you get out," he tempts me, because he knows I'll need it.

No doubt, Cassidy will want her revenge for this. If not now, then five, ten, fifteen years down the road. She will seek me out for throwing her under the bus. I broke the most significant rule. I ratted her and Logan out.

"And you expect me to believe anything that comes out of your mouth?" I grumble.

"You agree, and I'll get the paperwork here immediately. Everything will be on paper this time."

I won't be out for four fucking years. The bastard knows it's a difficult bargain to say no to. I deserve everything that's coming for me. There are no excuses for the actions I've taken in my life. If this is the only way to keep Calla safe, keep my family safe. I'll do it for them.

Mark's lips lift at the corners like he knows I'm about to accept. He's done this before, and he knows how to make people crack under pressure, how to use everything they care about against them. I open my mouth to give up my freedom, but at the exact moment, the door flies open, and Nik charges in like a knight in shining armor.

Behind him is a police officer with wide eyes and a terrified face. His first day on the job, I'm guessing. Mark stands straighter and places his hand on the holster around his waist.

"Nik Stryker, Ace's attorney," Nik introduces himself to Mark. "From now on, you won't be talking to my client unless I'm present. Everything my client has agreed to or said is inadmissible as he didn't have his attorney present. I need a list of the charges that have been brought against him, and I will need a minute with my client. Alone."

Mark's face turns blank, and his mouth sets into a grim line. He glances at me and then Nik, and I swear I notice his jaw twitch. He storms out of the room and closes the door behind him, leaving me alone with Nik.

"I thought I fired you." I meet Nik's stare.

A wicked, knowing smile spreads across his face. "Nice to see you, too, brother."

29

Nostalgia

Calla

I've been on edge since I left Nik's apartment. Mia is home when I stumble through the door, and she blasts me with questions. I attempt to summarize as best as I can while still being vague. It's not that I don't trust her, but once again, it's not my secret to tell.

Nik was different. I needed his help, and the only way to get it was to use the family card. Nik needed to know everything so he isn't blindsided by the revelations later. He also deserved to know everything before deciding if he wanted to take the case. I'd never downplay the situation so he would represent Ace if that meant going against his morals.

I feel it was the right decision to make now that everything is crashing and burning to the ground. I hope I don't get proven wrong.

It's a little past midnight, and even with a city bursting with life outside my window, the darkness frames me. I wonder if I subconsciously chose this city for the reason that it's always alive, allowing me to feel like I'm not alone. Although I've come to realize you can still feel alone with people all around you.

Mia pops her head into my room as I'm lying on my empty bed. "Did you want company?"

I shake my head. "No, that's okay. I just need to be alone tonight."

She nods and casually adds, "I'm going to head over to Theo's."

I raise my eyebrows. "You've been spending a lot of time with him. Is it getting serious?"

She's barely stayed in this apartment in the weeks since I got back from the trip with Ace, and who knows if she was here at all when I was away.

"We're just having fun." She brushes my question off.

"Does he know that?"

Mia scowls. "I told him that I'm not ready for anything serious."

"What was his response?"

She glares at me, and that's all I need to know that Theo isn't delighted with that. We all have demons we must overcome. Mia's is to accept that a relationship with a man isn't that wicked. She's stuck on the idea that all men are pigs, but there's a decent one standing in front of her, and he's been there all along. Despite that, there's no point in trying to make her see my point. She won't listen. She must figure it out independently.

Once Mia leaves and shuts the apartment door behind her, there's no escaping the emptiness. I spend all night on my computer, mindlessly searching the web. I look at places in Switzerland and appreciate the picturesque scenery. It would be a dream to live in a country like that, and I begin to imagine myself with my laptop at a small coffee shop that overlooks the snowy mountains. So peaceful. No distractions or worries to strangle me.

I know what the right choice is—what's best for me. I've learned I shouldn't put other people first. It always ends up a vigorous mess, and I eventually despise them for making me sacrifice something. It all ends one way or another anyway. I have to be true to myself.

Dawn comes, and I'm still awake. My eyes are heavy, and my body's depleted, but my mind is running marathons. I continue staring at my phone, waiting for any updates from Nik, even though I'm aware less than twelve hours have passed since I saw him.

When I finally force myself to get up and move to the kitchen, I pause at the living room window. A blanket of heavy clouds covers the sky, promising a dreadful and stormy day.

Oreo brushes his head against my leg, and I take that as a cue to feed him and brew myself a cup of hot coffee. I allow myself to sit on the sofa until it's a reasonable time to get dressed. Pulling my jeans on and swapping my usual pair of heels for some sneakers, I grab an umbrella on my way out.

The cab drops me off in front of the white house with a black gate surrounding it. It's not until I've paid the cab fare and face the house that I begin to question what I'm doing here.

Pressing the doorbell, I wait. I smooth my top with my hand and quickly brush my fingers through my hair. I've been here before, but I haven't felt on edge like I do now. What is Ace's mom going to think of me showing up uninvited like this? God, I should just turn around and go home.

It's too late. The gate opens, and I'm forced to put one foot in front of the other. The front door flies open, and Ellie skips over to me and wraps her hands around my waist. There's an instant smile on my face. She looks better than she did the last time I saw her. Her cheeks are filled with color, and her hair is shinier—I hope that means good news. This family has already been through too much trauma. They deserve a flicker of happiness, at the very least.

"Hi, Ellie," I greet her, taking in her dark hair and beautiful blue eyes. Nik is unaware he has another sibling, but that's one thing I'm not prepared to share with him.

"Hello, is Ace with you?" Ellie peers behind me.

Pain shoots in my chest, but I keep the smile plastered on my face when I say, "No, he's busy today." My gaze meets Reese, who's standing at the door, and there's an understanding between us. She knows, but how much?

"Hello, Calla, darling. Come in. We were just making breakfast. Have you eaten?" Her motherly instincts remind me of how openhearted she is.

"I haven't, but—"

"Come eat with us," Reese offers with a small smile and leads us inside.

We walk through the hallway, and the smell of toast, eggs, and coffee permeates through the house, greeting me and my grumbling stomach. The thought of food should make me nauseous after last night. Nik and I devoured everything he ordered, including dessert. However, I'm starving.

Toast, eggs, bacon, waffles, and fruit are laid out on the table with two plates set, Reese reaches into the cupboard and pulls out another plate for me. She tucks her neat hair behind her ears and motions for Ellie and me to sit at the counter.

"Thank you," I say.

"How was your trip? Ace told me you visited Paris and Italy." Reese makes conversation but is careful of what she says around Ellie.

I wonder if Ellie has heard about Ace. His name is splattered across the tabloids, and everyone's talking about him. She's not stupid, and I bet she has some kind of device she uses to go online.

"It was amazing, everything from the food and culture to the scenery. I miss it already," I admit, but I know I don't miss the beautiful places. It's the person I visited them with I'm longing for. I shut the thoughts down immediately.

She smiles. "I understand that. You can get lost in beautiful countries, wondering if you could just start a life there instead of coming home." Her eyes seem to wander into the distance as if she's recalling her own memories from a lifetime ago.

"Have you traveled a lot?" I ask.

"Once. A long time ago, all I did was travel for a couple of years with—" She glances at Ellie, and I understand she's talking about her ex-husband.

It makes me wonder what their relationship was like. Has Ace's father always been a dreadful human, or did something make him the way he is? I look at Reese and see a loving, gentle person and a wonderful mother. It's hard to imagine her with someone like Ace's father. Perhaps he was different when they first met. Or maybe, her kindness clouded her judgment of his character.

"Let's eat." Reese sits next to Ellie and takes a bit of toast.

"I start ballet classes next Saturday." Ellie grins at me, and then her face drops as she remembers. "Ace was meant to take me. Will he still…be busy?"

The food I swallowed feels like it's going to come back up.

"I can take you. If your mom doesn't mind," I suggest in an attempt to get her mind off Ace. I glance at Reese, hoping I'm not overstepping, but she grants me a thankful smile.

"Really?" Ellie exclaims, her face gleaming with hope. "Mom?"

"I'm sure Calla might have other things to do," Reese says.

"It would be my pleasure."

Ellie grins at me. "It starts at nine."

We finish eating breakfast while Ellie tells me about how excited she is for her ballet classes. While I help Reese with clearing the table, Ellie rushes to her room to put on her outfit so she can show me.

I want to ask about Ace, but I don't know how to go about it. Reese seems to sense this, so she tells me herself. "He told me it was a misunderstanding, but I know him well enough to know when he's lying through his teeth. I just hope he can get himself out of the mess that he's gotten himself in," she says with no empathy in her voice. It makes me wonder how much she knows about the situation.

"Have you talked to him recently?"

"Yesterday morning, when he told me not to listen to the news." Of course, he did.

"How's Ellie? Does she know? And how's her treatment going?"

At this, she exhales. "She doesn't know much, but it's hard to shield her from the news. Everything's going well with her treatment. She had a checkup the other day, and the doctor said it's best for her to get back into activities that kids her age do, hence the ballet classes. We just have to keep going for checkups regularly to make sure there isn't a relapse."

Ellie races down the stairs flaunt her outfit. She has sheer white tights on with a baby-pink leotard over the top. It sparkles as she skips toward us.

"Wow." I motion for her to twirl.

I spend the rest of the day with Ellie and Reese. It's easy to be around them. We watch movies and play board games while the storm rolls in at full force. The TV is turned up, but we can barely hear it over the raging thunder. I find myself laughing throughout the day, even though it's the last thing I feel like doing. Guilt pierces me each time. Ace should be here. The emptiness in my chest lingers, clinging to every bit of darkness and intensifying when I think of him.

Just because Ace and I aren't on good terms at the moment, it doesn't mean I shouldn't be here. I promised Ellie last time that I'd come back.

Ace knew what he was doing when he said those words to me, and even though it might have been part of his grand scheme to protect me, I'm tired of the lying, of him pushing me away. No matter how many times I express to him that I want him to talk to me, he persists in ignoring my requests.

Perhaps I'm asking too much, but considering our past, I think it's fair to ask that of him. I made it clear from the start I'm not going to sit back and let him make decisions for me, and that's what he did. He decided it was best for me to be left in the dark. Well, I've decided that men aren't going to make decisions for me anymore.

"He has a good lawyer. Everything will be fine," I reassure Reese on my way out, not sure who I'm trying to convince.

"Thank you for coming." Reese hugs me, and I inhale the fresh and vibrant tones of her perfume.

"I will do everything I can." Without him knowing that I am.

"You're the best thing that's ever happened to him. I just hope he knows it." She squeezes me one last time.

There's a heaviness inside my chest, and all I can manage to say is, "I'll see you next Saturday."

✦ ✦ ✦

The week drags on immensely, and there's no news on Ace's case. Nik tells me he's working on it, and he'll contact me when there's something to report. I do everything I can to take my mind off it, mostly work. Some nights I don't get home till midnight. It's a way to distract myself, and I could use the extra money.

At the moment, there's only one sure thing—Nik isn't letting Ace take any deal he's been offered. They both have connections to some of the most influential people in the country, but will it be enough?

There's a delivery to my apartment halfway through the week. After a long day of work, I climb the stairs to my floor to find the delivery guy standing in front of my door. He keeps glancing at his phone, as if checking this is the correct address.

"Are you Calla Maven?" he asks when I approach.

I nod.

He picks a large red box off the floor and hands it to me. I don't need to know what's in it to have an idea about who sent it. I wonder how Ace still manages to do this when he's in custody.

"Thank you."

I walk into my apartment and open the box. Inside are more red roses than I can count. On top of one is a sticky note with a key—Ace's apartment key. The same key I gave back to him.

I'm sorry.

I roll my eyes. A lousy apology without an explanation. I'd rather not have one at all. I keep the flowers since they make my apartment smell like a florist. I throw the note away.

Friday is when I finally hear from Nik. He calls me while I'm working on an article about the latest cheating scandal some athlete has gotten himself into. I can't wait until I'm writing articles on issues that matter, providing a voice for those who don't have one.

"Are you free for lunch?" Nik asks when I pick up the phone. His tone gives away that he has news. I try to get a sense of whether it's good or bad.

"Sure." I'm already packing up the stuff on my desk.

"I'll pick you up soon."

An Audi R8 waits for me outside when I depart the building. I have until the middle of next week to give *The Times* a response about their offer. My decision is already made, I've handed in my notice to Jennifer yesterday, and the only thing left to do is call Timothy.

Nik hops out of the driver's side when he notices me and walks around to the passenger side to hold the door open for me. A small smile etches its way across his remarkable face. "Hello, sweetheart."

A charcoal suit clings to his figure, his jacket buttons are undone, and a light-blue shirt peeks underneath. It's impressive to watch Nik carry himself with self-assurance and virility. To this day, it intrigues me that I still don't know much about him or where he came from, what his childhood was like or how many serious relationships he's been in. Come to think of it, I barely know him at all. It surprises me that I came to trust him and feel at ease around him when he's almost a stranger. Yet, there's something in his character that allows people to see how kindhearted he is.

"Hey, is everything okay?"

Nik nods in response and closes the car door behind me when I'm in the seat. "How have you been?" he asks when he begins driving through the streets.

"Yeah, trying to keep my mind busy. I've decided to take the offer in Switzerland."

He glances at me while we wait at a red light. "You'll love it. I have a holiday cottage there. I don't visit as much as I'd like to."

Where doesn't he own properties?

Nik takes us to an expensive restaurant in the middle of Manhattan. Before we step in, I already know I'm severely under-dressed. This place is extravagant and lavish. There aren't many people inside, and those who are, seem like they're conducting crucial business meetings.

Nik doesn't start talking about Ace until we've ordered and our drinks are in front of us. I opted for sparkling water with lime.

"I wanted to talk to you about this in person," he begins. "They have frozen all his accounts. He has nothing to his name. But you do."

"What?" I ask, mystified.

"Two weeks ago, he placed his assets in your name."

Another piece of the puzzle unveils itself. "That can't be true. Why me? He has family."

"It would have been too suspicious if he'd transferred all his assets to his immediate family. The FBI would seize them immediately without question."

"And now it's not…suspicious?"

"It still is. However, he made it seem like part of the deal he made with you and *Satire Times*. The FBI are doubtful, but they'll leave it alone for the time being."

I sip my drink, attempting to take in everything Nik is telling me. I like that he isn't keeping anything from me. He's always been straightforward, a rare attribute I've come to appreciate.

"There are two things I need you to do," he continues. "The first being to transfer ten million dollars for his bail."

God, ten million dollars. I've never seen that kind of money. "I suppose it's in my account?"

Nik nods. "Ace also set up an account for you two weeks ago and transferred some of his money there. There's enough to cover bail and leave some extra."

"And the second thing?" I prompt.

"They don't have much evidence. However, Ace made me aware of a problem that needs to be taken care of."

"What kind of problem?"

"A flash drive that he didn't have the chance to destroy before all of this happened. It contains vital information that the FBI would love to get their hands on."

"You want me to destroy evidence?"

He glances around, confirming no one overheard. "I'd never ask you to do that, sweetheart. Just acquire it and give it to me. I'll deal with it."

"Why can't you do it?" I question, not because I'm not willing to, but I want to know the risks.

He raises a brow. "Tell me how this sounds. A lawyer goes to his client's apartment while his client is behind bars. It will be too obvious, and my every move is currently being watched. It won't look strange if you go to visit *your* new apartment," he emphasizes.

My new apartment. I don't particularly like the sound of that. I exhale, absorbing everything. "Okay."

"You'll need to do it before Mark decides to go take another look. He'll probably do that before Ace gets released on bail, to check in case something was missed."

I nod once again.

"I'm sorry for throwing all of this on you, and I wouldn't ask if there was another way."

"I'm the one who got you into this mess, Nik. I'm thankful you took his case, and I'll do anything I can to help out."

We have lunch together, and the conversation turns more lighthearted. Nik chats about the times he's been to Switzerland. "Perhaps I'll have a reason to visit my holiday house now, especially after all this blows over," he says with an impudent grin.

I smile, twirling the straw in my drink before meeting his eyes. "I wouldn't mind having a familiar face in a foreign country."

Nik drops me back at the office after our lunch, reminding me about the flash drive. I plan to stop at the apartment after I finish work this evening.

Once I leave the office, my phone buzzes in my bag, and I check the caller ID before answering. It's Mia. "I need you to get me a pregnancy test on your way home," Mia speaks as soon as I press the phone to my ear.

"What!?"

"I know. I know. I missed my period, and it's probably just nerves, but I'm freaking out. I'm not ready for a baby. I don't even know where Theo and I stand. I'm not ready for commitment, let alone a baby! A baby, Calla!"

"Relax, breathe. I'll be home as soon as I can."

I purchase a few pregnancy tests from a corner store before heading for Ace's apartment building. Using the key he sent me the other day in the box of flowers, I unlock the door. I begin to question whether that apology had an ulterior motive. Did he know Nik was going to ask me to do this? The thought of it makes me furious. Ace pushes me away, and then when everything comes crashing down, he decides to reel me back in. I'm utterly confused about what his thought process is.

The apartment is hollow without Ace. There's no sign the FBI has already been here. However, Nik informed me they have. I set my handbag and the plastic bag with the pregnancy tests on the table and slowly walk around the space. The memories hit hard. I head toward Ace's room, where the flash drive is, needing to get out of here before the feelings I'm not ready for roll in like a thunderstorm.

My phone buzzes with yet another call. I don't remember the last time I've had this many calls in one day. It's Nik again.

"Did you manage to get it?"

"Yes, I'm leaving the apartment now."

"If you don't want to run into Mark, I suggest you get out of there. Fast."

I don't bother asking him how he knows that Mark is on his way here. There's no time for questions. I grab my bag off the counter and rush out the door. My heart beats out of my chest in the elevator, and when the doors open, I sigh in relief when I don't spot Mark's face. The flash drive in my bra—the only place I felt safe putting it—is like a bomb waiting to explode, and with every step I take out of the building, the timer ticks.

Only once I'm marching on the sidewalk toward the subway station do I realize I left the plastic bag with the pregnancy tests on the counter in Ace's apartment. It's too late to go back. There's too high a risk I'll run into Mark. So I stop at a pharmacy on the way home and buy more pregnancy tests.

"What is that?" I eye the bottle of wine on the counter with two glasses next to it when I step into my apartment after a long day.

"I'm getting ready to celebrate," Mia announces.

"Celebrate?"

"Celebrate that I'm not pregnant."

"Are you on birth control?" I ask.

Her face scrunches. "Kind of."

"What's that supposed to mean?"

"I keep forgetting to take it. I'm not used to having sex with men and not using protection."

I take a deep breath. There's a good chance she's pregnant. "Now, would it be that bad if you're pregnant?"

Mia stares at me like I'm speaking a different language, repelled by the words coming out of my mouth. She snatches the boxes out of my hands and heads to the bathroom, not bothering to shut the door behind her.

"The answer to your question is yes. It would be awful and..." She shudders, unable to find another word. "I don't want to get fat, and... God." She places her head in her hands. "I don't know what Theo would say."

"I'm sure he'll be more accepting of the idea than you are."

She scowls, and I lift my hands in defense. Mia pees on the stick and leaves it upside down on the counter.

"You do one with me." She shoves the stick in my hand like we're doing a shot together, or something that requires a team effort, and pushes me toward the toilet. I roll my eyes at her but do as I'm told.

I force myself to pee on the stick for support and click the lid back on it, setting it carefully on the counter next to hers. Without thinking much about it, I head toward the kitchen and open the fridge. No food. I haven't been grocery shopping in a while. Takeout it is then, for the fourth time this week.

I turn to find Mia with her eyes wide, clutching the two pregnancy sticks as if her life depends on them. Her mouth opens and then closes, and then opens again. "You put yours the closest to the edge, right?"

"I think mine was the one farther away," I articulate.

She stares at both of them. "One of them has two lines."

30

Burning Out

Calla

The next two tests both return negative. Mia and I are puzzled about how this could happen, and there's no point in taking another test and receiving a different result. It will only equate to more stress. I convince Mia to book both of us a doctor's appointment, and the earliest one we can get is next week.

I'm almost certain that if someone is pregnant, it's Mia. She's the one who hasn't been taking her birth-control pills and has missed a period. When was *my* last period? I begin to question myself, tugging my mind for every opportunity I could have forgotten to take a pill. One pill, that's all it takes.

"Don't look at me like that," I say to Mia when she's sulking by the window. "You're the one who has symptoms!"

"You have been extra moody this past week." She arches an eyebrow.

"That's a given considering everything that's happened in the last couple of weeks," I remind her.

She groans. "I just can't be pregnant! I've never even considered having a baby. There are so many things I still want to do without having someone relying on me."

"There are other options you can consider if you are. Try not to stress about it until you know for sure." I drop next to Mia and take her hand to soothe her.

"God, how could I be so careless?"

"Well, when the dick is good, your rationality kind of gets thrown out the window," I state with amusement tugging at my lips.

She snickers. "Oh, I'm sure *you* would know."

On Saturday, I rise earlier and head to Reese's house to take Ellie to her ballet lesson. The sun shimmers with no clouds evident in the sky. I hope it stays like that for the remainder of the day. It's been gloomy the past week, and I wonder if that's some sort of omen.

I wear a summery dress with sandals, and as I sit in the back of the cab, I reflect on everything that's about to change. I've gradually started packing for Switzerland, although I'm not leaving for another three weeks. A part of me is desperate to escape to somewhere more tranquil, and the other part is uncertain whether I'm making the right decision.

I've also been anticipating a call from my dad. I assume he's already seen the news regarding Ace. If there's been any chance of him having a change of heart previously, this will prove his original point. Every possibility of my dad accepting Ace has vanished.

The cab arrives in front of Reese's house, and Ellie jogs to greet me. "You came!" She wraps her tiny arms around my waist, and I return the embrace. She's in her pink ballet outfit, and her dark hair is slicked into a perfect bun that's held in place by a pink, glittery scrunchie.

"Of course, I did," I say with a smile. She spins in a circle, parading her outfit, and the sunlight catches the sparkles in the fabric. They dance in greeting and delight.

Ellie's eyes widen as she looks behind me. "Ace!"

A sudden heaviness expands in my chest, and I freeze in place. This is the last thing I planned for today. There was a part of me that knew I'd have to face him eventually, but perhaps I was hoping I'd have more to say to him when that happened.

Would I have been able to leave without saying goodbye?

"You're here! I didn't think you'd come." Ellie's excitement peaks.

"I told you I'd take you to your dancing lessons. Have I ever gone back on my word?" Ace asks. His voice sends a feeling of nostalgia through me—igniting everything I endeavored to extinguish.

I force myself to slowly turn and face the man I love to the point of no return. It's a dangerous kind of love—one that has the potential to shatter me in pieces. I'd say that's the worst kind.

His eyes connect with mine, and a dark enigma shines in them. Then Ace drops his guard, and I see everything—the apology behind the darkness and the pain behind the smile. Everything he hid so well from me the last time I saw him is out in the open now. It's as if he's too exhausted to conceal it, too presumptuous to see what he's done.

Ace and I are the same. I've known that for a while. Perhaps from the first time I met him. We're both damaged, messy, and shattered to the point of no return. We're flames that keep battling to stay alight, but two flames don't cool each other—they burn until there's nothing left.

And I'm burning out.

"Calla," he drawls my name like it's the only word he desires to speak for the remainder of his life.

Goose bumps coat my skin, and I tremble in response. "Good morning, Ace." I turn to Ellie. "I might just go now that your brother is here to take you."

Ellie laughs as though I'm joking. "You're coming with us!"

"We can go get something to eat after," Ace suggests cautiously. His sensual mouth forms into a line, but a soft curve is present at the corners.

I glance from Ace to Ellie, and I don't have the heart to leave. Ace and I have our issues, but it would be selfish to bring them up in front of Ellie. So I agree, for her sake. "Sure."

The soft curve at Ace's lips evolves into a genuine smile, which displays the prominent dimples on his cheeks. I glance away from him to halt the heartache building inside.

"I'll be right back. I'll have a word with Mom," Ace tells Ellie.

"Don't be long, or I'll be late for the first class."

"Yes, ma'am," Ace replies. He moves past me toward the front door. I step out of his way, but his arm still brushes against mine. I never thought such a simple gesture could ignite me in more ways than one, but it also solicits everything I've been trying to avoid.

I've never mentioned it, and I've barely admitted it to myself, but I was ready to sacrifice everything for Ace the day I came to his apartment. I was willing to tell him it didn't matter what my dad thought. It didn't matter what would happen in the future. I wanted this to work so desperately that I was willing to put him before everyone, including the only family I have left.

But I guess we're not on the same page. Perhaps, I'm asking for too much. I can't be with someone who lies to me, no matter the reason behind it. No matter whether they think they're trying to protect me. You could say I have trust issues, but that's already a known fact. It's a given considering the things I've been through.

Some people need validation and compliments, others need to be showered with gifts. The only thing I need is openness and honesty.

We're meant to be a team, but I've come to realize we were never a team. Ace always kept something from me. I never knew the whole truth when I was with him—not four years ago, and certainly not now. To me, that's an indication that maybe, just maybe, we're not meant to be.

"Calla…Ace isn't going to prison, is he?" Ellie asks.

I glance at Ellie, and she's looking up at me with a curious look. I'm unsure of how to answer her question. I'm uncertain of the situation myself. I only know what Nik's told me, and everything is still ambiguous with his case.

I squat in front of her, slanting to her eye level. "I don't want to tell you that everything will be okay, because I don't know myself. I don't know what's going to happen, but I know that everything will get better, even if it gets worse before it gets better. Behind every storm is sunshine."

Ellie wraps her arms around me and embraces me tightly. She smells like flowers and sweet candy. I hug her back and blink away the tears that are forming before she notices. "I'll always be here if you need me, even if it seems like I'm a thousand miles away," I promise.

Ace approaches us, and I stand. Ellie smiles at me, and I wish I could fix everything to keep that smile on her face. Out of everything that's happened, she's always been the one stuck in the middle of the chaos. She knows more than everyone gives her credit for.

Ace's G-Wagon is parked across the street. He opens the passenger door for me and then for Ellie. There's so much to say on the drive there, but we all seek words that will make everything better, only they don't exist.

"You know, Calla is better than you at Scrabble," Ellie reveals from the back.

"Oh, is that so?" Ace raises his brows and glances at me.

"She beat your high score," Ellie says.

I press my lips together. Did Reese tell Ace I spent last weekend with them?

"We'll have to change that," Ace says.

The ballet class only has five people, and Ace and I remain outside the studio, viewing through the vast window. The ballet teacher is a woman in her late twenties. She performs a dance for the girls, and they all watch her in wonder. Her moves are graceful and match the music elegantly as she spins around on her tiptoes.

It's only Ace and me and another two moms here. Occasionally, they glance at us, at Ace, but he doesn't seem to notice or care. As I sit there next to him watching Ellie—I wish our lives were normal. I wish we'd met under different circumstances. I wish we'd done things differently.

We sit for half an hour without saying a word.

"Calla—" he begins. My hands become the most exciting thing in the world as I avoid his demanding gaze.

"Ace."

Silence falls upon us as he searches for words, but nothing can undo what's already been done. "Are you pregnant?"

Oh God, the pregnancy tests I left on his counter. I've forgotten about them. I place my head in my hands. He notices my hesitation, and before he says anything, I meet his eyes and explain, "They were for Mia."

"Oh." A flicker of disappointment crosses his face, but it vanishes before I have the time to decipher whether it was genuine or something I'm fabricating in my mind.

"Can we talk?" he prompts.

"I don't have anything to say to you."

His eyes bore into mine. "I have a lot to say."

"It's too late for talking." Too late for explanations.

He raises a brow. "I can show you how sorry I am without saying a word. I'll even get on my knees for you, Calla."

I squeeze my thighs together. Damn him and his stupid words. Ace notices, and a wild smirk spans across his mouth.

"It's not the time," I state.

"I'm not the one with the dirty thoughts, love."

"Ace!" I hiss.

"You're right. I'm sorry. I'm trying to lighten the mood. I'm going to spend the day with Ellie and my mom, but I need to talk to you tonight."

"I'm busy."

"Tomorrow then."

I shake my head. I don't want to talk to him, because his words make me vulnerable. He knows all the right things to say, and I don't want my head clouded. I don't want to have doubts about my decision to leave.

Once Ellie finishes, we head to a café down the road from the ballet studio. We take the booth away from everyone, at the back. The café is bright, a light-blue theme with vintage wooden tables and chairs. There aren't many people here, and they are mostly elderly. They pay no attention to us. I order a coffee, too consumed by Ace's presence to stomach anything else. Ellie chitchats about how much fun she had, and she's excited to go back next week.

Ace sips hot chocolate out of a mug, and foam covers his upper lip. "You got—" Ellie tells Ace, motioning to her face, laughing.

"What?" Ace grins and takes another sip, purposefully coating more of his face with the foam. Ellie giggles, and a smile scrapes its way onto my face.

"You have a mustache," she admits, grinning.

"So do you," Ace says.

"I do not!" Ellie defends.

I laugh, unable to stop as Ace tries to *lighten the mood.*

Afterward, we stroll down the street toward Ace's car. "I'll just get a cab home from here," I say.

"I can drive you home." Ace opens the door of his car for Ellie.

"It's fine. Go spend time with your family. I need to do some grocery shopping anyway."

"Tomorrow?"

"I'll let you know." Ace opens his mouth to object, but I take a step back. "Bye, Ellie." I wave at her.

She waves back smiling, and I turn, walking in the opposite direction. This time, I'm unable to hold back the few tears that escape.

✦ ✦ ✦

My feet hit the pavement as I run through the mossy-green parklands. My heart races with adrenaline, and I push myself to go farther and farther, even though I'm near to collapsing on the ground. Music blasts in my ears from my phone. It's on full volume to suppress every thought that's been circling my head the last couple of days. I can't take it anymore. The constant voices echo in my mind, and it's exhausting. It's driving me insane.

I'm lost to the point of no return. Ever since Ace came back into my life, it has been nothing but chaos. I was doing fine before him. I was content with my life, and everything was on track. I wouldn't have thought twice if I got offered a job in Switzerland. I would have taken it in a heartbeat.

So why am I having second thoughts now? Why does Ace always have to be my weakness?

Hiking up the stairs of my apartment building, I wipe the sweat off my forehead with the back of my hand. This is something I'm not going to miss, a billion flights of stairs every day. I unlock my apartment and swing it open, still struggling to catch my breath from my five-mile run—something I haven't been doing often anymore.

"Oh my God!" I shriek when I spot the scene unfolding in front of me. "What the— My God!"

Mia and Theo are doing the dirty on the sofa. On *MY* sofa. Theo turns, and my face reddens in terror—everything is out on display. I cover my eyes with my hands, slightly peeking through to make sure Theo covers up at least some of his assets. I don't care about Mia's. It's nothing I haven't seen before.

"Shit, I'm sorry. You said you'd be out for a while." Mia tosses Theo's boxer briefs in his direction. He catches them and pulls them over his ankles.

"You said you were going out for dinner!?" I exclaim.

She smiles at me sheepishly. "Uh, yes. We're kind of running late." She slides her silky pink dress over her body and fixes her hair.

"Kind of late because you decided to make babies in my living room?" I raise an eyebrow to indicate that she possibly has already made a baby. Mia narrows her eyes at me behind Theo. "You know what?" I move back toward the door. "I came at the wrong time. I'm going to head back out. You two continue—"

"You don't have to do that," Mia assures me.

"Yeah, Calla. You don't have to do that. We were just leaving," Theo interjects.

I frown. "If there's anything on that sofa that's remotely close to your bodily fluids when I come back, you owe me a new one," I say to Theo.

Theo quickly glances at the sofa. I scrutinize Mia and Theo from head to toe—once, twice, and then turn, heading out. I shut the apartment door behind me and lean against it, exhaling. That was…eventful.

Knocking on Betty's apartment door, I wait in my sweaty clothes for her to answer. I haven't been spending much time with her apart from checking in every couple of days. Guilt begins to eat at me when I realize I'll be leaving her in a few weeks.

The door swings open. "Hello, dear." A blue apron is tied around her waist, and she holds the door open for me to come in.

It smells delicious in her apartment—a rich chocolate fragrance spreads from her kitchen. Betty is always baking something, trying new recipes. She says it brings her serenity in her old age.

"Good evening, Betty. How have you been holding up?"

"Oh, you know, the same old. Waiting for my judgment day to come," she replies.

"You might be waiting a while. You still have a good twenty years. Probably more," I reassure her.

She laughs, waving me off. "If I live another five, I'll call the devil to take care of me himself."

Betty sits me down at the counter where I've spent countless days and sets some tea in front of me. "The chocolate brownies will be done in about ten minutes," she says. "Now, what is it, dear? You look as though you haven't slept in days."

"Oh, is it that bad?" I hang my head in my hands.

"I wouldn't say bad, but you do look worn out and not—" she glances at my gym clothes, "—from exercising."

"A lot has been happening, as you know," I say. I've filled Betty in on the main things that have happened since my trip to Europe.

"I'll tell you a story," she begins, sitting down next to me. Betty takes a sip of her tea and smacks her lips together before beginning. "When I was younger, about your age, I met a man while I was on holiday. We hit it off. He was rich, successful, had a lot going for him, but he also came with emotional baggage. We kept in contact after my holiday. We talked every day. He came to visit me more than once." Betty stares off into the distance and takes a sip of her tea.

Betty has never talked much about her youthful days. She's only told me stories about her late husband.

"There came a point in our relationship where one of us had to sacrifice one of our established lives. It ended up being me. I gave up my city, my career, left my family behind and moved across the world for him. It was good for the first couple of months. We were madly in love." She smiles, recalling the memories from decades ago.

"However, soon after, I realized there were a lot of problems in our relationship. I was constantly putting his mental health before mine. For years, I tried to heal him and help him get healthy because I loved him. I loved him so dearly…"

I expect her to continue, but she doesn't. "What happened?"

"Oh—" she waves her hands, "—I found him in bed with our therapist."

My mouth gapes open at her revelation. "What a pig."

She laughs. "What I'm trying to say is that you should never compromise your own future for someone else. You should never put someone else before yourself. There's a saying that my mother told me—bless her soul—that I still hold to this day," she says. "Your biggest commitment must always be to yourself."

Betty and I continue talking. She tells me more stories and fills my stomach with homemade brownies. I head back to my place after I'm sure Mia and Theo have left.

After a much-needed shower, I stand in front of Nik's apartment with the flash drive I retrieved from Ace's apartment. Well, one that looks exactly like it. Ace didn't ask for it, so I decided to take care of it myself. It's gone. I didn't look at what was on it, even though I was tempted to. However, I'm taking it upon myself to find out whether I can trust Nik completely.

In my hands is a clean flash drive that I bought this morning from the store. Nik opens the door and invites me in. "Good evening, sweetheart." I look him over twice. Do both brothers not own a shirt? I guess it'd be easy to get them presents for their birthdays and Christmas.

I hand over the flash drive to Nik. "I'm sorry it took me so long. I've had a lot on my mind."

He waves a hand to dismiss my apology. "It's fine." He continues toward the kitchen, and I trail him. A tumbler of ice and bourbon rests on his kitchen table.

"Big day?" I eye the glass.

"Something like that." Nik takes the flash drive apart with the utensils he has in the kitchen and removes the memory card. He grabs a pair of scissors from a drawer and cuts it in half and then in half again. A smile grows on my face.

"Drink?" Nik offers me when he's done butchering the flash drive's empty memory card, not realizing what test he's just passed.

"I'll just have water, if you don't mind."

"Of course."

"Thank you for helping. I mean it. You didn't have to do all of this."

"I did." He passes me a bottle of water from the fridge and sits at the counter, and I do, too. "My mother died when I was ten, my father… He wasn't around until recently. I didn't have family here, so I got moved around in foster homes," Nik begins, exhaling.

"I'm sorry. You never told me…" I'd never have guessed Nik grew up in foster homes. People look at him and see a confident, successful man. From a distance, his life, his success, seems easy in a way. Though the more I uncover, the more I realize he's worked extremely hard to get where he is now.

He shakes his head. "I'm not telling you this so you feel sorry for me. Ace is my little brother. I wondered why even though he hated my guts, he still wanted me around as his lawyer."

"Does he know that you know? Did you tell him anything about me?"

Nik shakes his head. "I told you I wouldn't. Ace was already waiting for me to figure out we're related, but I would have never guessed."

I nod in understanding. "Again, thank you. Even if you felt obliged to help out, I'm still thankful you did."

"Of course, Calla. If there's anything else that you ever need, I'll help in any way I can."

"I'm glad to have met someone like you." I genuinely mean that. No one else would have treated me like Nik has. Even after what happened between us, he still regards me with respect and has never once looked down on me for choosing Ace over him.

"You're saying that like this is goodbye, sweetheart."

I look up at him. "I hope it isn't. I've come to enjoy your company."

"Likewise, sweetheart."

"Perhaps I'll see you around Switzerland."

A crooked, cunning smile forms on his mouth. "Perhaps you will."

"I should go." I stand to leave and lose my balance.

Nik steadies me with his arm, and my hand flies to his shoulder for stability. His calloused fingers snake around my waist, and I freeze. His eyes are on mine, sharp yet enigmatic and highly seductive. His grip tightens around me, and I draw in a breath.

He's still sitting on the stool at the counter, and I have ended up standing in between his legs. We stare at each other, both knowing if either one of us moves forward, it will result in nothing but trouble. But trouble has always had a way of reeling me in.

Nik's gaze flickers toward my lips, and my face heats in response. I can't move, my body isn't responding. He pulls me closer, and I squeeze my eyes shut when his warm breath grazes against me—sweet bourbon mixed with his own alluring pull.

"Tell me to stop, and I will."

I don't say anything, too stunned by the situation. I'm unsure where my head is at. I can't figure out whether I want him to continue, and it's making the room whirl around me. My hand is still on his shoulder, and Nik inclines toward me.

"I'm sorry. I have to go." I'm the first one to step out of his grip, and he releases me reluctantly. My heart hammers out of my chest. I need to get out of here. I grab my bag from the counter and rush for the door.

"Calla, wait." Nik catches up to me. "I'm sorry. I shouldn't have done that."

"I'm sorry, too. I-I shouldn't have given you the wrong idea. I don't know what I was thinking. God, I'm sorry." I clamp a hand over my mouth, where Nik's lips almost touched me a moment ago. Everything is all over the place, and nothing seems right. And it finally dawns on me that my mind has declared war against my heart.

"You didn't give me the wrong idea. I knew what I was doing. I can't get you out of my mind."

I shake my head, dismissing his words. "I can't do this right now, Nik." I turn away from him, open the door to leave and find myself face-to-face with everything I've been seeking to avoid.

Everything that's… "Ace."

31

Supernova

Calla

I haven't known Ace for very long. You could say I've known him for four years, but the time we've spent together hardly equates to a fraction of that. Yet it's not about time. It could have been a week. From the moment I first met him, there was a connection between us. Like we understood each other without knowing one another. Like we've crossed paths in another life.

So when I open Nik's apartment door to leave and see Ace there, it takes three seconds. Three seconds for Ace's mood to shift three times. From confusion to anguish and then darkness—a thick blanket of nightfall that conceals everything. Except I'm learning to see past that too, and when the rage radiates off him, my gaze penetrates right through it.

His eyes flicker from Nik to me, and a smirk crosses his face—a taciturn, heartless smirk. Ace doesn't look at me when he speaks. Instead, his eyes pierce into Nik, but it's clear who his words are directed at. "My car is parked downstairs. Go wait there."

"No," I reply.

There's no predicting what Ace might do when he's left alone with Nik in this situation. He won't listen to anything, he won't reason. He won't allow himself to hear the facts. I know this must look extremely bad. Ace couldn't have come here at a worse moment.

"Calla." His eyes dart toward me. A fire burns inside of them, ready to smolder this entire place.

"No, Ace," I repeat firmly. I'm not going to leave Ace and Nik alone, especially not right now.

"You shouldn't order her around like that. She can make her own decisions," Nik states.

I hold my breath. Does he have a death wish?

"Oh, and I guess you know her so well?" Ace challenges.

Since I'm the one who opened the door, I'm standing in front of Ace, and Nik is to the side, marginally behind me. Ace clenches his fists at his sides. If I move, I doubt Ace will hesitate to pounce on Nik. He needs to calm down. He needs to understand that nothing happened. It came close, but *nothing* happened. And I'm glad it didn't.

I take a step toward Ace, and his eyes flicker toward me once again. "Take me home."

I'm not sure what the situation is between the two brothers, but from the way Nik spoke about Ace earlier, they appear to be sorting through their differences. This doesn't help, and I'm desperate to get Ace out of here before his irrationality takes over. I don't want to be the reason their relationship is hindered even further.

Ace doesn't move, so I take another step toward him and grasp his hand. "Let's go, please."

He looks down at my hand that's holding his. For a short second, I believe he might recoil at my touch, but his grip tightens around mine.

A sigh of relief washes over me.

He veers away from Nik and pulls me with him. I manage to provide Nik with an apologetic half smile over my shoulder. I shouldn't have come here tonight. I had no idea it would result in something *almost* happening. Or that Ace would come here. The former was a misstep. My feelings are clear, I don't want to be with Nik. Yet the hesitation on my behalf was an ominous mistake.

Ace and I step into the elevator, and the silence envelops us, bouncing from wall to wall. My hand is still in his, and I find myself unable to let go, not *wanting* to let go. I missed his warm, welcoming touch. I missed the way it makes me feel—like everything is suddenly right in the world. Right with us.

But I have to remind myself that it's not. Perhaps it has never been.

Still, I don't let go. I savor every second I get to be with him, not knowing what the future holds or whether I'll ever get to do this again. My body is slightly in front of him. The warmth of his chest exudes through me, burning a fire inside my core. How? How can he make me feel like this all the damn time?

"Nothing happened," I feel the need to say. I sense his penetrating stare upon me. I don't look back to meet it, afraid of what other emotions might erupt through me.

He tugs my back closer into his chest, and that solitary movement has the power to destroy my barriers. I don't allow it to. I flatten my breathing as the fire burns through my lungs.

"I know."

"How?" My voice is too loud in the confining space between us.

"Nik had a disappointed look on his face. No man would look like that if something happened between you and them." Ace's voice holds an edge to it.

"Oh."

"Have dinner with me?" There's a question behind the demand. He's allowing me to decide for myself whether I'd like to, whether I'm prepared to talk to him.

"Okay." It's the most rational thing to do.

Downstairs, Ace's Lamborghini is out the front of the building. He must not have planned to stay here long, and I wonder why he visited in the first place.

"Takeout is fine. We can order it to your place," I suggest.

I understand being out in public might be uncomfortable for Ace right now. Everyone gawks at the famous boxer who's been arrested and charged. They don't know the truth, yet everyone enjoys speculating, and sometimes that's substantially worse. Going back to my apartment is a gamble, in case Mia and Theo are back from dinner. I hope they go back to his place instead.

Ace nods and drives toward his apartment, which isn't very far from here. On the way, I order food to be delivered and consider the many ways the conversation between us may go. There's so much to talk about, but we both keep quiet on the drive. I stare out the window, watching the lights flicker as the car moves.

Ace strokes his hand against my thigh to make sure I'm still here, to validate that this is real. I glance at him. He keeps his eyes on the road, yet his grip tightens around my thigh. My chest constricts, and it's difficult to concentrate. The lines between us are hazy once again.

He parks in the basement and leads us toward the elevator. His hand hovers on my lower back, his touch making me delirious, but I welcome it—perhaps for the last time.

As we stand in the elevator, I'm reminded of Paris, and I grind my feet to the floor. I'm unsure why I'm having these thoughts now, of all moments. I know it isn't the time. We have much larger issues at hand, but I can't physically block out the memories.

It seems so long ago that we were in a different country, eluding the inevitable, getting lost in something so delusory. Even though I was trying to save myself from precisely this—heartbreak and pain—I knew having any connection to Ace was asking for turbulence.

"What are you thinking about?" His breath caresses my neck from behind.

"Nothing." I swallow.

He chuckles, but it's not the usual lighthearted sound I'm used to. Instead, it's dark and chilling. "Do you want to know what I'm thinking about?"

I have an idea. "Mm-hmm." I clear my throat.

Ace seizes this as an opportunity. "I'm thinking about the night in Paris." His fingers faintly caress my shoulder. "Precisely about what I told you in the elevator."

I. Can't. Breathe. My body is numb, except for the areas he touches.

"Do you remember?" He tugs on my waist, turning me to face him. "Hmm, love?" Ace cocks his head, and a deliberate smile appears on his captivating mouth.

God, do I remember? I could *never* forget, even if I were compelled. His words embedded themselves into the filthiest parts of my mind the instant he spoke them.

The elevator doors open. I nod in response but place my hand on his chest. "Ace…we need to talk."

"I thought it was too late for talking?"

My glance plunges to his lips. He's too charming for his own good.

The undeniable yearning for one another is like a heady elixir, and we're treating it as a distraction. We both know there's a conversation that awaits us that will change everything, and we're both trying to elude it.

"This…this isn't going to change…anything." I don't know what to call it. This isn't going to change what I need to tell him or what I need to do for myself. This isn't going to alter my already made-up mind.

Ace understands. "Okay."

"Okay?"

"Okay, Calla. I'll take what I can get."

And with that, his lips are on mine, hungry and governing. His tongue dips its way inside, and I'm unable to stop myself as I explore him with the same determination. It's been too long, too long without his touch, too long with me seeking to keep my distance, too long holding back.

Ace shifts his fervent mouth from my swelling lips to my jaw and down to my neck, leaving wet kisses everywhere he treks. "You don't understand how irritated it made me seeing you at his apartment," he growls in my ear.

He picks me up, and I wrap my legs around him. Ace strides toward his apartment like a man on a mission and unlocks it with ease. He shuts the door behind us and presses my back against it. This dominating, jealous act of his turns me on, and my body aches to be touched by him.

"I was helping him with your case." I'm out of breath.

He pulls away, yet he still holds me against the door, searching my eyes. "You… You're the one who asked him to take it. He wouldn't have done it otherwise." Ace realizes.

"I couldn't just do nothing, Ace," I explain, my own hands clutching his body.

Why is it so simple to talk when we're like this? It's like we're so intimate that nothing we say can ever take this away from us.

He shakes his head in disbelief. "Calla, I lov—"

I heave his face back to mine, not allowing him to finish. I don't want to hear those words—not like this and not right now. My hands progress up his shirt, and his body strains. All I can feel is heat underneath my hands.

Ace sinks his teeth into my bottom lip, tugging on it, and I claw my nails into his back. "Ace, I need you to be rough with me. I need you to fuck me." I mumble against him, hauling him closer to me.

His cock twitches in response against my stomach. I need him in every way possible. Everything that's been piling up inside of me for the last weeks is fighting for release.

"It's like you're reading my mind, love."

Immediately, he grabs me by my waist and carries me to his sofa. He sets me down and bends me over it. My heart flies out of my chest with the ache for him.

One of his hands is on my waist, supporting me, and with the other, he lifts my dress up. He glides his fingers down my bare skin, toward my naked ass, and down in between my legs. I lean into his touch. "So eager." He chuckles, his voice alluring and low against my neck. His palm collides with my bare ass cheek, spanking me.

I hiss into my hand from the sharp sting.

"How can you deny the obvious connection between us, Calla?" He rubs me through my pink lace panties. The friction of his warm, calloused fingers and the sheer material creates a molten feeling.

"Ace…" I have no words as I arch my back.

"Take off your dress," he orders.

I promptly do as he asks, slipping it off my shoulders and

allowing it to pool around my ankles. My back is still to him, and he bends me over again. This time, he reaches over, grabs my nipple in between his forefinger and thumb, and squeezes it, allowing the sensation of pure rapture to pulse through me.

Fuck.

A moan escapes my lips. Ace slides my panties off and kneels so I can step out of them. My legs shake, and he grips my thighs with both of his large hands, spreading them wide open. My heart quickens inside my smoldering chest.

I'm bent over the sofa, unable to see what he's doing, and I steady my hands in front of me. "Ahhh." I suck in a sharp breath when his wet tongue meets my sex, licking up to my opening and then gently sucking, swirling his tongue. "Oh God."

"So good, Calla. You have no fucking idea how good you taste. It drives me insane. Like I'm an addict." He stands and slides one finger inside me with ease, and only then can I sense how wet I am. His finger is drenched in my arousal. He grunts. "Fuck. And you're so wet."

I can only imagine the smirk on his face.

"Don't move," he instructs as he pulls away.

"What?"

"Calla, don't move," he repeats sharply, walking away from me. I don't have to wait long before he returns, and I twist my head to look behind me. He roughly grabs my ass. "I told you not to move."

In his hand is a small vibrator. "I got this for you before, but…I didn't get the chance to use it." He presses the button, and it begins to vibrate in his hands.

I bite my lip in anticipation. I've used vibrators before, that's not the issue, but I've never had anybody use one on me.

"Oh my God," I shriek when he places it to my most sensitive spot—where he previously licked. It vibrates against me, and I pant louder.

"Stay still," he cautions, the dominant trait spilling from his voice. He holds the vibrator and slides a long finger from his other hand in me. The movements are unhurried, but there's an urgency to them. He's in control, and he's relishing it, appreciating the way I respond to him. The feeling in my core soars and intensifies with each pump of his finger—each vibration.

"Ace," I moan his name louder, which warrants me another finger inside my slick opening. He thrusts both of his fingers in and out, curling them, hitting my G-spot continuously while sliding the vibrator up and down. My legs buckle beneath me, I've never been this stimulated. My arousal seeps down my leg, and I need him inside of me. *Now.*

I grab the back of his thighs from behind me, hauling him closer, and mutter, "Please."

He doesn't stop. Instead, he tightens his grip around me, disregarding my demands.

When I reach the edge of my climax, he brings his thick erection against my opening and slams it inside of me. I cry out his name in both pain and decadency. The feeling of euphoria erupts inside my core. I squeeze my eyes shut and muffle my screams with the decorative pillow in front of me.

"Fuck, I missed this," he grumbles. "I missed feeling *you.*" He stays inside of me for a second without moving and brushes his lips against my shoulder. "Are you okay?" Ace strokes his fingers down my arm gently.

"Yes," I rasp, barely able to form a coherent word.

Ace sets his pace, filling me with his considerable length and then pulling out, repeating the movement over and over—striking the highly sensitive spot each time.

"Harder," I gasp.

He tightens his hands around my waist, and he drives harder, quicker—our clammy bodies colliding with each other, the slippery sound reverberating in the silent apartment.

"Harder, Ace," I moan, and he obliges. He needs me as much as I need him. It's unhealthy the way our bodies crave to be touched by each other and only by each other. We'll never be satisfied by someone else. We'll always crave more because we know there *is* more.

"Do you like that? Do you like me pounding into your tight pussy? Do you like that I'll think about this moment until the next time we do this?"

His words coerce my walls to clench around him firmly. "Yes," I breathe and bring my fingers to my clit, rubbing it with two fingers.

Sweat builds on his body, I feel it against me as he slams his pulsating length into me, over and over with insistence and craving. I'm so close to combusting, the orgasm circles me, and I squeeze my eyes closed as it erupts.

"Fuck." He digs his fingers into my hips, and my head collapses into the pillow again as he releases into me. We're both riding out our high, but there's a time when it must come crashing down. And drag everything down with it.

There's a great difference between surrendering and understanding when you've had enough. There comes a time when I finally must start putting myself first. It's easy to help everyone else and forget about yourself, forget about what matters to you, and forget about everything you've ever dreamed of.

I'm not going to be someone who looks back on their life and wishes they took that job, moved to that new city, experienced every opportunity life offered. Instead, I'll look back on my life and have the memories of that new job, that new city, and all the opportunities I've taken.

"Shower?" Ace murmurs in my ear.

I nod. Simultaneously, there's a buzz from the intercom, informing us that food has arrived.

"I'll get it. Use the shower in my room. I'll be right up." His hands graze my bare waist, and he retrieves his clothes from the floor near the sofa. I ascend the stairs and turn the shower on.

My hands tremble as I reach for the shampoo. Maybe I thought I could fuck Ace out of my system so I wouldn't crave him. I guess it didn't work. It made things worse. I've been ensnared by his touch.

Tears roll down my face. I squeeze my eyes shut, letting the hot water hide the evidence. Ace strolls into the shower—melancholy circulates us, sweeping over us. We both recognize that prior events were just a diversion. Now we have to face everything we've been trying to escape.

Ace takes the shampoo bottle from me and squeezes some into his hands. He lathers it through my hair, and I tilt my head into his hands. My emotions are all over the place.

The thing is, Ace hasn't healed. Or perhaps he has, but our relationship hasn't. *We* haven't. I thought this time would be different. I *wanted* more than anything for it to be different. I wanted to start clean, with no lies, no secrets. But I guess we can't have what we want. I can't hold another tear, and it rolls down my face, immediately rinsed away.

When Ace finishes with my hair, I do the same for him. Neither of us talks about the issue that got us here in the first place. We know what talking will bring, and I need to be dressed for that conversation. I squeeze shower gel into my hand and track my palms over his impressive chest, over his taut shoulders, over his whole body. The muscle beneath me contracts while Ace observes me. I don't risk eye contact.

He catches my hands with his. "Calla."

I inhale and hold in the tears that desperately try to fight their way out. I'm exhausted from crying.

"I think I'm done here." I evade his touch and walk out of the shower, drying myself with the towel he left for me. One of his shirts is sprawled out on the bed, along with a pair of boxers.

"I assume you want to be comfortable for dinner." Ace is right behind me.

"Thank you." I drop my towel. I feel Ace's gaze on me as I get dressed, but I'm too exhausted to make a joke. My chest is heavy with the knowledge of how the rest of this night is going to conclude. We're heading toward an explosion—a supernova.

We set up the food in front of the immense window in his living room, where we ate the first time I was here. I stare out at everything I'll be leaving in just a couple of weeks. The constant noise of a city that's alive, the place I've come to call home even though it doesn't feel like home. And the man I'm deeply and irrevocably in love with.

It's getting harder and harder to face the facts, to understand the complexity of the problems between us. There's so much more beneath the surface. But even if I had the chance to go back in time, I still wouldn't be able to stay away from him. He's embedded in my energy, his touch ingrained in my skin.

We were continuously gambling with borrowed time. And now

the clock has stopped, and time has run out.

"Let me explain," Ace begins after we finish dinner. He's been scanning my face for over twenty minutes, searching for any indication of how this will go.

"Let you explain?" I ask, standing in the vast living room. "You decided that keeping secrets would solve everything. That keeping me in the dark once again would somehow protect me, even though you knew you'd hurt me in the process. You thought I'd forgive you over and over for something that could've been so easily avoided with just a straightforward conversation. Did I sum that up correctly?"

Nik told me everything about Ace, about the deal he took from Mark Stanton. Nik told me everything Ace should have.

Ace stares at me blankly. "Don't walk away from this, Calla. Don't run away from your problems like you always do when things get too hard for you."

I pierce him with my glare, fighting fire with fire.

"What else am I supposed to do?!" I frantically question, wanting an answer, a solution that won't leave us destroyed. Every path we take together leads to obliteration.

He shakes his head, unable to give me one. "I'm not giving up on us."

"There is no us, Ace. There was never an us. There's you, and there's me. You always said that. Why can't you ever tell me the truth? In college, I opened up to you about everything. How could you keep such a secret from me when you knew how much I needed closure?"

It's not about his mistakes anymore. It's about the lying, the constant dishonesty over and over. It has become a habit, an unhealthy issue. He doesn't know how to stop even when presented with the chance.

"I couldn't tell you." He grits his teeth. "I tried to, but I couldn't let the words out. I knew everything would change once I did, and I couldn't let you go after getting a sense of you. A sense of a life with you."

"Am I some kind of obsession for you?" The feelings that Ace has toward me, are they all because of guilt? I mull over every word we've ever shared, every moment we've spent together.

I haven't seen you so fascinated by a girl before, the words were spoken by Logan four years ago—the guy who was with Ace the night of the accident. Does Ace love me out of guilt?

"Yes, you're a fucking obsession. You're in my mind twenty-four seven. All I think about is you. All I see is you." He tugs on his hair in frustration. "Every time I look at you, it's like I'm staring at the universe. Do you think any other person has ever brought me to my knees?"

I shake my head. There's a lump in my throat and pain in my chest.

"I've always been rapt by the stars and the universe because they gave me a sense of optimism. When you came into my life, it was like for the first time, I saw everything clearly," Ace rationalizes as he paces the room.

His breathing is rapid, frantic. I have the urge to calm him, to wrap my arms around him, but I avoid the impulse.

"I saw you, and I saw the pain I caused you. Something in me shifted. It felt like I had to do anything and everything to take that pain away from you," he explains.

"Were you ever going to tell me?"

"Yes. Fuck!" His voice is on the verge of rupturing.

"When? Please tell me when you were going to tell me? I said I don't care about what *you* did, but…" I shake my head. "When we met again, I thought you understood all I ever wanted was the truth. I've never resented you, but we picked up from where we ended."

And this is where everything comes out. The tears, the pain, everything I've been afraid to tell Ace because I know he'll close himself off even more.

"You make decisions based on what you think will be best for me without consulting me. That's not a partnership, and that's not something I want to be a part of." I don't care how my words emerge anymore. It's too late to tread on eggshells around him.

"I'm sorry! I've always been by myself. I've always had to make decisions for myself, for my family. It's difficult to get out of that mindset."

"No, Ace. You don't have to make decisions by yourself. You choose to."

His jaw stiffens. All the emotions are open on his face for me to read. There are too many—pain, responsibility, remorse, among others. It's like looking in the mirror. I feel every single one of them. Darkness surrounds us, pulling us deeper into the enigmatic coma of each other.

"I got offered a position with *The Times* in Switzerland for eight months. I'm going to take it." I hold my breath, afraid of what his reaction will be.

Ace's eyes widen, and he drops on the sofa. He rubs his forehead and then finally meets my gaze, finally understanding.

"I'm in fucking love with you. I just got you back, and you're going to walk away from everything that we have?"

I can't believe he thinks that's what I'm doing. I'm doing both of us a favor. We'll ruin each other otherwise. And I need to do this for myself, to follow my dreams. He, out of all people, should be able to understand.

"Don't. We're not going to do this. If you loved me, you wouldn't keep things from me when you know it's what broke us in the first place. When you're presented with the chance to tell me things, you choose not to."

"That's not true."

"Isn't it? Why didn't you tell me you made a deal with the FBI?"

"It was decided last minute." He doesn't meet my eyes.

Another lie. How many more?

"When you called me that night at my dad's, did you know?" I persist, trying to prove a point.

"Calla…" he warns.

"Did you know?"

He closes his eyes again. "Yes."

"You keep lying, Ace! You can't help yourself, can you? And you expect me to trust you?"

There are other things, too. He visited my dad to confess, and he hasn't mentioned this to me the entire time. He kept so many things from me that involved me.

"I didn't want you to worry. I wanted to get rid of this part of my life for you. We could have started over. I wanted to start over with you. I need you!" he yells the last words, and they echo through his apartment, against the walls that are suffocating me.

"No, you need to see someone. You clearly don't want my help. You don't want to talk to me until it's too late. About anything! The nightmares, your feelings, your secrets, the constant guilt that you haven't gotten over. It's like a game of tug-of-war with you. You give me an inch but then take it all away. You don't fully let me in. You don't let anyone in, and I don't know what to do to help you!"

This might be the most we've ever spoken to each other, and it feels liberating but also excruciating it had to come to this.

He runs a hand through his hair like he wants to rip it out. "I'll go see a therapist if you want me to. I want to try and be better for you."

"You don't understand. That's the problem! I don't want you to be better for *me*. I want you to be better for *you*." My vision blurs, and I blink, forcing more tears to spill down my cheeks.

"I need you…" he declares softly this time. He moves to reach for me but then changes his mind.

"It's not healthy to depend this much on a person," I say, even though I'm not much better. He's all I think about. My mind and thoughts are owned by him. My body responds only to him.

How can we be so alike and yet so lethal together?

"I'm not going to walk out of your life completely. I promised you I wouldn't. I'll always be here for you, but I'm taking the position in Switzerland. It's my dream. I need to do this."

"You have to be fucking joking. I can't be friends with you, if that's what you're suggesting," he scoffs. "It will kill me."

"I can't give you more." At least, not right now, not like this. In the last couple of months, I've been spiraling into everything I healed from. "It will kill *me*, Ace."

"When did you decide this?"

"Why does it matter?"

He shakes his head. It doesn't. "So what then? This is goodbye?" His eyebrows furrow in disbelief.

He must have seen this coming. It's not like it surfaced out of nowhere.

"Can't you see, Ace? Maybe we were always meant to say goodbye. We just keep prolonging the inevitable. I'm exhausted from fighting against it."

"Calla…" He drops his head into his hands.

I take his apartment key from my bag along with a simple sticky note, the one he gave me back in college and leave it on his kitchen counter. **Maybe we'll meet again in another life. When the stars align**. There's nothing more left to say.

Ace doesn't look at me when I walk toward the door, not until I pull it closed behind me. In that fraction of a second, when his eyes collide with mine, I find my past self and everything I've learned to leave behind.

32

Tying Loose Ends

Calla

Billions of stars scatter the sky—more. And all of them are steering me in the right direction. All of them are glimmering and thrusting me toward some ending as though my time in this place, this part of the world, has come to an end.

But every end is a new beginning, a time for new ventures and openings. We all like familiar places. We're creatures of habit, after all, and that's where opportunities and dreams crumble. To succeed, you must be willing to accept change, even if it challenges you in unimaginable ways.

I don't want to confess that I hoped Ace would offer to come with me. To meet me there or present another solution. It's selfish and greedy, not to mention it's utterly impossible with everything being so uncertain at this point.

I can't overlook the fact that Ace is on bail. It's looking better and better every day, but there's still a chance he may go to prison. I hope Nik won't allow that to happen.

And even if it were possible, would I let Ace leave everything behind—his family, his career here, his whole life—just to follow me as I pursue my dreams? I doubt it. I don't have it in my heart. Everyone must do what's best for them. Everyone must put themselves first at least once in their life. Otherwise, what's the point?

Nik has been straightforward with me since day one. From what he's told me about the case, the FBI doesn't have much evidence against Ace. So if all goes to plan, Ace could get off. Going to prison is the least of his worries though. Ace knows the people he's involved with aren't just going to let him go without a second thought. Without holding him accountable.

Each day, my mind crosses into the despair of the unknown. I'm anxious with every phone call I receive, hoping it's not someone calling to let me know something has happened to Ace. Even when I'm away from him, it's impossible to eradicate him out of my thoughts. Is this how it's always going to be?

I head to the subway after work. The city changes with every corner I turn. It flicks between affluence and poverty. Some streets are filled with smooth glass exteriors of fancy stores, the kind of places I wouldn't dare step foot into on my current salary.

My phone buzzes in my pocket. I take a breath, holding it in before looking at the caller ID. My shoulders relax once I see it's my dad.

I answer.

"Hey, Cals."

Our relationship has become more strained than ever, and there's nothing I can do to fix it. The weight on my shoulders is gone, but now there's a barrier separating us.

We've only spoken once on the phone since I came to visit him and revealed the truth that had been clawing its way out for years. However, neither of us has brought it up again. My dad is blatantly ignoring the fact that I told him I'm seeing the person who caused the accident. Our biggest tragedy. And I can't bring it up again. I also don't feel the need to tell him that Ace and I are over. In fact, I don't feel the need to speak of him at all.

"I got offered a job in Switzerland for eight months with *The Times*," I tell my dad after the small talk is over. I haven't mentioned it to him, perhaps because I thought I'd change my mind, but now there's no going back. I'm set on this, set on my future, and I'm excited about where this new adventure will take me, what other doors it will open.

"Are you going by yourself?" my dad asks with an edge to his tone.

I've been expecting this question. He hasn't brought up Ace's case, but I know he's seen the news. He just doesn't want to speak of him. He doesn't want to admit that his daughter is—was—dating a criminal. I understand.

"Yes." I don't elaborate.

"Hmm." He sighs into the phone. *Hmm* is his way of churning the thoughts in his head. "I'm so proud of you for chasing your dreams. Your mom would be too," he finally says. "I'll find a way to come visit you, Cals. Maybe we can spend Christmas together there. You're making the right decision."

I chew on my lip. "Of course, I'd love that. I'll have to double-check if I'll be there for Christmas. Part of the job requires me to travel to other countries in Europe for a couple of days at a time."

I've read over the contract they have sent me, and it's honestly a dream come true. All expenses are paid for, I get my own place, and once every few months, I'm required to travel to countries assigned to me. I get to build my portfolio while living in beautiful places. It's more than I could've ever imagined, and I'd be foolish to refuse this opportunity.

"Of course, you'll have to let me know." He pauses. "This is a lot to take in, Cals. Why didn't you tell me sooner? When do you leave?"

"I've only received the offer not too long ago. I was still deciding. I leave in two weeks." I hear the reception cutting out as I get onto the subway.

"What was there to decide? I'm glad you're doing this, New York doesn't seem like the place for you. Besides, I don't believe there's much keeping you there, is there?"

He hasn't asked outright, but I know what direction this question is heading in, and I have no desire to elaborate.

"No, there isn't. I'll call you later, yeah? I'm getting on the subway, and the connection is cutting out."

"Let me know if you need any help with anything and—" the connection drops out entirely, and I'm glad for it. There are some things my dad will never understand, and that's okay. I don't expect him to, especially in this situation.

✦ ✦ ✦

By Wednesday, I've forgotten about the doctor's appointment Mia and I have booked, that is, until I get a text from her on the way home.

Mia: ***Meet at doctors. I'm on my way there.***

The commotion of New York City surrounds me, but at this moment, all I can hear is the thumping of my heart. It all comes down to this.

I'm ninety-nine percent sure I can't be pregnant. That's the exact statistic of how effective the pill is. Yes, I looked it up when I saw one of the tests had two lines, and I haven't missed any pills.

There's more probability it's Mia, since she admitted to not taking the pill consistently.

Yet that one percent has me in a frantic whirlwind of emotions. This has the potential to change everything, and my mind becomes foggy with possible consequences.

I can't help but reflect on all the choices I made leading up to this moment. What will happen if I'm pregnant? There's also no doubt in my mind who the father could be. It's a no-brainer. The only man I've ever used no protection with is Ace.

Mia waits for me outside. Her face is drained of color, and I know mine mirrors hers. This isn't an ideal situation for either of us.

"Hey, there's no one else I'd rather be doing this with," she says, attempting to lighten the mood.

I force a smile. "This isn't something I wanted to do just yet."

"And what? You think I did?" She fidgets with the straps of her bag. Her hair is messy, like she's been continuously jerking on it on her way here.

"You know, you have to face the fact that if anyone is pregnant—it's likely you. I've taken all my pills on time. You haven't," I explain as we walk through the doors of the clinic.

It's stuffy, and the air has a hint of bleach. I've never been more anxious to set foot in a clinic, and I wonder if that has something to do with how radically this could change my future. This visit holds power over my whole life.

"Do not say that," she hisses at me. We make our way to the reception desk to check-in.

"I'm preparing you for the worst." I shrug. Our banter is the only thing keeping me sane at the moment.

"I've been doing that since I took those freaking tests, Calla." She glares at me. The terrified expression on her face indicates precisely that. I thought I was petrified of this, but looking in Mia's eyes, I get the drift that this may be the worst thing that could ever happen to her.

I know that in the future, perhaps a far-far-away future, I'd like to have kids. It's something I've always thought about. But Mia is set on not having kids at all. It's not something she sees for herself. Perhaps that's why she doesn't want to be in a committed relationship with Theo. Theo is a family-orientated man. Mia doesn't want to take that away from him, even though I bet he'd sacrifice everything for her.

I see her point. If Theo sacrificed ever having children, they might be happy for a while, they could perhaps thrive for years, but eventually, there would come a time when something would be missing for Theo. Mia knew he'd begin to resent her for forcing him to make that decision.

It's not long before we're sitting in front of the doctor. She's a young woman with a professional smile, one that's cold and distant. Her blond hair is neatly tied in a ponytail behind her, not a strand out of place.

"How can I help you today?" she asks, glancing at the files on her computer.

"We, umm…need to get a pregnancy check," Mia says.

"The both of you?" The doctor slides her chair out from the desk and folds her hands in front of her as she waits for an answer.

"Uh, yes," I say for both of us. Mia goes on to explain the situation, including the tests we took almost a week ago.

"Very well then, I'll test both of you and give you the results at the same time, if that's okay?" She glances at us for confirmation.

We nod.

"Have you told Theo?" I ask Mia as we wait for the results.

I'm desperate to talk about something so my thoughts stop eating me alive.

She glares at me, her bright blue eyes piercing through me as if that were the most insane question I've asked her. "Have you told Ace?"

"Point taken."

It would do no good to tell either of them before we know for sure ourselves. Men have a tendency not to react well when the word *pregnant* is thrown around. And in my circumstances, it would do more damage than good. I can't imagine how Ace would react to hearing that word.

My knees shake, and I pick at my nails.

"Stop it," Mia says. "You're making me want to throw up."

"Pregnancy sign," I manage to joke.

Her head snaps toward me, and I swear she's going to murder me. Better it be here than anywhere else.

In the time between my pregnancy test and my results being announced, I've picked the skin around my nails to the point of bleeding. I've moved on to chewing the inside of my cheek.

The doctor returns with a folder in her hand and the same generic smile.

"Mia Anson." The doctor glances at her. "You're pregnant. Probably around four weeks along."

She doesn't let the words process before turning her eyes on me. I can't breathe, I'm going to have an anxiety attack for both myself and Mia.

"And, Calla Maven…" She looks to her chart once again, perhaps for more dramatic effect. I barely hear her over the sound of the throbbing in my ears.

"Yes?" I prompt her just to give me the damn results. This

anticipation is unbearable.

"Your test came back negative. You're not pregnant."

This moment should feel more liberating, but one glance in Mia's direction is all I need to know. This isn't about me anymore.

"I'm assuming this was unexpected," the doctor says to Mia, placing her folder on the table and sitting down to face us. The smile disappears, and in its place is a consoling expression that she's practiced over the years.

Mia is pale, and her eyes are wide. She seems like she's going to pass out at any moment. I place my hand on her arm to let her know I'm here with her. She doesn't acknowledge me, doesn't look in my direction. She's lost in her own mind with her ominous thoughts.

"I would like to go through some options with you—" the doctor begins.

"I want an abortion." Mia's eyes dart toward the doctor. Her voice is shaky but nevertheless assured. I knew this would be her decision, yet it surprises me she doesn't even have the urge to think about it. But she's probably been thinking about it for the last week—weighing up all her options.

"Are you sure? There are support systems for single mothers. I can discuss other pathways—"

Mia shakes her head. "I can't go through with the pregnancy."

The doctor proceeds with an ultrasound and consent forms. She prescribes medication to Mia and explains how to take it. "You have three weeks to take it. The longer you wait, the less effective it is," she reiterates when we're leaving.

I walk out of the clinic with a weight off my shoulders. This is another push in the direction I sought—perhaps another sign that nothing is holding me back.

Mia said she was preparing herself for this, but I guess nothing can prepare you for the moment when your life becomes shared with something…someone else, especially when you're not ready for it.

"Are you going to tell Th—" I begin as we walk toward the subway. I look up into the sky. The clouds have formed, another stormy night ahead of us. Ironic considering the circumstances.

"No." Mia's eyes are distant, like her whole life is circling in front of her. Every decision, every word, every action that led up to this point, and all the choices she's going to have to face shortly.

"Why not?" I press my lips together.

"Because I know what his thoughts are on this," she answers tightly. Her hand clutches her purse to the point where her knuckles turn white.

I don't know how to console her in this situation. I have no words. I've never been in her position, and even if I were, I don't know what I would do.

Would I take the same option as Mia? Or would I opt for another path?

"And?" I prompt her to continue, to explain. I want her to keep talking, because I know the consequences of being stuck in your own mind. It becomes a dark and sinister place when all the odds are against you.

"I'm not keeping it."

"Are you sure? Maybe you should think about it. It's a big decision," I say—not to get her to change her mind, but so she doesn't regret this decision in the future. I want what's best for her. I always have.

"Are you crazy? It will ruin my life." She flails her arms.

"Don't you think Theo has the right to know?" I question

carefully. I'm treading in dangerous waters, but I'm always going to speak my mind around Mia. Always. We're not afraid of hurting each other's feelings. It's something we have always pledged to each other.

"Is he going to be carrying the fetus for nine months?" she snaps at me, pure hurt and fury in those deep-ocean eyes. I can't even imagine everything she's feeling at this point.

"No, but—"

"It's my decision, Calla." Her voice is icy, and I can't argue with her on this. Her mind is one hundred percent made up, and there's nothing anyone can say to change it.

"Okay." I squeeze her hand. "I'll support you no matter what."

Mia swallows her first pill when she gets home. We don't talk about it. She avoids all conversation. After twenty-four hours, she takes the other pills. Gone is her usual chirpy, gleeful self, and left in her place is someone who's experiencing severe heartbreak—not only for her decision, but also for the relationship we both know must come to an end. Theo will never forgive her, and I know Mia well enough to know she won't keep this from him for long.

I stay with her for the next few days. The atmosphere is thick, with emotions running high. We watch movies, order takeout, and I hold Mia's hand when bursts of pain flash through her.

I run her a hot shower on the second day when her pain gets unbearable, and there's nothing else I can do to help her. I stay with her through it all because I know she would have done the same for me. I suggest my therapist to her, but Mia declines my offer.

In the weeks that follow, I finish up at *Satire Times* and use the rest of this time in New York to pack my belongings and say goodbye to the city I've come to appreciate over the last year.

Nik calls me, apologizing for the night at his apartment. I

dust it off, not wanting to relive the memories. We fall into easy conversation, and I'm relieved to learn Ace's case is not as grim as it first seemed. Nik is quite sure the evidence against Ace is weak, and the powerful status of both brothers will help. But I know the consequences Ace is suffering are severe and beyond the legal sense. His whole life, Ace has been paying for his mistakes in one form or another.

Guilt over leaving New York, over leaving Ace when he's so far from okay, consumes me. I don't know how to help him. He won't let me. He scrapes everything off to the side. He's been doing that for the last six years. He refuses to seek help, to talk to a professional.

If I stay and attempt to fix him, there's no predicting what will happen when everything finally comes crashing down. I'll fall back into the mental state I desperately tried to escape, and both of us will spiral once again into an endless cycle of self-destruction.

Mia returns home at two in the morning one night. She climbs into my bed, tears streaking her face. "I told him. We're done for good," she mumbles. "He was so mad. I've never seen him like that before. He looked at me like he didn't know who I was."

I barely decipher her words as she mumbles them into the pillow. I can't blame Theo. It's unimaginable what he'd feel finding out Mia was pregnant and at the same time discovering a decision was made without him. I don't blame either of them, though.

Sometimes, people come together when they're not meant to in the first place. They fight with odds, but they lose the battle. Mia and Theo are two different souls whose paths collided and formed into one, but maybe it's time for them to take a step back and look at the bigger picture.

"You can come to Switzerland. I do have accommodation all

paid for there," I offer Mia, hoping she'll consider coming with me. She doesn't have emotional support here, and I'm afraid leaving her will send her rocketing down after the events she's faced these last few weeks.

"What would I do there? I feel so lost," she mumbles again.

I shrug. "Find yourself. What do you have to lose?"

Mia is not the one to stay in one place for too long. She wants to explore the world, that's always been her dream. She's a free spirit. Perhaps she's lost because her heart is still searching for more, more meaning.

She lifts her head and faces me. Mascara is smudged down her cheeks, and black patches cover the pillowcase. She reaches for my hand and nods. We fall asleep like that.

Ace doesn't make contact, nor do I expect him to. Perhaps it's better this way since we've already said our goodbye.

I hate goodbyes, yet I'm forced to say them to Betty, who's promised to take care of Oreo for as long as she lives. I say goodbye to Mia even though I'll be seeing her again in a few weeks. She's going to finish up her shifts at her job, deal with ending the lease and packing up the apartment, and then come to Switzerland for the year.

The cab driver winds down his window. "Airport?"

I nod. "But I have one quick stop on the way."

There are two more goodbyes left.

Shifting from one foot to another, I knock on the wooden door. After a few moments, footsteps echo, and the door opens. Reese smiles. "Calla."

She looks from me to the cab that's still waiting on the other side of the gate. The understanding flows through her. "You came to say goodbye."

I don't know how she knows. Perhaps Ace told her. But I didn't only come to say goodbye. "I don't know what else to do or who to go to. Ace is pushing everyone away."

I wonder if his mom knows how much he's been hiding under a smooth and shiny exterior. Pretending everything is okay while everything inside tears him to shreds.

"Ace has always been one to push the ones he loves away. He'll reel in and then push away. It's what he does. He's been doing it to me all his life. I stick by him because I'm his mother, but I don't expect anyone else to," she says. Her voice is calm and soothing. "Maybe the events that occurred in the past few months will finally make him realize that he has people around him."

Ace has his mom, Ellie, Theo, Josh, and now Nik. I offered to be his friend because that's all I can give him right now, but it isn't enough for him.

"I-I…" I can't force the words out without having a meltdown. I don't have time for it when the meter of the cab is still running.

"I know you love him. No one would have stuck around for this long if they were put in your position." She embraces me. "Especially with all that history."

Ellie appears in the doorway. Her eyes sparkle when she sees me. Another heartbreaking goodbye. She deserves one, though. I can't leave again without saying anything.

"I'm going to Switzerland," I say to Ellie.

She creases her eyebrows.

"But I'll visit when I can, and we can talk on Facetime," I tell her.

"I'll miss you," she says, a hint of sadness lingering.

I take her small hand in mine. "I'll call you so many times you'll get sick of me," I promise.

She laughs half-heartedly. "Okay."

I hug them again and jog toward the cab, turning to wave one last time. Emotions dash through me at the speed of light. I remind myself I'll see them again, that this is not forever.

I walk toward the terminal, dragging my luggage through the airport. This feels surreal. Yes, I knew this moment would come, but now that it has, I'm excited and terrified.

"Calla!"

I freeze. It's his voice, but it can't be. He can't be here.

Slowly turning, I double-check to see if my mind is playing tricks on me. But it's not. Ace jogs toward me. Each time I see him, he doesn't fail to make my heart skip a beat, no matter what has happened between us.

Yet the darkness still surrounds us. It's like a predator circling its prey, preparing to pounce.

"What are you doing here?" My voice is barely audible, stuck in my throat.

"I couldn't let you leave before I had the chance to say what I needed to say." He stops in front of me.

People turn their heads to stare at us, at him. He doesn't notice them. His eyes set on me. They pierce through me, and I hope he doesn't ask me to stay. I don't know how much of my self-control remains.

"I know I've fucked up on multiple occasions, kept things from you that you deserved to know and have hurt you in the process. I'm sorry about that. There's no excuse. I was selfish and thought keeping things from you was the only way I wouldn't lose you. But now I see it was the only thing that was pushing you away. I never wanted to hurt you. Ever."

"I know."

"I don't want to ask you for time, because I'm not sure how long it will take. I've never forgiven myself for the things I've done, and I don't know where to start, or if I'll ever be able to. But I'll figure it out."

"I know you will."

He takes a step forward and wraps his arms around me. I've missed them every night since I last saw him.

"I'll find you. Whether it be in this life, or another…I'll always find you," he vows into my hair. His voice is low and gentle near my ear.

"I'll always wait, Ace."

There'll always be a part of me that will pine for him, a part of me that will always feel empty without his presence. Our souls will always find each other. If not in this lifetime, then the next.

Ace holds me tighter.

Time is ticking, and I already arrived at the airport late. I don't want to miss my flight. "I have to go."

Tears run down my face. This moment is bittersweet. Time is all we have, yet it can be a cruel thing. It can be taken away without any warning and disappear as quickly as it comes. We look back and ask where it all went, but it's right in front of us, and we're willing to make the naïve assumption it will always be here.

I reluctantly pull away and meet his gaze. His eyes speak entire galaxies. Ace leans toward me, his hand on my waist, and his lips brush my cheek, exactly where the tears have streamed.

"Take care, love."

Time is temporary—only fate can bend it. And perhaps in the future, fate will bend it for us once more.

33

End of the Tunnel

Ace

I take a detour to a liquor store on the way back to my apartment. I haven't touched alcohol in six years. I'm unsure of what's driven me over the edge on this occasion. Perhaps realizing I've ultimately reached the bottom after evading it for so long.

I settle for the most expensive bottle of whiskey in the store, intending to drown in it. When I arrive back at my apartment and twist open the lid, memories from the last time I touched it splinter around me. All the fuckups, all the wrong decisions, everything that changed my life—it all twists in a vicious vine in front of me.

It doesn't take me long to feel the effects of the alcohol. My empty apartment spins, my vision zeroing on the piece of paper Calla left here after our fight. My own writing scribbled on a Post-it note.

The doorbell rings, and I groan in frustration. Who the fuck is that?

I want one fucking day with no phone calls, no disruptions, no reminders of what I have managed to lose once again.

The doorbell rings again. I rise with a groan and stumble toward the door to see what idiot doesn't value their life anymore. It's late afternoon, and the sliver of sun slips gradually behind the horizon.

"You look like shit."

My brother stands at my door in an expensive suit with a slim briefcase at his side. He's the definition of what my father wanted of me—a skillful, notable lawyer who's never lost a case. I can't halt the resentment, the envy that shadows around me. It's been years, and I still allow the hatred for my father to affect other factors in my life.

Nik isn't a bad man, but he's everything I'll never be—respectable, intelligent, and well-educated. He attained his goals without taking shortcuts. He's an honorable man in that respect, no question about it. He doesn't have blood on his hands, and the only immoral thing he's ever done is help me despite knowing I'm guilty of every charge I'm facing.

Without thinking, I retract my fist and collide it with his well-proportioned nose. Satisfaction percolates in me. I've wanted to do that since the day I discovered he was involved with Calla.

He touched her.

He fucked her.

He took what was mine.

The monster within me is unleashed from its den, and all I see is red. My self-control is nonexistent at this point as I hit him again. It's sloppy, and when I follow through, I stumble forward. I can barely feel my body, it's numbed by half a bottle of whisky that I drank.

Nik returns my punch with one of his own, striking me in the jaw with force. Fuck. Where did he learn to hit like that?

I'm so fucking drunk, and I stagger again, tripping over my own feet and taking him down with me.

"Stop this," he grumbles on the ground next to me, wiping the blood that trickles down his chin.

"No, I think I'm quite enjoying myself." I drive my fist again, aiming for his nose, but he twists, and my fist collides with the timber floor. The shattering sound doesn't sound good, but I can't feel it.

We're grappling on the floor, him in a suit and me in nothing but boxer shorts. It must be a sight to see from an outsider's perspective, two grown men scrapping like teenage boys.

I attempt to drive my fist into him a few more times, but he avoids my advances and elbows me in the ribs. Eventually, I'm over it, and I collapse on the floor and stare up at the ceiling. My breath is ragged, and so is Nik's.

"I didn't know you were my brother," he admits.

"Would it have made a difference?" I wipe my face with the back of my hand, smearing the blood.

"I don't know," he answers truthfully.

"It wouldn't have."

"It would've definitely made me think twice."

I scoff.

"I'm not sure about you, but family is important to me," he says.

He proved that by taking my case. I wasn't an easy client, but as soon as he found out I'm his brother, he set aside our differences and charged in the interrogation room like a man on a mission.

"We're in love with the same woman."

"But she's in love with *you*," Nik states in a definitive tone.

"Too bad I fucked that up."

"Calla needs to do this for herself. It's not about you."

I open my mouth to say something contradictory, but I know he's right. Calla deserves this. It's everything she's wanted from day one. I'm not going to get in the way of her dreams, but I wish I could be there with her.

"I'm glad I have a brother."

"You're not so bad yourself," I mutter under my breath.

Even though I've forced myself to think of Nik as bad, I can't deny that so far, he seems nothing like our father. Thank fuck for that.

"So what now?" I ask.

"Now we clean this shit up."

The months tumble like the snow lurching off a hill. Fast, but not without repercussions. Every day, there are things that remind me of what I've done, what I've lost, and what's to come.

I begin to see a therapist even though I don't believe in them. Perhaps I'm willing to give it a try for her in hopes that it's not a complete waste of my time. Even if one positive thing comes out of it, then it's worth it.

The man, perhaps in his late fifties, has an outdated office. Bookshelves and file cabinets cover the cream walls. He's behind a grand wooden desk and presses the button on the voice recorder.

Sitting across from him, I can't stop shifting in the brown leather seat that swallows me up. This is my second session, I'm not any more thrilled about being here now than the last time.

He scratches his receding hairline and shifts in his seat so he can lean forward. "It's time to focus on renewal. Everyone has made mistakes and has things they aren't proud of. You've been subjecting yourself to rumination and self-hatred for the last six years, and it's time for you to heal from that. I'm going to give you a goal that I want you to accomplish in the next few months."

"A goal?"

"A goal," he repeats. "By the sounds of it, everything has come relatively easy to you the last couple of years in terms of your abilities. You want to retire from your boxing career because it's not stimulating you the way you need it to. You earn more than enough money and are beyond comfortable."

You have no fucking idea.

"How about you find something that will challenge you? Push yourself to your limits."

Over the weeks, I think about his words more than once. Somewhere in the back of my mind, I know the therapist is correct. I need something to occupy myself. I need something that will challenge me physically and mentally.

I go out of my way to help the people I'll be leaving behind when the unlawful part of my life is over. I pay for their scholarships, use my connections to offer them deals with *legal* clubs. I try to assist in any way I can. In essence, I make amends. Not nearly enough good deeds to take away the wicked, but it's a start.

I keep training, even though I don't know if or when I'll be fighting again. It's a way for me to get out all my anger. It always has been. Fundamentally, fighting for me hasn't only been about the money, although that was the starting point. It has been about a release of anger, resentment, and fury that found residence inside of me.

"I was meant to tell you last week, but I didn't get the chance to. They want you in the octagon," my trainer says one afternoon after we finished sparring.

The UFC octagon, an alien world for me. It requires a different set of skills. It would be challenging to deviate from the abilities that I've acquired over the years and transform them into something I can use in a completely different field.

I wipe the beading sweat off my forehead with a towel and squeeze my water bottle, taking a mouthful. My trainer's eyes are on me, waiting for a response.

"Tell them I'm in."

✦

"What's got you in a shitty mood?" Josh asks Theo.

Theo has been distant recently. Josh and I've been trying to get him to tell us what the matter is, but he blames it on work. I didn't think anything of it at first, since he gets into moods like these when there's a deadline. I assumed there must be one.

"Mia was pregnant." Theo leans against my kitchen counter, shutting his eyes. "And then she got an abortion without discussing it with me."

"Jesus fucking Christ," I mutter under my breath.

I recall the pregnancy tests at my apartment and Calla telling me they were for Mia. I didn't think twice about them, assuming the result was negative.

"Wow, man," Josh chimes in.

"I'm angry at myself for being angry, but I can't help it. You know?" Theo explains. "I shouldn't be mad, it was her decision to make, but I would've liked to be in the fucking loop. But I understand why she did it. I wouldn't have made it easy for her. I've always wanted a family of my own. I would have said anything to convince her to keep it."

"I'm sorry." I apologize for his loss and for being so consumed with everything that was going on with Cassidy, Logan, and the

FBI that I didn't realize at the time that I maybe should have told Theo about the pregnancy tests.

Everything is starting to line up. Ellie is cancer free and happy again. I'm focusing on my training, which in turn is somewhat taking my mind off *her*. I wonder how long I can hold out. How long can I stay here knowing she's only a plane flight away? But if I get on a plane, we'd go right back to square one. I need time to sort my shit out.

Cassidy and Logan are in prison, but even I know it won't be for long. Both of them have connections. Both of them made deals with the devil.

They'll seek revenge for my disclosure, if not now, then soon. It's only a matter of time before they set all hell loose.

And I'll be ready once they do.

34

When the Stars Align

Calla

There comes a time when you have to take the world in your hands and chase all your dreams. It may be inconvenient at first and remarkably confronting at times, but as long as one foot is placed in front of the other, it means you're moving forward. And once you do, don't look back.

I've been in Switzerland for just over six months now. The air is clearer here, and it's easier to breathe. I thought I would miss New York. I thought I would miss hearing the city that never sleeps. I thought I'd miss my apartment, but in reality, I don't.

Here, it's quiet and tranquil. Fewer people rush to work, and more people spend their mornings with their significant others, families, or at small cafés.

I do.

Every morning, I head to a café down the road from my place and spend the better half of the morning working on my laptop. Occasionally, I stare out the window and people-watch.

I can easily make out the locals among the tourists. They don't get sidetracked by the views this place has to offer—the greenery in summer, the snowy mountains peeking through in the distance.

Working for *The Times* is proving to be everything I've imagined and more. The months here have confirmed to me over and over again that I made the right decision. In fact, I've been contemplating staying in Switzerland after the eight-month contract is up. I didn't realize how much I missed the peace and quiet. You don't get that in New York. Everyone is always on a mission—late for a meeting or work, rushing to get home in the evenings and get some rest before repeating the same thing the next day.

It's different here. People value their time. They'd rather spend it enjoying their lives and each other's presence instead of fretting about everything that can go wrong.

My work is flexible, and I get paid a lot. Or maybe I think that because I was paid minimum wage when working for *Satire Times* and worked overtime.

I have spare time for hobbies. Seven months ago, I didn't know what that was. Now, I have a greenhouse in the backyard that came with the place, and I hike some days.

Some nights, I lie outside and stare at the stars, wondering if Ace ever does the same thing. I've forgotten how bright they are. New York and other major cities have diminished their value, and you have to drive hours away to experience the beauty of the night sky. Even then, nothing can compare to the way they are here. Clear, vibrant, and utterly breathtaking.

I've exchanged skyscrapers for the stars, and they provide me with serenity and a sense that nothing in the world matters except for them and the secrets they hold. Philosophical, I know.

Sometimes, I swear I can feel Ace when I look up at the stars, and I wonder how his life is. I call Ellie at least once a week, and she's doing really well. Her cancer is gone, but they are keeping a careful eye on her just as a precaution. I try and sway any conversation with her away from Ace. I try to ignore the empty void inside of me that's screaming, making me realize I've lost a part of myself once again.

He hasn't called or made any contact, and I'm not going to be the one to contact him. I believe he needs time, time to heal, to find himself, to stop blaming himself for his past mistakes, and to begin to understand everything happens for a reason—only then will we stand a chance.

I keep in touch with Nik. We talk on the phone now and then. Everything turned out better than expected for Ace. Without much evidence, the judge threw the case out before it escalated to a trial. However, there are eyes on Ace twenty-four-seven, waiting for him to make one wrong move, to step out of line. He won't be so lucky the next time.

I've thanked Nik over and over, but he says he should be the one thanking me. Apparently, the relationship between him and Ace is thriving. Who would have thought?

They've bonded over poker and football. I didn't even know they were into that, but then again, the reality is I haven't known either of them for very long.

Nik was a fling, someone I used to get my mind off Ace. It sounds harsh, but it's the truth. I wouldn't have done it if I knew there would be feelings involved. I certainly wouldn't have done it if I knew he was Ace's brother. Lesson learned. Perhaps men are more susceptible to emotions.

And Ace… Our relationship was like a tornado. It was intense, destructive, and insanely hurried. Both times, we didn't get to date for very long, not long enough to get to know each other appropriately. We acted on the magnetic force that pulled us together at rapid speed. Now I realize that perhaps if we'd taken a step back, it might have turned out differently.

It's New Year's Eve, and Mia and I have decided to go to one of the town's bars. Our lives have changed here. Previously, we would have gone to a nightclub and gotten wasted while dancing the night away. Now, we both aren't in the mood for that, so casual drinks it is.

"Red or black?" I hold up two mini dresses. They both have sleeves, and both have a faint sparkling sequence, not too much to blind you, but adequate for this sort of occasion.

"It's New Year's Eve. Go all out," she says, nudging toward the red one.

I hang the black one back in my wardrobe.

I pair the dress with knee-high boots and a warm, full-length coat for the short fifteen-minute walk. It hasn't snowed in a few days, so the path is clear to walk along.

"Maybe you should let loose tonight," I say to Mia as we walk.

She hasn't so much as looked at another man since what happened in New York. I've tried to talk to her about it, but she instantly shuts me out. Perhaps some memories are best forgotten.

"What do you mean by *let loose*?"

This place is good for Mia, too. She's found a part-time job as a tattoo artist, but she's also found a passion for painting on the side.

"I don't know, have some fun." I shrug.

"I do have fun!" She seems upset by my suggestion. "We've been having fun."

We have been. We've gone sightseeing, skiing, explored national parks—all the touristy things that are a must here.

"I mean… You know, find someone to have fun with. Just for a night."

"You mean have sex? You want me to have sex, Calla?" she asks outright.

"If that's what you want."

"That's a little hypocritical, since I don't see you having sex. The vibrators don't count," she reminds me.

I groan. "I'm just suggesting it. You used to enjoy one-night stands, exploring other people..."

Mia rolls her eyes. She's grown out her blond hair, and her pink bangs are now absent. It makes her seem older. Yet her vibrant eyes still resemble a teenager hungry for what the world has to offer.

I don't want to say I understand what she's gone through, because I don't. But she got through it. Now, it's just a road to recovery within herself, and that might be the most challenging part of it all.

The bar is packed tonight with tourists and locals. When we open the door, the music flows toward us. Surprisingly, it's not too bad. Something along the lines of rock mixed with a modern touch.

My eyes land on the booth in the corner that's vacant. There are empty cups on it, an indication someone has just left. I yank Mia toward it before it gets taken.

"I was thinking I might save up some money and open up a little gallery somewhere," Mia reveals once she orders the first round of cocktails for us.

"Here?"

It was my dad's idea after he saw Mia's paintings via Facetime. It's no secret she has a talent for art. She conveys her emotions and feelings through her work.

My dad was unable to visit for Christmas, so we spent the entire day celebrating through Facetime. It wasn't as awkward as I thought it would be. It's like we've completely forgotten about the conversation we had the last time we saw each other. But I know he didn't. Perhaps my dad thinks I've finally come to my senses. I don't tell him otherwise.

She shrugs. "Maybe I'll go back to New York."

"Oh."

It's the last thing I expected from her. New York seems to come with dreadful memories for her, and I didn't think she'd want to live in a city that possesses heartbreak and grief.

"There are more opportunities there, especially for this type of thing. People actually buy artwork."

I guess she's right. We banter and laugh through the night, ordering cocktails and enjoying each other's company.

Mia has always been my person. No matter how much time has passed, no matter what shitty things we've gone through, we're always there for each other. I'm glad I met her back in college, because I don't particularly have other friends. I've always liked my own company.

My head spins a little from the alcohol, enough for me to gain confidence but not enough for me to be unaware of my surroundings. I explore the menu at the bar, wondering what cocktail to pick this time. I've had three different ones so far. Maybe I need to slow down, but it's New Year's Eve, so what's one more?

Mia saves our booth this time. We take turns ordering at the bar, since we never know who might steal our booth.

It's less busy now. People have moved on to livelier places to welcome in the New Year, but there's still a crowd here.

The bartender comes over to me. He's somewhere in his early thirties. A copious beard fills the better half of his face, and his thin lips are almost obscured by it.

"Do you have any plans for the rest of the night? I get off in thirty minutes. Maybe we can get to know each other."

I scrunch my brows. Those are the only words he's spoken to me the whole night. I'm flattered by the gesture and also weirdly confused. He doesn't even know my name, but perhaps names are not necessary for one-night stands.

"I'm sorry. I'm not single," I lie. He glances toward the booth I've been sitting in with Mia all night, trying to decipher if I'm lying.

"That's my girlfriend," I add, and I notice his entire expression changes, sinking like the *Titanic*.

"Oh." He scratches the back of his head. Once again, he glances from Mia and back to me. His eyes light up with a thought. I glare at him, hoping he doesn't dare suggest it.

I'm rescued when another customer approaches the other side of the bar, and he shuffles to serve them since I'm still deciding on a drink.

"I hope that's not the case, because I've been gathering the courage to talk to you all night," someone speaks beside me.

My head spins toward the familiar husky voice.

His voice.

Ace sits on one of the barstools next to me. Has he been here all along?

I can't think. My lungs twist, forbidding air to pass. I blink rapidly, wondering how drunk I actually am. Am I imagining things?

Ace is here. I repeat that internally to understand the situation's reality, yet I'm still unable to grasp it fully.

His arm leans on the bar, and my gaze wanders over him, drinking him like one of the cocktails. The white dress shirt he's wearing is like a second skin. His sleeves are rolled up, revealing the black ink that covers his muscular arms. My gaze drifts toward his face. Short, dark stubble covers his chiseled jaw, and his arresting mouth coils at the corners into a haughty smirk. He's amused at how speechless he's rendered me.

I don't dare meet his alluring eyes yet, aware that I'll get rapt in them. My heart stops and starts again, speedier than ever before.

"Aren't you that cocky boxer?" My voice surfaces surprisingly calm, fooling the both of us.

His spellbinding eyes gleam in satisfaction at the game we're playing. "If I say yes, will you allow me to buy you a drink?"

"Hmm," I consider, drumming my fingers on the counter.

I glance back at our booth in the corner, where Mia's talking to a woman who appears to be in her late twenties. They're leaning in, engrossed in conversation. I smile to myself. At least she's taking my advice. It'll do her some good.

"I do like a man who can work up a sweat."

He chuckles at my remark. "So is that a yes to a drink?"

I nod, finally unable to speak.

"Anything in particular?" He spins his chair to face me. Has he been working out more often? Is that even possible?

"I've been drinking cocktails from the list all night. Choose one for me." I slide the menu toward him. My hands shake from the abrupt and unexpected turn of events.

Ace reaches for it, and the edge of his hand brushes against mine.

The magnet snaps back into place, and I instantly succumb to him as nothing has ever changed. He scans the list just as the bartender advances to serve us.

I feel the dirty glare slicing into me like a razor blade. A couple of minutes haven't even passed since he made his move and I told him I have a girlfriend, now I'm flirting with another man.

Ace browses the cocktail list and grins. "Sex on my face," he drawls, his eyes settling directly on mine. They're filled with everything that makes my skin hot—desire and longing.

My toes curl in my boots.

He holds my gaze, and the smirk widens on his delicious lips. Why did he have to pick the most sexually named cocktail on the whole freaking menu?

I swallow hard. As I think about the words that have just spilled from his mouth, heat fosters deep inside the pit of my stomach, licking at the edges. Alcohol always seems to make me aroused quicker. But maybe alcohol is a very irrelevant factor in this situation.

And there's the fact I haven't had sex in six months. Every time I've gotten myself off, my thoughts have *always* been of him.

The bartender grunts a sound of annoyance and begins making the drink.

"Red suits you," Ace comments, deliberately eyeing me up and down. My body heats further.

"So I've been told," I reply under his captivating gaze.

We haven't talked for six months. I haven't so much as heard from him, and now he's here, in front of me like nothing ever changed.

I can't peel my gaze away from his, so we stare at each other, conveying every unspoken word. There's no game when he observes me like the entire world is directly in front of him. We can't pretend we don't know each other because our eyes speak eternal volumes of our past.

The bartender sets the drink in front of me, but Ace doesn't immediately drag his gaze away. Instead, he lazily turns toward the bartender with a superior expression, tapping his card to pay for my drink.

Mia approaches us, glancing from me to Ace. I can't distinguish whether she's surprised to see him here, which forces me to wonder if she was in on this.

"Hi, Ace."

He nods in greeting. "Mia."

A small scheming smile coats her face, the one that makes her bite her lip to hide it. And it's not difficult to solve that she indeed had something to do with this.

She turns to me. "Umm, I'm going to head out. I'll text you. You better take the booth before someone steals it."

I glance to where the woman Mia has been talking to is waiting. Ah, I understand.

"Have fun," I say.

"Yeah, *you, too*." She makes it obvious when she looks from Ace and then to me.

Ace and I move to the booth. He lowers in the seat across from me, setting his drink on the table. It's the first time I've ever seen him with one.

Even after everything that's happened, I've never been against him drinking—remaining sober has always been his choice. Has he finally decided to close the doors to the despair that lingered?

"What are you thinking about?" Ace leans closer.

The scent of his cologne creeps up on me, making me delirious. He smells like a man of power. Like a man not playing by the rules. My head spins, overwhelmed by everything.

"I can't believe you're here."

He tilts his head. "You don't want me here, Calla?"

"I didn't say that." I hold his gaze. "It's just very unexpected."

He nods in understanding. "Did you not think I would keep my word?"

"I didn't think it would be so soon. Last time it was four years. I wasn't sure if it would be the same this time."

"You were prepared to wait four years for me?"

Was I? I'm not sure. I shrug in response.

"It's midnight soon," I observe, glancing at the watch on his wrist. "Any New Year resolutions?"

"To start over," he answers honestly.

"Start over?" I stir the straw in my drink.

"Perhaps build another life. One I'll be proud to share with someone."

In another life.

I smile. "That's deep and earnest. I didn't expect that answer."

"It's the truth."

Everything I've ever asked for from him.

"I like it," I tell him.

Ace watches me play with the straw in between my fingers. I wrap my lips around it, sucking slowly while looking up at him. I slide my foot toward his thigh under the table. The alcohol is making me bold.

He coughs, swiftly catching my leg with his hand and digging his fingers into me. I smile. "Are you alright, Ace?"

"Just need some fresh air." He narrows his eyes.

I finish my drink, all while keeping my gaze on him. He shakes his head with a menacing smile, a promise he'll get his way with me later. I clench my thighs together. *Control yourself.*

He stands, glancing at me. "After you." He motions for me to proceed in front of him. He guides me out the door. The faint touch of his calloused fingers on my back forces me to suck in deep breaths.

"The sky is beautiful tonight," he murmurs in my ear once we're outside. The close proximity of his hot breath against my neck hurls goose bumps up my arms and then the remainder of my body.

Glancing up at the sky, I recognize a pattern. Three bright stars are prominently assembled in one line. They are so bright and obvious that I realize they must be planets. For them to align like this, is extremely rare.

When the stars align.

"I have the best view of them at my place," he says.

"I'm not sure I'm comfortable going to a stranger's house." A smile plays on my lips.

"You're right. I'm sorry. How about you show me your place?" he suggests.

I can't help but laugh. "Does that always work?"

"You tell me," he says, waiting for my answer.

"This way," I submit as I lead him back to my place.

His mouth curves into an even larger smile, and when his fingers brush my hand, electricity sprints along my skin even through my thick gloves.

"How long are you here for?"

"I've moved recently."

This sparks my curiosity. Moved? How long has he been here?

"A few weeks ago," he clarifies. Ace has been here for a *few weeks*, and we haven't bumped into each other?

"And you like it?" I prompt.

"I'm leasing a house by the lake. The view is noteworthy, especially at night."

"You'll have to show me another time."

"And you? Do you like living here?" he prompts as we walk past some people drinking on the sidewalk.

"I'm happy here. For now."

"For now?"

"I don't like being stuck in one place for a long time when there's a whole world to see," I explain. "It makes me feel trapped."

He nods in understanding. Before he can muster a response, fireworks erupt in the sky.

It's midnight. A new year. For some, a new life.

Ace takes my hand in his, brushing his thumb along the back of my hand, and we advance toward my house while watching the fireworks.

I unlock my front door, slide my shoes off, and switch on the light.

"Nice table," Ace remarks.

I furrow my eyebrows and glance at the table. It's a nice marble top with architectural wooden legs. It came with the place—all the furniture did. However, I don't know why that's the first thing Ace has decided to mention upon entering my house. Perhaps because of the arched skylight above it.

I head into the kitchen, not bothering to switch on another light.

"Do you want anything to drink?" I open the fridge. I still can't believe after all these months, Ace is here in Switzerland.

I'll always find you.

He shakes his head, and I take one bottle of water from the fridge. "I'm glad you're here," I say, meaning every word.

"So am I."

I take a sip from the bottle, and as I do, I watch Ace move toward me. The dim lighting shadows his facial features and projects the enigma bordering him.

"I want us to try again," he cuts through the shit. He curls his hands around the kitchen counter as he waits for my response.

"Try?" I prompt.

He nods. "These six months have felt like six years. I want to try with you because what we have together is rare. I'll never be satisfied with anyone but you. It won't be fair on them."

Ace shuts his eyes, and when he opens them, I see everything there. Yet, I allow him to explain.

"I'm not going to say I can't live without you. These years apart and these past months have proved that I can, but I've never felt this need to be a better person as much as I do when I'm with you."

The openness strikes a spot in my chest. It seeps inside and makes a warm feeling erupt through me. "Are you trying to convince me to give us another chance?"

"Is it working?"

"You convinced me when I saw you at the bar."

In reality, I've known for a long time that no one can ever compare to him. I've been waiting for him to find me as he promised he would.

His mesmerizing mouth erupts in a wholehearted grin.

"It's always been you, Ace. I've never had a need for someone like I do for you. And I get what you're saying about not being satisfied with anyone else. Even if I find a way to love someone else, they'll always have to share my heart with you. They'll never have all of me, because a part of me belongs to you."

The day I met him, everything clicked into place. Our futures have been aligned from the day of our tragedies. The timing wasn't right the two times we tried to make it work.

The first time, we were both broken. The second time, I found a way to heal myself, but Ace didn't. Perhaps the third time is the charm, because I know a life with Ace will be the most fulfilling.

"I want to do this right this time. Take it slow. I want to go on dates with you. Spend days just watching movies in bed. I want to get to know you slowly, without missing any detail."

I move my hands up his arms, savoring the feeling of him and convincing myself he's here. He cups my face and brushes his thumb over my lips like he's doing the same. He tucks a strand of my hair behind my ear, and I rise on my tiptoes to meet his lips, unable to be away from them for any longer.

He tastes like an addiction I never want to recover from. And every time I taste him, it grows stronger.

"Is anyone coming here?" he asks.

"Not anytime soon." I'm almost positive Mia isn't spending the night here.

"Good," he says with a wicked smile, and my legs shudder in response.

Ace picks me up, takes me to the table, and sets my ass on it. His mouth is on mine, and his tongue slips inside as he pulls me closer against his body. I run my hands up his arms, feeling every muscle. A groan escapes from the back of his throat, and I melt at the sound he's making because of me.

"I thought you wanted to take this slow," I mumble against him.

"This is slow considering I've been thinking about touching you for six months. Do you know how deprived I've been? At the bar, I almost convinced myself I could go without this for a few more weeks." He grips my thigh, his thumb drifting higher above the hem of my short dress. "But then I saw you in this dress, and all thoughts of going slow disappeared."

He grazes his finger against my inner thigh, teasing me, and I suck in a deep breath.

"Have you..." I chew on my lip. Would it bother me if he's slept with other women while we weren't together? Of course it would, but it's not like we agreed to be celibate. I can't expect it from him.

Ace seems to know what I want to ask without me having to question it outright. "No."

"For six months?" My mouth drops open.

"What do you take me for? Some sex addict?" He furrows his eyebrows.

"I just thought… six months is a long time." Especially when he's used to sleeping around.

"Have you?" There's a sharpness to his tone, and his eyes suddenly appear greener. Jealousy looks extremely sexy on him.

"No," I quickly say.

"So you've been using that package I sent you?"

My eyebrows crease in confusion, and then it clicks. Oh my God. I should have known it was him. A whole box of vibrators and other toys showed up at our door about six months ago. When I told the postman we didn't order anything, he was adamant it was addressed to me.

My cheeks flush. Mia and I halved them.

Ace smiles. "Good."

Did he send them to distract me from other men even though I had no interest in any other man? Ace is ruthless.

His fingers dig into my hips, starting a fire. "Perhaps you can show me precisely what you did to yourself when I wasn't here to take care of you."

I wrap my hands around his neck. "Let's see if you can keep up."

His eyes sparkle at the challenge. "How many orgasms have you had in one go?"

"By myself?"

"By yourself or with anyone previously," Ace clarifies.

The most orgasms I've had was with him…that night in Paris. "Five."

He runs his tongue over his bottom lip. "That's barely a challenge, Calla. How about we try for ten tonight? After all, tonight is a celebration. Some people say what happens on New Year's sets everything up for the rest of the year."

The thrill is erratic beneath my skin. Ace's hand moves farther up my dress, and he brushes his fingers against my underwear. I lean farther into his hand. I *need* him to touch me.

His mouth is back on mine. It moves lazily, like he has all the time in the world. A whole lifetime.

Something about him is different. The way he moves, talks, touches me. He's more content. I allow myself to drown in the taste of him. Ace mixed with a hint of a sweet scotch is better than anything I've ever imagined.

Breaking the kiss, I lift my dress over my head and throw it to the floor. Ace's gaze drinks me in. His fingers move down from the hollow of my throat, brushing my collarbone, down to my matching bra, trailing along the edges of it.

"Tell me what you want," he says deviously. He circles my nipple through the material, and it instantly hardens. Ace smooths his hand over my back and unclips my bra with his skilled fingers.

"I want your mouth." My voice is heavy with an undeniable desire for him.

He raises an eyebrow. "Where?" His fingers trace around my nipple. And he leans down and trails wet kisses down my neck toward my collarbone.

"Ace," I plead. He knows exactly where I need him.

He bows his head, catching my nipple in his mouth. His hot tongue swirls around the tip. "Here?" he dares to ask.

I part my lips, and a moan escapes me. I swear if he keeps this up, I'll orgasm purely from nipple stimulation. I've heard it's possible but never experienced it myself.

I'm panting, "Lower."

He trails kissed down my bare stomach, torturing me with the tip of his artful tongue. And then he moves farther down, stopping when he reaches my underwear. Finally, Ace drops to his knees, and his fingers go around the thin band.

A wry smirk plays on his mouth. "Do you like seeing me on my knees for you?"

"I've dreamt about it most nights," I admit, pressing my palms to the marble table.

"Is that so, love?" he taunts. He pulls my underwear down, and his eyes turn hungry.

"What else have you dreamt about during these months?" He doesn't wait for me to answer before his full mouth is on me, and I gasp. His tongue strokes my opening, licking all my arousal and flicking against my clit, teasing me.

Ace groans at the taste of me. He's still fully clothed, and even though he's below me, power radiates from him. His arms lie over my thighs, keeping me in place as he feasts on me like he's been starved—fucking me with just his tongue.

I tilt my head back and look through the skylight that's above the table, gazing toward the stars that are aligning for us. Then, bringing my attention back to Ace, I tangle my hands in his dark hair.

"Does that feel good?" he murmurs against me.

"Mm." I'm on the verge of losing myself to him.

"Tell me how good I'm making you feel, Calla." His voice against me is low, and I push my hips toward him, unable to stop myself.

"So fucking good. Your mouth is incredible."

He chuckles against me, and the vibrations pulse into my core. "I see *your* filthy mouth is still here. Perhaps when it's filled with something else, it won't be so obscene."

Ace's sharp tongue works directly on my clit, and the thought that he just deposited in my mind sends me over the edge. He prolongs the pleasure by filling me with his fingers. I quiver around them and moan his name as he watches me come undone.

"That's one," he states as I calm my breathing.

I can't imagine surviving nine more, but Ace has always been a man of his word, and if given a challenge, he'll always win.

He helps me down from the table and offers me his hand like I didn't just come in his mouth. He's in no rush to continue this, perhaps pacing himself.

"Lead the way to where you want your second one."

We end up in my room with me perched on my bed. I grip the waistband of his pants and look up at him. His jaw tightens.

I slowly pull down his pants and boxers as I run my tongue over my lips, wetting them. Ace is rock solid in my hands, and I glide my tongue over his cock from base to tip, observing how the thick ridges protrude. He swears, running a hand roughly through his hair, tugging on it. I wrap my mouth around his tip and flick my tongue over it.

Ace steps away from my grasp. "This isn't going to work for me. Not after six months without you."

Instead, he lays me on my back and kisses me. He moves his hands downward and slides a finger inside of me. He makes me come three more times before finally giving in and sliding his length into me.

Ace fills me completely and flips us over so I'm in control. I set my hands on his chest, digging my nails in, and his eyes pierce mine.

Perhaps it's not enough in this moment to tell him I love him, because this is more than love. I can't describe it. All I can say is that I've never felt so much at once. It's like every part of me is at his mercy, but at the same time, he gives me himself. We're so connected that there's no coming back from it. No pulling away.

Ace positions his hands on my waist and guides me against him. I lower my mouth to him gradually. Tasting him over and over.

For the first time, we truly make love, or whatever this is, because it's so much more than just four letters.

✦

We stand on my porch in the backyard. It's about three in the morning. I have an enormous warm blanket wrapped around me. I offered some to Ace, but he didn't want it. Apparently, he's warmer than he's been in months.

"So what now? Where do we go from here?" I lean into him. His skin is indeed hot even outside in the middle of winter.

"Wherever you want, Calla. I'll follow you anywhere you want to go to chase your dreams." He circles my bare shoulder with his fingertips.

"What about your family?"

"I can visit whenever I want. I've offered to buy them a house here, but they have a life back home. Ellie has school, friends, dancing lessons. They are happy there." He doesn't sound regretful.

"Your work?" I continue.

"I can work from anywhere. My meetings are usually virtual anyway. The only thing that will require traveling are my fights."

"You've thought of everything?" I ask, looking up at him.

I finally recognize what's different about him. He's somewhat happy within himself—more than he's ever been before. Energy radiates off him like a burning fire, but there's a sense of calmness to it, like he can warm anyone with it.

He skims my cheekbone with his thumb, and his mouth coils into a satisfied grin. "I made the stars align for us, love."

35

You Can't Outrun the Law

Calla

This feels like a new beginning between Ace and me. Something we can build upon and flourish. Undeniably, there are still issues we must work through. It's not going to be easy, but it seems like we have left the most challenging times behind us.

Obstacles remain in my relationship. I haven't told my dad about Ace and me, but it's something that looms over me every day in the form of a black, enraged cloud that persists to expand. My dad's opinion won't alter how I feel about Ace, but it will hinder both relationships in more ways than I'd admit. He won't ever accept Ace, that's clear to me, and I won't ever ask him to. I have no right.

I'm questioning if it's best to keep Ace from my dad for the rest of my life. Because what good can come out of telling him that I'm once again seeing Ace? It didn't go well the first time. How is this time going to be any different? Yet, my conscience wrenches at my chest.

Ace and I booked our first therapy session together, it's a step in the right direction. I was surprised and proud to hear that Ace has been attending therapy independently during our months apart. I know that it's something he avoided for years, even back in college.

It's already helped him tremendously in healing and forgiving himself for everything that he's blamed himself for in the past.

"I'll fly with you to Idaho," Ace says.

We're lounging by the fireplace of the lake house he's leased in Switzerland. The fire glows with a bright, radiant flame, and we're tangled in the thick blankets, facing it. The grand window to the side provides us with views of the wrathful snowstorm seizing everything in its path, and in the distance, the lake covered in inches of ice is barely visible to the naked eye. It's truly breathtaking to witness such a sight in the comfort of the man that I love.

"Why?" I ask. I'm meant to leave for Idaho in a week to see my dad for a few days. I wasn't counting on Ace coming along with me. I doubt he means that he'd come to my dad's house with me. We both know that's not advisable.

"I need to see Dean. I haven't seen him in a while, and there are some things I need to discuss with him."

I study him, searching for clues of what the discussion with Dean might involve. Ace vowed to stop keeping things from me, endeavored to be better—to do better. I'm working on building trust with him, but I'm unsure if it will ever be to a full extent.

Only time will tell.

"I want to convince him to convert the illegal fighting club to a lawful one. To get a license, to stop taking risks," he explains. "I already tried once, but he brushed it off, not wanting to take money from anyone. He's set in his ways. Perhaps this time will be different after what happened with me."

I frown. "Be careful. I don't want you falling back into that lifestyle again."

"I won't," Ace promises, tucking a strand of loose hair behind my ear. "That part of my life is over, Calla. I'll never sacrifice what we have right now for anything. And for the rest of my life, I'll do everything in my power to compensate for my previous mistakes."

I lean down and kiss Ace with a feverish need, growing lost in the existence of him, in the surroundings encircling us, and in the hope for a better future.

✦ ✦ ✦

We arrive in Boise, Idaho, on a stormy Friday afternoon. Ace plans to drive to Bridgevale while I'm going to spend time with my dad. However, once we get off the plane and pass customs, my eyes zero in on one person I didn't expect to be here.

Standing by the glass exit doors is my dad. He's in uniform. The shadowy material causes authority to stream from him. Anyone would recognize him as a man who upholds the law. A man who only offers mercy alongside justice.

What is he doing here? I intended to get a cab to his house.

My dad doesn't seem surprised to see me with Ace, which in turn, bewilders me. His face remains cold as stone, unmoving. Unrelenting.

There are officers beside him, all wearing the same expression. All standing, waiting for my dad to give orders. Their posture is straight and solid—their eyes are focused and alert.

And then it all occurs too quickly for me to register. The officers next to my father stride toward us, one of them bearing handcuffs in his hand. The flicker of badges blur in front of me in violent flashes, it's like I'm sinking, and I'm only able to decipher the hazy outline of the figures in front of me.

"Ace Blackwell, you are under arrest…"

I don't hear anything beyond that point. I don't hear if and when Ace consents to his Miranda rights. I don't hear when one of the officers orders me to step away from Ace. Instead, a sense of numbness floods me in the form of a waterfall.

"Dad…" I manage to utter. My eyesight clouds from the tears that torrent down my face with absolute conviction.

"I'm sorry, Cals. No one comes before the law and certainly not someone who destroyed our family. Justice must run its course. It's the only way."

Everything tumbles into place. My father set all of this up. He must have been molding this from the minute I told him about Ace. I should've known… I just thought that after everything, I'd finally catch a break. But I was naïve to believe that my dad would let this go.

He undoubtedly discovered a loophole. Something that will make Ace pay for his crimes. Something that will, once again, plunge our relationship on the testing lines. How much more can we survive without yielding?

Ace doesn't say anything. He doesn't tell me to call a lawyer. He doesn't resist his arrest. Did he know this would happen? He couldn't have… I refuse to believe that he was aware of this.

How did I, out of all people, not expect this? It seems like every time I begin to feel a fraction of happiness, an eruption of chaos follows. Perhaps it's a punishment for taking the law into my own hands, for betraying my mother and falling in love with the person who I should hate, for betraying my father and disregarding his principles. And finally, perhaps it's a punishment for permitting my feelings to obscure the grave reality of the situation at hand.

I've waited years for the stars to align, and it didn't strike me that when they finally would, it's inevitable for them to separate in a matter of seconds.